THE DIVINE NEWLYWEDS SHOW

A GAME OF LOST SOULS
BOOK NINE

LISA SILVERTHORNE

Lisa Silverthorne

The Divine Newlyweds Show

A Game of Lost Souls

After Azrael's guard is betrayed and death angels are murdered, Talia returns to Heaven to recapture an escaped rogue archangel who stole the Book of Secrets. Now commanding a legion of demons and remnants of his former guard, Samael's unholy alliance threatens to reignite Lucifer's promise to defeat Heaven and destroy Earth.

Meanwhile, back on Earth, Jack deals with his own demons and the drama of a new season on his reality TV show. But when an unlikely visitor asks for his help, Jack becomes embroiled in the hunt for Archangel Samuel, battling demons and former costars-turned-demons.

Will they stop Samuel before it's too late
or will Lucifer finally usurp the powerful Book of Secrets?

The Divine Newlyweds Show is the ninth book in *A Game of Lost Souls*. Dark, irreverent, and always romantic, this action-packed fantasy romance stars two lovers entangled in a mythic battle between good and evil that begins with a simple wager with the King of Hell.

THE DIVINE NEWLYWEDS SHOW

Copyright © 2021 by Lisa Silverthorne

Published by ElusiveBlueFiction.com

Elusive Blue Fiction Logo designed by Samantha Romage

Cover Design by Lost Souls Studio

Cover Imagery by Brusheezy, Benny Productions, Creative Fabrica, Deposit Photos, Obsidian Dawn

ISBN-13: 978-1-955197-09-0 (Hard cover)
ISBN-10: 1-955197-09-1

ISBN-13: 978-1-955197-08-3 (Trade paperback)
ISBN-10: 1-955197-08-3

Novels by Lisa Silverthorne

Standalones:

ISABEL'S TEARS

LANDFALL

PACIFIC BLUE TATTOO

A Game of Lost Souls series:

THE CINDERELLA HOUR

THE PRINCE CHARMING HOUR

THE EVER AFTER HOUR

THE FALLEN HEARTS SEASON

THE RISING SPIRITS SEASON

THE ETERNAL SOULS SEASON

THE ROYAL WEDDING HOUR

THE HEAVENLY HONEYMOON HOUR

THE DIVINE NEWLYWEDS SHOW

THE CELESTIAL COUPLES SHOW

THE ENOCHIAN APOCALYPSE SHOW

Curse and Crown series:

THORN & BLADE

1

A DIRE CHORUS RANG OUT FROM HEAVEN, CALLING ALL ANGELS HOME. To battle.

Talia hadn't heard that song since Lucifer's march on Heaven. The Maker's angels may have turned back the tide and kept Lucifer from exerting control over their realm, but now, Lucifer had set his sights on destroying the Creation instead.

Talia knew that Lucifer hadn't stopped his bid to claim the ethereal world as his own. Lucifer was trying to destroy the Creation as a step toward dominating Heaven. And she knew he would ruin it without even a passing concern. He hated humanity anyway and blamed God's Chosen for everything that had happened to him.

Jack Casey most of all.

The May air was cool and smelled of brine, the sheltered cove along San Juan Island's west side serene and shady as the sea whispered against the rocky shore. The wondrous place where Talia had spent her honeymoon with the man she loved. Her grey angel battle robes fluttered in the breeze. She had worn them for the show's last honeymoon challenge—in case another battle with Lucifer's archdemoness was imminent. To human eyes, her robes looked like a short grey dress. Only Jack knew the dress was her angel robes.

The beach was empty, the show's cast back in their cabins, preparing to return to Los Angeles, and the crew breaking down sets and packing up equipment. All around her, angels of death took flight, soaring through the crisp, spring blue sky toward the Heavens. Answering Azrael's urgent call.

Frowning, Jack moved beside her, Muriel, and Kesien to her left as they let their conversation dissolve into angel notes. Protecting him from himself, Talia knew. She feared that he'd get entangled in this terrible situation with Archangel Samael and his turncoat guard. She shuddered. And Lucifer.

"What's the matter, babe?" he asked, looking confused, his face pale as he watched all the angels taking flight. "Movie night at Eolowen? Or have the seraphim already turned Archangel Samael into a piñata?"

He looked so sexy in that grey Henley, faded Levi's hugging his leanly muscled body. He had on his favorite navy blue hoodie and those blue Vans slip-ons, a hint of cedar cologne hanging in the air between them. His smoldering, light green gaze narrowed, that light blond hair tousled by the wind as he gripped a smooth, blanched piece of driftwood in his hand. His gold wedding band glistened as sunlight momentarily bled through the clouds.

Her husband. Now until forever.

She winced. And now, she had to leave him behind and return to Heaven. For how long? She had no idea. It made her eyes sting and her stomach knot, remembering all those months that he'd been away from her—in Hell. It had been hell for her, too. And later, when Lucifer took control of her, she'd spent weeks trapped in the Middling...and away from him.

This was the first time that she had to return to Heaven and he couldn't follow.

And it hurt.

She pulled in a breath, her eyes turning watery as she gripped his hands, her heart already aching.

"Jack...I..." she began, trying to explain what was happening—what his human ears couldn't even hear—but her breath caught in her throat and her voice trailed away.

That stony game face slid across his beautiful oval face, light green eyes piercing as he moved closer, that heady hint of cedar cologne washing over her, making her lightheaded. And ache all over.

She only wanted to stay with him.

How long would she be away from him? Was this Heaven's way of telling her that she and Jack couldn't remain together? And without her and her squad, who would protect him from Lucifer's demons while all the angels of death were back in Heaven? He had Lucifer's mark on his arm and it was active, causing Jack fevers and announcing his location to every demon in the supernatural plane.

"Day job's calling you back to the office, isn't it?" he asked, offering her his best *everything's fine* smile. "Guess we both knew this moment would happen sooner or later." He glanced down at his feet and looked up at her through that thick fringe of dark blond lashes. "How long will you be gone?" he asked.

She heard the little wobble in his voice that he'd tried to hold back. His mouth quivered and he ran his hand across it to hide his emotions. She hadn't seen his game face slip like this before.

He bit his lip and looked past her at the waves whispering against the rocky cove as another squad of death angels took flight.

"Oh, God, Talia…please tell me this isn't the end." He pulled in a shaky breath. "The end of us."

His voice cracked and he turned away, hands on his hips. Staring at the sea.

"Oh, Jack, no—" she cried and slid behind him, wrapping her arms around his waist, holding him close. "No, of course not!"

He was shaking, hands trembling as he laid them on top of her arms. She heard him swallow a breath, trying to gain control of his emotions. In that moment of turmoil and hurt, she'd never loved him more. To see him so broken up over that possibility showed her how much he loved her. He pulled in a sharp breath. And another.

"The call home just rang out from Heaven," she said, trying to make him understand the urgency and importance—that it wasn't an excuse to leave him behind. "The call is summoning every angel back to the ethereal plane. Every angel, not just angels of death." She sighed. "Jack, it's a call to battle that I must answer."

"Of course," he said in a tight but understanding voice. "You're an angel of death. A soldier. This thing with Samael's huge. I understand, babe." A deep sigh rattled through his chest and he turned around in her arms, pulling her against his chest.

He held her so tight, like it was the last time he'd ever hold her. And it made her eyes well with tears, turning to crystals that fell against the sand.

"Just…" He pulled in another shaky breath. "Come home to me, okay? I love you, Tal. Now until forever." He laughed softly. "And if I don't hear from you in a human week, I'm flying up there to find you. Got me?"

"You promise?" she said, holding onto him.

"With everything I have," he said. "I can't lose you, Tal."

He pressed his mouth to hers in a frantic, aching kiss that burned through her heart and shot down to her wing tips.

She gripped his face in her hands, memorizing the soft curve of his oval face and those sexy, bow-shaped lips that turned up at the corners. The intense burn of those pale green eyes and his strong, squared hands holding her against his chest.

"Oh, Jack," she said, unable to hold the back the trembling in her voice. "I'm terrified to leave you—especially right now with Lucifer's bounty and every demon from here to Hell hunting you. Including that archdemoness." She winced. "I can't stand the thought of flying away without you beside me."

She felt him pull in another hard breath. He was struggling through this sudden separation, trying to hold his head high and keep that game face in place. But this time, it was slipping.

"Azrael better take good care of my wife up there," he snapped.

Again, the call to battle rang out from the Heavens.

She had to go. It made her ache all over, but she had to leave him now.

"Promise me you'll stay safe, Jack," she said, holding him out at arm's length, memorizing his face and the feel of his arms around her.

"That you won't go looking for Dumont and Hughes or any other demons. That you'll be here when I get back. No matter where in this world you are, I will find you, Jack." She kissed him hard on the lips again. "My bond with you will locate you anywhere. I love you, Jack Casey. Now until forever."

He forced the corners of his mouth into a sexy smirk and laid his hand against her cheek, cupping it in his warm fingers.

"I'll be at my shithole apartment, waiting, babe. Kick Samael's ass and come home to me. I love you, Talia."

Still smiling, he laid his hand against his heart and held out his open hand to her. Holding out his heart to her.

She bit her lip as she reached out and grasped his hand in her closed hand. She pressed his hand against her heart, cradling it a moment.

"Talia, we really have to go," said Muriel as she landed beside her on the beach. "Sorry, Jack. Azrael's calling all of us back to Eolowen. For the record, I hate this and none of us are happy about leaving you unprotected. Especially with all of Lucifer's demons and an archdemoness gunning for you."

Talia turned toward Muriel, took two steps toward her, and then rushed back to Jack, throwing her arms around him one more time. He held her.

"I can't do it, Muriel," she cried. "I can't fly away and leave Jack unprotected like this. Not with all of Hell hunting him. I can't!"

Muriel pointed behind him and she turned her head as Jack shifted his body.

Standing behind him were six Watchers with blue eyes and an assortment of pale hair colors from white to light brown. Some were dark-skinned, others light, and others with a tawny cast, wings crisp and white as the flock hovered around him.

"Jack," said Muriel with a relieved smile. "Looks like Azrael sent Watchers. They'll alert Heaven the moment they sense demons approaching. We can have cherubim blink into an interception almost instantly. With your seraphim powers, you'll be fine until Talia can get back to the Earth."

To Talia's surprise, Armand Gianni moved toward her and Jack from the footpath that meandered up to the overlook and its cabins. He couldn't see all of her guard taking flight. Just her and Muriel. Kesien and Deemah had already left for Heaven alongside Anahera and Daidrean, leaving her and Muriel as the last stragglers. If she didn't hurry, Azrael would be furious.

"Don't worry about Jack, Talia," said Armand, laying his hands on Jack's shoulders. "I'll make sure he's okay. When we get back to L.A., Izzy will be spending time with her family, so I'll keep watch on Jack until you're back."

"Thanks, dude," said Jack as Armand let him go.

"Thank you, Armand," said Talia, relief in her voice. "That's a great comfort."

"Be safe, Talia," he said with a nod and moved back toward the footpath, giving her and Jack a few last minutes alone.

Jack turned back to her and slid his arms around her waist, nodding. "See, babe, with Gianni on my six, I'll be fine." His gaze moved to Muriel. "Keep my wife safe, Muriel. She means everything to me."

"I will, Jack," said Muriel in a quiet voice. "I give you my word." Muriel patted Jack's shoulder as he reluctantly let go of Talia.

"I love you, babe," he said, that game face in place at last, and nodded toward Heaven. "Now, go kick some traitor archangel ass. And give Samael a punch in the face for me."

Talia leaned over and kissed him one more time. Turning away, she unfurled her wings and lifted off the beach. Her heart ached, eyes filling with tears as she flew away from Jack toward the clouds and Eolowen. Answering Heaven's call to battle.

To locate and apprehend Archangel Samael. And the Book of Secrets. Before both ended up in Lucifer's hands. In Hell.

2

JACK PACED HIS SHITHOLE STUDIO APARTMENT. OUT OF HIS MIND worrying about Talia and the guard confronting that traitorous bastard Archangel Samael. Without him.

It was a short trip around the five hundred square-foot space with its lack of furniture and amenities. About fifteen paces from the creaky Murphy bed to the worn-out Harvest Gold appliances in the kitchen. Twenty-five or so across hellhound-scuffed floors to his demon-torn green couch and the white clock that hung crooked above it.

Where was Talia right now? Flinging Holy fire at that loser archangel that had abused Heaven's trust to side with Luci? Was she fighting off demons? Had she stepped into a trap? Fallen into Lucifer's hands again?

God, his mind was on fire with the thousands of terrible things that could be happening to her right now!

The old, beat-up pine floors, marked by hellhound claws, creaked as he made another lap past the green couch, *whup whup* of helicopters passing over in the night as he headed toward the bed. His footfalls softened against the tan area rug that he'd thrown over the deepest demon and hellhound claw marks gouged into the hardwood floor.

Was Talia safe? Was she protected by seraphim wards?

A million horrible thoughts rushed through his head and he tried to keep them at bay. But at night, when the gunshots started popping above the helicopters and constant hiss of cars rushing past on the freeway, his imagination wandered.

Outside, beer cans crashed against concrete, the loud woofing of the neighbor's sasquatch-sized dog, Bruce, temporarily drowned out the gunshots and screaming kids next door. Eased by the skunky smell of weed wafting underneath the broken weather-stripping along the patio door.

What scared him the most was Samael's boss. Lucifer. The King of Hell was behind the whole High House jail break and archive heist. Archangel Samael was little more than a pawn, following his boss' orders. But why bother to jail break Samael out of High House?

Archangel Samael was one surly archangel among dozens. Might have been tough to find one that had a price on his or her loyalty after Raziel bought it, but still, it was one archangel. And maybe it was Samael who recruited Raziel?

Maybe Lucifer needed some of the death angel guard's numbers alongside a shitload of demons to assault the archive and take the Book of Secrets? Jack thought he remembered Pravuil saying that book had been locked up tight by the seraphim. How had a valuable book like that ended up lying around in the archive where almost any angel could grab it? Like that douchebag, Samael.

It's not like that part of the Heavens was in east L.A. or something. It was supposed to be a lawful place, where everyone did the honest and right thing. Even so, Pravuil said that book had been locked up by the seraphim. Probably after that dickhead Raziel had changed Heaven's landscape with his betrayal—right alongside Samael.

He groaned. Remembering something else that Pravuil had said. Back in his and Talia's cabin. God's Scribe had said that they consulted that book to cure Talia's demon paralysis.

And from the vineyard to the island, he and Talia had been herded.

He was damned sure of it now. Led down a carefully orchestrated path and hit with a series of painstakingly crafted incidents.

To get the Book of Secrets out of God's vault—into someplace where it could be stolen.

That's why Lucifer sent Zanth the angel executioner after him. To scare the shit out of the death angels. And get Zanth close enough to hit Talia with something that required information from the Book of Secrets.

Like demon paralysis. Damn.

The big, scary angel executioner had never intended to execute anything but Lucifer's misdirection. To boost that book and bust out Samael. But why? To what end?

He felt like he was in an *Ocean's Eleven* film.

And now the manhunt—er, angelhunt was on, every single angel combing Heaven and the surrounding areas for Archangel Samael.

Was the dude long gone?

If that was true, Lucifer would already have the Book of Secrets. Dude would be blowing up his phone to brag about his success.

Jack's pocket vibrated, the ringer turned off. Startling the hell out of him.

He shifted the hem of his hunter green Henley and fumbled his phone out of his front Levi's pocket, expecting *Sympathy for the Devil* to screech through the apartment. He wasn't in the mood to banter bullshit with Lucifer right now.

He glanced as his phone screen. Text from Gianni.

> *omw to your place, Jack*
> *be there a little after 8*

He glanced at the time. 7:57 PM. He smiled. So, Gianni kept his word.

Jack had been afraid that after Gianni and Izzy got back to L.A. from the islands, Gianni would be too freaked out by the demons and angels to ever talk to him again.

He texted Gianni back, thumbs flashing across the onscreen keyboard.

c u soon dude

Tonight, he was glad to have the company. Especially after his wife of one week was off battling demons and traitorous angels of death. While he waited for Herb's call on whether or not the network ordered episodes of *The Divine Newlyweds Show*.

Then he noticed the five other texts he'd missed. He sighed. All from Evan Bellows.

Today 5:32 PM
> *Jack, I'm begging you...please respond*

Today 5:37 PM
> *Time's running out for the show*

Today 5:58 PM
> *Jack! Listen, I'm sorry about firing you—twice*

Damn, dude! Rubbing the past in his face wasn't exactly endearing him to the idea of returning to *SanFran Confidential*. Especially since it was directly competing in the same time slot as his current show. That might change with the new iteration of Herb's show. Regardless, not even two point one million an episode was a grand slam home run in his book.

Today 6:49 PM
SanFran Confidential needs you, Jack

THE PROFIT-MAKING machine needed him because the whole thing was going under now that Lare Dumont's new role was Lucifer's newest demon minion. How ironic that the fallen Hollywood star they cast aside like spoiled milk was the only one that could save the show now?

But now that he and his costars were all married, the network worried that he and Talia weren't ratings gold anymore (along with

Gianni and Banks). That the show had no more sexual tension—or any tension for that matter.

He hated to admit it, but he couldn't completely dismiss Bellows' offer. He had to at least meet with the dude, find out what was on the table, and negotiate—in case the network didn't greenlight the new show.

Today 7:24 PM

Jack, please text me something to let me know you at least read this

Sighing, Jack tapped out a response.

Evan, contact Phil Getz, my agent about this offer and we'll talk

The knock at the door jolted him. Demon bounty hunters didn't knock. Or angel executioners.

He shoved his phone in his jeans pocket and hurried to the front door, throwing it open.

Gianni rushed past him, a six-pack of beer in one hand, a pizza box, and another six-pack in the other. He wore a black polo shirt, jeans, and black tennis shoes. Cary Grant looked like he'd just stepped out of a war zone.

And he had. After all, this place was south of the Fashion District.

"Jack!" he cried, glancing around him like he was being pursued by a horde of demons. "My God! I can't believe you live here." He tried to catch his breath as he walked ten paces to the rickety round kitchen table and set down the pizza box and beer.

"Welcome to the palace, prince charming," Jack said with a smirk and closed the door. "Hope you brought your royal Glock."

"This place is practically a war zone," said Gianni, still looking a little shell-shocked.

He followed Gianni over to the table and snatched a cold beer bottle. Whoa, Stone Brewing Belgian white—the good stuff! He twisted off the cap and took a long swig.

"Don't mind the gunshots and freeway noise. Drowns out the copters and the screaming."

Still looking shaken, his dark brown hair unusually disheveled, Gianni grabbed a beer and twisted off the cap, taking a long drink.

"First thing Monday morning," said Gianni as his hurried breathing began to slow down, "I'm calling my realtor and getting her started on finding you and Talia a new place. Before you get killed down here."

Jack clinked his bottle of beer against Gianni's. "Cheers, dude," he said. "To good friends, new places, and high ratings."

And no demons.

At last, a smile lit the taller soap star's face, illuminating his Cary Grant silver screen good looks. He tapped his bottle against Jack's and tipped it to his lips.

"I'll drink to that." He frowned. "Unless you're talking about SanFran Confidential."

Jack shook his head, letting the icy cold beer soothe his throat. "No way. Talking about Heavenly Honeymoon Hour. Wonder if Herb has seen any sweeps numbers yet."

Gianni shrugged and took another swig of beer. "Hoping they're good enough to greenlight the new season with its new format."

"Without Rachel Daniels," Jack added and set his beer on the table.

"Amen to that, Jack," said Gianni, gazing around the shoebox-sized apartment.

"Good taste in beer, dude," said Jack, the Cali craft beer smooth and a little citrusy.

Like a taste of summer at the Santa Monica pier.

He picked up the other six pick and put it inside the fridge beside an ancient jar of pickles and two cans of Natural Ice. A clear glass pitcher of water stood on the shelf above it, a six-pack of Coke beside it. He closed the old Harvest Gold refrigerator and slid over two steps to the kitchen sink.

"Thanks," said Gianni, leaning against the table. "Nothing but the best for my costar—and the man that saved my wife from demons."

Jack laughed and opened the faux pine, particle board cabinet to the right of the scuffed and lusterless stainless-steel sink and pulled out two red plastic plates. The mark on his right forearm began to burn. Dammit. Not a good sign.

"You'd have done the same for me."

"I'd have tried my damnedest, Jack."

Jack grabbed the roll of white paper towels off the dull butcher block countertop and carried it to the table as the spicy scents of pepperoni and sausage warmed the room.

"Wow, Bezos! Affording two meat toppings on one pizza? Look at you."

Gianni smiled. "And my Bugatti's parked out front by your yacht."

Chuckling, Jack picked up a hot slice of pizza. It had onions and mushrooms, too. He loved deluxe pizza—even with the green peppers. He grew up eating pizza from a local Indiana favorite called Sorrento's Pizza. Thin crust. Cut in squares. Lots of toppings.

He took a big bite as his pocket buzzed. Evan Bellows must have gotten his text.

"Any word from Talia?" Gianni asked in a quiet voice.

Jack shook his head, setting his slice on the red plate, and picking up his beer bottle. "Not a word. And I'm worried out of my mind."

"Bet she is, too," said Gianni. "About you."

He shrugged, feeling his wings shift against his back. Talia cast some angel magic on them before she left—to keep his wings hidden. He hoped it didn't wear off. She was probably worried sick about all of Lucifer's demons still gunning for him, trying to collect that bounty. While she was a million or so miles away. Gianni had no idea about any of that though.

The taller soap star fixed him with an unblinking gaze as he set down his bottle of beer.

"Hope we don't have to fight off any demons tonight."

"Same here," said Jack, taking another big bite of pizza. "How's Izzy?"

He worried that Lucifer would overwhelm him with demons and run him out of seraphim power until he was power drunk and empty. And then drag him off to Hell. Or kill him outright. But even then,

Lucifer couldn't take his soul. He sighed. Or could he? The King of Hell wasn't exactly playing by the rules anymore.

He glanced around the studio apartment, not seeing even a pale blue eye-flash of Watchers. No whisper of wings. He shuddered. Or scritch of demon claws. He was alone for the first time in nearly a year. It made him feel...exposed and vulnerable. And without Talia beside him, he felt a little lost and a lot sad.

"She's doing better," said Gianni between bites of pizza. "Said to tell you hi and that she missed you and Talia already."

He nodded. "Tell her I hope to see her soon on the set of The Divine Newlyweds Show." He glanced at Gianni. "Glad you're here, dude. I know it's only been a few days, but I miss you and Izzy, too."

And Talia. He had no clue when she'd return to him, either. It could be weeks. He winced. Or even months. He had no way of knowing or contacting her.

"She'll appreciate hearing that, Jack," said Gianni, pulling out a chair.

Jack sat down at the table, chair creaking, and grabbed another slice of pizza. He plopped it on his plate and took another sip of beer.

"Not going to lie," said Jack, setting down his beer bottle. "I'm worried that demons will attack and overwhelm me, force me to run out of seraphim energies." He fixed Gianni with his unblinking gaze. "Dude, if we get attacked and you hear me badly slurring my words like I'm drunk, get out of here fast, and don't look back. Understand me?"

Gianni glared at him. "I am not going to turn tail and run out on you, Jack. Forget it!"

Jack reached across the table and gripped his sleeve. "Seriously...if I'm slurring my words like a drunk, it means I've hit my power limit and can't summon anymore power. It means it's over. The demons want me alive to collect a bounty, so they won't kill me right away. You, on the other hand, they wouldn't hesitate to end."

"But if we still fight together—"

"There'd be too many of them," said Jack, shaking his head. "We'd be overwhelmed. Trust me, I know. They overwhelmed me once before and dragged me off to Hell. Gianni, you have to promise me that you'll escape."

Jack took a big bite of pizza and set the slice back on the plate.

"Forget it!" Gianni shouted at him, gritting his teeth.

"Someone has to make it out," he said, chewing, "to get word to Talia or the Watchers, dude." He swallowed the bite of pizza. "You're the only one that can do that. Promise me, Gianni!"

Gianni shook his head and crossed his arms. "No. I won't be the one to face Talia and tell her you got dragged off to Hell. That would kill her."

Dude had a point. He wouldn't want to deliver that message either.

"And I don't want to watch them kill you while I'm incapacitated, dude."

Gianni frowned. "What is this bounty you're talking about?"

Sighing, Jack ran his fingers through his blond bangs, pushing them out of his face.

"Lucifer marked me for his demons and put a huge bounty on my head. A spot high up in Lucifer's army? First shot at me? I don't know. All I know is that every demon in existence has come looking for me since Talia and I said *I do*. With her and my angel of death bodyguards gone, I'm worried they'll attack in heavy numbers and drag me back to Hell."

Gianni's eyes turned intense, his voice softening. "The angels told me everything you did, Jack. I still can't believe that Hell is real."

Jack nodded. "It is. Real Hollywood-style fire and brimstone. Lava glowing bright red alongside red demon eyes and tons of souls packed into a small, cavernous place. Burned out buildings. Bridges made of bones. A little less screaming and evisceration than the 405, but it's all real, dude. I was the only living human there and…it was brutal."

"Jack…I'm stunned."

Maybe Gianni thought he'd been damned to Hell like Lare and Hughes for selling their souls to Lucifer?

"You understand that I didn't sell my soul or anything, right?" Jack asked.

Gianni nodded. "Muriel said you sacrificed yourself to protect Talia."

Jack slid out of his chair and began to pace the apartment again. He was uncomfortable talking about that place, but he had to make Gianni understand that he wasn't damned. He stopped beside Gianni's chair, studying him a moment.

"Talia was forced into a couple of wagers with Lucifer," he began, trying to compress all of this into a story that Gianni could understand.

"Wagers?" Gianni cried. "With the devil?"

Jack nodded. "If she lost, she fell from the Heavens."

Gianni rose from his chair, looking surprised. "Like a fallen angel?"

"Exactly!" Jack replied. "Like Lucifer. Well, she lost the second wager and fell from the Heavens."

"But she still has her wings," said Gianni, brow wrinkling. "I saw them!"

"Because she has a rare angel power that allowed her to grow them back and regenerate her halo. That's what Lucifer was after. To get his own powers back. She was his test case."

Gianni's big brown eyes began to glaze a little, the confusion beginning. And this whole thing was so complicated.

"She was able to regrow her wings?"

Jack nodded. "Lucifer was counting on it. He showed up here." Jack motioned around the apartment. "Right here with his demons and hellhounds, determined to drag her off to Hell. So, I hid her at the angel-warded beach house in Malibu for The Ever After Hour. Until Lucifer and a legion of demons breached the wards and came for her."

"A legion of demons?" The fear burned bright in Gianni's eyes as Jack began to pace again.

"Legions," said Jack, his tone sobering. "We couldn't hold them off in the escape room."

"They dragged you out of the escape room?"

He nodded.

Gianni stared at him, a mixture of shock and surprise on his face.

Jack could almost see him flicking through his memories of the Malibu beach house and that den-turned-escape room.

"That's where I…"

His breath caught and he sucked in a breath, remembering that moment so clearly. So painfully.

"You what, Jack?" Gianni asked softly.

He pulled in a breath. "I pushed Talia into Azrael's arms and launched myself at Lucifer." He winced. "So, he'd take me instead of her."

Gianni stood up, studying his face a moment. Then he gripped Jack's shoulders, his gaze a little sad and emotional. "My God, Jack—you sacrificed your immortal soul and an eternity in Hell to save Talia?"

He nodded, a little overwhelmed. "I wasn't dead, so not my soul, but I'd have been stuck there for eternity. And I'd do it again, Gianni," he said in a tight voice. "She means everything to me, Gianni."

"Jack…" Gianni stared at him for several long moments. "You really did give up everything for Talia, didn't you?"

His face contorted. "I couldn't stand the thought of her burning in Hell. Forever."

"I'm in awe," Gianni said finally, letting him go. "But how'd you get out?"

Jack let a smile curl across his lips. "I played the long con on Lucifer and escaped when he assaulted Azrael and Talia's death angel guard. Where I lured Lucifer into a trap."

"You conned Lucifer?" Gianni's eyes were wide. "That would explain all those angry phone calls, wouldn't it? I remember Muriel telling me what you did, Jack, but hearing you tell it—I have no words…" He shook his head. "But how did you escape?"

Jak shrugged, staring at his hands a moment. "I lured Lucifer into this walled garden near Heaven, intending to fuse the gate's lock with him inside. But I couldn't get Azrael and the other death angels clear." He shoved his hands into his jeans' pockets. "So, I had to blow the lock from the inside, trapping myself in there with Lucifer."

Gianni's face turned as white as the paper towels.

"Lucifer killed me for it, too."

"Killed you?" Gianni looked sick.

Jack nodded. "But Talia used her rare angel powers and somehow brought me back. I don't remember much after Lucifer used my face as a shovel."

Silence descended as Jack continued to pace. Gianni still looked pensive, like he hadn't quite let go of the story that Jack had told him. Finally, Jack returned to the table and picked up the rest of his second slice of pizza. He finished it as Gianni returned to his chair and downed the last of his beer. Jack grabbed two more bottles from the six-pack on the table and slid one across the tabletop to Gianni.

"Dude, let's drink to living to tell the tale," said Jack, twisting off the bottle cap on his second beer.

Nodding, Gianni opened his bottle and held it out to Jack.

"Here's to living to tell the tale," said Gianni and clinked his bottle against Jack's beer. "And succeeding in Hollywood without selling our souls."

Jack smiled. "I'll definitely drink to that." He took a long pull off his beer as Gianni took a big swig from his bottle.

The doorbell rang, a faint, tinny sound that barely rose above the sputtering fridge and the freeway noise.

"You order an uber or more pizza?" Jack asked as he rose to his feet and started toward the front door.

Gianni shook his head and gave Jack a wary look. "You expecting more company? Like Evan Bellows?"

"Doubt Bellows would come to South Park—even for me." Jack felt his stomach drop. "No," he said with a sigh. "Whatever's at my door probably has red eyes and horns."

Gianni scrambled out of his chair, eyes wide as he crouched beside the table. "Don't answer it."

"They'll just come through the walls," said Jack as he moved toward the door. "But open that closet door beside the Murphy bed. There's a little souvenir from The Prince Charming Hour inside."

The taller soap star rushed over to the closet door and pulled it open. "Yes! Perfect, Jack!"

Jack got three paces toward the front door when Lare Dumont and Tyler Hughes materialized through the closed and locked apartment door.

"Hello, Jack," Lare sneered, red eyes gleaming.

"Yeah, sorry we had to rush off like that at the crossroads," Hughes said, glaring at him.

Lare thumped his chest and squared off with Jack. "Well, we're here now. And you've got some payback coming, Casey. Before I collect your bounty."

"And put you on the next redeye flight to Hell," Hughes added.

Lare chuckled as he and Hughes advanced on Jack. "Get it, Casey? Redeye? You're about to—right in the face."

3

TALIA FLEW OVER THE CRYSTALLINE ROOFTOPS AND SHIMMERING WHITE walls of Heaven and swooped, flying low, toward Eolowen's long nave. When she reached the terrace, she landed alongside the growing numbers of death angels in her guard. She glanced around the terrace's white stone walls and the dais where Azrael stood, tall and commanding, as he awaited the arrival of the entire guard.

Heaven's clean, crisp air had a trace of brimstone clinging to it, a haze hanging over the glistening white buildings. In the distance, smoke cast a pall against the shimmering white spires and fleecy clouds scuttling past.

Long, gold trails of liquid light stretched across the terrace's white stones and pooled in the grass. Angel light had been spilled here—a lot of it. Talia's eyes welled with tears and her heart clenched.

With that much angelic light spilled, she knew that several angels had been erased from existence. After Archangel Samael's guard of death angels had defected from Azrael's guard and assaulted High House. They must have taken the entire guard by complete surprise when it happened.

In order to have broken Archangel Samael out of High House, they had to join forces with legions of demons. Enough to overwhelm the seraphim long enough to release Samael and reunite with their traitorous archangel commander.

How many angels of death did Eolowen lose today? How many were slain by Archangel Samael's guard? And demons? Had they lost any seraphim or cherubim in this ambush? And what about Pravuil and his archive angels?

How many had they lost at the archive, protecting the Book of Secrets?

On the terrace, Kesien fiercely paced the stones, fury burning in his grey eyes, his mouth set in an angry line, hands clenched as his Eternean armor glistened in the sunlight warming Eolowen.

"Forgive me, archangel," said Kesien, pain radiating from his voice as Deemah landed beside him, a hand on his shoulder as her long, dark hair fell over her shoulders. "If I had known—"

Azrael looked enraged, grey eyes molten and steely, soot grey wings twitching against his stiff posture.

"It isn't your fault, Kesien," said Azrael, an edge to his voice as he rounded the dais. "You couldn't have known that the scores of death angels that joined my guard were traitors. No one in Eolowen—or the Heavens—expected you and Deemah to vouch for every single angel of death from Samael's guard. This carnage was not your fault."

Talia stared at the gleaming pools of pale gold angel light in the grass and the trails crisscrossing the terrace like human blood. It had been a slaughter. It made her furious—and wanting justice for the angels that were erased from existence right where she stood.

Gritting his teeth, Kesien turned toward the archangel, his hands balling into fists. "But I should have known!"

He turned away, his heartsick gaze shifting from the light staining the white stones toward the smoke on the horizon from the spires. His shoulders hunched, his tall, lanky frame looking wilted. And shame burned in his kind grey eyes.

"You can only know your own heart, Kesien," said Talia, moving beside him, a hand on his sleeve. "And you aren't responsible for their choices."

Kesien patted her hand and turned back toward Azrael, looking determined.

"Sir, I give you my word that I won't rest until I've hunted down every single traitor from my former guard."

Azrael nodded at him. "That's a task for another day, Kesien. Right now, we have more pressing matters. Like caring for the injured ethereals that survived this ambush. And the stolen Book of Secrets."

Talia looked up as a flock of cherubim in eagle form landed on Eolowen's rooftop. The round room. Carrying three injured angels, their pure white wings dripping light as the cherubim descended through a portal into the room below.

She peered into the room.

Inside, beyond the billowing white curtains, Berith and Oseira worked feverishly to heal a roomful of injured angels. Her stomach twisted into knots when she realized that many of them were archive angels. And worse. Pravuil, God's Scribe lay motionless on a cloud-like pallet closest to the terrace entrance. A huge gash cut across his forehead and disappeared into his thick, short white hair, pale gold light dripping from it.

"Sir?" she cried, turning back toward Azrael. "Is Pravuil all right?"

Azrael gritted his teeth, holding onto the cold white fire of anger that burned through him.

"He was fortunate, Talia," said Azrael in a clipped tone. "If the cherubim hadn't stormed the spire when they did, those demons and traitorous angels of death might have caused irreparable damage to our Maker's Scribe. Berith's tending him with her rare healing powers and Oseira is supporting her. He'll be fine, but his anger is white hot for Archangel Samael."

"And so is mine," said Kesien, pain in his voice.

Muriel stepped toward the dais, her dove grey wings unfurled and spread wide behind her Eternean armor.

"Has that miserable traitor been located yet?" Muriel asked in a bitter tone. "And the rest of the death angel dung that used to be part of our guard?"

Muriel reached over and gave Kesien's arm a reassuring squeeze as the remaining numbers of the guard crowded around him and Deemah in solidarity. The guard's show of support eased some of Kesien's anger and pain that was visible on his face. She'd never seen Kesien like this before.

Azrael spread his wings wide and folded his hands behind his back as he renewed his pacing around the dais.

"Watchers alongside the cherubim report that Archangel Samael, his surviving death angels, and a horde of demons fled along the Garden road. Past the haunted woods and well beyond the Garden walls."

There were so many areas that Samael and his forces could retreat to, fading into Heaven's landscape. It would take angel-months or longer to find him—much less apprehend him. She feared they'd never see the Book of Secrets again.

"Fortunately," Azrael continued, his voice growing louder, "the seraphim cut off his escape route toward the crossroads. And the road to Hell. They closed ranks with the cherubim and cornered him in the sepulcher leading into Purgatory."

"Purgatory?" Muriel replied, eyes narrowing. "He can't just walk into Purgatory! Even he should remember that souls have to invite angels and demons into that shadowy place." A smile lit her face. "Then that means we've got him right where we want him! Trapped."

If that were true, then it was the first good news Talia had heard since demons and the rogue death angel guard broke Archangel Samael out of High House.

Azrael turned toward Muriel, a grim smile lighting his face.

"Yes, it does, Muriel." His silver-black hair billowed as the wind blew it off his neck. "As soon as the seraphim summon us, *this* death angel guard will respond. Blinking across the Heavens, past the Garden, and down the road to Purgatory. To apprehend him and the rest of those traitors in the sepulcher. And then, Archangel Samael will finally face the consequences for his actions."

Azrael felt the same way that Talia did. Archangel Samael had a lot to answer for and she'd grown tired of his unanswered acts of betrayal against Heaven and her guard. Retribution was long overdue and had been since Jack escaped Hell into archangel politics and betrayals.

Where the seeds of this ambush had begun, she realized.

She glanced over at the round, white stone room off the terrace, the memory of Jack recovering in that space warming her thoughts. Holding him in her arms after all those months had been amazing after thinking that she'd lost him forever.

After feeling him take his last breath in the Garden.

Despite tremendous odds, she hadn't lost Jack, but that small comfort did little to ease her trepidation at leaving him behind—a human—without ethereal protection against legions of demons hunting his soul.

After what had transpired here on Eolowen's terrace, it terrified her to be away from him right now.

But she had no choice. When a call to battle rang out from Heaven, she had to answer it.

She'd sent two dozen more Watchers out to keep watch over him and alert her at any sign of demons. So far, their voices had been silent. And she worried that they had been overwhelmed by Lucifer's demons.

She glanced over at Kesien who had a grim smile on his face at Azrael's revelation.

"Sir, when do you expect the seraphim's summons?" Kesien asked.

"Any time now, Kesien," said Azrael, looking beyond Eolowen's rooftops. "It won't be long. They're storming the sepulcher as I convey this information. They'll call us in to escort the traitor and any of his surviving forces back to High House."

The seraphim couldn't directly assault Samael if they wanted him to survive their burning Holy Fire. They needed a cherubim escort and the death angel guard to bring Samael and his guard back to High House.

"Archangel," said Muriel. "Can I pull up a chair and watch from the pyre when God's Scribe gets hold of them? I'd rather be burned up by the seraphim than face Pravuil's fury. At least the seraphim Holy fire would be quick. I have a feeling Pravuil's justice will be long and painful."

The guard laughed.

Azrael's smile widened into a grin. "Couldn't agree more, Muriel. I'll be seated right beside you, watching justice be served. It's been a long time coming."

The archangel's gaze traveled across the hundred or so angels of death standing on the terrace and surrounding him in the grass.

"We lost a lot of members of this guard today, angels," Azrael began, his tone sobering. "Several angels of death were wiped out when Archangel Samael's guard suddenly went back on their loyalties to Heaven. And to Eolowen. Without warning, they turned on my guard. Called in a demonic horde and overwhelmed them. We will not forget this act when they are apprehended either. We await the seraphim's judgment and will abide by their decision, but we will not forget what happened here today."

Kesien stepped forward and turned to face the guard as Deemah moved beside him, head held high, long, walnut brown hair blowing in the breeze. He glanced over his shoulder at Azrael and then dropped to one knee. Deemah slid to one knee, her right shoulder against his left pauldron.

"Deemah and I formally pledge our loyalty to Archangel Azrael and this guard. Eolowen has become home and we will never forget the true sense of grace that this guard embodied when it accepted me and Deemah with open arms into its ranks. When Archangel Azrael treated us like seasoned members of his guard from the moment we arrived."

Deemah nodded and laid her hand against her heart. "We serve the Maker. Now and always. And we pledge our loyalty to Azrael and this guard. All of you accepted us without condition, treated us like we'd always fought beside all of you."

"And we will always have your backs," Kesien continued. "We will be leading the charge to apprehend Samael and those betrayers. They have a lot to answer for and Deemah and I intend to hold them accountable."

Talia rose from the terrace and flitted across the stones toward them. She landed on Kesien's right and put her shoulder against his in solidarity as she turned to face her guard.

"Guard," she announced. "As Azrael's second in command, I support Kesien and Deemah." She held her head higher. "No, I stand with them as equals. They are an integral part of this guard. I fight at their shoulders and I shield their backs. We are one guard. Now and forever. Samael will never change that."

The guard cheered and surged around Kesien and Deemah, bumping wings and thumping pauldrons.

"Thank you, Talia," said Azrael, his voice filling the eerie silence settling across the terrace. "If any member of this guard feels otherwise, speak now. I need to know right now whether there is cohesion or derision in the ranks of my guard."

Not a single angel note rose around them. Muriel nudged Kesien's breastplate with her shoulder and ruffled the feathers of Deemah's dove grey wings.

"Deemah," said Muriel, a hand on her hip. "You and Kesien are two of the best things to happen to this guard in more than a century." She smiled. "Well, that and Jack Casey joining the guard."

At last, Kesien's mood lightened as he glanced from Deemah to Muriel and finally, Talia.

"Thank you, Muriel," said Kesien as Deemah nodded. "And Talia. Your support means so much to us, especially right now."

A chorus of angels sang a requiem that pierced the silence, roiling across the terrace in a series of tense, anxious soprano discords. Azrael's gaze snapped toward the clouds, his expression hardening.

It was the seraphim's summons.

"It's time, guard!" Azrael shouted. "Assemble into your squads. I want phalanx formations in the air and shields to the sun. In formation and await my orders. Move!"

The sound of more than a hundred wings beat the air as angels of death lifted off the terrace and took flight. Five-member squads assembled above Eolowen's crystal rooftops, golden shields of light burning against the crisp, Parrish blue sky, smell of smoke and traces of brimstone still tainting the wind.

Azrael lifted into the air as another flock of cherubim landed on the atrium roof, carrying more wounded archive angels.

"It's time to bring Archangel Samael down," Azrael announced in a booming voice. "Make him accountable for the loss of angels and for spilling so much light across the stones of Eolowen."

Talia took to the air and blinked to the front of the guard. Where Muriel, and Anahera hovered in a phalanx line, waiting for the rest of the squad. She let Deemah and Kesien shift into formation in her squad before she took her place in the center of the line. Muriel and then Anahera floated on her right as Kesien and then Deemah completed the line to her left.

For a few brief moments, Azrael descended into the atrium room. Probably checking on Berith and the wounded. In a heartbeat or two, he shot out of a roof portal and blinked across the nave's rooftop to the head of the guard.

"All right, guard," Azrael commanded, soot grey wings flexed and beating the warm air currents. "Swords at the ready. Shields to the sun."

The golden gleam of more than a hundred shields of light glimmered above Eolowen, reflecting the sun. Talia held her shield aloft in her left hand and clutched a guttering sword of white Holy fire in her right hand. The rest of her squad held newly forged Eternean swords. Only she possessed the archangel's ability to summon a sword of Holy fire like Azrael.

"Tight phalanx formations," Azrael shouted with a wave of his arm. "To the sepulcher."

"To do some pest control," Talia added.

Muriel chuckled as Talia's wings caught the wind ahead of her. "Who knew there were winged rats in Heaven?"

"That's offensive to rats, Muriel," said Talia as Muriel soared beside her. "I like rats, not traitors like Samael and his guard."

"Good point," Muriel replied and stretched her wings to catch a warm updraft. "I'll take rats over Samael any day."

Talia followed Azrael closely, her squad in tight formation as the entire guard shot across Parrish blue skies, past scuttling Constable clouds. Toward the Garden. And the road to Purgatory.

4

Jack sneered at Lare Dumont, calling up two murder marbles as he glanced around the apartment, expecting to be flanked by demons. Knowing the place was about to get torched—like the honeymoon suite in Seattle.

"You two really want to try me?" he said, rolling the gold orbs between his thumbs and forefingers, keeping them connected to the Holy fire as long as possible.

"You're more talk than a threat, Casey," Hughes said with a snarl as he moved closer, red eyes glinting. "And I'd give my soul all over again to shut you up."

The moment the murder marbles disconnected from the light, they'd start building into an explosive force. He didn't want to outright trash his apartment, but no matter how much noise he made, it would never compete with Bruce the sasquatch dog's barking next door above the gunshots and helicopters.

"I get that a lot, Hughes," he said and kept the murder marbles tight in both fists, still connected to the seraphim Holy fire.

He didn't want to blow a hole in the wall on either side of his apartment. To his right, they'd be buried in an avalanche of Natural Ice cans and Bruce's sunbaked dogshit bricks. To the left, a hole would create a giant bong and they'd be higher than the Empire State building from all the weed his neighbors smoked. For months.

"Lucifer said the first thing he'd do when he got hold of you was rip out your tongue," said Lare as he halted about three feet from Jack, teeth gritted, body stiff and tense.

Keeping a little distance? Looked like Lare was afraid of him.

Jack grinned. "Nah. After talking to you, douchebags for five minutes, Luci would really miss talking to me."

"Bullshit! He hates you." Hughes.

"That why he calls me all the time?" Jack asked.

Behind him, something rustled against the patio door.

Damn. He knew that sound anywhere.

The scritching of demon claws and hellhounds. This was going to be like the night that Talia fell out of the sky and all her angel buds showed up for movie night. Until demons crashed the party. At least, Lucifer couldn't show up this time. He cringed as he glanced at the pine wood floors.

Shit! He was out of area rugs to cover the damage.

"He calls you because he hates you and wants you to know it," said Lare. "If you give up now, Jack, I promise not to kill you."

"Dude, Lucifer would use your body as a throw rug if you took that pleasure away from him. So, I know you and Hughes won't try to kill me. Now, me on the other hand, no promises…"

Lare took a step toward him. "Maybe so, but that doesn't mean I can't kick your ass the whole way back to Hell. Hard."

Jack sneered at him. "You and Hughes? Not so much."

The back door began to rattle and shake.

"Oh, I came prepared, Casey," said Lare, his mouth quirking into a smile. "I've got a demon horde on the other side of that door, just waiting for you to make the first move. So, they can beat the shit out of you." He held up his hand and motioned Jack forward. "C'mon, Jack. Take a shot at me with those murder marbles. See what happens."

"Yeah, you ain't got no angel backup this time, Casey," Hughes said with a snarl.

They were daring him to take the first shot. That meant there were a couple shitloads of demons surrounding his place. That was bad. Could he handle that many alone long enough to take them down? Without his death angel wife's rare angel powers? Or her squad's backup?

Guess he was about to find out.

Suddenly, he felt Gianni standing at his right shoulder, something silver flashing in the warm wash of lamplight that filled the apartment. He glanced at the taller actor, his Cary Grant poise unfaltering as he stared at Lare and Hughes in silence. His right hand was behind his back, cold steely anger hardening his brown eyes. Jack hadn't seen that much fury in Gianni's eyes since they'd battled that possessed bodybuilding firefighter on *The Prince Charming Hour*.

"Maybe not angels," Gianni replied in a deathly calm voice as he glared at Lare and Hughes. "But he's definitely got backup."

Lare motioned toward Gianni and snickered. "What? You gonna sprinkle some salt or Holy water on us? Or act your way out of a demon beatdown?"

Gianni gave him a slow shake of the head as he slid the sword from behind his back. He raised the blade across his body in a defensive position, holding the hilt loose against his fingers.

It was the razor-sharp blade that Jordan Bellamy almost killed Jack with on *The Prince Charming Hour*. Set coordinator, Steve Kosinski gave it to him after filming wrapped. Gianni had been a fencer in college and had proven on that show that he was damned good with a sword. Lare and Hughes would soon learn how well he wielded that blade, too. Like a pro.

Gianni set himself, lifting the sharp blade higher. "Not salt," he said, fixing Lare with an unblinking stare. "I'm going to sprinkle your body parts across Jack's floor."

"We prefer the direct method of dealing with demons," said Jack, giving Gianni a firm nod as he clutched murder marbles in each fist. "Now, we could call some roach exterminators, but we'd prefer to stomp both your asses ourselves."

Didn't want them to think that Talia and her angels of death weren't a shout away.

Something skittered across the patio and thumped hard against the back door. Startling Gianni whose glance shot over his shoulder to the patio door and back again.

Jack didn't even turn to look. He'd seen this horror movie before. He wasn't opening the closet door this trip. Besides, they'd bust through that door whether or not he turned toward it.

"You cheap bastards! Didn't even bring a bag of chips to this party," said Jack. "And Gianni and I don't feel like sharing our beer." He rolled both murder marbles across the tips of his fingers.

Lare's eyes narrowed, the red glow deepening as the loud crack of splintering wood echoed above the freeway noise, letting in the *whup, whup, whup* of helicopters and Bruce's constant barking. And the skunky weed smell as Jack set himself.

"Guess that's it for the icebreaker portion of the evening," Jack replied with a shrug. "Let's skip the swimsuit competition and go directly to the talent portion. Hope you packed your evening gown and heels, Lare, 'cause you're gonna paint the town red tonight. In demon goo."

Smirking, Jack flung the two murder marbles at Lare and Hughes as assassin demons busted through the patio door, flooding into the apartment. Hellpoodles followed, snarling, baring pointy teeth.

"Run!" Hughes shouted.

Lare and Hughes both leaped away from the blast as it shook the apartment hard.

Filling it with smoke.

Gianni's eyes got huge as he turned sideways, sword raised, gaze shifting around the apartment.

"Jack…what's happening?"

"You can't see them, can you?" Jack whispered.

He shook his head, but his frenetic gaze tracked left to right. He felt them around him even though he couldn't see them.

"Here, let me fix that," said Jack, herding Gianni to the right, toward the Murphy bed.

That was probably the apartment's most defensible spot. No doors or windows. And the bathroom and closet were off to the left. A possible plan B if they had to barricade themselves against a legion of demons.

But this time, there was no cavalry to call. No angel of death wife to drill the fear of Holy fire retribution into these bastards. No archangel to throw down unending waves of Holy fire. No seraphim to nuke the site from orbit either.

It was just him against all these demons. They might be screwed this time.

Jack waved his hand around the room, using seraphim powers to reveal every demon as it stepped into the apartment.

Gianni's mouth gaped as he backed toward the Murphy bed that was closed and upright against the wall.

"Here," said Jack, reaching toward the sword. "Let's even the odds a little." He touched the blade, calling up his seraphim powers to imbue the blade with flames of Holy fire.

"Whoa!" Gianni cried. "Nice!" When he looked past Jack, his expression hardened, mouth pressing into an angry line. "Oh, God—I preferred the demons when I couldn't see them," said Gianni with that Cary Grant nonchalance that almost made Jack laugh.

Lare and Hughes ran at them as the lights throughout the apartment dimmed.

Jack held up his hand, palm up, and slammed Lare with a gold shield of light.

"Shield bash is my favorite," said Jack with a snicker.

Gianni laughed and lifted his sword, clocking Hughes in the face with the hilt. "Mine, too," said the taller actor. "With a little improvisation."

"Just hope my neighbors don't swat my apartment over the noise," said Jack as he threw three murder marbles into the shadowy horde of assassin demons crouching in panther form.

Snarling Hellpoodles trotted behind the shadow panthers as the murder marbles clattered against the pine hardwoods.

"Tell them you're having a party."

Gianni lunged forward, blade arcing.

He cut through three shadow panthers and reduced them to ash. Already, the air was thick with sulfur as more demons flooded into the apartment from the patio.

"You wanna throw a party, huh?" said Jack as he dropped to one knee and slammed his left hand against the pine floor, sending a cascade of Holy fire across it. "Let's set the mood with a little candlelight and music then." He tapped his phone in his jean's pocket. "Siri, play my demon-splattering playlist."

Electric guitar riffs warbled through the room as the wave of Holy fire hit the demons and hellhounds. They screeched and whimpered, Jack's seraphim power knocking them around the apartment like bowling pins as an electric guitar thrummed an anthem. Drum kit pounded out a throbbing bass beat, cymbals ticking as a raspy voice filled the apartment.

Gianni grinned at the thumping rhythm as the apartment walls began to shake, the floor quaking to *You Shook Me All Night Long*.

"AC/DC?" Gianni asked, sword arcing, taking down another rush of demons. "You weren't even born yet."

Jack rocked his head to the beat as he shield-bashed Lare and Hughes again.

"Metal forever, dude," he said with a grin and glanced at Gianni. "Let's get this party started."

As the song crescendoed through the apartment, Jack whipped a handful of murder marbles into the writhing mass of demons that tried to overwhelm them.

"Duck!" Jack shouted, dropping to the floor.

Gianni fell to his knees as Jack's wings unfurled over top of them. The explosion shook the place again.

"Damn you, Jack!" Lare shouted. "Turn off this noise and stop lobbing missiles at us!"

"Siri, max the volume," he said, tapping the phone with his seraphim powers. "And don't forget, Lare—you started this."

The room filled with louder electric guitars and booming base, the

AC/DC song looping as it thumped through the apartment. Jack flexed his wings and lifted off the floor, pulling Gianni up beside him.

They were swamped by another line of assassin demons and more Hellpoodles. Must have been at least fifty or more.

Jack held up both hands, palms up, and slammed the tangled mass of demons and hellhounds with another blow of Holy fire. The knockback shot the whole horde across the room and into the kitchen.

Something metal crunched and Jack winced.

"Hope that was the stove and not the fridge," he replied.

Gianni lunged forward, thrusting his sword at a rampaging shadow panther that leaped at him. The blade pierced it and it shattered into a burst of smoke. He turned, swinging at a hellhound. Felling it.

Jack shield-bashed Lare and Hughes again, throwing them back about thirty feet.

"Dammit!" Lare snarled. "This is ridiculous! He's human! Take him!"

Jack leaned over to Gianni. "Watch this," he said with grin.

Holding out his hand, palm turned down, Jack extended his index finger. And summoned omnificence. The maelstrom of data and images and information flooded over him, threatening to swamp him like a tsunami.

But he held onto it, sweat beading his face as he focused all that power down to the room. To the floor. And him.

His hand began to tremble as he cast his own image out in front of him. Another one off to the right. A third one to the left. And a fourth one behind Lare and Hughes.

Surrounding them.

"Let's rock, Lare," he said, gritting his teeth to steady his voice.

"What the hell?"

Lare whirled around, turning in a circle as Hughes leaped at one of the images. Faceplanting against the old pine wood floors.

Laughing hard, Gianni bashed the hilt of his sword into the jaws of an attacking hellhound. He pivoted left and ran an assassin demon through with the blade. It screeched, dissipating into smoke.

Furious, Lare leaped at Jack's images that surrounded him as Jack crept toward him from the left.

"Careful…" Gianni said with a growl, running two more hellhounds through as Jack blended into the glow of the images surrounding Lare.

Trying to fight each apparition of Jack, Lare slammed his fist into the images, but it passed right through them as he tried to hit their faces.

"Try this one, Lare," Jack said with a snarl, cocking his fist.

He slammed it into Lare's stupid demon face, popping him right on the chin. Red eyes crossed as Lare crumpled to the floor.

"That's for Izzy, dude," said Jack, wincing as he held his fist against his chest. "Damn, does every demon have a glass jaw or what?"

"You bastard!"

Hughes leaped at him, body-slamming him against the Murphy bed.

Jack rolled clear as the whole bed screamed like the dead and dropped away from the wall. Smacking Hughes right in the head. He went down like a sack of flour. Out cold.

"That was for Talia, bitch!"

Grinning, Jack fluttered his wings and rose into the air as *You Shook Me All Night Long* looped again.

"Two outs on the double play," Jack called out and threw himself into another rushing horde of shadow panthers trying to devour Gianni. "Leaping catch at third for the last out!"

"Jack!" Gianni yelled as Jack disappeared into a tangle of shadows and red eyes.

With an angry shout, Gianni charged into the smoke and demons, sword swinging like a scythe.

Jaws bit into Jack's arms and side, hellhounds swarming him as he spun in a circle, tossing murder marbles.

When he saw Gianni enter the fray, he lunged for him, grabbing him around the waist. He blinked out of the mass of demons and hellhounds and hit the floor hard with Gianni beneath his wings.

Moments before a thunderous blast of murder marbles exploded through the apartment.

Burning the walls. Shattering every lightbulb and splintering most of the furnished portion of the apartment into sawdust. The whole apartment went dark.

"Oops," said Jack, sliding back as Gianni struggled to his knees. "Might have unleashed a few too many murder marbles."

Gianni's perfect hair was dusty with ash, his face splattered with a fine spray of red demon goo. His brown eyes were filled with a mixture of anger and concern.

"Might have?" Gianni shouted. "Trinity had less kilotons!"

Jack frowned. "Trinity?"

"First nuke test?" said Gianni, shaking his head. "Your murder marbles made that detonation look like a thunderclap."

You Shook Me All Night Long looped again as the smoke cleared throughout the apartment. Jack stood up, surveying the damage as Gianni got up from the floor, still clutching the sword in his fist. Jack reached out his hand and used his seraphim powers to restore the light bulbs. Warm light snapped on throughout the charred, ashen studio apartment.

Lare and Hughes were both out cold on the burned, gouged pine floors—that were ankle-deep with ash.

He and Gianni walked toward the kitchen. The stove was bowed in where something big had slammed into it. He turned the knob on one burner and it ticked on with a twitch of blue flames. He turned it off. A huge dent crowned the Harvest Gold refrigerator that still gurgled and groaned through its chilling cycle. He smiled. Made those 70s appliances like battle tanks.

He groaned when he saw the burned and smoking green couch. The old answering machine was charred slag on the floor, the crooked wall clock a melted white lump beside it. But the dresser his dad had made and the old round dining table hadn't moved an inch. Pizza box was still on the table. Two bottles of Belgian white beer were still nestled safely in their six-pack container.

Jack grabbed both bottles and twisted off the caps. He handed one to Gianni.

"To metal and winning," said Jack, clinking his beer against Gianni's.

At last, Gianni smiled and clicked his bottle against Jack's beer. "And knocking Lare Dumont and Tyler Hughes on their demon asses. For Izzy and Talia."

"I'll drink to that."

Jack guzzled his beer, still cold. He set down the bottle and pulled out his phone, pausing the music. When quiet had descended throughout the smoky, sulphury studio apartment, he slid his phone back into his pocket and opened the pizza box, grabbing another slice of pizza. Gianni took another piece, too, taking a big bite.

Jack bit into his slice when *Sympathy for the Devil* screeched through the silence.

Aw, dammit. Lucifer.

"Uh, Jack…" Gianni said stepping behind him.

"I know," he snapped, making a face as he fished his phone out of his jean's pocket again. "I'm not answering it. I've had enough from Hell tonight."

"But Jack—"

"Forget it," he replied as electric guitars and Mick Jagger's voice roughed up the quiet. "I'm not dealing with demons AND Lucifer tonight."

"Jack…" Gianni persisted. "We've got another problem." His voice trailed off.

"What now?" Jack demanded and turned toward Gianni.

In the threshold, standing on top of the splintered patio door, was Zanth. Angel executioner.

A smoky haze clung to the air around her, demon-red eyes glowing as she gazed around the ruined apartment and then fixed Jack with her unblinking stare.

Jack sighed as *Sympathy for the Devil* continued to screech from his jeans pocket. "Looks like this game's going into extra innings."

5

Talia flew behind Azrael as vanguard in a tight phalanx formation with the other four members of her squad. With Muriel and Anahera to her right and Kesien and Deemah to her left, they banked over the dark, foreboding walls of the Garden and soared along the dusty road that made several serpentine turns through fields and darkening wilds. Already, the air's sweetness was tainted with sulfur and smoke.

The road rolled over the surrounding steep green hills that tumbled into a valley that became a deep rupture in the soil as it branched in five directions, one fork cutting through the clearing of a thick, steamy rainforest.

Five trenches about six feet deep gouged the soil. She knew this place well. The Mortise of Souls. Where every soul that didn't rise at death stood and chose a path. Most of the time, the paths along this road eventually led to redemption and back to the Corridor of Pervasive Light. The paths' soil reflected their final location. Sand, silt, still water, twilight, and stars traced along the depths of each channel and disappeared into places where angels and demons couldn't follow.

Only if a soul summoned them.

The sandy path led to a sheltered location beside the vast ethereal ocean, a place of deep contemplation where souls overcame regrets and missed opportunities. The path of silt led to the Shade River Delta where the flow of time ran close, allowing those still tied to their human timelines to observe the outcomes of the world and witness its events. The path of still water meandered around Spirit Lake, a place of rest, reflection, and communing with other lost souls. To face the issues that each soul left behind or had avoided in life.

Above them, high over the rainforest, seraphim burned in the overcast skies. Awaiting Azrael and the guard's arrival. Talia knew that the seraphim could not approach Archangel Samael and his guard or risk burning them out of existence. The seraphim made it clear that they wanted these traitors apprehended and their wings and power stripped from them—so they couldn't harm anyone through their chosen allegiance with Lucifer.

Azrael banked over the path of stars, where a river of stars flowed into the cosmos, allowing souls to touch the future of the worlds that they left behind and see what thrived throughout the Creation—and beyond their place in it.

Turning in a wide arc, Azrael angled toward the path of twilight. This shadowy path led into a dusky half-light through the rainforest and stopped at a towering stone structure deep in the wilds.

Where the entrance to Purgatory stood, silent and dark. A doorway that only humans could enter. Angels and demons could only enter Purgatory if invited by a soul inside. The only way souls exited Purgatory was by an angel of death opening a door into the Corridor of Pervasive Light. Back to Puriel.

The structure looked like an ancient, abandoned temple built from smooth, charcoal grey stones that reminded Talia of river rocks. It had a tall tower at each end and a connecting nave between them. The temple was covered in moss and tangled with vines, casting its long, lean shadow through the rainforest and onto the path of dusk.

The path to Purgatory.

Azrael slowed his descent and flew into the dusky trench that cut through the wilds, illuminated by the distant glow of seraphim as the rainforest darkened. Talia and her squad followed as he flew deep into the rainforest's steamy warmth and watery mist that hung in the air. Until the ruined temple rose out of the fog and shadows.

"Guard, hold positions," Azrael chirped out, hand up as he halted the guard a safe distance from the ruined grey stone temple.

Talia fluttered in the air between Muriel and Kesien. She gazed over at Kesien who looked so determined, his jaw set, curly black mop of hair so dewy in the mist as his gaze bore into the temple ruins ahead. His body stiffened, wings moving faster than the rest of the squad—or the guard. He was ready to be unleashed. Eager to bring his former guard and commander to justice.

She understood. She couldn't imagine the turmoil he was going through right now. Especially knowing that these angels of death had extinguished the existence of several death angels that had trusted them.

Deemah was troubled, but Kesien felt responsible for their actions. And that worried Talia.

Azrael hovered, a hand against his ear as he gazed at the ground. His lips moved in silent conversation with the seraphim floating high above them. To keep the angels of death safe from their overwhelming Holy fire.

"Guess the seraphim need us to round up these idiots," Muriel said in a soft voice as she surveyed the area. "If the seraphim handle it, we'll be sweeping up Samael and his guard from the sepulcher as piles of ash. But honestly, that would make me very happy right now."

Talia nodded. "We're fortunate that we get the opportunity to bring them in," she said, still watching Azrael for the signal to press forward. "The cherubim usually handle these sorts of breaches."

"I'm grateful for this chance to atone for their corruption," said Kesien, his usually calm voice tight and angry, grey eyes steely and hard.

Talia reached out and laid her hand against his shoulder, squeezing. "Kesien," she said, shaking her head. "You did nothing wrong. You didn't know what they were planning and you weren't a party to it. You aren't responsible."

He sighed, running his fingers through his hair as he bowed his head. "But I should have known what was in their hearts. I've crossed over tens of thousands of humans, knowing their hearts. Why should my squad and my guard be any different? We're beings of light! How did I miss all those shadows?" He balled his hands into fists, wings beating the air harder. "How?"

"There will always be shadows among the light," said Talia, still gripping his shoulder. "And without that light, you wouldn't have seen those shadows at all. Samael and his remaining guard could have wiped out so many more angels."

Finally, he nodded. "You're right. I just—feel…responsible. I brought them to Eolowen. I thought I was doing the right thing for them and for all angels."

"You did do the right thing, Kesien," said Muriel, floating beside him. "None of this is your fault."

"You weren't responsible for your guard, Kesien," Talia added. "Only yourself. This is on Archangel Samael—and the angels of death that chose to follow him against Heaven. And we choose to stop him. Here. And now."

"Here and now," Kesien repeated. "We won't let these monsters escape and join Lucifer's cause."

Muriel poked his shoulder with her fist. "Got that right."

Talia nodded as she let go of Kesien's shoulder. "We're here for a little old-fashioned angel of death Holy retribution, Kesien. With you as the tip of that lance."

At last, the beginning of a smile lit his face, those grey eyes softening into a more familiar expression.

"I'll gladly strike the felling blow," he said. "They must atone for what they've done, but more importantly, we can't let them deliver the Book of Secrets to Lucifer. With that Book in his possession, all Lucifer needs is an angel that can read it. And cast resurrect, severing his tether."

That outcome terrified Talia.

"Lucifer already has a fallen angel with rare angel powers in Hell," said Talia, her tone wary. "Procel the Fallen. Granted, he lost most of his power when he fell from Heaven, but he can still read the Book."

Muriel's mouth gaped. "What? I didn't know there was still a fallen angel in Hell that can read the Book of Secrets!"

"Unfortunately, yes," said Talia, sighing as she met Muriel's fearful gaze. "Procel's story is in the Book. His story helped me find a piece of the resurrect power, so we have to assume that Lucifer will have a piece of resurrect in his possession—or he knows where to obtain it. But without Procel's angel powers, he can't awaken resurrect. Or find the other pieces of the power which can only be obtained in Heaven by an angel of rare power."

Kesien's brow furrowed as the anger fled from his face, replaced with concern.

"That's very disturbing," said Kesien, his gaze tracking toward the ruined temple and back to her again. "Even if Lucifer can't get at all the pieces, he has some malevolent reason for getting the Book. We can't let it fall into Lucifer's hands."

Again, Talia nodded. "Lucifer has no way to obtain all the parts of resurrect because they are in Heaven. But if he got them all somehow, Procel could cast resurrect on Lucifer's tether until he broke it. With most of his angel powers gone, it might take a very long time to break the halo tether. It wasn't impossible. Because of that slim possibility, we have to make sure that Samael doesn't escape with the Book."

Muriel groaned. "I agree on all counts, but at least Lucifer can't escape Hell after breaking his tether."

Talia frowned. "What do you mean?"

"Azrael said that Abaddon locked the gates to Hell when he returned to Heaven," Muriel replied.

"You're right, Muriel!" Talia cried, her spirits lifting. "But he must be scheming ways to try and open that gate—with the Book of Secrets somehow."

Was that it? Was that the reason?

"Attention, guard!" Azrael called.

Talia and her squad returned their attention to Azrael who floated in front of them, soot grey wings flexed, silver-black hair fluttering in the air currents as he pointed toward the ruined temple.

"As most of you know," he began, his voice commanding, his charcoal grey eyes intense. "Inside that structure is a stairwell leading to the sepulcher and the door to Purgatory. Archangel Samael and the remainder of his guard have taken up defensive positions in the chamber. In front of the door."

Azrael's voice was strong and clear as a breeze rustled through the rainforest trees with a strong gust. Talia found human forests so different with all the insects buzzing and birds trilling. These forests had no creatures because they were part of the angel-inhabited areas of Heaven. She had no idea what forests were like where the Risen resided. She imagined that they had lots of animals and birds and reptiles, but the forests where angels dwelled were silent and serene.

"Seraphiel has given the order," said Azrael. "On my mark, we blink into the ruined temple and storm the sepulcher. And we apprehend Samael and take the Book. At. All. Costs. Is that clear?"

Talia felt a chill flutter across her wings. That meant at the cost of their existence as angels. She shuddered at the thought of having her light extinguished. Never seeing Jack again. That would destroy him.

She closed her eyes, reaching through the light and the air currents and the Creation. Telling him that she loved him. Now until forever.

Her eyes snapped open and she gasped, feeling the bursts of seraphim powers exploding at a great distance. And the dark presences surrounding him.

"Jack!" she cried.

"Talia, what's wrong?" Muriel replied under her breath.

"Jack's being attacked by demons," she said, her face contorting. "I feel it through our bond, even at this distance. It's Lucifer's bounty! And that angel executioner."

Muriel's eyes widened. "And we can't go help him."

She winced. "Why didn't the Watchers report back?"

Closing her eyes, Muriel pressed her hands together as if praying, her halo spinning faster. Suddenly, she gasped and her eyes snapped open.

"Talia, the Watchers!" she cried. "I'm not detecting any of them around Jack." She shook her head. "I can't feel their presence in Heaven either."

That meant the Watchers had been destroyed by demons. The realization chilled her to the bone.

"Jack's alone…at the demons' mercy!" Talia felt tears sting her eyes. She couldn't go to him. Her heart was breaking.

"Be ready to blink into the temple on my mark," Azrael commanded, lifting his hand into the air as he angled his body toward the ruins ahead.

"Talia," said Kesien, gripping her arm. "Have faith. We'll get to him in time. Right after we capture Samael and the Book."

Her heart dropped into her feet. She had to hope Kesien was right. And that she survived this fight to return to Jack. But she couldn't stop thinking about demons dragging him back to Hell.

"Three, two, one…mark!" Azrael shouted.

He blinked through the mist toward the looming grey stones of the temple.

Slow to respond, Talia forced herself to focus on Samael and blinked deeper into the rainforest behind Azrael. He was a hazy shadow that moved through the dusky light into the open stone structure. She followed, landing on the crumbling, winding stairwell that twisted into the shadowy depths below. Toward the stone-carved door that led into Purgatory.

But her thoughts went back to Jack as she felt more bursts of Holy fire popping. He had to be all right. He had to be.

Ahead in the twilight, three or four dozen figures shuffled through the shadows, wings rustling, halos burning.

She shot forward behind Azrael, feeling Muriel and Kesien a flutter or two behind her. Already, a hint of ozone and brimstone tainted the clean, rain-scrubbed air.

In moments, she floated on Azrael's right side, more and more of her death angel guard filling the basement of the ruined structure. Facing Archangel Samael and his guard. Also, in tight phalanx formation.

Archangel Samael clutched the Book of Secrets against his chest, the Book's starry, midnight blue cover glowing in the twilight. His long white hair cascaded around his shoulders and tumbled down his back, soot-grey wings looking so black in the sepulcher. His soot-grey eyes were so wild, flicking from Azrael to her as he held the Book tighter against his grey angel of death robes.

"Surrender, Samael," Azrael ordered. "By order of High House."

"It's over," said Talia.

Amusement lightened Samael's gaze as he glanced at his guard and then back at Azrael again. And Talia.

"Is it? Lesser angel?"

Azrael bristled, charcoal grey eyes narrowing. "Says the former archangel, surrounded in Purgatory's sepulcher. About to be turned to ash by the seraphim."

The hint of a smile lifted the corners of Samael's mouth. "Are we now, Azrael?"

By the Maker, he was so smug! She wanted to punch his condescending, defiant face.

"There's no way out of here, Samael," Azrael replied, motioning behind him. "Even if you manage to take down me and my entire guard, you can't escape. The moment the seraphim feel your energy outside this temple, they'll incinerate you with Holy fire."

Archangel Samael and his guard backed away until their wings pressed against the door to Purgatory, halos fiery in the dim-lit sepulcher.

"Who says we're planning to escape from this ruined temple?" Samael replied.

His coy responses were getting on her last nerve. Talia called up a burst of Holy fire that writhed in her hand and aimed it at Samael.

"Who says we aren't planning to incinerate you right here, right now?" Talia fired back, cocking her arm.

Samael's gaze shot toward her as he held up the Book. "You wouldn't dare! Not when I'm holding the Book of Secrets."

Time to take a page out of Jack's playbook.

She smiled and let the Holy fire gutter brighter in her hand. "I'd rather see it destroyed than in Lucifer's hands. Traitor."

Kesien slid his Eternean sword from its sheath and stepped beside her, brandishing it at Samael and the death angels surrounding him.

"I couldn't agree more," he snapped, glaring at Samael.

"Well, look," Samael cried, chuckling. "The mighty, righteous Kesien, Maker's soldier and pawn. This act satisfy your conscience, Kesien? Over all those lost angels of death? It was all your fault, you know."

Kesien's jaw sharpened, gaze hardening, but he didn't move a muscle in response. He wasn't going to rise to Samael's needling.

"He knows better, you flying sack of traitorous garbage," said Muriel, sliding into position beside Kesien as she drew her Eternean sword from its sheath at her left hip.

"And soon to be pile of ash," Talia added.

She slammed the ball of Holy fire against the stone wall an inch above Samael's head, but close enough that it creased his forehead. His white hair began to smoke, but didn't catch fire. A shame. She'd have to work on her targeting.

"Give up," she demanded. "Now."

Azrael grinned. "You heard my guard. Surrender. Last chance and then we burn all of you into compost."

Talia watched the fear wash across Samael's face and the remains of his guard, but then, the fear strangely receded. Replaced by a sudden calm expression. And...she frowned...a smile? Why was Archangel Samael smiling at them? He was surrounded by angels of death inside and seraphim and cherubim outside. What could he possibly have to smile about inside this sepulcher?

"A shame we can't stay and debate this outcome," said Samael with a shrug. "Another time, angels of death. Follow me—if you dare."

Talia blinked toward him, another burst of Holy fire in her fist. Kesien, Muriel, and Azrael blinked right behind her.

She was less than a foot from grabbing Samael when he and his death angel guard began to shimmer. No. No! And fade.

She tried to grab hold of Samael, of the Book, or even his long, flowing white hair. But all she came up with was a handful of air as they dissolved into the dim light of the sepulcher.

"Where'd they go?" Talia shouted, glancing around, expecting them to be behind her with swords raised.

But they had vanished.

Her gaze shot to the door into Purgatory. The heavy stone door was closed tight, the rusted iron ring on the door unmoved and undisturbed.

"Oh, no," Azrael said with a groan. "It can't be!"

Talia moved toward him. "What can't be? Azrael, where did they go?"

He laid a hand against his forehead, rubbing as his face scrunched into a look of pain.

"This was all planned!" Azrael shouted as he lunged at the unmovable door and pounded it with his fist.

"Planned?" Talia replied, shaking her head.

Azrael nodded, but the look in his eyes was white, fiery rage.

"Planned," he nearly spat. "Right down to this moment of escape. Into Purgatory."

Muriel shook her head, Kesien beside her, looking angry. "But sir, that door never opened."

"It didn't have to, Muriel," said Azrael with a growl, sounding disgusted. "They got a soul inside Purgatory to summon Samael and his guard. Into Purgatory. Souls can summon demons or angels into Purgatory to ask for help."

With a roar of frustration that startled and silenced the entire death angel guard, Azrael shouted and slammed his Eternean sword against the door.

"He's daring us to go into Purgatory after him," said Azrael finally.

With the Book of Secrets in Archangel Samael's possession, they had little choice but to follow him into Purgatory.

"Then let's go!" Kesien replied, moving toward the door. "Let's give him what he requested. Obliteration inside Purgatory."

Azrael shook his head. "I wish it was that simple, Kesien," said Azrael. "Let me see if the seraphim can open this door."

Talia heard the trill of clear, tenor angel notes rise as Azrael called out his question to the seraphim.

"What?" Azrael replied, grimacing. "Not even a seraph can open this door? What about getting God's Scribe to take this to the Maker? Or surely, Puriel can open the door?"

"What about getting Zephana out here? The armorsmith?" Talia cried. "She could take the hinges off the door with her Aeonium tools."

Anahera stepped forward, shaking her head.

"Talia, no angel can open this door," said Anahera in a soft voice. "Not even seraphim. And that's by design."

"Why?" Talia demanded, arms crossed.

"Because this is a realm of souls," said Anahera, motioning toward the door to Purgatory. "If angels—or demons—could come and go as they pleased through this place, no souls would ever come to terms with whatever issues brought them to Purgatory."

Muriel nodded. "Unfortunately, Anahera makes a good point."

"Anahera's right," said Azrael, his shoulders slumping as the anger left him. "When a soul leaves Purgatory, an angel of death ushers them into the Corridor of Pervasive Light." He pointed at the heavy door. "And this door never moves."

With a sigh, Kesien leaned his hand against the door and hung his head. "So, only humans can open this door?"

"When their souls cross over, they can open the door into Purgatory," said Anahera. "But they can't open it *out* of Purgatory."

Azrael propped his hands on his hips. "Then we take this issue to Pravuil for discussion while the cherubim and seraphim guard the entrance. If there's a way to open this door, Pravuil will know how or know who to ask." He pointed toward the stairs. "Let's go home to Eolowen, guard," Azrael said with a sigh. "Prepare to blink."

Talia nodded. And then she would blink down to the Earth to await Azrael's next summons. Immediately. Before anything terrible happened to the love of her life.

"Talia," Azrael called. "I need you in this discussion."

She frowned and turned toward him. How did he know where she was headed?

"But sir, I feel—"

"Watchers are standing sentinel over Jack. At the first sign of demons…"

His voice trailed off, an alarmed look spreading across his face. "Destroyed!" he cried with a growl, his eyes turning stormy. "All of them. Go. Quickly! The angel executioner approaches."

Her heart hammered against her chest as she turned and blinked across the Heavens, her squad right behind her. Headed toward Earth.

6

Jack pulled Gianni behind him and spread his wings around the taller actor.

"A little late to the party, Zanth," said Jack and pointed at the empty cardboard container on the table. "We already obliterated all the demons and drank all the beer. So, unless you brought more, it's time to go home."

"Nonsense," said Zanth in that sultry alto voice, her French accent like worn velvet as she sauntered into the kitchen and threw open the dented Harvest Gold fridge door. "There is still beer in the fridge, so the party is not over yet. Jack Casey."

She pulled out a beer and twisted off the cap, tossing it onto the round dining table. She wore a short, sleeveless white satin dress cut halfway up her shapely demon thighs. With a smile, she brought the bottle to her demon lips, red eyes sparking, and took a sip.

"Dammit, Gianni," said Jack, glancing over his shoulder. "I told you we should have gotten more beer—in case an archdemoness showed up or something. What kind of terrible hosts are we anyway?"

"Dial back the antagonism, Jack," Gianni said in a quiet voice, glaring at the archdemoness as he gripped the sword hilt tighter—

preparing for another round. "I'd hate to have to call Izzy and tell her we're both dead."

Jack smiled. "I knew I could count on Cary Grant to keep this situation cordial and light."

"Oui, I appreciate that, too, Armand Gianni," said Zanth as her gaze drifted back to Jack. "And I love a cold beer after hunting humans," she said, one hand on her hip as she set the beer bottle on the table.

"Like it was hard to find me or something?" Jack snapped and shook his right arm with Lucifer's mark at her. "This thing sends up flares to every demon on the planet. And you call this hunting? It's like the Vegas Strip for demons."

She wiped her mouth with the back of her hand and stared through him. "Correction. After killing humans."

She held up both hands. Her claws extended like she'd pressed a button, releasing sharp, glinting, jagged talons about seven inches long on each hand. Blood red.

Jack sighed. "Well, I'm glad we cleared that up," he said and curved his wings tighter around Gianni. "If it's still a little hazy, I'd be happy to shine a little Holy fire on it for you. Okay, a lot of Holy fire. In your face."

She picked up the beer and took another long drink. With glistening red lips, she smiled at him.

"And I would enjoy that immensely, Jack Casey. Like a cat toys with a mouse."

"Jack!" Gianni said with a hiss. "This is not good. I saw what this woman did to your cabin on San Juan Island—and you. We need to get out of here. Fast."

"To where, dude?" he asked and pointed at his forearm, where Lucifer's mark burned like neon on his skin. "I'm like a beacon with this thing." He nodded toward the door. "I'll throw down some Holy fire. Give you time to make a break for it. Don't stop until you get to New York."

"What?" Gianni snapped. "And leave you to be slaughtered? Forget it."

Zanth began laughing. "How sweet. Considering that both of you are about to die."

"The only thing dying here tonight," Jack said, turning back to the archdemoness, "is your ego. Last warning and then I open fire with seraphim-level wrath on your demon ass. Until you're a glowing red puddle on my kitchen floor."

"You talk a good game, Jack Casey," she said and set down the beer bottle. "How do you say in English...*bring it, bitch?*"

Jack couldn't help but laugh. "Sounds so sexy when you say it, Zanth. Gives me chills. Too bad it won't stop me from kicking your demon ass."

Sympathy for the Devil screeched from Jack's Levi's pocket again.

Zanth sighed and crossed her arms, nodding at him. "You had better answer him. The longer you keep him waiting, the more time you shall spend on the rack in Hell."

Sighing, Jack slid his phone out of his pocket and answered the video call.

"You're interrupting my party, Luci," he said with a growl. "I was just about to hang up the piñata, too. You know? Zanth? Your angel executioner."

Lucifer's pale blue eyes bore holes through him from the FaceTime screen.

"I hate talking to you," Lucifer replied, British accent sharp.

"Then why do you keep calling me, Luci? Lose my number already! But you can't, can you? Because you're still obsessed over me, aren't you? I can hear it in your voice. You just can't stand to be away from me for so long, can you? You miss me, admit it."

"I miss you hanging on my wall, Jack," Lucifer snapped. "As artwork! Silent artwork. That doesn't speak or talk in stupid human euphemisms and slang. That doesn't utter a sound."

"It's my hella good looks, isn't it? That's why you can't stop calling me. Luci, we really need to see other people."

"Shut up, Jack!" Lucifer shouted. "I called to give Zanth a message."

"Damn, Luci, you're so cheap that you can't get your angel

executioner her own smartphone. How'd you text her before this? Stone tablets delivered by gargoyles?"

Lucifer's eyes began to glow red, tiny horn buds appearing on his forehead.

"Enough!" Lucifer shouted. "Zanth, find out how much power he has left. Now."

"Wow, dude—time to switch to decaf. Or take an anger management course. You got time, being tethered in Hell and all. Time to finally deal with those daddy issues of yours, too, before it really affects your health."

"Either you shut him up, Zanth or I will!" Lucifer's voice was grating now.

"You gonna come up from Hell to my place and shut me up, Luci? Oh, wait—"

"Zanth! Now!"

And the phone went dead.

"That's the third time in a week that he's hung up on me," said Jack, sliding his phone back into his pocket.

"Do you have a death wish, Jack?" Gianni cried, a horrified look on his face. "That's the devil, right?"

Jack shrugged. "Yeah. So?"

Gianni shook his head, his horror changing to shock. "He could crush you, Jack."

"If I were you," said Zanth, moving toward him, "I would listen to your very astute friend. Ethereal beings are very different from physical beings that bleed. And die. Including Lucifer, once the most powerful angel in existence. Who hates humans more than anything. Especially you, Jack."

If she was sent to kill him, why hadn't she made any moves on him? And Lucifer asked her to find out how much seraphim power he had left. Had Lare and Hughes shown up here to test him? He glanced over at Hughes and Lare, still out cold on the floor.

Lucifer knew he was alone tonight, without any angelic wingmen. Either the King of Hell was afraid of his seraphim powers (not likely) or Zanth was sizing him up for something. But what?

Or maybe this whole thing was another misdirection by Lucifer, using his anger to cloak what he was really after?

And why hadn't Zanth made her move? Last time, she didn't waste a single breath on him. She'd gone straight for the jugular. Kind of like Rachel Daniels. Why was she stalling this time?

It made him nervous.

"Why you passing out advice to me like a concerned aunt, Zanth? Instead of trying to remove my liver through my nostrils like last time?"

Her red, glowing demon eyes sparked as she turned to smoke and disappeared into the hazy, dim-lit edges of his apartment.

He called up some Holy fire, but she moved around the room. Away from him.

Was she spinning a huge demon trap around the room? And he was just letting her do it.

"Stop whatever you're doing! Now!" he shouted, pulling back the sphere of Holy fire, ready to fling a fastball right over the plate at her.

Her movements left a red, sparkly trail behind her that floated up from the floor to the ceiling and coalesced into an undulating curtain. Cloaking the walls.

Was she putting up demon wards?

When all four walls had been cloaked in red, billowing energy, she zipped across the floors and then flew across the ceiling until floor and ceiling shimmered red. When she finished, she materialized an arm's length from him. Staring.

"I have buffered this space, isolating it from Hell and all demons," she said and took a step toward him.

Jack stood his ground, not flinching. Holy fire guttered in his hand as she stood less than a foot from him.

"Why?" he demanded.

"So, that our…conversation remains private," she said. "Are you planning to use that?"

She pointed at the writhing sphere of Holy fire that he held in his hand like a baseball. Could he put it out? He turned toward it and blew on it. The flames shuddered and went cold before winking out.

"Private? As in *away from Lucifer?*" he asked, grinning. "Do tell, Zanth."

"Aren't you the least bit curious about what is happening in Heaven?" she asked.

"Changing the subject," he replied. "All right. I am curious, but my angel of death wife will tell me all about it when she gets home from work."

"Your angel of death and her squad went into the sepulcher to drag out Archangel Samael and his guard at the behest of the seraphim."

Jack nodded. "Sounds about right."

Zanth sized him up again. "That is the entrance to Purgatory."

He shrugged. "Is that important?"

"Of course, it is important," Zanth snapped and crossed her arms. "Neither angels nor demons can open the door into Purgatory. Souls must invite them into this shadowy world. Humans, Jack—like you. But once they have crossed over, they can only open the door to enter Purgatory. Getting out requires an angel of death and they can only open a door into the Corridor of Pervasive Light."

"Uh...pervasive what?"

"Light, Jack," said Zanth, her voice still patient and even. "It takes them to a place of souls where they shift into other parts of Heaven. Or they fall into Hell."

Jack brushed his blond bangs out of his eyes. "Why you telling me all of this in your...your demon cone of silence?"

At last, she sighed, looking annoyed.

"Because, Jack Casey, Archangel Samael and his guard disappeared through the door into Purgatory and your Archangel Azrael is incensed about it. Because he cannot get to Samael or the Book unless a soul invites the angels into Purgatory."

So, Samael escaped the wrath of the seraphim by fading into a place where only souls resided? How'd Samael manage that? Bet Azrael was Holy-fire furious right now, wondering how they'd escaped. Was that where Talia was right now? In this sepulcher? Dead-ended by a door that no ethereal could open?

"Again, why you telling me about this? You got a line on the soul that invited that little bitch into Purgatory? Or are you just playing me? With Lucifer navigating everything?"

Sighing, Zanth stepped forward and grabbed him by the shoulders. "Yes, Jack Casey! I know the identity of this soul! He is my human lover, Tre Sheridan and he invited Samael and his guard through that door into Purgatory. He gave his life to help Lucifer hide Samael and keep the Book of Secrets out of angel hands." Her eyes darkened, flashing a deep red now. "He was to be rewarded for his great sacrifice with a high position in Lucifer's army. And to be at my side for eternity. But Lucifer did not tell Tre that he could not open the door out of Purgatory once he entered."

She looked enraged, her body shaking with anger.

"So, your human lover died for Lucifer's cause? But nobody told this dude the truth about his sacrifice, so now, he's trapped in Purgatory? Is that what you're telling me?"

"Oui, Jack Casey. That is why I came here under the guise of testing your seraphim power. To bargain for your help. You are the only one that can help me rescue Tre."

He couldn't halt the smile from curving across his face. "Let me get this straight. You're asking me to bargain with a demon?"

"Oui," she repeated.

"Not in this lifetime, Zanth. Forget it!"

"I need your help," she cried, sounding almost desperate. "I could have killed you in that cabin back on the island. Along with your angel of death wife and best friend. I chose mercy."

"For your own gain," Jack replied, eyes narrowing. "Like every single demon I've ever encountered." He laid his hand against his chest. "So, why me?"

"Because," she said, her voice sharpening, "you are the only living and breathing human being in existence that can open that door into Purgatory and out again."

"Me?" he cried, shaking his head. "How can I do that?"

"Because you are not dead and you have angel powers channeled through you," Zanth explained, holding out her hands. "That allows you to walk both the physical and ethereal planes. With one foot in

Heaven and one on Earth, you are the only being that can walk in and out of that door again. Long enough to let Tre walk out of that door with you." She pulled in a breath. "And back into my arms again." She bowed her head. "Otherwise, I will be separated from him for eternity."

Her words stabbed him right through the heart. He remembered a time when he thought that he and Talia would never see each other again. That they would be forever separated, him in Hell and her in Heaven.

Was Zanth playing him? Or was this human lover real? Lucifer could be riding around in her head right now, doing his best to con Jack into a trap that would separate him from Talia for eternity.

"What's stopping him from inviting you into Purgatory?" Jack asked.

She sighed. "Nothing, Jack Casey, but it is not forever. And it is not freedom. Ethereal beings cannot stay for long in that realm."

So, Azrael and his guard could camp the entrance to Purgatory for Samael and eventually, he'd get ejected into their custody. He had no idea how long *not forever* was to a demon though. It could be centuries.

"Why not just get an angel of death to open the door to this corridor of light?" Jack offered. "Then your lover tells the angels he wants to go to Hell."

She shook her head, the frustration rising in her voice. "His actions define where his soul migrates, not his preference. His biggest crime was loneliness, Jack. He took his own life, so that he could be with me forever. He did not care where as long as we were together. Suicide does not land a soul in Hell. Only in the Between."

Jack was stunned by her admission. He'd never even considered that demons felt love, much less felt it as deeply and completely as he did. Or Talia. But most demons were fallen angels, so it made sense. Ethereals were as emotional as humans. They just refused to admit it —especially Lucifer. Most of them were like humans with wings and raging egos.

"Wow, he killed himself?" Jack replied.

"Oui," she said, nodding.

Suicide…intentional overdose…the line was very thin between his own circumstances and this Tre Sheridan. It made him uneasy.

Regardless, he gave Lucifer a lot of shit about being thrown over for humans, but Jack understood that hurt more than he'd ever admitted. His own mother chose her daughters over her youngest and only son, forgot about him completely when she divorced his dad. Even when he was seventeen and his dad died of cancer, she didn't offer him a place to live. Didn't even check to make sure he had food and that he wasn't living on the streets somewhere. Just forgot about him.

No, he understood Lucifer's hurt over being *replaced* and then being kicked out of the house. But Lucifer wanted humans and angels to pay for that rejection and that was the difference between them. Jack hadn't sought revenge. Only a cure for feeling abandoned—which became a flake addiction and a few bad relationships.

But he understood how Zanth felt right now. And he found it strangely disturbing to have sympathy for a demon. Even so, he couldn't trust her with the possibility of Lucifer riding around in her head. Orchestrating the situation. Baiting the trap.

"I'm sorry, Zanth," he said, shaking his head. "I feel your pain, but I can't fully trust that Lucifer isn't still riding around in your head."

"Jack, please—" she cried, gripping his shoulders. "You are the only one that can help me. I need—"

The flutter of wings echoed from the patio and reverberated through the dim-lit, smoky apartment.

He grinned. The cavalry. Right on cue.

Zanth's head swiveled toward the back door. She let go of him, her gaze fixed on the threshold.

"Another time, Jack Casey," she said. "We shall speak again."

She faded into smoke as Talia blinked through the back door's threshold, a terrified look on her beautiful oval face, those intense grey eyes glassy as her squad landed on the patio.

"Jack!" she called through the haze and the smoke. "Jack, please! Are you all right? Answer me! Jack!"

He relaxed his wings, letting Gianni step out from behind him.

"Over here, Tal," he called.

In an instant, she blinked through the wreckage that was his apartment and threw her arms around him.

"Oh, Jack!" She held him tight. She was trembling. "When I saw that broken door, the scorched walls, and charred furniture, I was terrified that Lucifer had overwhelmed you!"

He held her as close as he could. Everything felt better with Talia in his arms.

"Nah, Luci's still tethered to his playpen. But Lare and Hughes showed up for a pissing contest." He pointed toward the two unconscious figures on the scarred pine floor. "Couldn't hold their liquor though—er, Holy fire."

She kept him close as she glanced around the ruins of the apartment, searching for something as Gianni let the sword fall to his side.

"Where is she?"

He frowned. "Who?"

"The angel executioner," she said, her gaze scrutinizing the haze and dissipating smell of brimstone. "I feel her presence."

"Relax, babe," he said. "She's gone. Allergies."

Talia's face scrunched into a look of confusion. "Allergies?"

He nodded. "Apparently, she's allergic to feathers and ass-kickings. Who knew?"

Gianni chuckled, but Talia didn't seem convinced. She motioned for her squad to fan out through the apartment—all 500 square feet of it. She opened her mouth and sang those angel notes he couldn't hear, so he had no idea what instructions she'd given them. He felt like he had a seat at the kiddie table again.

He glanced over at Hughes and Lare. They turned to smoke and disappeared from the apartment.

"Guess Lucifer decided to claim his luggage," Jack replied and pointed.

"Where'd they go?" Gianni demanded, his eyes wide.

He rushed over to where Lare and Hughes had been on the floor.

His gaze shifted as he surveyed the dark apartment for a sign of Lare or Hughes. They were long gone. They didn't have the balls to take on five angels of death. Or even one.

"Turned to demon smoke and took the redeye back to Hell," said Jack as Talia's grip tightened around his waist. "Trust me, babe, Zanth's gone."

He needed to tell her about the soul in Purgatory that became Samael's alibi, but he wanted to leave out the part where Zanth had asked for his help. Talia would be livid. And he didn't want to watch Talia's eyes burn white with Holy fire, in case some of that Holy retribution got aimed at him. He just hoped that Gianni wouldn't offer up that information to her before he had a chance to ease it into another conversation. It was a little much and even he was still processing it.

"We're making sure, lover," she said, wings wrapping around him. "Muriel, Kesien, I want those seraphim wards in place in a hurry."

"On it," Muriel called out, a story gem in her fist, as she worked quickly beside Kesien to drench the ruined studio apartment in white seraphim light.

"I should have used my seraphim powers to ward the place," he replied. "Never thought about that until now."

Talia shook her head. "It requires too much power, Jack. You'd be power drunk if you warded this place."

"Good to know," he said with a smile.

"Anahera, are you still detecting the angel executioner?"

Anahera turned around, short red hair bright in the glow of the first seraphim ward.

"Nothing so far," she answered in a soft soprano voice.

"Babe," he said, knowing he'd have her full attention in a moment. "I know she's gone because she let something slip that Azrael and the seraphim need to know."

"What did she say, Jack?" Talia asked, her gaze still evaluating the apartment and scrutinizing her squad's activities.

"Lucifer had a soul planted in Purgatory that invited Samael and his guard through that door," Jack explained. "That's how they escaped from your guard."

Movement in the whole room ceased as all the angels turned toward him. Talia took hold of his shoulders, a look of surprise widening her intense grey eyes.

"What?" she cried. "Lucifer placed a soul in Purgatory to help them escape capture?"

Jack nodded. "Yep, said that it had all been planned. I even have the name of the dude that killed himself to be there when Samael needed an escape route."

Muriel, Kesien, and Deemah blinked across the room and stood in front of him, their expressions fearful. Except Kesien who looked murderous, an expression he'd never seen on the tall, normally, and laid-back angel's face before.

"All of this had been planned and orchestrated!" Kesien shouted, shaking his fist at the room. "Right down to entering Purgatory!"

Deemah laid her hand on his arm and tried to calm him, but Kesien was furious.

"Sorry, dude," said Jack. "But at least you know their clock's ticking in there."

"That's a very good point, Jack," said Talia. "Angels and demons can't remain in Purgatory. We need to ask Pravuil about how long that timeframe is and be there when they're expelled."

Kesien's eyes narrowed. "I'll be there to drag them back to High House to answer for the carnage they unleashed on this guard. So many angels were erased from existence when they turned on us and assaulted the spires!"

Angels had…died over this jail break and heist? That made him queasy. He thought angels were eternal. He slid his arm around Talia's waist and held her closer.

"I'm sorry," he said. "I didn't know that."

Talia held him closer. "It was brutal, Jack," she said in a sad voice. "We lost several angels when they turned. A horrible act for creatures of the light to commit."

"And it will be met with exacting retribution," said Kesien, a determined glint in his charcoal grey eyes. "I pledge myself to bringing every one of them to justice."

He meant those words.

Guilt began to poke at Jack, especially when he glanced over at Gianni who gave him a stern look.

"Isn't there more, Jack?" said Gianni in a sharp tone.

Jack sighed. After this news, they needed to know the rest. He couldn't keep this from Talia or angels like Kesien. Maybe he could help them go into Purgatory and get Samael? Make that salty bastard pay.

Talia's eyes narrowed as she glanced at Gianni and then back at him. "Jack…"

He nodded. "There is." He shoved his hands into his Levi's pockets and began to pace.

Talia crossed her arms and exchanged a wary look with Muriel.

"Why am I already scared?" Muriel replied.

"Okay," he said, not looking at Talia. "I haven't even begun processing this yet."

She was going to freak. He only hoped it wasn't at him.

"Processing what?" she replied. "You're scaring me, Jack."

"Zanth came here tonight…to ask for my help."

"What?" Talia's response was shrill and frightened.

"A demon wants your help?" Muriel replied. "And not just any demon either. An angel executioner."

Kesien stepped in front of him, anger burning in those grey eyes. He grabbed Jack by the shoulders, looking all angel of death intense and retribution-focused.

"Spill it, Jack!" he shouted.

Jack met his angry glare. "Dude, chill," he said in a calm voice, almost like the tone he remembered from Kesien. Always so consistent and laid-back. Not like this. "I'm getting to it."

"We're wasting valuable time, Jack," he said, insistent. "No games."

Jack felt his anger spark. "Dude, when have I ever played games with you? I may have spared Talia some hurt a few times, but I'm a straight shooter. You should know that by now."

At last, Kesien nodded, the intensity in his face dissipating. "You're right. Forgive me, Jack." He let go of him, turning away. "I've witnessed so much over the millennia and thought I had seen everything. Until I flew back to Eolowen and saw all of that light spilled across the terrace stones. Angels obliterated by their own kind. To side with evil. It...it..." He laid his hand against his chest. "It hurts. And I feel responsible—and I don't know who to trust anymore."

"Angels obliterated?" Jack replied in a quiet, calm voice, hoping to acknowledge what Kesien was going through right now. "Dude, I can't even imagine how horrible that must have been. Must have felt like a war zone. Like it did that day during the battle for Heaven."

Kesien shook his head, his voice so painfully quiet. "It was worse, Jack. Because I brought them into Azrael's guard. Me."

He turned toward Jack and Jack saw the hurt burning in those grey eyes. He looked so wounded. So broken.

"And without warning, they turned on the guard," said Kesien, looking so disturbed. "During training. Ran their sparing partners through with swords and hit them with bolts of Holy fire until the light poured out from their bodies and drenched the stones. And emptied from their eyes." He winced, bowing his head. "Azrael couldn't stop it. He tried, but they attacked and fled, leaving the guard powerless to defend the spire when demons and my former guard broke Samael out of High House. And then assaulted the archive. For the Book." His hand smashed into a fist, teeth gritted. "All those angels lost—for a book!"

Jack reached out and gripped his arm.

"You're not responsible, Kesien," he said in an insistent tone. "You had no way of knowing that those bastards were hollow. That their hearts were rotten. That this had been part of Lucifer's plan all along."

Kesien's gaze jerked up from the floor and the six-foot-six angel stared at him in shocked silence.

Jack nodded. "Yeah, dude, it was planned. All the way back to that dickhead, Raziel. Lucifer was maneuvering Samael into position even then. We just didn't know it. Because that king of bastards always has a couple of contingency plans in motion. Samael was his—in case Raziel didn't follow through. And in case he failed to take Heaven."

"My God," Kesien said with a hiss. "You're right, Jack."

"Sucks when you feel played like this, but you had no way of knowing your former guard was positioning itself for an inevitable attack—if things didn't go Luci's way. Raziel was supposed to deliver the Book of Secrets along with Vassago. When that didn't happen, Luci moved other pieces into position. This wasn't your fault, Kesien. It's Lucifer's. Lucifer killed all those angels. Not your sense of angel justice. It isn't broken. It works just fine. You couldn't have known or sensed his plan."

The corners of Kesien's mouth lifted in a brief smile and he patted Jack on the back. "Thanks, Jack. Now, tell us what else happened."

Jack sighed. "Apparently, I have another unique ability that I didn't know about."

Talia spun him around to face her. "What ability?" she asked, staring into his eyes.

"According to Zanth, because I'm a living, breathing human that stands with one foot in Heaven and the other on Earth, I'm the only one in existence—besides God, I guess—that can open that door into Purgatory."

"But Jack," said Talia. "Every human sent to Purgatory can open the door into that realm."

Jack nodded. "But apparently, only I can open it back out again."

"Out again..." Muriel cried, sounding shocked. "Talia...Jack can open the door outward. I never even considered that."

"Zanth did," he said, continuing. "Because the soul that killed himself to be in Purgatory when Samael needed an escape route is Zanth's human lover. Who wasn't told he'd be stuck there instead of going to Hell and being reunited with his demon lover."

"Whoa! Seriously!" Muriel shouted. "Are you serious?"

"Deadly serious," he replied. "Zanth said his actions hadn't earned him an address change to Hell, so right now, she only has visitation rights in Purgatory. She wanted me to help her get him out."

Talia shook him. "Tell me you said no, Jack."

"Babe, I don't make deals with demons. Even for love."

She let go of him, hands on her hips. "Yes or no?"

"No, Tal. I said no."

Gianni stepped beside him, a hand on his shoulder. "I'm a witness, Talia. I heard him tell that archdemoness no."

Jack frowned. "So, now, I need witnesses? Should I call a lawyer before the guard reads me my rights?"

Talia's angry expression faded into a smile as she held up her left hand. "Your rights are to love, cherish, and respect me. While telling me everything. Now until forever."

"You say that in a closing-the-penitentiary-door kind of way."

She gave him a deep nod, that smile widening into a grin. "Marriage is a life sentence, Jack Casey. You're stuck with me."

He laughed. "Happily ever after stuck with you, Cinderella," he said, leaning down to kiss her as she slid her arms around him.

"Oh," he said, snapping his fingers. "Forgot one last thing."

"Uh, oh," said Kesien with a groan.

"Brace yourselves," Muriel replied, closing one eye as she pulled back from them. "Talia preparing to smite him in three, two, one…"

"Relax!" Jack cried and turned back to Talia. "Tal, she said his name was Tre Sheridan. Figured you could look up his archive book for more information. Might get you dudes closer to Samael."

Talia's eyes widened and she stared at him in surprise. "You have the soul's name?"

He nodded.

Grinning, Kesien ruffled Jack's hair. "Jack! That's fantastic! That's an incredible lead. If we can get into Purgatory, we can easily locate this soul's tie to Samael. It should lead us right to the archangel and my former guard members."

"I let Azrael know what Jack told us," said Talia.

In moments, Azrael materialized in front of Jack, startling the hell out of him. The archangel looked formidable in his clear gold armor, soot-grey wings extended, and charcoal grey eyes steely with determination as his attention focused solely on Jack.

"Jack!" Azrael cried, taking a step toward him. "Is it true? Do you really have the soul's name that invited Samael into Purgatory?"

He nodded. "His name is Tre Sheridan. Committed suicide to end up in Purgatory."

Azrael's demeanor shifted and he turned his gaze toward the Heavens, staring for several moments. Finally, he looked down at Jack again.

"Jack, Pravuil wants a word about this situation."

He glanced around, looking for the white-haired, gold-eyed archangel of the archive.

"Where is he?"

Azrael shook his head. "In Eolowen, Jack. To talk about you opening doors."

Jack turned toward Gianni. He'd seen and heard all of this. Probably understood about half of it, too, like Jack had when he first started seeing angels and demons. The guard let Gianni see them this time.

"Be safe, Jack," said Gianni, casting a glance at the angels and then at Talia. "Take care, Talia. I'm going to head home to Los Feliz and Izzy. We'll talk as soon as Herb gets the word about whether the new show is a go."

Jack patted Gianni's shoulder. "Dude, take care. Thanks for being my bodyguard and kicking demon ass with me tonight. And thanks for the beer and pizza."

"Let's do it again soon, Jack," he said with a smile. "With less demons and more beer and metal."

"You're on," Jack replied.

"But not at my place," said Gianni, shaking his head. "I don't want to try and explain a mess like this to Izzy."

"I'll make sure my next place is warded first," said Jack.

"Take care, Jack," said Gianni as he leaned the sword against the wall and shuffled out of the apartment.

"Muriel, can you send some of your guard to make sure no demons mess with him and Izzy? No Watchers."

"Already handled, Jack," said Muriel. "We've got some of the guard stationed around his residence. We'll make sure that both of them are safe." She glanced around his apartment. "In the meantime, this guard will see if we can put your place back together, too, starting with the back door. Anahera and I are starting to get the hang of door repair."

"Thanks," Jack replied.

"Ready, Jack?" Talia asked and wrapped her arms around him.

He kissed her lips and extended his wings. "Let's go visit the in-laws, babe."

Azrael and Kesien stepped beside them and together, they blinked out of the apartment. And up to Heaven.

TALIA KEPT CLOSE TO JACK AS THEY FLEW OVER EOLOWEN, MURIEL AND Anahera on point, Kesien and Deemah on flank. Trails of dark smoke still hung in the skies over the Heavens, turning the crisp Parrish blue skyline almost gunmetal blue. It dulled the sunlight and the gleam of crystalline rooftops. Even the distant spires that had always glistened white on the horizon had turned dusky grey in the aftermath of Samael's assault.

Shock still hung heavy along the air currents, the angelic choruses barely a whisper. The hush of song gave her some comfort, but an eerie atmosphere still clung to her home, one she hadn't felt since Lucifer had marched on the Heavens.

And across the Heavens, the smell of brimstone lingered like ozone.

The loss of so many angels cast a painful reflection throughout the clouds and across sun-drenched meadows. And sent a frightening message. Not even paradise was safe from Lucifer's darkness.

What terrified her more than anything was that Samael's escape had been planned and engineered.

Even when Lucifer had been trapped in the Garden, his nefarious plans were in motion and playing out from every direction. And that meant, even after his failed bid to takeover Heaven, Lucifer still had destructive goals in mind. Carefully laid out and orchestrated. Like the Phoenix shifts. Like the wagers. Even Jack succumbing to a cocaine overdose.

In every one of those situations, Lucifer had been clear about his intentions. He was trying to takeover Heaven. But now? No one had any clue what Lucifer was trying to accomplish.

What did Lucifer gain in helping Samael escape? Why did he want the Book of Secrets? The parts necessary to awaken those powers were only located within Heaven. It made no sense. But it terrified her.

She motioned Jack toward the atrium room where he'd once spent a lot of time recovering and training with the guard. Right now, the circular room was setup for healing. More than a dozen soft white pallets dotted the white stone floor, injured angels stretched out on them.

Berith and the cherub, Oseira flitted around the room, caring for the injured, and closing wounds that leaked gold light like human blood. Oseira, skin dark bronze and eyes bright yellow, sang out angel notes of healing as she treated and bandaged wounds. She wore a long white angel robe beneath a burnished gold breastplate, her wings snow white against the mottled grey robes and dove grey wings of the angels of death surrounding her. Cherubs could shift form into an eagle, an ox, a lion, and a human form and Oseira appeared human. Like all cherubim, when she did shift form, it was instant and chilling.

Looking tired and frazzled, Oseira struggled to carry angels through the room and over to pallets along the walls, requiring angels of death to assist her.

Had she been injured in the attack?

Normally, cherubim were stronger than most angels—except seraphim. After Oseira had settled the latest casualty, she moved toward Berith. And God's Scribe lying in the bed against the wall. For a moment, Oseira leaned against the wall, eyes closed.

Talia frowned. That was odd.

Cherubim were stronger than archangels and angels of death

combined. If Oseira was struggling, why didn't she shift into her oxen form? Only a short while ago, Talia had watched Oseira fly into Eolowen carrying two injured angels from High House.

So much prolonged and intense healing must have taxed her powers. Talia turned her gaze to Berith.

Berith's mottled grey robes stood out against all the crisp, bright cherubim- white robes, rose-gold halo spinning fast. She was the only angel in the room without any armor—at her behest. Berith said she'd grown weary of the constant state of war in Hell and refused to don battle armor—even back in Heaven.

Berith sat on the edge of the bed where she'd tended Jack several times, caring for Archangel Pravuil this time. She applied ribbons of gold healing light to a thick, deep gash across Pravuil's forehead. Oseira's gold healing light looked a little pale and almost tarnished. The cherub needed rest.

God's Scribe looked livid, face taut, and those piercing, gold archangel eyes flashing with fury. A thin trail of pale gold light leaked down the side of his face and disappeared into his short white hair. She and Oseira had to hold him down to keep him in bed.

"I don't care! Let me up!" Pravuil shouted, struggling to rise from the bed.

"Lie still," Oseira cried, two hands pressing his shoulders and wings back against the bed, but Pravuil was winning the tug of war. "You're leaking light from your injuries."

Light leaked from both of the Scribe's white wings, feathers sliced away, and jagged slashes cutting across both wings. His face was shadowed, but the anger burned hot in his gold eyes.

"Too bad!" the Scribe snarled, "I'm going after that winged turncoat if I have to inch across the airstream to do it!"

"Scribe, please—" said Berith, looking disheveled and unnerved by the number of wounded and what had happened at Eolowen.

Azrael rushed to Oseira's side and pushed Pravuil back against the bed.

"Scribe! Listen to reason—you can't fly like this," Azrael insisted, pressing against Pravuil's shoulders.

Jack landed beside Talia, gaping at all the injured angels. He hadn't seen a scene like this since Lucifer assaulted the Heavens. Even then, he'd been too busy trading fatal bursts of Holy fire with Lucifer in the haunted woods and hadn't seen the toll that any of these skirmishes had taken on Heaven's angels. He looked worried and unnerved and hadn't uttered a sound.

"Azrael, let me go!" Pravuil yelled, struggling against his hold. "I want that monster's head on a platter! So, I can file it in the archive under loser."

At last, Jack smiled, but his amused expression quickly faded as his worried gaze returned to the number of injured angels in the room.

"Sir," said Talia, calling to Azrael. "You called for us?"

"Ah, Talia," said Azrael, looking up at her from Pravuil's side. "I'll be with you and Jack in a moment."

"Jack?" the Scribe exclaimed. "Jack Casey?"

"Yes, Scribe," said Azrael. "I called them back immediately when you—"

"Jack Casey, get over here right now!" Pravuil ordered, slapping his hand against the bed. "I want to talk to you."

Shrugging, Jack glanced at Talia and she nodded him over.

He hesitated, but then walked over to Pravuil's bedside as angels darted past him on all sides.

"What'd I do this time?" Jack asked with a groan, standing beside the bed.

"Nothing yet," said the Scribe, that twinkle returning to his gold eyes. "But you're about to, young man."

Jack's eyebrows pressed into a frown, those luscious, bow-shaped lips turning downward as confusion shadowed his clean-shaven face.

"Won't that get me smited?" he asked in a quiet voice that brightened Pravuil's dark, angry expression.

"Hardly," said Pravuil. "It might get you knighted—that's a figure of speech. No knights in Heaven." Pravuil pressed his fingers against his forehead, a pained look rising and falling on his face. "Listen, Jack, Samael and his traitors nearly destroyed me when they ransacked the archive and stole the Book of Secrets. I threw everything I had at those vermin, but there were too many. Thank the Maker that Berith got to me in time. Before those monsters extinguished my light entirely—like they did to several of my staff."

That possibility made Talia shiver. Heaven had come so close to losing God's Scribe.

"That little bitch, Samael has some real payback coming," Jack said with a growl.

All the angels in the room paused to stare at him, looking a little surprised and unnerved. Jack glanced up, noticing how quiet the room had gotten.

"Guess vengeance isn't very divine, is it?" he said in a sheepish voice. "But I'm human and I'm not sorry. Samael created this mess. And I'm going to make sure he cleans it up, too."

Oseira patted his shoulder as Berith smiled at him.

"Angels don't judge, Jack," said Oseira. "We shepherd and soldier. The seat of judgment is reserved for the Maker."

Berith laid her hand on his arm, squeezing. "I think the room appreciates your…colorful determination, Jack."

Talia moved to his left side and slid her arms around him. "Especially this angel," she said and held him close.

"Thanks, Mrs. Casey," he said, leaning over and kissing her.

"And I appreciate your willingness to kick Archangel Samael's ass all the way back to Baladon, Jack," said Pravuil in a sharp tone, startling the roomful of angels again. "Now, tell me about this planned attack and this latest unique ability of yours."

Berith's eyes widened and she glanced at Azrael. "What new ability? Jack, you be careful. This situation is almost as dire as the day that Lucifer marched on the Heavens."

"Yes, Mom," he said and gave Berith a quick hug. "I'll wear my jacket and look both ways before I kick Samael's ass."

Azrael and God's Scribe laughed, but the hard look from Berith made Azrael's frown return. He cleared his throat, looking stern again.

Pravuil grabbed Jack's arm and hauled him over to the bed. He pulled Jack toward him, forcing him to sit on the edge of the bed.

"The ability, Jack," Pravuil snapped. "Tell me what that demon said to you."

"Demon?" Berith's eyes got huge and she turned to the archangel. "Azrael, what demon?"

"According to Zanth the angel executioner, I can open the door into Purgatory," said Jack with a shrug. "And apparently, I can open it out of Purgatory, too. Because of my unique position of having one foot in Heaven and one on Earth."

"By the Maker!" Pravuil cried, his gold eyes animated and bright. "That's true!" The Scribe turned his attention to Azrael, glaring. "Azrael, why in the Heavens am I hearing about this from a demon?"

The archangel shook his head. "Wish I knew, Scribe. We only found this out a few minutes ago."

That sexy smirk lifted the corners of Jack's mouth, a mischievous glint in those smoldering, light green eyes.

"That's because it took love to discover it, Scribe," said Jack. "Must have killed those demons when they realized that the light was still winning."

Pravuil frowned. "Love? Explain."

"The angel executioner came to me tonight, asking for my help. Said that her human lover was the soul that had invited Samael into Purgatory and allowed him to escape Heaven."

"Human lover?" Pravuil raised an eyebrow. "I need more explanation than that, Jack. Continue."

The room had gotten very quiet since Jack started talking.

"Her human lover committed suicide—"

"Well, paint me with Holy fire and call me a seraph!" Pravuil exclaimed. "Those demons got a human mixed up in this debacle? Convinced him to kill himself—so that ragged-winged traitor could escape his well-earned consequences! This is an outrage!"

Jack laid his hand on Pravuil's sleeve, gaining his attention. "Scribe, this dude wanted to spend eternity with his demon lover, Zanth. The angel executioner. Lucifer promised him a place in the power structure and at her side if he landed in Purgatory and opened the door for that douchebag, Samael and his dickhead followers."

Talia heard some chuckles and angel whispers throughout the room.

"Well said, Jack," said Pravuil.

"So, this demon asks me to help her get him out," said Jack, motioning toward the crossroads. "Said I was the only one that could help her because I could open the door into Purgatory. And I could open it out of Purgatory. Long enough for this dude to escape with her. A match made in Hell, but hey, love is love. I don't judge."

"Pravuil, this is huge," said Berith, stepping behind Jack and laying her hands on his shoulders.

"What do you mean, Berith?"

She smiled. "This angel executioner is willing to risk everything and break ties with Lucifer to rescue her lover. When she does that, Lucifer will put a bounty on her head like he did Jack's. Then every demon in Lucifer's army will hunt her and her lover."

Azrael stepped forward. "If she's really turned toward love and not darkness, then she and this soul will need our protection. One less demon in Hell is a victory I'll take any day, Pravuil."

"What the archangel said," Jack replied. "We do this right and they see we're not self-righteous, unwavering blowhards that only care about rules. Like Lucifer's tried to convince the world about Heaven. If Zanth and Tre see we're all about love and fairness and atonement not vengeance, then maybe they'll join our fight?"

Both Azrael and Pravuil were smiling now.

"Azrael, hire this young man for our public relations department immediately," said Pravuil.

Azrael shrugged. "I don't know, Pravuil. He used the word *we*. Sounds to me like he's already part of the team."

Talia wrapped her arms tighter around him. "He is, archangel."

That smirk on Jack's face brightened. "Married into the family business, what can I say?"

She leaned over and kissed him.

"And I'd marry you all over again, Mrs. Casey," he replied, but his gaze turned serious as he returned his attention to Pravuil. "Scribe, this dude gave up his life to be with Zanth. Not to help Lucifer. And

Lucifer royally screwed him—like that's a new thing. What if we can get this soul on our side right now? Get him to lure Samael to him in Purgatory. Where Talia and her squad will be waiting for him. Let into Purgatory by me. Samael will run like the little bitch he is, so we pursue him. And herd his ass right out that door and into the guard's custody."

Pravuil was grinning now. "Jack Casey, I like how you think. What about it, Azrael?"

A smile touched the archangel's face, those charcoal grey eyes brightening.

"It's risky," he said, rubbing his chin. "Jack, Talia and her squad could get overwhelmed by demons in there. But Jack has the power to open that door, whereas the demons do not. And the guard and the seraphim would be waiting on the other side of that door. That Jack could open for us, too. I think it's our best option right now."

"It's our only option," said Talia, rubbing Jack's wings. "We can't let Samael escape to Hell with the Book of Secrets."

"Agreed," said Jack. "But if we go in and set a trap for Samael, I want all of you to know right now, that if I agree to help Zanth— which I haven't decided about yet—I will open that door and let Tre Sheridan escape through it when I leave. I'm not going to be like Lucifer or the demons and double-cross Zanth. If I agree to help her, I intend to follow through with my promise."

"Fair enough, Jack," said Pravuil. "Let me discuss this with the seraphim before we agree to anything." God's Scribe reached over and patted Jack's arm. "Don't want anything going into your Book of Life and Death that will jeopardize your afterlife, Jack."

Jack nodded. "Appreciate that, Scribe." He looked over at Talia who stood at his left shoulder, and gripped her hand. "I also don't want anything added to my book that will separate me and Talia. Got it?"

Pravuil's eyebrows lifted. "What if you've earned a place with the Risen, Jack?"

Talia stiffened. If Jack's soul was among the Risen, then his soul would ascend to the highest place in Heaven. Far, far above where she could touch in the ethereal plane. Allowing them only stolen moments and brief encounters at best. It made her chest ache to think that he might someday ascend for eternity and leave her behind in Heaven's lower reaches where only angels dwelled.

"Especially that," said Jack. "If she can't stand beside me as my wife, then I'm not going there. Period."

He laid his hand to his heart and then held it out to her. She clasped his hand in hers and pressed it to her heart.

She loved this man more than her own existence.

"I'm never going to stop falling in love with you, Jack Casey," she said to him in a quiet voice.

"And I'm never going to exist a day without you, Talia," he said, squeezing her hand. "Or go someplace where you can't follow. I love you too much."

Pravuil squeezed Jack's arm. "Not to worry, Jack," he said. "We'll keep your Book real. And I promise not to submit your name for sainthood."

"Saint Jack?" Jack said with a chuckle. "That might give God a really good laugh. Besides, anybody that knows me will tell you that the moment I opened my mouth, I'd erase any chances I had at...uh, leveling up. I'll be lucky if they let me in the upstairs window at the end of the day."

"Not to worry about that, Jack," said Pravuil. "Unless you do something really stupid. Like side with Lucifer."

Jack laughed. "I think I'm off Luci's Christmas list. More like his shit list. Dude's hung up on me three times already this week."

Azrael's brow furrowed and he looked alarmed.

"Jack, Lucifer's called you three times?"

"That I answered," he replied. "He called to give Zanth a message. Didn't like me poking him, I guess."

"What message?" Azrael replied and moved toward Jack.

Jack shrugged. "He wanted her to find out how much seraphim power I had left after Gianni and I fought a shitload er, boatload of demons at my place."

"His place was smoking wreckage when we left for Eolowen, sir," said Talia. "I left some of the guard to put it back together, but it may require Jack's seraphim powers to fix everything back the way it was."

Azrael's mouth pressed into a worried line, those steely grey eyes looking pensive now as he stared past Jack, deep in thought.

"Something wrong?" Jack asked, glancing from her to Azrael.

Azrael folded his arms against his chest, soot-grey wings twitching.

"I'm not sure, Jack. That just seems odd to me."

"What seems odd?"

"That Lucifer would be testing your seraphim powers again. Hadn't he seen enough at the vineyard when you used omnificence to bargain with him and Abaddon simultaneously? That took much more power than a simple fight with Lare Dumont and Tyler Hughes —and some assassin demons."

Talia felt a cold chill settle against her wings. What was Azrael getting at? It frightened her. A lot.

"Azrael? What's the matter?"

"It's like Lucifer's running an experiment of some kind," said Azrael finally, not turning around. "Throwing demons at Jack and then observing how much power he has left. Then throwing his angel executioner at him. And gauging how much power he drained in that fight." Finally, Azrael turned around. "Like he's tailor-making the right sort of assault to throw against Jack that will completely drain him. Rendering him powerless."

Now, she was terrified.

Lucifer was still fixated on Jack. Way beyond this vendetta he'd protested way too loudly about. No, he wanted something from Jack. But what? Lucifer was a master of subtlety and misdirection. He'd had millennia to perfect his craft and watching Jack poke him with verbal sticks made her ache all over. Lucifer wouldn't allow a human to best him for long. He would hit back. Hard. When Jack least expected it.

For the first time, she was glad that Jack had seraphim powers. He wasn't an easy mark for Lucifer, but human limits were easier to hit than ethereal limits. Lucifer was trying to figure out where that limit was for Jack.

For what purpose? She doubted that it was solely for petty revenge. Lucifer had a goal, but she had no idea what he sought. Or why. Beyond killing Jack.

"Is he that hell-bent on revenge?" Jack asked. "Going to all those lengths to drain my power and kill me?"

"Yes, Jack," said Pravuil. "He would. You represent everything that made him fall from the Heavens. And you're one of God's Chosen, so if he strikes at you, he hurts God, too. And hurting Him is still one of Lucifer's primary focuses. Along with destroying anything connected with humanity because he doesn't want it to replace angels."

Jack shook his head and gripped Talia's hand tighter. "Wow, dude has the worst abandonment issues I've ever seen." He bowed his head. "Hate to say it though, but I do understand how he feels."

"What?" Azrael cried. "You're empathizing with that monster?"

"No," he snapped, his gaze shifting to the archangel's angry eyes. "I can just understand how it feels for one of your parents to dump you, that's all. But instead of wanting to crush them out of existence, I want to fix it somehow. I'm just saying that I get what eats at him, that's all."

The archangel seemed to relax at the rest of Jack's statement.

"Azrael," Pravuil called, motioning toward the terrace. "Gather your guard together and start training them for some heavy demon fighting. Because that's what they'll encounter in Purgatory. If Lucifer planted a soul in there, then he's got the place crawling with demons to protect Samael and our Book. You need to send your best five-angel squad through that door and station the rest of them outside it."

Azrael blinked over to the bed, arms still crossed, and stared down at Pravuil.

"Why only five angels, Scribe?" he asked. "If it's going to be an all-out war in there, why not send the whole guard?"

"And panic that schmuck into running with that Book? Forget it!" Pravuil's face flushed red, his voice rising. "We need a small strike team to go in there, locate this soul, stake him out, and hit Samael when he least expects it. They won't draw a lot of demon attention or stand out that way."

Azrael was nodding. "True, true. A large force of angels might alarm Samael."

"Exactly," said the Scribe, his attention sliding from Talia to Azrael. "Then when that putz runs—and trust me, he will—your strike team will herd him right out that door and into the guard's trap."

Talia nodded at the Scribe. "I agree, Azrael. Five angels won't stand out and a squad is nimble enough to move fast and move quietly."

The Scribe pointed at her. "Just what Talia said, Azrael," he said to the archangel. "And then Jack suddenly opens that door out of Purgatory and Samael won't think twice. He'll bolt like a jackrabbit through it. Right into the open arms of your guard. With the Book of Secrets."

Azrael studied Talia a moment. "I think you and the Scribe are right, Talia. A five-angel team can be swift, but keep to the shadows."

Her gaze shifted to Jack and he looked concerned.

"So, you're planning to keep me on the sepulcher side of the door, aren't you?" Jack said finally.

The Scribe and Azrael both nodded.

"When I have seraphim powers and can help protect your squad?"

"You're human, Jack," Azrael replied. "It's too dangerous. We have no idea how many demons are inside there."

Jack turned to Talia, staring at her with those sizzling light green eyes. "Tal, what do you think?"

She nodded at Azrael. "I'd feel better if you were safe with the guard, Jack."

"Okay," he said with a sigh. "I'll sit this one out. With the guard."

"Then it's decided," said Azrael, unfurling his wings. "Talia, Muriel, mobilize the guard. Put them in their squads and run them through every single drill the guard runs. I want training around the clock. I'll be observing throughout the exercises and I'll select the best five-angel squad to enter Purgatory."

"Understood, sir," said Talia.

"On it, sir," Muriel announced and spread her wings, lifting off for the rooftop.

Azrael nodded at Jack. "We'll keep Jack in Eolowen for now. In case, Lucifer decides to run more experiments. Or send his angel executioner for another test run."

Talia slid back from Jack as he rose from the bed and stuffed his hands into the pockets of those faded Levi's that hugged his leanly muscled body in all the right places.

"Jack?" Azrael called as he turned away. "I do want you back in Eternean armor though. I don't want to take any chances."

"I'll get Jack's armor out of the gear room," said Kesien. "It's hanging right beside Talia's Eternean armor."

"Thanks, dude," said Jack, glancing around the room, a funny look on his face, one Talia couldn't quite read. "I'll..." He glanced around. "Sit under the willow tree and look busy."

He flexed his wings and flew through one of the portals onto the roof.

Talia frowned. He looked a little lost. Was he upset at not being part of the strike team? Or relieved? She wasn't sure what was going on in that actor's head of his, but as soon as she got the guard divided into squads and training, she'd find out what was bothering her new husband.

8

Jack flew across the terrace and through the smoky haze toward the willow tree that draped its delicate boughs over the cold, bubbling stream that ran along Eolowen's winding white stone pergola. He landed and folded his wings against his back, settling against the gnarled, grooved trunk of the ancient tree. Feeling a little useless.

Okay, a LOT useless.

Even with seraphim powers, they didn't want him anywhere near the fight to recapture Samael and his guard. Or Purgatory, a place that, as a human, he'd be the most useful to them. Especially when they located this soul that had invited Samael into Purgatory. He understood this dude better than anyone. A few extra turns of the wheel and that could have been him.

Tre Sheridan had recently died, so he'd definitely relate better to Jack than angels. Lucifer had probably filled this dude's head with lies about them, too, so Jack expected him to be wary of angels. And only thinking about what he'd lost—the love of his life. Jack related to that better than any of the angels. Except maybe Talia and Azrael.

God, he felt confused right now. He felt like everything was slipping through his fingers. First, Talia being called back to Heaven. And no word from Herb on the new show.

Had his newfound fame burned itself out when he married Talia on live television? And when Talia had to rush back to Heaven without him, he felt like his life had come full circle. Returning to all the bad stuff.

Right back to where he'd begun this crazy journey, too. Alone. In his shithole studio apartment south of L.A. With no one but Evan Bellows wanting to hire him—for a cameo. Where it all began.

Heaven still hadn't responded about him and Talia staying together and he feared that they would keep calling her back here, more and more, longer, and longer, until they grew apart. And became polite strangers. Or hated each other and wanted to put worlds between them—like his parents.

Before, Azrael had included him in the guard. This time, he'd felt like an observer. Almost an outsider. After all, he was only the doorman for this operation. Nothing more.

Not that he had to be the center of it all, but he felt so much distance this time. And that disturbed him. He liked being the honorary member of the guard. Not the Make-a-Wish guard for a day feeling he'd had today. Like they'd plopped some fake wings and a lopsided halo on his head to make him feel included.

And he even hated the idea of Talia going in there after Samael without him. Of her battling that double-crossing douchebag archangel and his backstabbing, murdering band of death angels. That little bitch had screwed over most of Heaven and he'd use every dirty trick he had to escape them. And he wasn't afraid to erase angels from existence either, especially angels of death—which seemed to be his new hobby.

He couldn't take it if Muriel and Kesien came back without Talia. He wanted to be there to make sure the only angels that got erased from existence were Samael and his guard.

He plucked a long blade of deep green grass from the ground and twisted it around his fingers as he watched the angels of death fly in and out of the round room off the grand hall. Overhead and across the terrace, they gathered in five-angel groups, gold shields of light clutched in their hands, wings beating the air that smelled a little like woodsmoke and ozone with traces of sulfur.

Sunlight cut through the smoky haze, burning it away, and reflecting off that clear gold armor that Heaven's master armorer, Archangel Zephana, had made for the battle against Lucifer.

His phone vibrated.

He slid it out of his Levi's pocket and glanced at the screen. Three texts. All from Herb.

Today, 8:36 PM

Jack, show swept the ratings again. Huge numbers. Network still being cautious though. Ordered 6 episodes of Divine Newlyweds. Show's officially a go.

Today, 9:59 PM

Contracts for you and Talia sent to your agent with a nice per episode salary increase.

Today 11:21 PM

Filming will be on set at Studio 22 and on location around L.A. Rehearsals will start sometime in MID-JUNE.

PLEASE tell me you haven't spoken or met with Evan Bellows.

He glanced at the signal on his phone. Still had two bars—even in Heaven. His thumbs flicked across the onscreen keypad.

Good news, Herb
Tal n I will get contracts back asap
And no, haven't spoken 2 Evan...c u soon

Almost immediately, his phone buzzed with Herb's response. At least, this time, Herb wouldn't have to wait days for his response.

Relieved!

    Thank you and take care, Jack

He tapped out a quick response.

u2 Herb

When no more texts appeared, he slid his phone back into his pocket and leaned against the rough tree bark again as the sunlight began to sparkle through the willow tree's tiny leaves and delicate branches. He watched Talia soar across Eolowen's rooftop, drawing squad's together in phalanx formations, and directing them through drills. Shield-bashing. Sword thrusts. Dodging blows. Her guard had probably been through these exercises a bazillion times.

He watched Kesien go through shield bashes and sword thrusts with almost frenetic determination, his grey eyes lit with fire. Samael's wholesale killing of death angels had upset Kesien in a way that Jack had never seen before. Dude was adamant about bringing these douchebags down. By himself.

Jack understood.

Kesien felt responsible for what happened. Guilt gnawed at him. Jack saw it in his face. Along with the beginning of those terrible second guesses that were haunting him. The kind that woke Jack up at 3 A.M. The *what-ifs* and *why-didn't-I's*. Guess even angels had regrets. Kesien had always been so laid-back and calm. This carnage had changed him. Jack hoped that the Kesien he knew and appreciated made it through to the other side.

The world didn't need another vengeful angel like Lucifer. Not that Kesien was anything like that. He hoped Kesien understood that none of what had happened at Eolowen was his fault.

Jack watched the angels of death train, dove grey wings and clear gold armor filling the Parrish blue skies as the smoke dissipated, clash of swords against shields ringing out like thunder throughout the Heavens. Pushing up the sleeves of his navy blue hoodie, blue Vans slip-ons propped on a tree root, he tried to relax. But he had a nagging feeling that everything was about to come apart at the seams.

What was Lucifer's goal with all of these attacks?

An assault on the archive. A jailbreak. Marking him and putting another bounty on his head. Samael would have never had the balls to attack God's Scribe on his own. No, Lucifer was behind all of it—including taking that Book of Secrets. And not even God's Scribe had a clue why.

It made Jack queasy. Because Lucifer only set his sights on big scores. And whatever he was up to right now was big. Huge.

Dove grey wings fluttered overhead.

He glanced up, smiling. Talia.

She landed beside him in the grass and knelt in front of him.

He patted the cool shady grass to his right. "Hey, babe," he said with a smile. "Wanna share some shade with me? We can make out while no one's looking."

She laid her long, tapered fingers against his face, brushing them across his cheek and across the curve of his jaw.

"Hope that's just a warmup, Mrs. Casey," he said and pulled her into his arms as her wings flattened against her back.

"It is," she said against his ear. "Until I can get you alone."

"When would that be?" he asked with a chuckle. "We haven't been alone for..." He paused and stared into her intense grey eyes. "Well... never."

"True," she said, leaning over and kissing him hard on the lips. "But I'm determined to make that happen."

He slid his arms around her neck and gazed into her luminous grey eyes. "I like a woman who's motivated."

His kiss was deep, urgent, everything feeling so fragile and fleeting. He remembered the time he'd spent underneath these branches once, feeling broken and lost after Lucifer had taken control of Talia and took her away from him. He'd almost lost her.

And it felt like the end of the world, something he never wanted to feel again.

That time had passed, but he felt something dark stirring at the edges of the crossroads, along the roads that skirted the Heavens. An evil growing like a cancer. Straight out of Hell. He didn't know what any of it was, but he felt it—deep in his soul.

And he knew he was powerless to stop it.

"Jack?"

His gaze met hers and he realized that he'd just shut down on her. He felt distracted and worried. Uncertain about what she'd face in Purgatory. And dammit, he wanted to be beside her, protecting her. He didn't want to be separated from her again. The thought of that scared him to death.

"Jack?"

"Yeah, babe," he said finally.

She snuggled deeper into his arms and laid her head on his shoulder, staring up at him with those scrutinizing, angel of death grey eyes. She knew something was up.

He couldn't hide it any longer. He wasn't that good of an actor.

"You completely disengaged from me just now," said Talia, eyes wide. "Right in the middle of a very sensual kiss. What is it? You've never done that before." Worry shimmered in her luminous grey eyes. "Is it me?"

He shook his head emphatically. "God, no, Talia!" He cupped her chin. "I'm so sorry. You always make my blood boil."

"But…" she said, staring at him.

"Guess this thing with Samael has me worried," he confessed. "And I hate being separated from you again. Plus, the fact that I won't be beside you in there."

He bowed his head. He sounded like an insecure teenager with his first girlfriend. But he and Talia had been through so much, fighting to stay together, fighting to reunite, fighting to find the middle ground between Heaven and Earth.

She pressed a gentle kiss against his lips. "I knew something was up."

He sighed. "There's more," he said, glancing down at the grass.

Her eyes widened, fear creeping into her face now. She kept quiet though, nodding for him to continue.

"This thing with the guard," he began, trying to find a way to express what he felt. "Am I going to wake up alone most mornings? Eat dinner alone? Live my life with only brief visits from my angel of death wife until we're just two strangers wearing the same ring?"

"Jack, I—"

"Because if that's our future…tell me now," he said, an ache in his voice. "I don't want to wake up one morning a year from now and realize that it's our first anniversary. And I haven't seen my wife for months. And I didn't notice."

"Oh, Jack…no," she said, her eyes glassy, her arms tightening around him. "I won't let it be like that."

"It may be beyond your control, Tal," he said with a groan.

Tears gathered in her eyes, turning to crystals that clung to her long, dark lashes. He reached over and brushed them off her cheeks.

"So, if Heaven is planning to wield you full-time in its fight against Hell, tell me right now. So, I can start training for the next fight of my life. Because I'm going to enlist. If that's the only way we can stay together, then I'll be the best damned human member of the death angel guard that Heaven has ever seen."

At last, she smiled through her tears.

"You would do that?" she cried, her voice barely above a whisper.

He nodded. "I'd give up everything for you, Mrs. Casey. To be with you. And if they demand you be here full-time, then they're gonna be stuck with me in their ranks, too."

"I love you so much, Jack Casey," she said, holding him close.

She kissed him hard on the lips.

"Don't forget that I can fly here without a ticket and they can't keep me out unless they drop me into Hell."

Her smile lit up the shady haven beneath the willow tree, brighter than the sunlight that filtered through the smoky haze and onto the grass.

"C'mon," she said and slid out of his arms, her wings unfurling.

"Let's go get your Eternean armor from Muriel and get you into my squad. I don't want you out of that armor while you're in Heaven."

He grinned. "Even if my room empties out and it's just the two of us?"

She leaned up and kissed his mouth. "Correction," she said with a playful smile and tweaked his chin. "I don't want you out of that armor unless we're alone."

"Challenge accepted, Mrs. Casey," he said with a smirk and flexed his wings, lifting off from the ground.

He was careful to avoid the willow tree branches as Talia shot into the air beside him. Together, they flew toward the terrace where Muriel stood, carrying his armor. He blinked onto the terrace, wings folding against his back, and moved toward Muriel.

"Thanks for getting my armor out of hock, Muriel," he said and held out his arms for the load of lightweight, clear gold armor that Heaven's master armorer had made for him. "Was afraid I might have to sell my soul to get it back."

Muriel laughed and placed the bundle in his arms. "The guard was excited when I brought out your armor, Jack. They were hoping you'd be fighting alongside us again."

He smiled. "Thanks," he said. "I appreciate that. But right now, Azrael wants me in armor because of the situation with Samael."

"I want him wearing that armor, too," Talia added, wrapping her arm around his waist.

"Tal, too. Nothing beyond that though…unless you count opening the door to Purgatory combat."

Breastplate, greaves, pauldrons, and gauntlets. It was all here and as shiny as a clear-coated gold coin. That inner Holy fire writhed at its core like flames, giving it almost a sparkle as he slid on the breastplate and fastened the clasps under his arm. Over his hoodie. He clamped on the pauldrons and gauntlets and then snapped the greaves over his Levi's.

Talia chuckled. "Never seen an angel in Levi's and a hoodie before, Jack," she said.

He was relieved not to wear one of those grey short robes.

Muriel frowned. "Aw, that's it? Just door duty?" She shook her head. "The guard won't like that at all." She glanced toward the crossroads. "We'd all feel safer knowing that seraphim powers were backing us up." She fixed him with her gaze. "Especially with Jack Casey wielding them."

"Sorry, Muriel," he said and held out his hands. "I'm staying Heaven-side with Azrael and the rest of the guard while one of your squads goes in on their snipe hunt for that douchebag, Samael." He nodded at Muriel. "I'm betting your squad will be the one that goes in though."

Muriel looked surprised. "Why do you say that, Jack?"

Jack pointed at Kesien who was knocking back all comers with his sword and shield of light, Deemah bashing them hard with her shield. "My money's on Kesien and Deemah to bring Samael down." He motioned at Talia. "Add my beautiful angel of death wife to that mix and you, Muriel? No contest." He nodded at Kesien. "Besides, don't think Kesien will accept sitting this one out. He's on a mission to capture these douchebags."

Muriel turned and watched Kesien's almost brutal blowbacks against the rest of the guard. Samael's betrayal and the carnage they committed had deeply affected Kesien. And Deemah. They were fighting hard to make it inside that door for the chance to right this horrible wrong.

"Yeah," said Muriel, still watching Kesien's almost frantic movements. "I don't see Kesien sitting this one out. He feels responsible and he needs to be the one to bring them to justice." She turned around and poked Jack's shoulder. "Kind of like this actor I know. Has a similar obsession with fixing things himself."

"He taller than me?" Jack asked, making Muriel smile.

"C'mon, Talia, let's get the whole squad on these drills. Including your husband there. When he stands around, he gets into trouble."

Talia smiled as she tugged Jack alongside her and into the squad's formation.

"Don't I know it," said Talia, leaning over and kissing him. "I try to keep him busy."

"I've got a few suggestions about that," said Jack as he returned her kiss. "It involves the angel mile-high club and that round room over there."

Talia blushed, making Muriel bust out laughing.

"Love embarrassing my angel of death wife," said Jack as he wrapped Talia in his arms and followed Muriel into her squad's phalanx line at the edge of the terrace.

9

TALIA AND HER SQUAD TRAINED FOR HOURS, KESIEN AND DEEMAH BOTH still in hyper-focused modes as they battled a dozen other squads. Jack tried to match pace with her squad mates, but by the end of the drills, he looked exhausted, his eyes haggard, and his movements slowed.

He did his best to try and keep up with all the ethereal beings around him. He did an extraordinary job, too, impressing her guard and Archangel Azrael, but by the end of the trials, his human body had exhausted its energy.

He couldn't continue at that pace without food and sleep.

Frustrated, he had to finally acknowledge his limitations. Especially when Berith pulled him over to the edge of the dais beside Azrael when Jack began to look unsteady and sluggish. Earlier, Talia had tried to get him to take a break, but he refused, not wanting to look weak.

After a dozen squad against squad drills, he was hurting.

Berith noticed and forced him out of the phalanx line. He was angry, but too exhausted to fight her, too. Berith handed him a cold glass of water and made him sit down on the steps.

"Can't believe he kept up with us that long," said Muriel, pivoting right, shield-bashing a sword thrust.

Talia nodded and lunged at two other death angels, disarming one with her sword of Holy fire and knocking the other backward. The death angel spread his wings and kept his body from hitting the terrace floor hard.

Each time she or one of her squad disarmed a member of an opposing squad, that death angel was out of that round.

For this round, there was only one death angel left now. Daidrean.

Kesien, Deemah, and Anahera had him cornered against the terrace wall.

Daidrean fought hard, shield-bashing, and swinging his sword back and forth, but the five members of Talia's squad quickly overwhelmed him. Disarming him.

That left four squads undefeated.

"Way to go, Tal!" Jack called to her as he leaned against the wall, pale blond bangs dripping with sweat, green eyes hooded. His face had gone from red to pale. He still looked winded and a little fragile.

She blinked across the terrace and gave him a quick but passionate kiss. And waited for the next match to start.

Azrael was in a quiet but colorful discussion with God's Scribe in the doorway of the atrium room, Pravuil looking a little weaker than she'd expected. And that surprised her. Judging from the Scribe's injuries, she wondered if Archangel Samael and his guard had intended to extinguish Pravuil's lifeforce in that assault.

Along with the other angels in her guard that he'd murdered.

She glanced at Kesien who crossed his arms and leaned against the wall, staring across Eolowen's rolling meadows toward the crossroads. No doubt aching to follow Samael into Purgatory and take him down. She'd never seen such anger burn in Kesien before. He'd always been focused and dedicated, but he seemed almost obsessed with bringing Samael down. But she understood. What Samael did was beyond atonement. It was reprehensible. It was calculated and deliberate.

And Kesien had dedicated himself to bringing the archangel to justice. And his murderous guard.

She felt the same way. She'd lost members of her guard.

It hurt, knowing their lifeforces had been senselessly snuffed out. Knowing she'd never see them flutter through Eolowen's halls or float on Heaven's warm updrafts again.

What happened to angels when their light was extinguished? Was there a special place in Heaven for those ethereal beings—like God's Chosen? Or were angels considered an acceptable loss? Used up like an empty ink pen and discarded.

If angels and humans were to someday walk beside one another as equals, she needed an answer to that question. From God's Scribe.

"All right, angels," Azrael shouted as he blinked across the terrace, back to his dais. He stood with hands behind his back. "Begin. Last squad standing earns the honor of entering Purgatory to flush out Samael and his guard."

Kesien turned at the sound of Azrael's voice and hurried back into phalanx formation beside Deemah.

Talia flitted across the terrace, wings flexing, and took her place as the vanguard of her squad, in the center with Muriel and Anahera to her right and Kesien and Deemah to her left.

The other squad flew at them in a burst of speed, shields raised.

Kesien moved in tandem with her, shield-bashing the line that rushed at them. Muriel and Deemah shifted to the outside of the line, shields up as they pushed the other squad back with a fierce counterattack.

Whirling around, shield in motion, Kesien carved a path right through the other squad, felling four of them.

Talia took down the last of the squad. And it was all over.

She moved beside Muriel and watched the other two squads battle each other across the terrace. Their fight went on for a long time until, one by one, each squad's line fell apart. It came down to a face-off between two seasoned angels of death, both females. But a well-placed shield bash dropped the taller, paler angel of death.

"All right, angels," Azrael replied as he held up his hand. "We are down to two undefeated squads. Last skirmish. The squad that wins goes in after Archangel Samael."

"When?" Kesien called out, arms crossed against his Eternean breastplate, grey eyes intense and burning in the sunlight.

Jack stared at Kesien, looking concerned. Talia understood why. She hadn't seen Kesien like this before either. Most of the guard, including Azrael, were sympathetic to Kesien's pain over this attack. They'd lost angels, already a terrible and senseless tragedy, but they also understood what Kesien was feeling right now. Everyone in the guard had shown him their support, but it hadn't defused Kesien's ultra-driven response to the attack—and hyper-focus on capturing Samael.

She knew that Jack wanted to help Kesien, too, but the tall, usually calm, and laid-back angel of death had become distant. Only focused on going after Samael—something Jack understood well, being human. Humans had that ability to obsessively focus, but angels of death were different.

They'd been trained to be objective and reserved. Qualities that Kesien had always embodied. But right now, he had one goal in mind—justice for the angels murdered in Eolowen. Atonement for the evil committed here in the name of greed.

She knew that he also felt responsible for all of it.

"Tomorrow, Kesien," said Azrael finally. "We have Tre Sheridan's Book of Life and Death now—thanks to Pravuil and the surviving angels from the archive." Azrael motioned toward the atrium room. "The squad that earns this assignment will be granted access to the Book immediately for study. Tomorrow, we march on the sepulcher where Jack Casey will open the door into Purgatory. And the winning squad will locate the soul of Tre Sheridan. Samael and his guard will be near this soul. They can't stray far from him, so you'll find the archangel somewhere nearby."

"That's all I need to know," said Kesien with a growl, taking a step toward the dais. "They won't hide from me—not even in Purgatory." Kesien white-knuckled his sword, his expression burning with anger.

"We need to help him," said Talia in a quiet voice as Muriel moved beside her. "If we don't, his anger will consume him."

Muriel nodded. "I know, but how? He isn't listening to any of us now. He's only focused on bringing the archangel to justice. And his former guard."

To Talia's surprise, Jack walked across the terrace and gripped Kesien's arms.

"Dude, you need to slow your roll," he said in a firm voice, shaking his head. "You go in there like Mel Gibson at Yom Kippur and Samael and his murdering flock of death angels will ambush you."

"Yom Kippur?" Muriel said, squinting.

Talia shrugged. "Must be a Hollywood reference."

Kesien's eyes narrowed and he glared at Jack, looking sullen and angry. She saw the anger in his grey eyes, knowing he only wanted to storm Purgatory and lay waste to Samael. And she understood that. But going in there unhinged might end his existence—and her entire squad. As its vanguard, she was as responsible for their survival and for capturing Samael on this mission. That meant protecting Kesien from himself.

But she knew Jack saw the writing on the wall. He feared for her safety in there—Kesien's too. That worry smoldered in his light green eyes. She could have seen his fear from a mile away. He didn't want to see her squad perish. Or Kesien.

She smiled. But Jack's primary concern was her.

"They must face what they've done," Kesien snapped through gritted teeth. "And it's my duty—my responsibility to apprehend them. Don't you understand, Jack? This is my fault."

Already, Jack was shaking his head. "Dude, no—it wasn't."

Kesien sighed and bowed his head. Jack shook him. Hard.

"Kesien!" he shouted, forcing the angel of death to look at him. "Dude, I get it. You feel like those angels got murdered because you brought your former guard here. But it wasn't your fault." Jack stared into Kesien's fiery gaze. "You did a good thing. You gave those douchebags a second chance they didn't deserve. And they just took a piss on it. Laughed in your face. And I know that makes you rage inside—even for an angel, that's gotta push all your buttons."

Kesien pulled away from him, glaring.

"No offense, Jack, but what do you know about any of this?"

Kesien's expression was raw and angry. "You're human. Granted the Maker's mercy and yet, you all go out and kill each other or yourselves in spite of it. How can you understand what angels deal with? A betrayal that erases all existence. A betrayal that may or may not be punished by High House. An unforgiveable assault on our own kind that may escape any sort of justice whatsoever. Because we have no divine gift granted to us, forgiving us, and lifting us out of the abyss of nonexistence."

The silence on the terrace was heavy.

Talia knew that every angel understood Kesien's pain—and every single one had felt almost envy for the spoiled humans that got a second chance when selfless angels got erased for all time. It seemed so unfair. She remembered feeling that way, too, once. That's what got her into that first wager with Lucifer. But in a way, it had also saved her—introduced her to the love of lifetimes, but this wasn't about humans. This was about angel greed. And being turned to the same darkness as Lucifer embraced.

Kesien motioned toward the terrace as if the memory of those angels' final moments still played across the white stones.

"Where is their forgiveness?" he demanded, shaking his hand at the traces of gold light still shining against the white stones. "Where is their moment of being lifted from the abyss of utter disintegration? Where's their second chance, Jack?"

Jack didn't shrink back from Kesien's unbridled anger. If anything, it spurred him forward.

"As someone who willingly climbed aboard the bullet train to oblivion, I stared that abyss in the face, Kesien—human or not. And believe me, Talia was the last person coming to look for me—and that was because of a bet. And I almost managed to screw that one up, too. So, I get it. Angels have no safety net. No game reload if one of them gets obliterated. Doesn't seem fair to me either. But they weren't made of darkness or blood. They were made of light and the one thing that still remains is that light. So, maybe they aren't gone for all time?"

Kesien squinted at him, pensive, shaking his head.

"The sunlight has never not shone on Heaven. On Eolowen." Azrael's voice joined Jack's. "Not for long anyway."

Jack motioned to the sunlight streaming through the scuttling Constable clouds, brightening the Parrish blue skies.

"Hear that, Kesien?" he said. "I think that they're still here somehow." He turned his hands over in the warm rays of sunlight bathing the terrace. "Here in this incredible glow of light that touches everything in Heaven. And when God's had enough of all our shit—humans and angels—then he'll reboot it all. And if humans go from blood to light as souls, then there's got to be a lot of angels in that light alongside them. Just waiting for God to shine them back into Heaven again. As angels."

Pravuil stepped out of the atrium into the jarring silence of the terrace, looking almost frail.

"Jack, your terminology is crude," said Pravuil, his voice sharp as he moved with slow steps, wings flat against his back. "But by High House, you're talking about resurrecting angels." His gaze snapped to Talia and then Berith and he pointed at them. "And Talia, you and Berith are the only two angels in Heaven that possess the rare angel gift of resurrect. Yes, it can resurrect an angel. So, call me a romantic, but Jack's rather simplistic speculation may be spot on."

Kesien's eyes widened. "Then they may not all be lost forever?" Kesien replied in a shaky voice. "The angels that were killed by Archangel Samael and my former guard?"

Pravuil gave him a sharp nod. "That's what I'm saying, Kesien. We are creatures of light and air. If we fall in battle, we return to that light and air. Like humans return to the dust of the Earth. All of it is part of the Creation. None of it is ever destroyed. It merely changes form. A form fueled by this eternal light."

"So, what Jack said then," said Talia.

Pravuil's eyes narrowed and put his hands on his hips, those gold eyes flashing with annoyance.

"Arrogant little humans think they know everything," he said in a piercing tone. "But by High House, Jack's right. The existence of resurrect proves it, Kesien. There is a path home again for those angels erased from existence. Some through our own powers—others?" God's Scribe sighed. "By divine gifts. There, I said it. Now, will you angels stop being so self-righteous and pick a winner, so I can watch Archangel Samael turn crispy on the High House pyre. While the seraphim take his wings and halo." Pravuil shook his head, tongue clicking against his teeth. "Might even pack a lunch and picnic in the cloud chamber for that one."

Talia laughed and Muriel joined her as Jack turned around to Kesien and shrugged.

"Dude," said Jack, "all I'm saying is get those bastards in Purgatory, but don't lose yourself in the process. It wasn't your fault they were dishonorable douchebags."

Smiling, Kesien slapped him on the back. "I like the particular phrasing of that advice, Jack. Thank you. Appreciate it, kid."

Jack's eyes darkened. "Not your goat, dude."

Kesien's laugh dissipated the tension across the terrace. He glanced at Talia. "Let's finish this," he said with a nod.

"All right, guard," said Azrael as he unfurled his soot-grey wings and gazed at the last two remaining squads on the terrace. "Show me the squad going after Archangel Samael."

Talia passed Jack as he moved toward the dais. She reached out and gripped his hand a moment.

"That was beautiful, Jack," she whispered against his ear and kissed him.

"Thanks, babe," he said, returning her kiss. "Can't say I'll be happy to see you win this sparring contest, but I'll be damned proud if you do. Just be careful in Purgatory, okay?" He squeezed her hands. "For me, Mrs. Casey?"

He laid his hand against his heart and held out his palm to her. Offering her his heart.

She closed her hand and pressed it against her heart.

"Now until forever, Mr. Casey," she said as he kissed her hard on the lips and let her join her squad for the final skirmish.

He moved beside Azrael's dais, his face tense, jaw line sharp as he waited for the fight to commence.

But the last squad didn't stand a chance against Kesien and Deemah. The moment Azrael set the last drill into motion, Kesien launched himself forward, Deemah beside him.

Shields connected all down the phalanx lines, but Talia's squad had been faster, bashing the other squad backward. Talia slammed her shield forward and then pivoted, following the blow with her sword of Holy fire. They quickly beat back the other squad, Kesien chewing through the line like a buzz saw, alternating shield bash and sword hack alongside Deemah.

Already, three angels of death had gone down.

Together, Talia and her squad pressed the line, wielding shield and sword, until the remaining two angels of death fell to their knees. Kesien drove both of them against the ground with a powerful shield bash.

And it was over.

Talia and her squad were going into Purgatory after Archangel Samael.

After they examined Tre Sheridan's Book of Life and Death. Without Jack. It made her feel a little strange, knowing he wouldn't be beside her this time.

It brought back his confession beneath the willow tree and she felt a tremor of fear at the memory of Jack's words. He was afraid that on their first anniversary, he'd wake up and realize that he hadn't seen her in months. And he hadn't even noticed.

She felt a chill brush across her wings. The thought of that scenario terrified her. How did he say it? *That they'd be strangers wearing the same ring?* That made her shudder. To prevent that, he'd been willing to enlist in the death angel guard to be with her, knowing he couldn't keep up.

And she loved him for that.

"The drills have ended," Azrael announced. "Talia, you and your squad step forward, please."

She motioned Muriel and Kesien toward her as Anahera and Deemah sheathed their swords and turned toward the dais. Her squad moved back into position with Talia at the center as its vanguard.

Together, they approached the archangel as an unbroken phalanx line.

Jack looked alarmed, but he stayed quiet, chewing his bottom lip.

"As champions of that battle exercise," said Azrael, "you and your squad have earned the right to face Archangel Samael in combat."

"Thank you, sir," said Talia as she motioned toward the atrium room. "We'd like to review Tre Sheridan's Book of Life and Death now. Get plenty of time to study it before we leave for Purgatory."

Azrael nodded. "By all means, Talia," he said. "Take your squad and consult with Pravuil. He'll grant you access to the Book. Tomorrow, at Earth's first dawn, we'll leave for Purgatory."

"Thank you, sir," said Talia and turned toward the atrium room. "We'll do our best to represent the guard and apprehend Samael quickly."

"You can bet on that," said Kesien with a deep nod.

Azrael stepped down from his dais. "All right, squads. Dismissed." He turned around and fixed Jack with a steely grey stare, silver-black hair tousled by the breeze. "And Jack, make sure you sleep before tomorrow."

"Dude, I'm just opening a door," Jack replied and pointed toward the crossroads. "How much sleep do I need for that?"

Azrael crossed his arms, his gaze hardening as his mouth pressed into a tight line of annoyance.

Chuckles rumbled across the terrace as a blush touched Jack's face.

"Er, archangel," he said.

Azrael sighed and turned toward Talia.

"Talia," said Azrael. "Make sure your husband gets some rest."

Talia slid her arms around Jack's waist. "Done, sir," she said, nudging him toward the atrium room.

And away from the archangel's probing gaze.

"You gonna help me rest, Mrs. Casey?" Jack asked, a mischievous grin lighting his face.

"Not the way you'd like me to—Mr. Casey," she whispered against his ear.

He frowned.

"Besides, the atrium is full of injured angels," she said and tugged him toward the atrium's portal. "A little too crowded for me."

"Every angel of death in Heaven passed through this room when I was staying in it," he replied, following her toward the opening. "Never bothered you then."

She turned around and kissed him hard on the lips. "God's Scribe wasn't convalescing in there," she said in a quiet voice. "And it wasn't full of cherubim either."

"Guess I'll live with a few stolen kisses from my wife until Samael's back in his cage, waiting to have his feathers plucked and his nightlight shut off." He squinted at her. "Why we going in here anyway?"

"I want you with me when the squad looks at Tre Sheridan's Book of Life and Death."

He glanced behind him as Muriel and Kesien blinked across the terrace. Toward the atrium room.

"I've never seen one of these books before," he said as Kesien soared onto the rooftop beside Muriel and disappeared into the atrium.

Anahera and Deemah landed after them and slipped through a portal into the room.

"I want you to see what's written in this one," said Talia in a soft voice, "since Zanth propositioned you."

She paused a moment. That came out like a jealous school girl. And Jack's eyes sparkled, confirming it even though he didn't say a word.

"Think there will be any notes about demons in this dude's book?" Jack asked, glancing at her, those light green eyes so animated.

"Possibly," she replied. "What's that look about?"

"What look?" he asked, sounding so innocent.

But she knew better. He'd picked up on her tone. It was written in his gaze and in his expression.

"That *wow, do you sound jealous* look on your way-too-handsome face," she said, crossing her arms. "Especially since I didn't hear this conversation between you and the archdemoness."

And there it was. That infamously sexy smirk curling the corners of his mouth. A sure sign that he was up to something.

"She was definitely flirting with me," he said, looking at her through a thick fringe of eyelashes.

And that expression of his could melt steel. She had to focus on the issue and not that bedroom stare that made her forget her own name.

"She wanted me bad."

Talia gasped, feeling the roil of Holy fire trembling through her. She'd smite that archdemoness all the way back to Hell if she laid a sultry finger on him.

"To help her get her lover out of Purgatory."

Her expression darkened and she glared at him, hands on her hips. "Jack Casey! You deliberately led me to believe that she was hitting on you to stir up my jealousy."

"Is it working?" he asked in an uncertain voice. "Otherwise, my wife's gonna fall in love with her career instead of her insecure actor husband."

By the Maker, he was so sexy when he was vulnerable, looking so innocent as those honest declarations tumbled out of his mouth. He was smiling, like it had been a joke, but she knew better.

She let her anger subside and moved slowly toward him. She slid her arms around his neck and pressed a long, gentle kiss against his hot mouth.

"It's working beautifully, Mr. Casey," she said in a husky voice and pressed her forehead against his. "And my most important job is being your partner." She nuzzled his nose with hers. "Because not even Armand Gianni can keep you out of trouble alone."

He shrugged and brushed a lock of black hair out of her eyes. "See, I'm a real handful. Can't be left alone for a minute. Just ask any of the directors I've worked with."

She nodded and kissed him again. "That's why Heaven sent its best angel to manage this job. One that specializes in trouble. Said it might take an eternity to resolve."

"She in your guard?" he asked.

She nodded as he pressed a steamy kiss against her lips, pulling her against him. She felt his arms tighten around her, an urgency in that kiss that made her body temperature rise and her wings tremble.

Until Muriel cleared her throat and Talia realized that the atrium room had grown quiet while she and Jack stood in the portal kissing.

She let go of him and he looked up, seeing the sea of angels staring at them from inside the atrium. And God's Scribe leaning against the wall, looking annoyed and anxious.

"Hey, we've only been married about a week, so chill already," Jack snapped. "This is the first time she's been away from me in a while."

Muriel smiled, but Pravuil didn't look amused. Even Kesien looked amused.

"God's Scribe doesn't chill, Jack," said Pravuil, his eyes narrowed. "He makes sure that putz, Samael gets taken down hard. And burns for eternity."

Jack laid his hand against Talia's face. "And you've got one of the best death angels in Heaven on the case, dude. Talia will take him down. That sketchy douchebag's done."

Thankfully, Jack didn't tell God's Scribe to chill again. He left that part unsaid, but it still made Muriel snicker. Even Kesien chuckled as Pravuil turned to her, shaking his head.

"Talia, tell me that means you'll make sure Samael faces justice," said God's Scribe as he cast a sideways glance at Jack.

She nodded. "That's the plan, archangel," she replied and motioned toward Muriel and the rest of her squad. "My squad won the right to bring Samael to justice."

"That's excellent news," said Pravuil, moving unsteadily over to the bed, and plucked a book out of the air.

God's Scribe held out the Book and Jack's eyes got huge as he stared at it.

Like all Books of Life and Death, this one had an animated cover, replaying moments of Tre Sheridan's human life. One cut short by suicide.

This human was of average height with shoulder-length stone-brown hair in his late twenties. He had a lean build and a long face. His sad eyes were a deep sapphire and stubble shadowed his strong jaw. His thick hair, parted in the center, hung in waves just above his shoulders and tousled around his face. On top, it was in long, shaggy layers and tumbled into an occasional curl.

Dressed in a light blue tuxedo shirt, navy blue tuxedo, and white sneakers, he had a top hat and black cane in his lap and sat alone on a bench in the middle of a crowd. Neon lights gyrated and pulsing overhead in an array of colors and patterns in the lonely night. His eyes looked bloodshot and he looked dejected and lost.

"Hey, that's Vegas!" Jack cried. "That's Fremont Street." He squinted. "Dude looks like some sort of stage performer."

When Talia touched the Book's cover, it opened, the pages spilling out around her and her squad, images moving, sounds carrying as moments and memories played all around them.

"Wow, it's like a film of this dude's life," said Jack as he glanced at her. "Are all these books like this?"

She nodded. The Book could be read in the traditional way, but with her whole squad present, she'd set the Book in motion. Allowing all of them to view it at the same time.

"Wow, mine must have been like a bad Looney Tunes cartoon," said Jack, shaking his head. "Lots of bombs stamped ACME and lots of falling off cliffs."

She gazed at him for a moment, remembering the horrible revelations from Muriel back on *The Cinderella Hour*. When she'd demanded to know how Jack's life ended and Muriel couldn't tell her everything. She'd looked at Jack's Book a few times since then, including when Lucifer had someone try to rewrite how his life ended. Thankfully, she'd been spared seeing those bleak moments when his life had been slated for a short, premature end.

Like this young man.

And she was grateful that she hadn't been forced to watch Jack's life end like his Book showed. Like all the others she'd watched over the centuries. She had no idea how his Book ended now and she didn't want to know those details yet. Not for a very long time. But she did wonder how Jack's transformation had changed that ending. Someday, she'd find the courage to ask, but for now, she didn't want to know.

"Your Book was terrifying, Jack," said Muriel. "An overdose cut your life short—at twenty-six. Until Talia saved you. For once, I was glad that Talia didn't have the power to read your Book when she appeared on The Cinderella Hour."

A sobering look darkened his face. "Does it mention Talia in my book now?" he asked.

"Why do you ask, Jack?" Pravuil asked.

"If mine mentions Talia, then I wonder if this dude's book mentions Zanth the angel executioner. I mean, how'd they meet? Why were they even together and why'd an archdemoness fall in love with a small time Vegas stage performer? Seems strange to me."

"In what way, Jack?" Kesien asked as he studied the pages floating around him.

Talia understood what Jack was asking. He was as anxious as she was about learning what this archdemoness' relationship with Tre Sheridan's soul entailed. Had Tre Sheridan really killed himself to be with her or to help Lucifer? They needed to know all the reasons why this man killed himself. And what brought them together initially.

"You want to know if they met by accident or if it was arranged by Lucifer," said Talia to Jack who was already nodding. "Was the entire love affair arranged by Lucifer to achieve this sacrifice or was their relationship a by-product of something else? Or just an accident?"

"Spot on, babe," said Jack, returning his attention to Pravuil. "We need to know if Zanth really loves this dude or if all of this was orchestrated by Luci to trap us in Zanth's web."

Talia nodded. "Exactly." She had no reason to trust anything this archdemoness said—especially when she was hitting on her husband.

"Although," Jack continued as he paced around the squad. "Zanth seemed pretty determined to rescue this dude. Seemed totally uninterested in Archangel Samael and his guard. Her focus was solely on this dude's soul. And me because I can open the door for him."

Talia bristled. She didn't trust this demon at all. And she didn't want her around Jack, not even for a few minutes.

"It's all in there, Talia," said God's Scribe, hands behind his back. "His Book is complete, so every last moment of his life has been recorded. And there is a woman in the last part of his story."

Pravuil leaned closer to the pages and plucked out a handful. "Like here," said Pravuil, pointing. "Looks like Tre Sheridan made a deal with a demon. Sold his soul for a year at the top. A fleeting trip around the horn of fame that became a busted dream for the magician and illusionist. Had his own show on the Vegas Strip. Won one of those television show competitions."

Talia squinted at another page. "Looks like he didn't read his contract very carefully. He didn't realize he'd sold his soul for a year of fame. He was angry. He was on his way to confront the demon that had tricked him."

Muriel laughed. "And he ends up foiling a mass shooting by colliding with the would-be gunman, knocking the rifle out of its case in the hotel lobby."

Azrael landed in the atrium room, Berith beside him. When she landed, rose-gold halo spinning brightly, she rushed over to Pravuil to inspect that deep gash on his forehead.

"A little well-placed angel of death magic," said Azrael.

Shocked, Talia turned around and stared at him. "You?"

Azrael nodded. "I was trying to foil that contract and put him in the room with this gunman. Tre surprised everyone by grabbing the rifle and training it on the man that would have open-fired three hours later in a huge, crowded casino. That's how he met the angel executioner."

"Dude, seriously?" Jack replied. "That's like—a Hollywood inspired meet-cute if I ever heard one."

"Except it caused a...demon meet-cute, as you call it," said Azrael with a groan. "Zanth had been in Vegas to orchestrate that mass shooting when the whole exercise got ruined by Tre Sheridan."

Jack smiled at Azrael. "So, hot and sexy archdemoness confronts the human that ruined her mass-murder night on the town. She's furious. Goes to confront this idiot who'd sold his soul and ruined her day. They make googly eyes at each other and fall in love. Lucifer sees an opportunity."

Pravuil looked a little confused as he glanced from Jack to the Book.

"That's right, Jack," said Azrael, nodding. "Not sure what happened after that event though."

Jack held up his hands. "Let me set the scene for you. Think Die Hard meets The Bridges of Madison County."

Muriel looked horrified. "Die Hard and Bridges of Madison County? Together? Are you crazy?"

"Picture it," said Jack with a smirk. "Shitloads of action, great romance, a shit-ton of explosions, and a lotta bad guys. But the ending is the worst love story ever written. Because this dude saves dozens of lives which elevates him out of Hell. Well north of his new demon girlfriend's neighborhood."

Talia grinned. "You're right, Jack. That act would have ensured that he didn't go to Hell."

Jack's eyes were bright as he nodded, continuing. "Exactly. Knowing that, Luci convinces this lovestruck dude that, in order for them to be together, he needs to take one for the team and spend the night in Purgatory. Only Luci *forgets* to tell him—and Zanth—that it's a one-way trip. Dude was all set to spend his evilly ever after in Hell with the archdemoness of his dreams. But Lucifer snatches their happy reunion away from his new first lieutenant and separates them for eternity. Because he needed a plant in Purgatory. *So* not a Hollywood ending."

Pravuil sighed and shook his head. "I need someone fluent in Jackspeak to explain that…explanation to me."

Talia shrugged. "That last part's even beyond me, Scribe."

"Okay, let me try again," said Jack, glancing around the room. "Tough crowd. Basically, Luci ruined a good love story by separating Zanth from her lover. He tricked Sheridan into killing himself and landing in Purgatory by promising him an eternity with his demon lover in Hell. And Lucifer totally pissed off his first lieutenant because of it. I have no clue what Lucifer's up to with this Samael distraction, but I think Zanth is sincere about trying to rescue her lover."

"It's the Book, Jack," said Kesien, letting go of the pages from Tre Sheridan's story. "Lucifer wants the Book of Secrets. We think it's to get resurrect."

Berith stepped into the conversation, nodding at Jack. "I agree with Kesien, Jack. Lucifer's after the Book. With Procel still in Hell, Lucifer has another fallen angel that can read it. And possibly awaken the resurrect power. If Procel succeeds, Lucifer will break his tether and escape Hell somehow. Despite Abaddon locking the gates." She reached out and gripped Jack's forearm. "And the first thing he'll do is come for you, Jack." She glanced at Talia and then the floor. "Then he'll come after Talia. For tethering him into Hell. And then me for betraying him."

Jack's gaze narrowed as he stared at Berith a moment and then his gaze shifted to Azrael. And finally, God's Scribe.

"I don't know why, but I think it's more than that," said Jack with a sigh. He ran a hand through his hair. "He's been misdirecting us again and again. Pushing us. Pursuing us. Herding us." He pointed to the right. "We look over here. He does something over there. I don't know what his end game is, but whatever it is, it's going to explode in our faces. Hard."

The atrium room fell deathly silent as Talia and her squad exchanged frightened, confused looks with each other. And Azrael.

"I feel it, too," said Talia. "I don't know what game Lucifer's playing, but he's got some goal in mind. Something much bigger than Archangel Samael and revenge on Jack."

Azrael's and Berith's expressions and her squad's continued silence spoke volumes. The other angels around her felt it, too. And so did Jack. But no one knew what game Lucifer was playing this time. Not even God's Scribe.

"Azrael," the Scribe replied, motioning him over to the bed. "Contact Abaddon. He's got to have some insights into this situation. And I want to hear them."

"Right away, Scribe," said Azrael, rising into the air. "Won't be easy though."

He darted through a portal on the roof and disappeared.

Talia hoped Lucifer' former first lieutenant could tell them what Lucifer's next move might be—or what he was after. Quickly. Before he got his hands on the Book of Secrets.

10

Jack didn't realize he'd fallen asleep in the grass under the willow tree until he started dreaming about Tre Sheridan. Dude looked a few years older than him in those videos streaming across the cover of his Book of Life and Death.

Later, as his sleep deepened, Jack's actor brain stitched those events together with the ones he'd heard Talia's squad talking about. And then he'd tossed his own spin on the events, too, his subconscious making it into a feature film.

First scene. A wide pan of the Vegas Strip as Sinatra sings his jazzy 60s version of *Luck Be a Lady*. With lots of brass.

Camera pans downward, pulling downtown in a wide shot to a bench at the Fremont Street Experience. Neon lights pulse and race overhead, drenching everything in movement and confetti colors.

Camera captures several clear plastic cups and dog-eared playing cards littering the concrete at the feet of a down-and-out, struggling magician with disheveled hair and a wrinkled navy blue tuxedo.

Close up shot on the magician as *Luck Be a Lady* crescendos. Long, windblown stone-brown hair. Blue eyes hooded and bloodshot. Collar of his sweaty, light blue tuxedo shirt is undone, bowtie untied and hanging. A top hat is upturned at his feet as he tosses playing cards into it. And misses. Over and over.

He's trying—and failing—to make it big in Vegas. On the Strip. But he's downtown and down on his luck.

A plastic cup skitters across the concrete in the wind as the scene transitions to a cup sliding into Tre Sheridan's shaking hand at a restaurant on the Strip.

A legendary Vegas-style buffet. And a new agent.

Looking sketchy and sus to everybody but the struggling magician. Even as *Luck Be a Lady* swells, horns brighter than a new penny in the July Las Vegas heat, the dark music behind it foretells trouble.

But between the shrimp cocktail, the ribs, and the dim sum, magician dude sells his soul to this agent/demon at that all-you-can eat buffet on the Strip. For a year at the top.

Transition scene. Neon-lit billboard along the Strip rapidly changes acts and dates, showing time passing. It's now fall in Vegas, the triple-digit heat dissipates to high 70s.

Cut to the money shot.

Dude wins one of those TV talent competitions and gets his own show in Vegas. His face is on billboards across the Strip with him drowning in a shower of Benjamins as the camera pans out.

Just like the demon/agent promised.

Fade to black.

Fade in with a calendar. Night shot of Vegas. More Sinatra. *My Kind of Town.*

This magician is now the hottest ticket in Vegas. For a year.

Scene fades to that same Vegas strip hotel with the legendary buffet. Successful Vegas magician, dressed in a slim-fitting blue Armani suit and black Hermes dress shoes. Runs into a gunman and his archdemoness escort. Hero magician does a sleight of hand and wrestles the rifle away, saving dozens and dozens of lives.

And pisses off the archdemoness that orchestrated the whole shooting spree.

Magician and demoness argue. Attraction is overwhelming until they kiss.

Scenes of a whirlwind romance flash across the screen to hip 80s songs as magician and archdemoness spend the weekend in her billionaire suite overlooking the Strip. Kind of like *Pretty Woman.* Only with demons.

Fade in the Hollywood Happily Ever After moment as they decide they want to be together forever.

Cue dark 90s grunge music as the suite darkens. Scene fades to a private table in a dark, smoky lounge.

Lucifer steps into camera frame. Dressed in a grey Brioni pinstripe suit, white shirt, no tie, and shiny black Hermes loafers. Suave and debonair, curly blond hair swept back in a smooth wave, he lays out his innocent little plan.

The King of Hell needs a plant in Purgatory. One soul to summon a douchebag archangel, so the traitor won't get bitch-slapped by all of Heaven.

With expert precision, Lucifer manipulates the lovesick magician into volunteering for this honor. Tre Sheridan agrees to kill himself as a path to spending eternity with his forever demon love.

Fade to night drone shot, circling the Strat tower south of downtown Vegas as Tre Sheridan stands on the observation deck. Intense music darkens with electric guitars and cellos as Tre Sheridan leaps from the Strat to his death.

Darkest moment as the camera fades in an overlay: two images of the separated lovers. Sheridan in Purgatory, Zanth in Hell.

Relationship seems over. All is lost.

Camera angle widens. Upbeat, frantic orchestra music swells. And like Richard Gere showing up in a limo like a knight on a horse to rescue his princess from the tower, Jack Casey flies through a dark, dusty sepulcher, silver-grey wings stirring up ancient dust and whispers. Smiling at the camera, he opens the heavy tower door. Reuniting the archdemoness with her dead lover's soul.

They kiss and live evilly ever after.

The End. Fade to black and roll credits as electric guitars rock out a heavy metal version of *I Will Always Love You.*

But somewhere between the gaffer and the grip credits, a cut scene explodes across the black screen.

Lucifer appears in the sepulcher. Laughing, he disintegrates his archdemoness angel executioner as Tre Sheridan screams. Lucifer binds Jack Casey in chains and drags Jack through the floor of the sepulcher. Down into the depths of Hell. Never to be seen again.

The movie screen shook. Hard.

"Jack? Jack, wake up!"

He gasped and opened his eyes, his clear gold Eternean armor creaking as he snapped up from the lush grass underneath the tree. Expecting to see Lucifer leering at him.

Talia leaned over him, smiling.

"Jack, wake up," she said, kneeling beside him. "You need to eat something and then follow alongside the squad as Azrael leads the guard to the sepulcher."

His heart pounded against his rib cage, the echo of Lucifer's laughter still ringing in his ears.

It was so real!

He ran his hands across his arms and torso, checking for chains.

"What's the matter?" Talia asked, looking concerned as she watched him flail.

When he felt the sunlight seeping through the willow branches to warm his face, he glanced up at the turquoise sky.

Still in Heaven.

No Hellfires burned around him. The air was scented with roses and gardenias, not woodsmoke and brimstone.

"Had a nightmare," he confessed, fixing her with his gaze. "About this Sheridan dude." He pulled in a pained breath, the moments so real as Lucifer dragged him through the ground and back into Hell's dark, burning depths. "And Lucifer."

She reached out, eyes almost sad, and caressed his face.

"Those images are gone now," she said in a soft voice, soothing his fear and panic. "You're safe here in Eolowen with nearly a hundred death angels surrounding you."

He smiled and slid his arms around her waist, pulling her against his chest. "Especially my ass-kicking, demon-smiting angel of death wife," he said and kissed her. "Good morning, Mrs. Casey. Missed waking up beside you."

That sad look touched her luminous grey eyes again. She reached out and ran her fingers across his cheek and along the curve of his jaw.

"I'm so sorry, Jack," she said, her voice heavy and aching. "I wish I could be beside you every single morning and every single night. Soon, okay?"

He nodded. "I'd wait an eternity for you, Tal," he said.

Her eyes turned glassy and she put her arms around him, holding him close. She smelled like new-fallen rain and lavender and he nuzzled his face against her wavy, raven black hair that smelled like sunlight.

"You say the sweetest things, Jack," she whispered. "I love you with all my heart."

"I love you more," he said with a chuckle and kissed her soft lips.

"Challenge accepted, Jack Casey," she said with a wry smile as she studied his face, those grey eyes turning intense.

She held out a small bundle of white cloth to him.

His brow furrowed as he unwrapped it, finding two small, round white cakes nestled in the folds. They were each about three inches in diameter and two inches thick. They looked like they'd been dusted with powdered sugar that sparkled with gold flecks even in the willow tree's shade.

"What's this?"

She ran her fingers through his hair and down his neck, stroking. "Breakfast," she said. "A couple of manna cakes for you."

"Manna cakes? Like Heavenly Ho-Hos or something?"

She laughed as he picked one up and sniffed it. "So much better than that, Jack."

Cinnamon, pecans, and honey. The cake was warm and moist. He took a bite. It tasted rich, not too sweet, a hint of cream filling against his tongue as the cinnamon and pecans mixed with the honey. The cake melted in his mouth, light and fluffy—almost like whipped cream.

"Talia…" he said with a gasp. "You've been holding out on me. This is the best thing I've ever tasted. Why wasn't our wedding cake made out of—whatever this is?"

She laughed. "I'm afraid I don't have a recipe for manna wedding cake, Jack. Here in Heaven, we can just—summon them."

"And this is the first time you're sharing this amazing ambrosia with me? The love of your life?" He sighed. "And I thought I meant something to you, Tal."

She bit her lip. "After you escaped Hell, I was planning to conjure some cakes for you, but then you went and conjured your own meals with those seraphim powers. Remember?"

"Okay, I'll admit that In-N-Out Burger is human ambrosia, but Tal —withholding the angel cakes?" He bowed his head. "I'm hurt."

She shook her head and gave him that *don't make me smite you* look. "Not working, Jack Casey."

"Damn!" he shouted, smirking at her. "I'll have to find another way to guilt my way into more Heavenly Ho-Hos."

"Guilt doesn't work on angels, Jack," she said. "Haven't you figured that one out yet?"

He downed the first cake and took a bite out of the second one. "I'm not leaving here until I get a recipe or a lifetime supply. So delicious."

He slid his arms around her and kissed her hard with a face-melting kiss that left her breathless.

"How 'bout a little newlywed seduction?"

She nodded. "Newlywed seduction is working," she said in a soft voice. "I'll talk to Azrael and see what he says about supplying my new husband with manna cakes."

He rose onto his knees. "Tell him I'll power wash Eolowen's terrace for manna cakes. Cut the grass? Weed the flower garden?"

She laughed and kissed his lips again.

Only when she sat back in the grass did he turn his attention to the other manna cake and devour it.

"Azrael wanted me to make sure that you got some nourishment before we left for Purgatory. He has the guard assembled on the terrace." Her eyes turned glassy again. "Before Samael's guard attacked, we were over two hundred strong in Azrael's guard. The largest and best death angel guard in Heaven, the envy of all the archangels of death."

Jack reached out and slid his arms around her, holding her against his chest. "Babe, your guard is still the envy of those archangels," he said in a soothing voice. "And it's still the best guard in Heaven. If it hadn't been for you and your guard, Heaven would be dust under Lucifer's boots right now. Never forget that—or how you made Heaven's victory possible. You, Tal."

She lifted her face from his chest, staring into his eyes. "Me? You were a huge part of that victory, Jack," she said and kissed his lips. "Without you, we might have lost everything."

He shook his head and offered her his best smirk. "I played my part, that's all," he said. "If it hadn't been for you, Tal, I wouldn't have been alive to even help fight Lucifer."

She held him close. "And I never, ever want to see you fall, Jack Casey. I never even want to think about having to cross you over." He felt her sigh. "With these changes that have happened to you, I hope I never have to, either."

He still couldn't quite wrap his brain around the fact that he had stopped aging, especially as he approached his twenty-seventh birthday in a couple of months. Or that these wings and halo were permanent fixtures in his life either. He wondered when the seraphim would get around to finding a way to remove their powers from him —after he'd accidentally drawn them out of the healing stone and into his body at the Santa Rosa vineyard chateau.

Heaven had a lot of anomalies to deal with and they all had his name on them. Except for Talia having a human soul. Her enduring a Phoenix shift and awakening all those rare angel powers, too. This whole journey had changed her in ways that Heaven didn't understand either. Maybe with all the complexities that the two of them faced, the seraphim would decide to let Talia forge her own journey beside him on Earth?

Or let him stay with her in Eolowen.

He winced at the thought of not being able to act anymore, the one love in his life before he met Talia. But he'd go anywhere and do anything to stay with her.

They just needed Heaven's divine blessing not to separate them. And a little divine intervention to keep Lucifer and his demon clown circus away from them.

"I don't think I could take watching you cross me over either, Talia," he said in a tired voice. "Knowing that you were going to send me off someplace else. Someplace you couldn't follow." He shook his head. "Even then, I'd refuse to go."

That made her smile.

"Come on," he said and nodded toward the terrace as he gripped her hand. "Let's go open that door into Purgatory and get that rat bastard and his murdering death angel posse. So, we can go back to being newlyweds again."

She wrapped him in her arms, the scent of sunlight and lavender wafting over him.

"I can't wait to be your wife again," she said against his ear.

At last, she let him go as her wings unfurled at her back. He let his stretch out behind him, catching the breeze. She lifted off from beneath the willow tree and he followed, wings whispering against the wind.

Ahead, the entire guard stood motionless on the terrace, across the rooftop, and in the grass, surrounding Azrael who stood on his dais, hands behind his back. In front of the dais stood Talia's squad, an empty spot in the center reserved for Talia.

Above the grand hall of Eolowen, cherubim shifted form from eagles to angels, carrying more wounded toward the spires. Berith had her hands full still healing injuries. And from the line of eagle-like cherubim winging across the Heavens toward Eolowen, there were still lots more injured to treat.

Talia landed at the head of her squad as vanguard.

Jack hung back, landing in the grass behind Azrael. He felt in the way of their operations and didn't want to cause any problems for Talia or her squad. Or Azrael's guard.

"All right, guard," Azrael called out in a booming voice, those steely grey eyes narrowed, silver-black hair curling in waves around his shoulders. "It's time. Phalanx formations. Shields out. Prepare to blink toward the crossroads at my command."

Jack watched the sea of gold light roll across the terrace and glimmer in the sky, the grass lighting up as the remaining guard brandished their shields of light.

"When Samael's former guard members turned on us during a training exercise, we lost a lot," said Azrael, pacing across the dais, hands behind his back. "Friends. Colleagues. Squad members. Our hearts are broken. Our trust is wounded. Our shock is evident. And our losses are great."

Azrael fell silent as he turned to gaze at the entire death angel guard gathered around him.

"But today, we also count our blessings," he shouted across the terrace. "God's Scribe did not perish. A once-fallen healer with rare angel powers still stands, redeemed, among us, healing the Scribe and so many death angels that we nearly lost forever."

He motioned toward Talia and her squad. "Five of the strongest death angels in our guard stand ready to confront Archangel Samael and his guard in Purgatory. I will lead the entire guard to the ancient temple as we stand silent watch at the sepulcher. To await the traitors when they emerge."

His gaze shot around the terrace until he turned and saw Jack on the steps leading into the grass. He smiled and held out his hand.

"And one brave human has volunteered to open Purgatory's door and usher our strongest squad into the realm of souls to pursue Samael." Azrael turned back toward the terrace. "The entire guard will position itself between the door and the seraphim situated above the ancient temple beyond the Garden. We will be the battle link between the squad and the seraphim, fighting relentlessly until Samael is apprehended and the Book of Secrets is recovered."

The soft flutter of wings was the only sound on the wind as Azrael stood in silence, eyes narrowed as he stared toward the horizon and the forbidding walls of the Garden. And the path that wound past it to places that Jack had never seen before.

But the walls of the Garden made Jack shudder, the memories razor-sharp as he remembered Lucifer beating him to death inside those walls.

"Angels," Azrael continued, his voice sharpening. "Our position is fragile with so many still wounded, including God's Scribe, and several archive angels. But our cause is just and our fight is true. It is imperative that we recapture Archangel Samael and recover the Book of Secrets. Before it lands in Lucifer's hands."

The archangel lifted his hands toward the sunlight streaming through the thick, fleecy clouds that floated through the crisp, turquoise sky.

"The fate of the Creation and our human charges now rests in our hands. Let us be swift to capture Samael. But let us be slow to judgment. For that sacred task belongs to the seraphim who will decide the fate of Samael and his remaining guard."

Jack heard his name whispered across the terrace.

He glanced past Azrael, seeing Talia and her squad motioning him toward them. But he kept his position behind the archangel, not wanting to distract him.

"To the skies, angels. Keep to your squads and formations and await my order to blink. We will regroup at the sepulcher door. May the Maker bless us and the battle ahead. Onward, angels! Let's bring retribution to Samael and his guard."

All around him, angels spread their dove grey wings and took to the air. Berith rushed out of the round room and threw her arms around Azrael, kissing him urgently. He held her tight, their halos entwining as the rose-gold mixed with the red-gold light.

The burst of color reminded Jack of an autumn L.A. sunset when the air turned cool and the sun burned low on the horizon, filling the sky with vivid oranges, reds, and purples, and giving the coast a fragile, ethereal glow.

Azrael let Berith go and she hurried back into the round room as he unfurled his wings and lifted into the air.

Hands grabbed Jack from behind, pulling him into an embrace. Talia kissed him hard on the lips and motioned toward the sky.

"Ready, Jack?" she asked, her eyes bright, wings fully extended.

"Let's make some fireworks like Azrael and Berith?" he said with a smirk.

"Fireworks?" she replied.

"Let's bump halos, Mrs. Casey," he said and returned her kiss.

Behind her stood Muriel, Kesien, Anahera, and Deemah.

"We're so not leaving without you, Jack," said Muriel, a hand on her hip as she clutched her gold shield of light. "C'mon. Before Azrael gets grumpy."

Jack patted the pockets of his Levi's through his Eternean greaves. "I can play my demon-splattering playlist for him to set the mood."

Kesien laughed as Talia slid her arms around his neck, shaking her head.

"I don't think the archangel will appreciate the finer points of heavy metal, Jack," said Talia. "Unless it involves Eternean ore and armor."

"Not even AC/DC?" Jack asked with a frown.

"Afraid not, Mr. Casey," she said, kissing him again. "He prefers the classics."

"You Shook Me All Night Long is a classic!" Jack replied.

This made Muriel break into a fit of laughter that infected the rest of the squad.

"I wanna hear this playlist," said Muriel.

"Lare Dumont and Tyler Hughes weren't very appreciative," he replied with a shrug. "Neither was Zanth. But Gianni loved it."

"That's right," Muriel replied. "Gianni fought demons with you that night in your apartment."

He nodded. "Had AC/DC on repeat. Lare was so pissed."

His comment made Muriel laugh harder. "By the Maker, wish I'd been there during the demon fights."

"Me too," said Talia, letting him go. "The one involving that angel executioner."

She had a jealous glow to her grey eyes, making him chuckle.

"Only because she was hitting on me and not with her fists."

Talia's eyes flared with anger. "Hitting on you with what? I want to know everything that happened and how it happened. I'm going to smite her all the way back to Hell if I see her again."

He smiled. "She was hitting on me with Hellfire, but I love that jealous gleam in your eyes, babe."

"They're going to turn white with Holy fire if you're not careful, Jack," said Muriel, glancing from him to Talia. "Good thing she wasn't at that monument when you fought Zanth last time."

He gasped, remembering when he'd kissed Zanth back—to find out whether Lucifer was still controlling her. Back at Roche Harbor Resort on San Juan Island. And dammit, Muriel was about to tell her all about it.

He waved Muriel off, shaking his head.

Talia's eyes widened and she stared at Muriel, the heat rising in her grey angel of death gaze.

"What happened at the monument, Muriel?" Talia demanded, hands on her hips as she cast a quick glare at him. "That Jack neglected to tell me about."

The look on Muriel's face shifted into an apologetic expression. She knew she was about to sentence him to sleeping on the couch for the rest of his marriage.

"We need to get in the air now," said Muriel, flexing her wings.

Talia grabbed her by the shoulders. "Don't you even think about leaving this terrace until you explain that comment."

He sighed. He had to tell her now. At the time, she was suffering from demon paralysis and he wasn't going to upset her with that story. But now, not telling her made it look like he was hiding things.

And he was. She would either be upset or furious—or both. Especially when she heard that he'd kissed Zanth back.

"Babe," he said in a quiet voice. "She kissed me again. Trying to seduce me."

"What!" Talia cried, rounding on him. "And you never told me?"

He shook his head, casting a glare at Muriel. "With that demon paralysis, I didn't want to upset you with that story." He cleared his throat. "Or the one that follows it."

Talia's eyes narrowed and she blinked in front of him, arms crossed. "One that follows it?"

"Yeah, just before you arrived with Azrael," he answered.

Okay, he was stalling. He didn't want to make her cry or hurt her. Or get smited.

"Spill it, Jack Casey," she demanded.

He pulled in a breath, watching as Azrael slid into his Eternean armor, Berith helping him.

"Zanth was being controlled by Lucifer, babe," he said, dreading the punchline of this story. "But I had to be sure. The only way I knew how to infuriate Lucifer and get him to show himself—through the phone—was to use his own game against him."

Talia was already frowning and shaking her head.

"What does that mean, Jack?"

He sighed and stared at his feet. "It means I…uh…kissed her back."

"You what?"

Her voice was so tight and quiet. And he could feel the heat from her Holy fire already churning into a bolt of smite aimed right at him.

"I…kissed her back."

The anger burned white hot through her, those grey irises catching fire.

He averted his gaze, wincing.

"Babe, it was the fastest way to infuriate Lucifer!" he said, holding a hand in front of his face. "He was absolutely incensed and blew up my phone with a screaming, scathing call. I had to know who was standing behind her that day, so I could fight it. Don't smite me—I was playing a part! Kissing her was like kissing a hellhound in the snout."

She grabbed hold of his Eternean breastplate and jerked him forward, an inch from her face. She studied his eyes, his face, his expression.

"Hellhound, huh?" she said in a sultry whisper.

He nodded. "Trust me, it was one of my greatest acting achievements."

"What about this?"

Her lips parted as she smashed her mouth against his, the force and heat slamming through him at five g's of acceleration and the explosive power of a 200-megaton bomb.

Until his whole body overloaded with fire and need and connection.

And everything went dark and quiet.

In a moment or two, he saw halos hanging over him and realized he was laid out on the terrace, staring into Talia's terrified grey gaze, Muriel laughing beside her. Kesien and Anahera chuckled at him, Deemah fanning herself.

"Jack!" Talia cried when his gaze met hers.

"What…just happened?" he asked, his whole body still pulsing.

She sighed and bowed her head. "I'm so sorry, Jack," she said. "I… was jealous and wanted to show you that angels were sexier than demons."

Muriel snorted she was laughing so hard.

Jack frowned and slowly sat up on the terrace.

"And…?" he said, shrugging.

"So, I…put a little Holy fire behind that kiss," she confessed, her gaze falling to the stones, a blush washing over her cheeks. "I wanted my kiss to be as hot as hers."

He couldn't halt his belly laugh. She stared up at him in surprise.

"You're laughing?" she cried.

"Damn," he said finally. "First time I've ever been knocked on my ass by a kiss. I'd marry you all over again, Mrs. Casey. That. Was. Epic!"

Grinning, she threw her arms around his neck and he held her close.

"We'll have to revisit this topic later," he said with a smirk. "Back at my place."

"All right, angels! Get ready to blink on my mark." Azrael's voice cut across the terrace.

Talia pulled Jack to his feet beside her.

"And…blink!"

In a blur of motion, angels shot across the terrace and through the turquoise sky. Jack was a step or two slower, but with his seraphim powers, he blinked ahead of them. And hovered above the crossroads until Talia and her squad appeared beside him.

When Azrael materialized behind them, he pointed toward the winding path that led past the haunted woods. And the Garden. With its creepy white light illuminating the overgrowth of vines and dead trees, the tall stone walls scorched and shadowed. The terrible memories of pain and fear and choking on his last breath filled his head again. And he wanted to just blink past that place toward whatever locations existed beyond it.

An ocean. A swampy, shadowed delta. A river of stars and a dusky lake. And some ancient temple that housed the door to Purgatory. He'd never seen any of these places—didn't know they even existed until now.

"All right, guard, stay in formation, shields out. Blink past the Garden toward the Mortise of Souls."

"The what of souls?" he whispered in Talia's ear.

"It's a deep network of pathways," she replied in a soft voice. "Leading toward the places where souls dwell—except the Risen."

Mortise of Souls…sounded like a low-budget, black and white B-movie. Starring Lon Chaney's son's cousin's brother's best friend. Sounded like a place where souls went to forget everything. Forget the lives they led before. Forget who they were and what they'd done while alive. He was almost glad he wasn't going into this fight and was just opening a door.

Almost.

11

Talia flew near Jack, but side-by-side with her squad in a phalanx formation. She kept Jack close on her left as they flew past the scorched, pocked walls of the Garden, hoping to get past this place quickly. She knew that Jack's memories of that place were still difficult and painful—especially now that Lucifer had a bounty on Jack's head and every demon in existence was hunting for his soul.

Of course, Jack tried to play off the whole situation with a joke or two, but she saw the hurt still hovering in his pale green eyes. Every time he looked at the Garden's stone walls, those moments flooded back to him. Lucifer's relentless attack and Jack unable to get away from him.

Even she thought about those moments whenever she saw the Garden, the memory of Jack gasping out his last breath still made her chest ache. And the memory of his beautiful heart's shuddering beats that slowed until they stopped made her eyes well with tears. She would feel the ache of that moment for the rest of her existence.

"You okay, lover?" she asked, leaning toward him as her wings thumped against the air currents.

He nodded. His silver-grey wings were graceful beside her, buoyant on the updrafts as he soared over the Garden like he didn't see it. But she saw those moments playing behind his tired eyes. And she knew that look. He hadn't gotten enough sleep. She remembered him jolting awake beneath the willow tree when she shook his shoulder. He said he'd had a nightmare about this soul in Purgatory—and Lucifer—but he hadn't said much beyond that.

And it worried her.

With preparations underway to capture Archangel Samael and his remaining guard, she hadn't had much time to even ask Jack about the nightmare. He'd played it off though, changing the subject abruptly. And kissing her.

Making her worry even more.

In moments, they were past the Garden, the rest of the guard whispering past it as the road sloped downward and into a sharp curve to the left. Over top of a thick forest with massive trees. Similar to California's Redwoods, but with delicate, frilly red and russet leaves. Like one of Earth's sunsets had pooled across the branches. These trees were very different from the spindly, skeletal trees and misty indigo twilight that clung to the haunted woods. This forest was tranquil and shaded, the air cool and almost sweet. Moss covered the tree trunks and carpeted the ground, fiddlehead ferns and wild flowers in reds and pinks growing in the shade. It had a magical, mystical feel to it and she wanted to lose herself in this forest.

"Does this forest remind you a little of California, Jack?" she asked.

"Quite a bit," he replied, wings beating the air harder to keep pace with her. "Reminds me more of the lush Pacific Northwest forests. Like in Washington State."

She smiled. After honeymooning there with Jack—despite the demon assaults—she had very fond memories of that area. It would always remind her a little of Jack. Like southern California. She would never think of Los Angeles without seeing his stunningly handsome face, those sizzling light green eyes, and his sexy smirk. Her husband. It hardly seemed possible that she had finally gotten to marry this man.

"Maybe we can go back there for our first anniversary?" he said, his eyes luminous against the Parrish blue skies, that sexy smirk tugging at the corners of his mouth.

He was already thinking about their first anniversary together, expecting Heaven to let them remain a couple. She loved him so much.

"I would love that, Jack," she said, reaching out to touch his face, wanting to feel his arms around her. "Wherever you want to go, I'll follow."

"Unless Heaven says otherwise," he said, sadness in his voice.

He was right, no matter how much she struggled against it. And that made her sad, too.

"And I don't want you to follow me, Talia," he said with a sigh.

She felt a cold chill shudder through her wings. "What does that mean, Jack?" she said in a quiet voice.

"No following," he repeated and she winced. "I want you beside me, babe. Never behind me."

She smiled, feeling more reassured now.

"You're my leading lady, Tal," he insisted and gripped her hand. "My costar. Equal billing." He chuckled. "Even though you're an angel of death that could smite me into next Wednesday. Should probably put your name first."

She loved him calling her his leading lady. It warmed her wings and made her halo spin faster.

FOR A LONG TIME, as vanguard, Talia led Jack and her squad along the winding road that meandered over hilltops and alongside the endless stretch of forest that bordered the northern steppes of the ethereal plane. Until the turquoise sky faded to a washed-out blue that soon became a soft, creamy grey as the outlines of trees gave way to misty forms that looked almost like ghostly outlines of trees.

More vapor than substance—a little like the haunted woods. But these trees had a lighter, wispy quality to them, feathery, almost like steam rising through cold air.

This far away from Heaven's glimmering white spires, she'd often thought that these ghostly stretches of forest looked almost like placeholders in the Creation for new trees and forest. Like this area was still an active part of the ethereal plane still being formed. In the process of being defined by the Maker. Almost like volcanoes creating new landscapes on Earth.

But she also knew that the change in the forests marked the beginning of the Shade River Delta. Where many souls congregated before moving onto the higher planes of the afterlife on their journeys to rise above their former lives.

So many souls left their physical lives in traumatic and sudden ways. Unable to quite process those events and transition through the Corridor of Pervasive Light, they chose to go it alone. Here. In this hazy, dusky part of the Creation where they struggled through remnants of unfinished lives. The heartaches and losses that prevented them from rising. Or many feared what judgment might bring to their souls, misunderstanding the angel, Puriel's role. So, they hid themselves away from the light. And the darkness.

Most of the time, angels of death only guided souls to the entrance of the Corridor of Pervasive Light. But they couldn't make them enter it—much less follow it to the doors leading to Puriel's soul refuge. Along the way, angels—and demons—could only reach out to these souls if called.

Until the Creation on Earth changed and was remade again.

Puriel's job wasn't to judge either. Her refuge was like a visitor's center for souls, routing them according to their Books and their hearts. Finding the best fit for each soul—unless all possible routes to redemption had closed. What lived in their hearts was what mattered most and that tinted the events of their Books of Life and Death—and their placement.

There were far fewer truly unredeemable souls that crossed over and were sent to Hell.

All of the souls that didn't go through the doorway that Puriel chose for them found themselves at the end of this road: at the Mortise of Souls, a deep trench with five paths. Each path led to a place with a structure that had a door. The path of sand led to a secluded beach resort along the vast ethereal ocean. The silt path led to a boathouse at the mouth of the Shade River Delta where a churning river wound through the swampy region. A place of denial and ignoring reality.

The still water path led to a glass and cedar lake house at the edge of Spirit Lake, a twilight region with a misty, still water lake where exhausted souls gathered along its banks to rest. The stars path led to a round observatory at the precipice overlooking the River of Stars, where the Creation met the cosmos and that sense of wonder burned. And the fifth path, the path of dusk, led to an ancient temple and its sepulcher with a door leading into Purgatory, a place of imagination and myths. Where souls hid from the truth and tried to forget their former realities—or wallow in them.

Souls could open the door into each of the five structures or gates and choose one realm to enter. They could look into each location and choose which one to enter. Or go back the way they came through the trench, ending up back with Puriel in the Corridor of Pervasive Light. Or call to an angel (or demon) to guide them. But once they closed that door, only an angel could return them to the Corridor of Pervasive Light. Demons could enter the location if called, but they couldn't take souls to Hell.

Only if High House had labeled a soul as unredeemable and sent them to Hell. Like Lucifer, they would fall from the Heavens into Hell. Very few were labeled unredeemable upon entering the Corridor of Pervasive Light. Most souls sent to Hell got there after traveling through the Mortise of Souls and spending time along one of the paths where they chose to turn their backs on the light.

And exhausted all chances at redemption—like Lucifer had done, leading to the Rebellion and his fall from the Maker's Grace.

Already, the sun had fled behind growing cloud banks, the air cooler here than Talia remembered as the road beneath her hollowed out, deepening into a ravine. The air grew smoky as the misty forms of souls flitted through what had become a trench that carved its way through the hilly terrain and valleys.

She wondered if Jack could see the souls below him. She reached out and touched his shoulder, nodding toward the rapidly changing landscape below.

"Jack, what do you see below us?" she asked.

Frowning, he squinted at the road, his wings spread wide as he floated on an updraft.

"Looks like a forest fire or something," he replied, glancing around at the forest.

"Forest fire?" she cried, shaking her head as the air grew hazy above and below them.

He nodded. "The air's got that smoky haze that carries for miles and miles when the countryside burns. But I don't see any trees on fire and no distant glow of flames. Just lots of smoke." He shrugged. "We deal with lots of wildfires in Cali."

"The road below us is turning into a deep trench," she said, pointing at the deepening scar that cut through the Maker's ethereal Creation. "That is where the Mortise of Souls begins."

He squinted, shaking his head. "I see a lot of smoke and mist down there, moving along the road. Maybe Luci's illegally burning trash in Hell again?"

He did see the souls. To him, it probably looked like roiling smoke, not clutches of souls traversing the trench as they traveled toward the paths. And a door into somewhere comforting.

"That isn't smoke, Jack," she replied. "Those are souls."

His eyes got wide, his mouth flattening. "Whoa, seriously?"

She nodded.

"So, are we getting close to Purgatory?" he asked, his voice sounding humbled and so serious.

"Yes, Purgatory is one of the paths in the Mortise of Souls."

His brow furrowed as he studied the road below more carefully as it became a cavernous channel that ended at another crossroads. This one was very far away from Heaven and Eolowen.

Azrael sang out commands to the guard in angel notes. Asking them to fly into the Mortise and follow the path of dusk to the ancient grey stone temple in the forest. Where the door to Purgatory loomed below—tucked into a shadowy corner of the temple's sepulcher.

"Hear that, squad?" Talia asked, gazing to her right and making eye contact with Muriel and Anahera.

She glanced left and saw Kesien and Deemah nodding.

"Got visuals on the dusk path," said Muriel as she tilted her body to the right, dipping one wing.

Jack frowned. "Mind translating that song for the kid's table?"

Talia turned back toward him as she angled to the right and kept a close line with Muriel.

"Azrael directed me and the squad toward the path of dusk. We're supposed to land and enter the temple, meeting Azrael and the rest of the guard at the door to Purgatory."

Brilliant gold light burned through the clouds off to the right and Talia didn't need to part the clouds to know that the seraphim floated above the temple. Awaiting the moment when Talia and her squad flushed Archangel Samael and his former guard out of Purgatory. Where the guard would be stationed to capture the traitorous archangel and his remaining angels of death for the seraphim. Returning them to High House.

She and her squad had to get this right. She didn't want to disappoint the seraphim. Or Azrael.

As soon as Jack opened that door, she and her squad would be inside Purgatory, on a mission to locate Tre Sheridan's soul. She sang out a soft melody of angel notes, imploring the rest of her guard to keep a close watch on Jack while she was inside.

"All right, squad," she said aloud, for Jack's benefit. "You can already see the seraphim floating in the distance above the temple. Let's enter the gallery and wait for Azrael to set this mission in motion."

Jack's wings thumped against the cooler air currents as he banked alongside her, flying low over the road as the trench expanded. Ahead, in the misty haze, the Mortise's five paths loomed, each one made from the different types of soil. Only the path of stars glittered back at her, the white and gold lights reflecting off the path of still waters' mirrored surface.

The first distant outlines of the five structures loomed out of the mist as she, Jack, and the guard followed the trench that sloped downward. Like a labyrinth, the five paths jutted into the furrowed ground, almost creating the spokes of a wheel. The path on the right was shadowy and led deep into the forest where smooth, charcoal grey stones, draped in vines, and covered in velvety moss and lacy lichens, stood tall on the horizon.

The temple was dark and empty, great tree roots spilling over the lichen-encrusted structure.

"Wow…incredible," said Jack in a hushed voice as they flew over the towers and around the massive structure in the shadows of thousands of trees. "This place reminds me of temple ruins in Cambodia or even Thailand."

She had seen most of Jack's world over the centuries, including these sacred places. All of them where shades of this part of Creation. She sang out to her squad for them to follow her into the tower on top of the structure and spiral through its gallery into the sepulcher below.

Reaching out, she gripped Jack's hand.

"Stay close and follow me in," she said. "We'll enter that tower on top and fly down through the structure until we reach the sepulcher below." She sighed. "And the door into Purgatory."

That door made her uneasy.

Heaven didn't quite understand the enigma that Jack had become, neither completely human or angel. He wasn't a Nephilim, the product of a human and angelic union either. They were still figuring that part out. But no one knew for certain whether Jack could open that door out of Purgatory. It was all conjecture. That angel executioner seemed certain enough, but everyone in Heaven had only speculations and theories.

Even God's Scribe.

Because of the uncertainty, she needed to stick close to him—in case he couldn't open that door out again. That's why she didn't want him going through that door with the rest of the squad—and risk him not being able to leave Purgatory.

A dark entrance loomed ahead at the top of the temple as she flew toward it. Jack stayed within a hand's grasp of her on the right. Between her and Muriel. As the squad neared the top of the temple, they closed ranks, flying in a tight phalanx formation like she'd asked. But also making sure Jack was well insulated on all sides. Thankfully, he hadn't heard that part either. She didn't want to offend him, but he meant everything to her and by the Maker, she'd protect him.

Like a flock of doves, they entered the tower, the temple's gallery dark and smoky as they moved through its thick, fluid shadows, halos lighting the way.

Jack stayed close to her as they angled their wings, folding them close to their bodies as they navigated tight turns and openings in the broken stone floors. The flutter of wings echoed in sharp layers through the temple's center crevasse as they moved downward.

Toward the sepulcher below.

The bottom of the temple appeared abruptly, looking like an abandoned well. She and Jack spread their wings wider to slow their momentum, landing with hard thumps of their armored boots against the stone floor. Scattering dust and shadows as they turned toward the massive stone door that led into Purgatory.

Sounds reverberated like gunshots through the silent, still structure. Only the whisper of wings and flow of souls softened the sharp silence.

But that silence made her uneasy. It was too quiet here.

"Wow, is this place ever creepy," said Jack, his voice echoing.

She nodded as Muriel and Kesien landed on either side of Jack. Deemah landed behind him, Anahera in front.

"Couldn't agree more, Jack," said Muriel, her grey gaze darting around the dark sepulcher lit only with the light from their halos.

Muriel's hair looked almost coal black in the sepulcher. Her hair had darkened so much since that night in the Chicago alley where Talia had lost two souls and felt no empathy for either of them. Something that made her cringe now. And made her heart ache.

Before Azrael made that first wager with Lucifer, Muriel's hair had been a chestnut brown color. But after everything she and Muriel had been through together, the color had darkened to a rich sable. Even the color of her eyes had turned a softer, creamier grey. Like most angels of death. But her stint in High House had accelerated that process quite a bit.

Would Jack's hair and eyes change? She prayed they would stay pale blond and that hypnotic light green that made her skin burn and her chest ache.

Jack's expression darkened as he studied the broken walls and dank, mossy floors of the sepulcher.

He shook his head, hands on his hips. "What soul in their right mind would look at this place and say, *Hey, this looks like home to me. Honey, pack up the kids, and we'll have a barbecue, make a lifetime of it.* Damn."

Talia chuckled. She couldn't agree more.

"It's sure not this lovely atmosphere, Jack," said Muriel with a snort, nodding at him. "Or the visuals that attract them—thank the Heavens." She motioned at the door. "It's the energy that pulls them toward this door. And the energy beyond it."

Three smoky souls walked past them, two others stepping through them as they opened the tall stone door with its huge, iron ring handle. The souls didn't even hesitate. They pulled open the door and went inside. Like they belonged there.

The door rasped across the stones, creaking, and shuddering. And then it closed with a thump, iron ring clanking as the sound echoed through the dark, silent temple.

Again and again, the door opened and closed. The stream of souls through it was constant.

Jack looked a little stunned as he watched them disappear and the door close—with more traveling behind them—but he didn't say anything.

"Tal, you sure about this place?" he asked finally, squinting, his gaze nonchalantly shifting toward the shadowed corners.

"Why, Jack?" she asked.

He shrugged and crossed his arms against his Eternean breastplate, casting more furtive glances around the sepulcher. Something was bothering him about this place, even though he was trying to act like everything was fine. In typical Jack Casey fashion.

"Jack? What is it?" She reached out and laid her hand against his face, caressing.

"Something doesn't feel right, okay?" he said finally in a quiet voice. "Don't you feel it, too?"

"Like what, Jack?" Muriel asked, glancing at Talia.

He tilted his head toward the lengthening shadows above him, the darkness quickly consuming the light, like a candle wick burning down.

"You said the seraphim were overhead, right?" he said, nodding toward the tower above them and the sliver of sky.

"We saw their light as we approached, remember?" Talia replied as Kesien and Muriel both nodded at him.

Anahera glanced around the space as she moved closer to Muriel. She looked uneasy, too.

"Those dudes light up the world like Vegas visiting Disneyland, babe."

Muriel chuckled.

"They lit up the entire forest as we approached the temple," said Talia. "Why?"

He held out his hands, shadowed from the rich, dark shadows enveloping the sepulcher. Shadows that drifted through the temple well and collected here in this tomb-like area. He turned his hands over and back again, palms up.

"Then where's the light, Tal?" he asked, glancing upward again. "The top of that tower we entered was open to the sky, so the seraphim should be lighting up this temple and the sepulcher like a Phish concert."

Talia frowned. A fish concert? What did singing fish have to do with the seraphim's light?

"Singing fish?" she replied, scrunching her nose. "I don't understand."

He sighed. "Like New Year's Eve in Vegas, babe. Where's the seraphim light?"

"Jack's got a point," said Kesien, looking intense as he gazed around at the deepening shadows.

Shadows that had grown thicker. Darker.

"Talia…" Muriel's wary tone cut through the confusion.

"What is it, Muriel?" she asked as Muriel fixed her with an apprehensive look.

"The stream of souls has stopped."

Jack's gaze flicked through the space as he moved closer to Talia. "What the hell does that mean?"

"Exactly," said Kesien.

"And Hell is exactly what it means. Jack Casey."

The velvety alto voice with a smooth French accent filled the sepulcher as Talia felt the sudden presence of Hell creatures. She gritted her teeth.

They were surrounded.

How had they suddenly appeared around them without her sensing their approach? How?

"Roundel formation," Talia said with a hiss. "Shields out. Form around Jack."

"Surprised to see me and my demon army, angels of death? This far into the Creation?" the angel executioner asked as she sauntered through the dim-lit tomb, her voice almost a purr. "An old archdemoness trick to gradually absorb the light and increase the shadows. Where my demons could hide until they were legion."

Talia and her squad moved into position, keeping Jack in the center as a legion of demons stepped out of the shadows all around them.

"Zanth!" Jack replied in a curt voice, pointing at her. "You threw us a surprise party, you crazy demon chick, you! How thoughtful. But apparently, no one thought to bring some beer. Or hell, even a bag of chips. You call this a party?"

Zanth stood about fifty feet away from Talia and the squad,

dressed in a short black party dress and pearls, fingernails blood red. Matching her lips.

"No," Zanth replied, crossing her arms. "I call this a massacre."

The corpulent slide of frog-like demon feet sloshed against the shadowy stones, the heavy footfalls echoing through the sepulcher.

The archdemoness glanced overhead and grinned, revealing sharp, pointy teeth.

"Ahhhh…and your guard will arrive right on time to be wiped out. Demons! Engage. Leave nothing but feathers behind."

Anger flashed in Jack's green eyes. "The only thing that's gonna be left behind is demon stains when we wipe the floor with you bastards."

Zanth laughed out loud, the rich, deep sound filling the silence.

"You still make me laugh, Jack Casey. Lucifer can't wait for your comedy as he flays your skin off in Hell."

"Too bad you won't be alive to see it, Zanth," said Jack.

"Or your angel of death friends, I'm afraid," she replied as an eight-foot, hulking Devourer of Angels stepped out of the shadows toward Talia and the squad. "Au revoir, angels."

Talia felt the fear sharpen around her as her squad hesitated, tightening formation.

"Don't you dare give ground to this demon bitch," said Talia, not taking her gaze off this smug angel executioner. "If we do this right, we can feed her to her own Devourer."

"I knew I married the right woman," Jack said with a laugh.

"Take them," Zanth ordered, pointing toward Talia and the squad. "Take them all down. Now."

Another flood of demons churned through the sepulcher as the Devourer of Angels screeched and lumbered toward Talia and the squad.

12

"Jack, you stay away from that Devourer!" Muriel ordered, raising her shield as Kesien unsheathed his sword. "The squad's got this."

A sea of red eyes filled the sepulcher's dark expanse, the Devourer of Angels screeching as it bared its pointy teeth and stalked toward them. Zanth stood in the middle of the tomb, grinning, hands on her hips, as waves of demons surged past her.

"Hey, don't come crying to me when you get eaten," Jack snapped at Muriel. "I think I've proven myself against these bastards. I leave a bad taste in its mouth—like most people after they meet me."

Why they insisted on keeping him away from this thing, he'd never understand. He'd wait until they engaged the other demons and then take it down. Talia was the vanguard of this squad, the nearest angel to this thing. He refused to watch it swallow his wife and all her angel of death pals either.

The stench of brimstone soured the air as it grew smoky and dark, shadows shifting around them. But the Devourer of Angels was huge compared to the other demons and it loomed over them as it lurched forward.

At the flutter of wings, Jack turned.

He was surrounded by angels of death, Talia at the front of this circular formation.

What was it called again? The name always reminded him of some 60s band…like the Supremes? The Temptations? The Rondells? Stuff his grandparents listened to as teenagers.

"You dudes aren't gonna break into a chorus of Get Ready or Stop in the Name of Love, are you?" he shouted. "What Kind of Fool?"

"What?" Muriel frowned as Talia gave him a confused look and returned her attention to the approaching legion of demons.

He sighed and held out his arms. "Since you've got me imprisoned in this Supremes formation or whatever it's called."

Guarding him might get some of these angels obliterated. Starting with the love of his life. Talia, the squad vanguard.

His head knew Talia was a warrior with centuries of battles fought with that sword and shield of light. Lifetimes compared to his short time at this demon fighting business. But his heart still wanted to leap out in front of her and protect her from the onslaught of demons pressing toward them.

Muriel started laughing. "It's roundel, Jack." She shook her head. "Supremes. Where do you get this stuff?" She turned to Talia. "If you divorce Jack, can I have him?"

"Forget it, Muriel," said Talia, her gaze still on the demons. "He's all mine."

"Thanks, babe," he called out.

Where in hell was Azrael and the rest of the guard? And why didn't the seraphim burn these bastards out of existence?

Jack sighed. Probably got hit with an even larger force of demons on the way into the temple. Looked like Lucifer had stocked up on demons at the last Black Friday sale in Hell—just for this occasion. That crafty bastard.

And Jack knew that they were way too close to the demons for the seraphim to act. Dammit!

From the outlines in the shadows and the shape of the glowing red eyes, he recognized the assassin demons. Even in shadow form. And the beady red eyes of a bunch of Hellpoodles that had massed around the assassin demons. But the rest? He had no clue what they were.

Until they emerged into the light where he could mow them down with murder marbles.

"Squad, shields to the sun," Talia ordered, her voice firm, but deadly calm.

"What sun?" Zanth replied. "There is no light left here or haven't you noticed? My demons and I have been busy absorbing all traces of it from this temple. Or hadn't you noticed?"

Talia glanced back at Jack with wide eyes and that *you were right, Jack* look of hers.

"We noticed," Talia said, her voice tight, her anger controlled. "But you forget we're creatures of the sun, demon. And we make our own light."

"That's brilliant, Tal!"

What if he threw down a good old-fashioned seraphim barbecue and angel-broiled these demons into oblivion? Briquet-hard!

Zanth's smile was condescending. "And how would you do that, little angel of death?"

Would his seraphim light make Zanth and her forces retreat from the sepulcher?

"Like this, bitch!" he shouted, closing his eyes. "Gonna be a regular disco inferno down here. Let's dance."

He held out his arms, calling up the glow of seraphim light around him. Feeling the light project outward from his body.

The angels of death surrounding him gasped. Wings fluttered. Halos spun faster.

"Jack, what are you doing?" Talia.

"Cover your faces!" he shouted, directing the force of light forward.

Toward Zanth, the darkness, and the sea of demon eyes burning red in the shadows.

"Jack, don't!" Talia shouted.

He held onto it as long as he could, but it slipped free of his grasp and careened toward the demons.

Like a Heavenly bowling ball, it rolled over the massive force of demons. Crushing many of them underneath the white-gold burst of Holy fire he'd just fired at them.

When he opened his eyes, the sepulcher burned with Holy fire in every crevice and corner. He'd mowed down a massive number of demons, but he hadn't taken down the Devourer of Angels or whatever skulked behind it.

Or Zanth.

But the shocked look on her face was worth it.

"Jack!" Talia cried, grabbing hold of his Eternean breastplate. "That was an insane amount of light you tossed at them."

"Just hammering your point home to our company, Mrs. Casey. It got a little Biblical. Sorry."

Muriel snickered. Even Kesien was smiling as the demons struggled to recover.

"That was epic, Jack," said Muriel.

Zanth turned toward them, those red demon eyes glowing brighter.

"So, you have more power than I expected, Jack Casey," she said as she sauntered past the burn marks charring the stone floor. "Lucifer will want to know all about it. Nevertheless, it should not take too long to drain it at this rate."

Jack shook his head. "Didn't you hear? Me and Talia got an upgrade when we became husband and wife. That union came with an endless well of Holy fire, too. Didn't Luci tell you? Guess he's too busy playing with the blinky lights and squeaky toys in his playpen to pass that along."

Muriel and Kesien both laughed.

"Squeaky toys?" Muriel said with a snicker. "By the Maker, Jack—no wonder he put a bounty on your head."

"Lucifer is counting the moments until he can take you apart piece by piece, Jack," said Zanth, smiling. "And meanwhile, another legion of demons has engaged your guard. A shame there will be nothing left of your squad when they finally reach the Purgatory door."

Jack shook his head. "Wow, Zanth...vindictive much? All because I didn't help your lover escape his new, self-imposed prison? For being dumb enough to trust Lucifer."

Zanth bared her teeth and took several steps toward him. "You leave Tre out of this!"

Whoa…hit a nerve.

Zanth lifted her right arm above her head and snapped it down again. "Next wave. Go!"

The Devourer of Angels screeched, the sea of red eyes turning dark as things rustled through the now-dying light in the sepulcher.

Unlike the seraphim, he didn't have endless energy to fuel the seraphim spotlights like they had. As a human, even his new, improved connection to Talia couldn't refill his well fast enough for a continuous burst of Holy fire like the seraphim. He may have seraphim powers, but he was nothing like them. And he had a failsafe that shut off the energy well, making him power drunk if he expended too much power. To keep him from killing himself.

Guess it was time for murder marbles and confusing them with omnificence until he passed out or Azrael galloped in with the angel cavalry. Or they just flew the hell out of here as fast as they could. Falling power drunk here in the middle of Demon Central might just end him.

"Get ready to blink above on my mark," Talia replied.

Looked like Talia thought that exiting stage right was the best choice, too. Otherwise, they'd be overcome by the waves of demons. There were just too many.

A shrill soprano scream pierced his ears. He glanced left.

Anahera!

The Devourer of Angels had stealthed across the room and grabbed her. How the hell had that hulking, eight-foot monstrosity done that with frog feet?

Kesien blinked, throwing himself at the Devourer as it lifted Anahera into the air and smashed her toward its gaping mouth.

She screamed again. That bastard was killing Anahera!

Jack leaped into the air, wings spread.

"Jack!" Talia shouted. "Jack, no!"

He conjured up a handful of murder marbles and flashed past the corpulent red demon's fat face as Kesien bashed it over and over with his shield.

The rest of the squad moved with lightning speed, slamming this monster with shields of light as hard as they could. Talia ran it through with a sword of Holy fire.

But not fast enough to stop it from putting Anahera against its gaping maw. It bit down, pointy teeth piercing both wings.

Anahera's shriek of pain was bone-chilling.

Talia blinked beside it, sword raised again.

But Jack launched himself at the Devourer's mouth, throwing himself between those teeth and Anahera just before it popped her inside like a Scooby Snack.

He hovered, shoving six murder marbles into its fetid mouth, and then hauled off and punched its fleshy face as hard as he could throw his fist.

It was like punching jello.

The Devourer squealed, dropping Anahera as it flailed and clawed at its face.

"Get down!" he shouted at the squad and threw himself to the floor, covering Anahera and Talia with his wings.

Muriel dropped down beside him, shield poised overhead. Deemah and Kesien rolled toward them, holding up their gold shields of light as all six murder marbles exploded.

The Devourer showered the sepulcher in demon parts and red goo as the patter of hundreds more demon feet scritched across the stone floor. Red glow of demon eyes cast an unholy radiance throughout the long, narrow tomb.

Jack heard one after another thump against the raised shields above them, bouncing off, the sound like hailstones hitting a tin roof.

All light left the room, the sepulcher going dark as the squad got swallowed up in a mass of writhing, attacking demons.

One by one, the shields fell as Kesien and Deemah battled the teeming mass of demons. Muriel defended them as best she could, but she peeled off to assault the next wave of demons.

Then Talia.

She engaged Zanth after leaping away from him and Anahera. Both of Anahera's wings bled white-gold light across the grey stone floor. She couldn't move. She was shaking, the light in her halo fading in and out as she crawled toward the wall, grey eyes hooded, breaths coming in gasps. She summoned a flickering shield of light, holding it out with shaking hands, and braced herself behind it.

Anahera wasn't done yet.

In an instant, Jack was surrounded by demons.

"Okay…if that's how you want to play it," he said with a growl, calling up murder marbles in each hand. "I can explode your asses all day long."

He flung a handful of murder marbles at the demons like he was chalking the first base line at Dodger Stadium, and called up a sword of Holy fire in his right hand. It guttered in the shadowy darkness as he swung it in a wide arc, cutting down several demons.

But there were a shit-ton more behind them.

He had to keep fighting them until his tank was empty. It was all he could do. Or become Luci's target practice dummy for eternity.

They had to hold out until the guard punched through the main assault. Azrael was a brilliant tactician. He'd see right through the demon forces stalling them and find a way to reach the sepulcher. And Talia's squad.

He was betting his soul on that fact.

Talia slammed Zanth with a massive burst of Holy fire. Throwing her back against the wall.

Zanth crouched a moment, shaking her blue-black hair, those red eyes sparking as a smile curved across her ashen face. With a snort, she leaped at Talia, talons slicing through the smoky darkness.

They tangled, bat wings and angel wings beating the air as they floated above the stone floor. Talia slammed Zanth backward again.

Zanth tumbled to the sepulcher floor. And became a shadow, disappearing like smoke into the shadows and the frenetic waves of demons.

Talia zipped through the room, tossing out bolts of Holy fire, and swinging that flaming sword. That blade was in continuous motion as it stretched into a long, curved blade. And became a scythe. And she reaped destruction with it.

With every swing of that blade, demons fell by the dozens around her.

"That's my wife!" he shouted with a fist pump and slammed it into the face of a shadow panther that leaped at him.

He rolled away from it and scrambled to his feet as an uneasy lull in the fighting descended. The sudden calm made his skin crawl as his gaze darted around the tomb, only the dim light of his halo illuminating the stones, the Purgatory door about fifty feet behind him.

"Find the angel executioner!" Talia shouted, turning toward her squad. "Now!"

Something cold and diamond-sharp snapped against Jack's throat, hands yanking him backward. Slamming him against the Purgatory door.

"All of you, stand down! Now!" Zanth shouted, arms stretched around him as shadowy bands wrapped around his legs, arms, and chest, immobilizing him. "Or I slit his throat. Stand. Down. Now!"

Damn. She'd outmaneuvered him.

Talia blinked across the sepulcher and stood an arm's length from him now, eyes glassy, mouth in a taut, flat line, scythe raised over her head.

"You're about to lose your head, demon," she said with a feral growl. "Let him go. Now!"

Zanth's velvety alto laugh filled the sepulcher and he heard the smile in her tone.

"You may get one swing of that scythe off, angel of death," said Zanth, sounding amused. "But not in time to stop him from bleeding out on this very floor."

That was a comforting thought.

He felt the burn of Zanth's blade-like talons against his throat, already nicking the skin and drawing blood. Like razor burn. If she even twitched, he'd get a tracheotomy and a one-way trip to Puriel's side of Heaven. Or overnighted to Luci's condo in Hell.

He did his best not to flinch. Dammit! This demon bitch had him in a game-ending headlock.

Either way, he was screwed unless Azrael got here. Fast.

"Jack…"

He heard the quiver in Talia's voice.

She looked helpless as she stared at him, an arm's length away, as the other angels of death gathered around her.

"Demons!" Zanth shouted. "Engage the death angel guard overhead. Now. Go!"

Like the sun rising, thick, black oozing shadows faded to a deep charcoal as the rest of her legion, her army, turned to smoke and floated up through the temple. Toward the sky. Where Azrael and the guard must have finally broken through their defenses.

Zanth lifted her left hand and coils of red light swirled out, encasing her, Talia, and the squad in a roiling spin of red light.

"Demon cone of silence again?" Jack asked, barely letting his lips move. Or his Adam's apple.

"Jack," said Zanth, her tone softening. "Please. Help me." She swallowed a breath. "I give you one last chance. Help me rescue Tre…*s'il vous plaît*. I will fight at your side throughout Purgatory. Help you capture Archangel Samael if you will only help my Tre escape."

His eyes narrowed. "Forget it," he snapped. "I don't negotiate with demons."

"Not even when you're about to die?" she countered.

Dude had a point. But no way. That was the quickest way to become Luci's favorite chair in Hell.

"At least I know I won't be on the bullet train for Hell if you kill me," he said.

"Jack!" Talia cried. "Don't—please!"

He braced himself for the tear of those bladed talons across his throat.

But Zanth didn't move. Didn't even flinch a fingernail.

"What if I give you something that you have yearned for?" Zanth asked.

He flexed his ring finger. "Happily married," he said.

"Your father is in Purgatory, non?"

He froze. "How did you know that?"

"I overheard you talking about it. So, I asked my love and Tre found him for me."

"You found my dad?" he said in a quiet, shaky voice. "In Purgatory?"

"Yes, Jack Casey," she replied with a purr, those talons still against his neck. "If you agree to help me, I will take you to him."

He could see his dad again!

Say the things he never got to say when Dad suddenly went from coherent to comatose at home hospice. He'd been at work, lifeguarding at the YMCA when Dad's condition had worsened. All week, Jack had been gathering up the courage, trying to find the words to tell his dad everything he felt. Everything he needed his ol' man to hear. But by the time he'd rushed home from work, it was too late.

In the end, all he could do was sit there and hold Dad's hand. And spill all the things out at once, his chest so tight he could barely talk, and his heart breaking into pieces as Dad's breaths turned shallow. His blood pressure started dropping. And in minutes, he was just— gone. He took one more breath. And then the next one never came.

And that was it.

Then the world expected him to just man up and move on with his life. Like when the lawnmower stopped working. Drop it beside the dumpster and go on. Move on already. It had been two months. *Why wasn't he over it yet?*

Over it. Like it was an illness—like the flu or bronchitis. Or a fight with his best friend. It lasted a few days and then it was gone, right? Then everything was back to normal.

From that first night that he'd spent alone in the apartment he shared with his dad, Jack knew that his life would never be the same again. It would be forever marked by the time *before* Dad died and the time *after* Dad died. And even though nine years had passed, he still felt that raw grief a lot, like that first night with the ol' man's palpable absence from his life.

Even now, Jack had trouble wrapping his brain around the fact that his dad wasn't in the world somewhere anymore. Somewhere he could text him and get an almost instant response. Ask him music or sports questions. Or just hear his voice again on the phone, telling him to pick up bread on the way home. To be careful driving because there were storms coming. And to be home by eleven o'clock, his curfew.

All that pain he'd carried for nearly a decade at such a pinnacle loss. And he'd have traded his fame a million times over to spend an hour with his dad again. To say the things he didn't even know he'd needed to say because he was just a kid back then.

"You have not said a word," said Zanth. "Did you hear what I have offered you? The chance to reunite with your father."

"Tal…" he called, his voice cracking. "Tal, I—"

"Jack," said Talia, so close that he could hear the spin of her halo now. "I know. I feel the pain you carry from that night."

"You can't be seriously considering that, can you, Jack?" Kesien demanded. "She's Lucifer's first lieutenant. She'll help Archangel Samael finish us off in there. And she'll drag you back to Lucifer with a big red bow tied around your neck."

"Jack, my offer stands," said Zanth. "The moment that Tre is free, he and I will escape together. Leaving Lucifer's army behind."

Dayum! She intended to betray Lucifer. To walk away from his army and Hell. She'd be hunted like him and Berith. Forever.

"Are you prepared to be hunted for the rest of eternity, Zanth? Where can you and your lover even go that Luci won't find you?"

"I love Tre," said Zanth, a shudder in her voice. "Freeing him is all that matters to me. He was promised an eternity at my side and got—this! THIS! His human life is over. And he does not want to ascend without me. We will be together again. And when he returns to me, we will disappear. Together."

Wow, she was crazy about this dude, Tre.

And no matter how hard Jack tried to deny it, he was a romantic at heart. Even he was a sucker for a good, old-fashioned demon love story. Especially one that screwed over Lucifer as the credits rolled on this feature film.

Looking into Zanth's red, glowing demon eyes, he saw only pain. She had let down her guard for him, showing him her heartbreak. Leveling with him about what her goal was and how she intended to achieve it. While swirled in this demon cone of silence.

But Lucifer would find out soon enough when Archangel Samael didn't come home from school and his face appeared on milk cartons and lava alerts all over Hell. He'd know that Zanth had betrayed him. Hard.

If Lucifer had only followed through with his promise, he'd have had a loyal first lieutenant for eternity. Not one about to ghost his ass for convincing her human lover to swan dive off the Strat and trap himself forever in Purgatory. Just to rescue that flying dickhead, Samael from his seraphim prison.

Was the Book of Secrets really worth all these betrayals?

"All right, Zanth," said Jack in a quiet voice. "You take me to my dad—no tricks—and help us route Samael's ass back to prison with the Book. Once Samael's in angel of death hands, I'll open the door for your lover. We got a deal?"

Zanth pulled in a quivering breath, her body trembling.

"Oh, Jack! Oui! Merci beaucoup!"

"You make one move to help Samael and I flame you out and that door stays closed. Got it?"

"Oui," she said in a quiet, shaky voice. "Merci, Jack—merci."

Kesien glared at him, those calm, patient grey eyes stormy now, anger burning across his face, halo light spiking as it spun faster and brighter.

"I hope you know what you're doing, Jack," said the six-foot-sixish angel of death, shaking his head, tousling that mop of black curls.

At last, Zanth let the blades slide away from Jack's throat, the swirl of red light still whipping around her and the squad. She held up her right hand.

"I give you my word that I will help you find Samael and take you to your father's soul."

Kesien glared at her. "That means so much coming from an angel executioner. And Lucifer's first lieutenant." He propped his hands on his hips. "And now, Jack's going to be in harm's way in there. He was only supposed to open this door. From the sepulcher, not Purgatory."

"You'll need him in there," said Anahera in a pained voice as she leaned against the wall, eyes hooded, light still dripping from both wings. "Without me."

Talia and Muriel rushed over to her, both casting healing light onto both wings.

"We'll get Daidrean then," said Kesien.

Jack frowned. What was with Kesien?

"Kesien?" he replied. "Dude, if you've got a problem with me, say it to my face. But don't talk about me like I'm not here."

Kesien sighed, running a hand through his black curls. "Kid, I don't have a problem with you. I like fighting alongside you. But I'm worried that this is all a setup by Lucifer to drag you back to Hell. I only want to keep you safe." He nodded toward Muriel. "Like Muriel and Anahera, I like having you around."

That made him feel better. "Thanks, dude. In most cases, I'd agree with you. I don't know why, but I believe Zanth. I always like to see love win. And I don't judge. Demons have a right to love just like we do, don't they?"

Talia slid her arms around Jack's neck and pulled him close. She was trembling.

"Always my hopeless romantic, aren't you, Jack?" she said. "Besides, this is an unconventional way to take down Lucifer's first lieutenant, wouldn't you say, Kesien?"

Kesien nodded. "Got a point, Talia. It's a divine solution."

Jack slid his arms around Talia's waist and held her close, feeling the race of her heart and the slowing spin of her halo.

"I keep thinking what if that was you trapped in Purgatory, Tal," he said in a soft voice. "And if I knew there was one person out there that could open that door, I'd bust up every choir in Heaven to find him. I'd make him open that door for me."

She leaned up and kissed him. "When you put it that way, how can I not agree to help. Love is love."

Jack glanced over at Zanth, the slow spin of sparkling red light still whipping around them. Her eyes looked glassy, a smile curving across her ashen face.

"Love frees all," said Jack. "Even demons apparently. Azrael's gonna spit Holy fire when you tell him."

Talia let him go, staring into his eyes. "When I tell him? You're going to explain this crazy little plan to him, Jack. All of it."

Muriel chuckled. "Can't wait to pull up a chair and watch Jack squirm his way through this explanation."

At last, Kesien's expression brightened. "Me either, Muriel. Can't wait to watch the kid give this Oscar-worthy performance."

Jack sighed. "Azrael's going to smite me when he hears this."

"Feeling a little inebriated yet, Jack?" Muriel asked. "Because I'd love to watch you explain this to the archangel while power drunk. We could do ambrosia shots every time he calls Azrael dude."

The whole squad broke up laughing, including Anahera.

"Did I mention how much I hate angels of death?" Jack replied.

He felt a little lightheaded from tossing out that massive blast of seraphim light, but he'd reined in the rest of his attack, using murder marbles, a sword of Holy fire, and his fist. No, he didn't feel a power drunk coming on. But he wouldn't mind a couple of whisky shots before having to explain this to Azrael.

Hey, Azrael, we've got a squad member down. Zanth the angel executioner said she'd fill in for Anahera. Cool? Cool! We're goin' in! Don't wait up.

He sighed. Dude's halo was going to spin up like the Hadron Collider.

13

TALIA COULDN'T HELP BUT LAUGH, WATCHING JACK SQUIRM AT THE thought of telling Azrael about this situation with the archdemoness. But she loved how romantic he was—even with a demon involved. She looked forward to her future with him, learning how deep his love ran as she got to see it in action. She wondered how it would evolve as the years passed. Would his attitude and feelings age even if his body didn't? She loved how consistent he was at such a young human age, rarely saying one thing and doing another.

Even with an angel executioner involved.

She cast more healing light on Anahera's right wing, trying to close the massive gash that had nearly severed her wing mid-span. Light bled out in a steady stream. The sight of it alarmed her. This was more than she could heal. It would require Berith's rare healing talents to restore Anahera's wings. She doubted her squad mate could even fly back to Eolowen.

Anahera laid her head against the slick stone wall and groaned. That greater demon had almost swallowed her whole.

If it hadn't been for Jack's quick response—and paying absolutely no attention to everyone telling him to stay away from that Devourer—Anahera would be gone now.

But she wouldn't tell him that. He would be even more emboldened and push his human limits well beyond their breaking point.

Still, he'd handled that greater demon like a seasoned angel soldier, despite she and her squad treating him like a delicate flower about to get trampled. As usual, he'd ignored them—and her. But that was her Jack. Most of the time, he scared her to death, but she loved—and hated—his selflessness.

Especially this agreement with the angel executioner.

He could have outlasted Zanth, knowing that she needed him alive, until Azrael arrived. But the angel executioner dangled the right bait in front of him this time. Talia knew how much the death of Jack's father still hurt him. It was even in his Book of Life and Death, listed as a catalyst for his drug addiction and a source of long-term despair that had never healed in him.

She wanted to review his Book again. See how these newer events had changed it. Especially after what had happened in the Garden. And after he received his wings and halo—and the seraphim powers.

Like dissipating storm clouds, the thick, inky darkness permeating the sepulcher lifted as light filtered down through the tower and into the long, narrow tomb-like sepulcher. The stench of brimstone and smoke faded as Azrael and dozens of the guard zipped through the broken walls and floors down toward them.

"Look!" Talia cried, pointing upward. "Azrael and the guard broke through!"

"Guess it's showtime, Jack," Kesien said with a chuckle.

Jack's light green eyes narrowed and he tossed an angry look toward Kesien as Muriel smiled, arms crossed, and leaned against the stone wall beside Anahera.

"Nominated for best actor in the most painful explanation to an archangel category...Jack Casey in Demonsplaining," said Muriel.

Talia and the rest of the squad broke into a fit of laughter.

"And the Oscar goes to..." Deemah said, motioning toward Jack as Azrael landed beside him.

"You dudes should have your own show," Jack said with a growl, glaring at them.

His response made them laugh harder.

Azrael's charcoal grey eyes were steely, narrowed, his body stiffening when he saw Zanth leaning against the wall beside the door to Purgatory.

"Guard! Phalanx formations! Shields to the sun!" He pointed at Zanth. "Prepare to engage!"

Jack held up his hand. "Relax," he replied. "She's no threat."

"No threat!" Azrael roared. "She's an archdemoness! Lucifer's first lieutenant." He pointed at Zanth again. "She's executed hundreds of angels over the centuries."

Zanth didn't move or react. If anything, she looked bored.

"And she just retired after a century of service," said Jack, glancing from Zanth to Azrael.

"Retired?" Azrael replied. "Angel executioners don't retire! They get obliterated by Holy fire." He motioned at the dozens of death angels that landed behind him. "Guard, prepare to bombard her with Holy fire! On my mark."

Jack blinked across the sepulcher and spread his wings in front of Zanth, arms extended.

"Dude, seriously—you need to listen first." He cried, hands splayed, a panicked look on his face.

"I'm an archangel! I don't need to listen to anything!"

Holy fire glowed white in Azrael's eyes, soot grey wings stretched wide, as more and more of the guard crowded into the sepulcher. His red-gold halo churned faster.

Jack's eyes were wide with fear, sweat threading his upper lip. "Dude, before you start splitting atoms and spitting Holy fire, hear me out, okay?"

Azrael's face was a mask of confusion. "Hear you out? About what, Jack?" He glanced at Talia. "Talia, please get your husband out of range. I don't want him to be collateral damage."

"Sir, please listen to Jack for a moment," she said, laying her hand on the archangel's forearm. "A lot has happened down here."

The white flames dissipated from the archangel's eyes, the steely grey color returning. His gaze narrowed as he studied Jack and then Zanth.

"Is this about the human soul trapped in Purgatory again?"

"Oui, archangel," said Zanth, stepping out from behind Jack's wings, that swirl of sparkling red light still whipping around her.

The circle widened until it had traversed the whole sepulcher with that demon-red sound dampener.

"Angels don't make deals with demons," Azrael said with a growl.

"They didn't," said Zanth, crossing her arms. "The human did."

Azrael groaned. "You mean Jack?"

Zanth nodded. "Oui," she said with a sharp nod. "In exchange for my taking him to his father in Purgatory and helping him capture Archangel Samael, he has agreed to open the door for the soul of my human lover, Tre Sheridan."

"Jack!" the archangel shouted, looking exasperated. "How many times have I told you never to bargain with Lucifer and his demons? How many times?"

Jack shook his head. "This isn't about Lucifer. Archangel...this is about love. About reuniting two lovers by opening this door. It's something only I can do."

Azrael's expression softened and he shook his head, motioning at Zanth. "It may very well be about love, Jack—but this isn't just any demon. This is an archdemoness. And an angel executioner."

Jack moved toward the archangel, a sad look on his face. He wasn't acting either. She could see the pain and conflict in those pale green eyes.

"I know," he said, holding out his hands. "I get it. But isn't redemption what all you angels keep preaching? About this divine gift of forgiveness and love?"

"That's for humans, Jack," said the archangel in a soft voice, almost like he was speaking to a child. "Not for demons. Not for creatures of the light that chose the darkness."

Jack glanced over at Zanth who leaned back against the door to Purgatory again. Like she'd expected this response and wasn't going to bother trying to debate it with an archangel. But those red glowing eyes took in everything. And she made no moves.

"She was never a fallen angel, were you, Zanth?" Jack asked, turning toward her. "Did you fall in the Rebellion?"

She shook her head. "Non. Lucifer created me from Hellfires and put me through the cage fights until I defeated every challenger. And then his champions."

"A beast by her own admission," Kesien snapped.

Her gaze shifted to the archangel's face, ignoring Kesien's comment, and stayed there, unblinking.

"I was never a creature of the light," said Zanth, waving her arm at the archangel. "Nor was I ever given a chance to choose. I became what I was taught. What was pounded into me by the demons I defeated to become Lucifer's first lieutenant."

Kesien glared at her. "See! She's a monster by her own admission."

"Monster…innocent, demon…angel," said Zanth with a shrug. "It is a question of perspective."

Jack's gaze narrowed, but he kept quiet as Zanth glanced down at the grey stone floor, crossing her arms against her chest like she was cold.

"I played the role I had earned until I ran into a human magician who sold his soul to Lucifer for fame. A year at the top of his game. It was the first time I had experienced this famed human emotion of love. And I have lived for it ever since."

"Dude, look at Berith!" Jack replied, turning toward the archangel again. "She fell in the Rebellion. Broke your heart for centuries. But she found a way to turn it around and redeemed herself. She got her wings and halo back. In a world where everyone said there was no redemption for fallen angels. If she found a way, then why can't there be a path for demons that want out, too?"

Azrael was quiet for a long time, but then, he sang out questions to the guard. To Talia, Muriel, and Kesien. To Anahera and Deemah.

To the seraphim.

"You're talking to each other, aren't you?" Jack replied with a shake of his head as he gazed at the angels surrounding him. "Don't want me to hear. You gonna spell out the big angel words, too? Like I'm at Heaven's kiddie table?" His eyes narrowed. "Well, just so you know, I intend to open that door for her lover's soul if she keeps her word. Because taking down Lucifer's first lieutenant with an act of love, rather than an all-out Holy fire war, is my idea of a well-fought battle."

Jack spun around and around, shouting toward the top of the temple so even the seraphim could hear him.

"All you high level angel types keep agreeing that love frees all! Well, prove it! Is it really all...or just some?"

He turned around, glaring at Azrael. "She's taking me to my dad in Purgatory. First time anyone's offered to do that one small thing for me."

That stung.

Talia wanted to reunite them, but there hadn't been time yet. She hoped he was excluding her from that list, but his anger over it bothered her.

"This is my chance to tell him all the things I couldn't as he died of cancer," Jack continued in a tight, pained voice, anger pinching his beautiful face. "When he was too weak and ill to know if I was even there beside him. And in exchange for that gift, I'm gonna bring the soul of her human lover out of Purgatory through this door. Because I feel her love for this dude every time she talks about him. Because love is love. And dammit, it should free all, not some!" He shouted toward the top of the temple again.

The silence in the sepulcher was painful. Azrael looked lost, like he had no response at all.

"Isn't love this gift you angels keep talking about? A gift way more than human love." Jack's voice carried through the sepulcher and rose in layers toward the tower. "That it isn't something you can earn or take. It can only be given. And don't you angels keep saying how humans are going to teach angels about love? It's the only thing we can give you dudes! What do you give the angel that has everything?"

The sepulcher remained deathly quiet, the guard standing stoically behind Azrael, wings folded at their backs, halos a soft buzz in the calm, smoky twilight. They seemed at a loss for words like her and her squad, too, looking to the archangel for a response.

"Well, I counted five dudes," said Muriel, stepping away from the wall. "So, that should tell you how serious Jack Casey is about this decision, Azrael. It was a five-dude explanation."

Chuckles erupted through the squad and rippled through the guard until even Azrael was smiling.

"A five-dude explanation?" Azrael replied. "That must mean it's important." He cleared his throat and the smile fled. "Jack, the seraphim want a word about this situation. Let me commune with them first. Talia, Muriel, a word please."

Talia reached out and ran her fingers through Jack's hair, soothing his anger. Then she leaned up and kissed him before she took flight, following the archangel up through the broken stones, Muriel behind her.

Jack nodded. "Fine. I'll be right here by the Purgatory door when you're ready to yell at me again."

WITH WINGS SPREAD, Talia rose on the warmer air currents, wings fluttering as she flew out of the tower. She soared above it as Azrael and Muriel sailed alongside her. Her gaze shifted to the soft blue skies and thin wisps of clouds, the seraphim high above them, burning the sky like a glaring sun. Even at this distance, she felt the heat of their Holy fire radiating. How had Azrael stood it in the cloud chamber when he had faced them on the platform? Or the pyre as everyone called it.

Now, she understood why.

"Talia," said Azrael, shaking his head. "That husband of yours is very passionate about this situation."

She smiled. Jack Casey was always passionate. To a fault. One of the things she loved about him.

"Five-dude passionate," Muriel remarked.

Azrael's dire expression lightened. "Yes, he wasn't a bit power drunk when he called me dude. I felt his conviction all the way through that tower. He feels strongly about trusting and helping this archdemoness." Azrael groaned and shook his head. "The seraphim are very displeased by his change of heart. And they're worried, Talia. Worried that he might be shifting loyalties. With seraphim powers, that could spell disaster."

"What?" Talia cried, unable to hide her shocked expression. "Jack would never support Lucifer and Hell. Ever. And besides that, this angel executioner is planning to betray Lucifer. She's walking away from Lucifer's army the moment she's reunited with the soul of her human lover."

Azrael nodded and his gaze flicked toward the distant seraphim and then back at her. She felt her breath quickening and her heart racing. If they felt Jack was a threat, they'd smite him. Or take his halo and wings, sending him to Hell. The act of removing a halo and wings greatly diminished an angel's power, turning them into a fallen angel. She shuddered. Forever banishing him from Heaven.

"Sir," she said. "Are they planning to harm Jack? Smite him? Take his wings? Because if they are, I—"

He motioned her silent and she felt her anger welling. He was conversing with the seraphim.

"Holy Hosts!" she shouted, turning her gaze toward the sky. "Jack Casey is right and if you condemn him for this, then you must condemn me as well."

"Talia!" Azrael cried, his eyes widening, alarm burning in those soot grey eyes.

"Talia, careful—" Muriel cried. "Or you'll end up in my old room at High House, waiting for them to glow up your eyes and reeducate you."

"We have the opportunity to take down Lucifer's first lieutenant without a single shot fired, Holy Hosts!" Talia shouted. "Without a battle and by upholding the Maker's golden rule of love."

The heat was staggering as a seraph blinked forward, hovering close. She felt the stifling wind blow hot across her face, nearly scalding her wing feathers. They curled up, her eyelashes and eyebrows singed.

But she held her ground. She would defend her husband to her last wing feather.

She felt Azrael grip her arm as she heard the seraph inside her head.

You have chosen to trust one that has hunted angels for sport. One that has executed angels for millennia. You act against every angel instinct. Why?

The voice pounded through her mind, the words hitting her like an avalanche. Demanding. Insistent. Impatient. From the looks on Muriel's and Azrael's faces, they had felt the seraph's words, too.

It was Seraphina.

"Because love has changed this angel executioner," she said, staring up at the sky.

Explain. This other seraph voice was sharp and forceful.

"A demon true to its nature would have threatened us and tried to force us to do its will."

This demon WAS true to its nature. It threatened to kill your human.

Talia nodded. "At first. But she learned that she had to earn our trust. She learned that to get help, she must first give it. And give it in equal measure. Because the love of a human has changed her."

How has love changed this demon? It was Seraphina's voice again, an edge to her words, a hint of impatience.

"At first, she hunted Jack and me. She paralyzed me as a show of force. She threatened Jack's friends in Lucifer's name. None of that made him surrender to her will. Only through an unselfish act of love did she win over Jack. And me."

What unselfish act? It was Seraphyron, his tone demanding and derisive. *To get what she desires? All demons act on their selfish desires.*

"The archdemoness has agreed to fight alongside us to recapture Archangel Samael and the Book of Secrets, but she is giving Jack a great gift of love by taking him to his father in Purgatory."

She is still a demon. Insisted the third seraph, Seraphiel, his tone matter-of-fact—like his pronouncements were a foregone conclusion. *This gift will only give her what she desires. That isn't love. It is a means to an end. She will show her true nature once her lover is free and collect Lucifer's bounty. Folly in humans is expected, but in angels, it is indefensible. You risk everything, Talia.*

Talia fervently shook her head. "No, it isn't folly. And she will not act against Jack or my squad."

How can you be certain! Seraphiel.

"Because if she collects Lucifer's bounty, she must return to Hell alone. The soul of her human lover cannot follow. Only damned souls can pass through the Gates of Hell. Besides, she knows how much Lucifer hates humans and would never allow her lover to live beside her in Hell. No, this love has changed the archdemoness."

The silence from the seraphim was intense.

Continue. Seraphina's voice was calm and collected.

"The archdemoness has done monstrous things to angels for millennia," said Talia, the heat sweltering. "And to humans at Lucifer's bidding. Like Jack, I won't ignore these terrible things and I haven't chosen to trust her. I have chosen to accept her help. And show love in return, to the unlikeliest of creatures. One of my greatest enemies."

A divine response. Seraphina. *Where did you learn this?*

Talia smiled. "Jack Casey taught me how to turn enemies through love."

Love frees all—not some. To quote the human. Proceed.

Seraphiel and Seraphyron both objected, their voices rising in a chorus that made Talia's head ache.

Enough! Talia and her squad walk a path intended by the Maker. Even if they stumble, the light chooses love. Go, Talia. Find Archangel Samael before he escapes capture and hands over the Book of Secrets to Lucifer.

"Thank you, Heavenly Hosts!" she called out.

Hold onto this strange little human, Talia. He might even change the face of God before long.

This was her moment. She had to bring up her relationship with Jack. And ask about their future. About staying together.

"Heavenly Hosts," she began. "About Jack. And me." She held out her left hand, her gold wedding rings glistening. "We married in front of Heaven and Earth, yet we live day to day with one wing in Jack's world and one wing in mine. He longs for me to be beside him as his wife."

"Seraphina," Azrael replied, barging into the conversation. "Jack Casey has endured so much to stop Lucifer. Even his physical form has changed in ways no one expected or understands. And don't forget how moved the Maker was at Jack's completely selfless prayer in the haunted woods as he fatally battled Lucifer to save Heaven."

Thank you, Azrael. We remember. Seraphina's voice was calm and steady. *Continue, Talia.*

"Every day, Jack broods about losing me. And I fear that one day, Heaven will demand that I return to Eolowen for all time. Leaving him behind. An act that would destroy him. And me. Please…grant us Heaven's blessing that we might stay together for eternity."

Talia felt her eyes welling with tears. The first crystals began to roll down her cheeks.

"Heavenly Hosts, haven't Talia and Jack earned the right to remain together?" Azrael said, his voice insistent. "Separating them now, after everything they've sacrificed and everything they've given would be… Hell."

The silence was palpable. She was terrified. She couldn't lose Jack.

Talia…it is unnatural for an angel of death to love a human in this way. Seraphiel's voice tore through her heart like a flaming sword of Holy fire.

And it goes against the order of humanity as ordained by the Maker. Seraphyron's voice pierced her human soul. The crystalline tears rolled down her face and disappeared into the tower's darkness.

No. No! She didn't care about rules and order and custom. She loved Jack more than her own existence. She wouldn't give him up. She wouldn't!

Yet, despite the rules and the order of things, you and Jack Casey forged this strange and magical bond. Part human. Part divine.

Seraphina's voice ached through her spinning brain and she wanted to dive into the tower and wrap Jack in her arms. And disappear with him. Like Zanth wanted to do with Tre Sheridan's soul. At that moment, she understood this archdemoness. No, she empathized with her. It trembled through her heart and quivered across the tips of her wings, sending her halo into a wild spin.

You are not the same angel of death that won a wager against Lucifer, Seraphina continued. *And he is not the same human whose soul you saved from oblivion. You have a human soul. He has wings and a halo. He gave his human soul to save you. You gave your wings and halo to save him. Changing the two of you for eternity. Each sacrifice strengthened and deepened a bond that no angel—or seraph—dares to sunder.*

Talia gasped, her gaze shooting toward the radiant glow in the sky as the seraphim shifted closer. But instead of brisk, burning winds of heat, she felt warm comfort.

We will discuss this union with the Maker, Talia. Seraphina's voice was gentle and soothing inside her head this time. *Do not lose faith now. The Maker could have sundered your bond long ago, but chose to watch it grow and develop. How you and this little human, forever changed, stay together is a discussion for another time. To ensure that his other human spirit bonds—family, friend, or animal—are not broken. Have patience, focus on Samael, and cleave to your mate. Love is winning.*

For several, long moments, Talia could barely focus, the words rushing through her head: *a bond that no angel—or seraph—dares to sunder.* The seraphim had no intention of trying to *fix* Jack or revert them back to some state before they fell in love. It was a bond only the Maker could sever now. How they stayed together was now the discussion. Not if.

She wanted to dance through the Heavens with Jack in her arms! The seraphim weren't planning to separate them or force her to leave him behind. She was so relieved that Jack wouldn't be cut off from the humans that he loved either.

"Thank you, Heavenly Hosts," Azrael called out, wrapping his arm around Talia's shoulders when she began to lose altitude. "Knowing that Talia and Jack will remain bonded is a great comfort. We'll discuss the how part of the equation later, once you've discussed it with the Maker."

Talia nodded, feeling a warm rush of joy wash over her.

"Thank you," said Talia, her heart too full to speak.

She laid her hand against her heart and smiled up at the seraphim as she held it out to them.

We feel what's in your heart, Talia. Seraphina. *And that insight has taught us a lesson in love. Including one about demons. Your empathy is strong. Angels walking beside humans is teaching Heaven a great deal. As the Maker intended. Or so Azrael told us once in the cloud chamber.*

Talia glanced up at the archangel. To her surprise, he was blushing.

Be vigilant, Talia. Seraphiel's voice thrummed through her head. *We watch your mission alongside this angel executioner with trepidation. And hope.*

The seraphim blinked away from the tower, the air cooling as their bright white light shone at a comfortable distance now. As they waited for her squad to flush Archangel Samael out of the Purgatory door. And into the awaiting force of her guard, backed up by the seraphim.

She squinted toward the road that wound into the distance. Back toward the crossroads. And Eolowen. A large force of angels approached. She felt their celestial light. It was the cherubim ranks. Ready to take custody of Samael and his former guard. And the Book of Secrets.

"I sure hope that Jack is right about Zanth," said Talia as Azrael descended into the tower, his arm still around her shoulders.

Muriel was at her elbow, looking concerned.

"If he's wrong, we'll have all the smiting power in Heaven outside that door to take her out. Either way, the problem will get resolved."

Muriel had a point. If Zanth double-crossed them, she and the soul of her human lover still had to escape through that door. Even for an archdemoness and angel executioner, that action would be demonic suicide. Unless Lucifer had an even bigger force gathering to mount a surprise assault. And the odds were high that the angel executioner would be the first demon obliterated in such an all-out war outside the door to Purgatory.

No, her intuition told her that Jack was right. That Lucifer had no idea his new first lieutenant was about to betray him for her human lover. Lucifer would go on a rampage as soon as he learned about it.

Good thing he was still tethered in Hell behind a locked gate, so that the Earth didn't pay in blood for his rage.

"Good work, Talia," said Azrael, smiling as he led her down toward the sepulcher. "Let's get you back to Jack—in case your husband decides to go Hollywood on us."

She frowned. "Hollywood?"

Muriel chuckled. "You know, Talia? Terrible, terrible idea, but looks great on film."

Talia sighed as Jack and the squad came into view, Jack pacing back and forth in front of the sepulcher door.

"That's Jack all right."

"Exactly," said Muriel. "Hence the reason we need to get back down there."

"Besides," Talia replied, a smile returning to her face. "I just want to hold him in my arms and tell him what the seraphim said."

"He'll be so happy to hear it, Talia," said Muriel. "I know he's been feeling really down about returning to his old apartment and having you up here without him."

He had. Talia hated leaving him back on the island when the call home came. They'd only been married a week. And the devastation in his eyes had run deep.

"Leaving him on the island hurt me, too," said Talia. "A lot. I hope I never have to leave him like that again."

Azrael nodded as they passed through the broken floor above the sepulcher door.

"He looked so lost," said Muriel. "I think he was relieved when Heaven asked for his help again. Even if it was just to open a door."

"Unfortunately, it's got to be more than that now," said the archangel as they floated toward the shadowy sepulcher floor.

"What do you mean?" Talia asked, fear rising in her chest.

Azrael shook his head. "With Anahera so badly injured, I need to get her to Berith fast. I was planning to go into Purgatory with you, too, so that leaves two holes in the assault team. The archdemoness and Jack will have to fill them now. There's no other choice. He'll get the chance to see his father after all. Besides, Jack's safer with the squad in there than out here. No telling what other demonic forces will challenge us now."

The archangel was right. The thought of leaving Jack on the other side of that door without the archangel there to guard him was terrifying. No, he was safer at her side. With the rest of her squad.

As they landed against the floor, Jack stopped pacing and turned toward them.

"Jack!" Talia called and blinked across the room toward him.

She wrapped him in her arms and kissed him hard on the lips.

"Missed you, Mrs. Casey," he said with a smile, but it faded as he glanced at Azrael and Muriel and then back to her. "Everything okay?"

"Everything is more than okay," she cried and kissed him again.

"I'm liking this conversation," he said with a smirk and returned her kiss with a sizzling smooch that made her weak in the knees.

She pressed her mouth against his ear and spoke in a soft, excited voice. "The seraphim acknowledged our bond, Jack. They said it was one they would never sunder."

His mouth gaped and he pulled her face toward his. "Does that mean they aren't gonna widow me by keeping you here full-time?"

"No, Jack," she said, grinning. "They aren't going to separate us."

That sultry smirk burned across his gorgeous face. "That mean it's Mr. and Mrs. Casey for eternity?"

She nodded and he threw his arms around her, holding her against his chest.

"I'm so relieved. I'd have died without you, Talia."

She held him tight, never wanting to let him go. "And I couldn't have existed without you, Jack."

As he twirled her around in his arms, her gaze fell onto Zanth. The archdemoness had a strange look on her face. It was part sadness and part anger.

Zanth stepped away from the wall and stood in front of her and Jack as he let Talia go.

"Talia, if Tre and I could have even half of what you and this human, Jack, have, I would be...happy." Zanth shook her head. "Happy is not an emotion I have understood until I began to hunt you and Jack Casey. But now, it is what I crave. With my Tre."

14

Jack was surprised by the range of emotions running across Zanth's face as she watched him twirl Talia around and kiss her. Including the envy flickering in her red eyes. But he also saw pain. She truly hurt at her separation from this dude that had committed suicide for Lucifer's plan to prison break Archangel Samael. So, he could be with Zanth forever.

And Jack was a little shocked that Lucifer would screw over his new first lieutenant's lover like this—especially after Abaddon had returned to Heaven and left the post unfilled. There were probably tons of demons vying for that position. Maybe even Archangel Samael? Dude had to be looking for a new line of work...other than being Heaven's most wanted.

Maybe this debacle was a test of Zanth's loyalty by Lucifer? And Zanth was using him and Talia to pass it.

Didn't Lucifer care that his first lieutenant was miserable alone? He squinted at her, studying her expression, her body language. Like Zanth wouldn't have found out immediately that her lover was trapped in Purgatory? That must have been a real blow when she learned about Sheridan's fate.

But it didn't make sense that she wouldn't know. Like Lucifer, all his demons were in the human-damning business.

Maybe Lucifer intended the shocker to hone Zanth's hatred into a weapon? Jack wouldn't be surprised if that was the sole reason Lucifer had hidden it from her.

Still, this made about as much sense as the game Lucifer had been playing since the vineyard in Santa Rosa. Jack had no idea what game it was either. Or what Lucifer was trying to achieve. But it had kept him and Talia running and off center for weeks battling demons.

What was Lucifer playing at?

At some point, he knew that they'd find out—the hard way. Like every interaction they'd had with the King of Hell. Tethering the dude back in Hell hadn't lessened the mayhem either. Jack hoped that it didn't involve him being dragged away from Talia again. And back to Hell.

That thought terrified him more than anything.

"Zanth," he said, turning toward her. "Why would Lucifer betray you and your lover like this, knowing his plan would trap your lover in Purgatory? Wouldn't he want his first lieutenant happy? And informed?"

"Lucifer equates happy with complacent," said Zanth, shaking her head. "There is no happy in Hell, Jack Casey."

Dodged that question.

The archdemoness glanced back at the great stone door leading into Purgatory as the stream of souls resumed toward it. She seemed anxious, on edge, fidgeting.

"Don't I know that," he replied. "Regardless, why would he betray you by knowingly trapping your lover in Purgatory?"

"It was not so much a betrayal as a…"

She paused a moment, crossing her arms as she watched the flow of ghostly human figures open and close the door, over and over. Like she wished she could simply reach out and open it herself.

"As a calculated risk."

So, Lucifer hadn't really intended to screw her and her human boyfriend over. She'd stretched the truth a little. His stomach dropped. What else had she stretched out of shape and led him to believe? Demons stretching the truth? Didn't see that coming…

He felt his annoyance spike as his patience began to drain away. When didn't demons shift the story around to suit them?

He frowned, glancing back at Talia and Azrael, and then returned his gaze to the archdemoness.

"Before, you said that Lucifer knew what would happen and didn't tell your squeeze. Now, you're saying this maneuver was a *calculated risk*? Which is it?"

Azrael moved closer to Talia, wings rustling as the archangel's steely gaze flicked from him to Zanth. Azrael looked surprised and concerned. Probably because he hadn't detected her lie. She'd hid it well from the angels, but not from a human's perspective.

Zanth moved away from the door, arms still crossed as she let a sigh escape.

"I told you what I thought you wanted to hear. I did not think you would help me unless I told you that Lucifer had betrayed me."

His eyes narrowed as he glanced at Talia again. Her posture had stiffened, an angry burn beginning in those luminous grey, angel of death eyes. It wouldn't be long before they were roiling white with Holy fire if this conversation unraveled any further. At least that Holy fire wouldn't be directed at him.

"Try again," he said with a growl.

"All right!" she shouted, lifting her taloned hands into the air. "I did not learn about your father in Purgatory until much later. And then I was afraid that the chance to speak to your father would not be enough of an enticement to help me," said Zanth, her gaze shifting from his face to the Purgatory door. "So, I invented a lie about Lucifer betraying Tre."

"All right, Zanth," Jack snapped, hands on his hips as he stood in front of her, blocking her path. "Either you level with me right now— all of it—or that door's gonna stay closed until Hell freezes. And I don't think Luci gets the Canada Goose Parka catalog in Hell yet."

Alarmed, her red eyes wide, she jerked her gaze toward his face, full red lips parting, a mixture of fear and despair on her face.

"All right, the truth," she said with a moan and called up that swirl of sparkling red light again. It enveloped the angels of death surrounding her. "All of it."

Talia was at his side now, her arm sliding around his waist as her halo lightened and spun faster.

"Don't forget that all angels have an inborn ability to sense lies," said Talia, her unblinking gaze on Zanth.

"I am an archdemoness," said Zanth with a knowing smile. "There are ways around those senses."

Jack frowned. "But not around my human bullshit detector. And right now, it's on overdrive, Zanth. Stop capping or the deal's off! Tre won't get paroled and all you'll get are zombie visitation rights. For eternity."

"Capping? Zombies?"

Zanth frowned, a confused look washing across her ashen face, one that matched Talia's perplexed expression.

Muriel leaned forward. "That's Jackspeak for keep lying and that door stays closed."

"Didn't I say that?" Jack replied with a shrug to Talia and then gazed around the sepulcher.

Kesien and Muriel were both chuckling as Talia shook her head.

Deemah leaned against the wall beside the door. "In a very Jack Casey kind of way. Wrong audience."

"I should have tried to translate," said Talia as her gaze met Muriel's. "But Muriel is more up on popular culture than me."

"Had nothing better to do when I was stuck in High House than sift through Hollywood entertainment news—and social media," said Muriel, shrugging as her eyebrows lifted into a light-hearted expression.

Jack felt annoyed. He was trying to get this demon to spill the truth, not hold a Heavenly debate on his word choices. He crossed his arms.

"Forget the terminology!" he said in a sharp tone. "Shoot straight this time, Zanth. To be fair, Luci's definitely my idea of a supervillain and none of this would be a stretch for him, but don't make him look worse than he is. That would make his day."

With an almost mournful look, Zanth turned to stare at the door and then she whirled back around. He was surprised—no shocked—at the glassy look in those red eyes that didn't spark so much right now. Like she was remembering something very painful. He'd never seen a demon tear up before. Was it just an act?

It took him by complete surprise. He had no idea that demons felt any sort of remorse or emotional pain. That would almost trouble him the next time he flung a murder marble at one.

Almost.

"Here is the entire truth, Jack Casey," she said, still staring at the door. "Tre and I...had a fight before he agreed to Lucifer's proposal."

"A fight? Like a couple's spat? Or like a demon battle?"

She nodded. "A couple's disagreement."

"Over what?"

"It was complex," she said.

"What? Little, like which side of the bed demons prefer or big, like which spoke of Hell got the least cool air in the afternoons?"

She whirled around, those red eyes sparking.

"You make jokes? What do you know about my kind?"

He took a step toward her, a hand on his chest. "I know plenty, Zanth. I spent months in Hell as Lucifer's latest Lego project, getting taken apart and put back together daily by him and his demons. Believe me, I saw it all."

The sparks in her eyes softened along with her temper. "I forgot that you spent time there." She still looked pissed at him for poking fun at her argument. "Our fight was over remaining in Hell for eternity." She bowed her head. "He was having second thoughts."

"Who could blame the dude? It's hotter than...well, than Hell down there. I mean, the dude was living in Vegas which is like Hell's northside, but maybe he wanted the possibility of someplace cooler? I sure get that."

"Perhaps. That's when Lucifer brought up Purgatory."

Jack scoffed. "That figures. So, did Luci tell him it was a permanent address change or just a timeshare? And that he should bring a sweater."

Zanth crossed her arms, looking sullen. "He told him it was permanent. I told him I would not stand for it."

"So, your boy toy defied you. Is that what pissed you off most, Zanth? That he defied you or that he didn't love Hell as much you did?"

"But he said he loved the hot weather!" she cried, waving her hands in the air. "That the desert weather was his favorite! I never dreamed the heat would be what would separate us like this."

Her hands fell against her sides and she slumped against the door, looking defeated.

"So, he didn't think it all through?" said Jack, walking toward her. "Didn't realize he'd only get conjugal visits? Changed his mind on the no A/C and no heat option?"

She shook her head. "You humans make no sense to me! You talk in circles. In rhymes. And you constantly change your minds! It is infuriating!"

"Welcome to my world," said Talia, sliding next to him.

"Wait a minute," Jack said with a chuckle, turning toward her. "Your world? You saying I'm infuriating, Mrs. Casey?"

She nodded, a smug smile on her radiant, winter-pale face, those grey eyes luminous.

"And you're constant trouble. Constantly changing your mind. Your emotions. Your attitude."

"And my clothes," he replied. "Who knew?"

She was trying to empathize with Zanth at his expense. He was willing to fork over his credit cards if it endeared this archdemoness to their cause and moved her farther away from Lucifer's plan.

"Humans!" Zanth cried, looking flustered. "They never see the big picture! How have you managed to stay with one this long?"

Jack gaped at Talia who was nodding. She was flat out agreeing with this demon. Against her loving, devoted husband of almost two weeks.

"Sorry you married me yet, Tal?" he asked with a smirk.

Shaking her head, Talia reached out and laid her hand against his face, stroking.

"Never. Zanth, a human's physical life is so much shorter than ours. Humans burn so bright for such a short time. Like fireworks. And butterflies."

"Butterflies?" said Zanth, frowning.

Talia nodded. "And they can't see the big picture because it's never been shown to them. Only tiny snippets and snapshots have flashed around them, hinting at possibilities. Nothing more." She cupped his chin. "Hinting at eternity. And I wouldn't have them any other way. Their souls burn hotter than the sun—like their passion, their devotion. Their love. That burn fuels my reason for existing. And it brightens my angelic light in ways I never imagined possible."

He grinned and leaned toward her, kissing her hard on the lips.

"Mrs. Casey, you're the best wife ever," he said and laid his hand against his heart, holding out his palm to her.

She pressed her hand against his, like she was gripping the heart he had offered her, and put her closed hand against her chest.

"And you are the love of lifetimes, Mr. Casey. Now until forever."

At last, he glanced at Zanth, expecting that demon look of disgust to shine in her eyes, but she looked amused.

"You celebrate each other's very different natures," said Zanth, motioning at him and Talia. "I must learn not to dominate, but to accept. And let his fire burn."

Jack nodded. "I learned early on that trying to change an angel of death was like trying to change the past. Just makes things worse." He glanced at Talia and smiled. "Besides, I love my black-robed, scythe-wielding, card-carrying death angel wife. Just the way she found me with a sarcastic hatred of humans and an arsonist's wit who didn't know who the hell I even was on Earth."

Talia rolled her eyes. "He's supposed to be some big Hollywood star, Zanth. Voted sexiest man alive two years in a row. They made a mistake."

His mouth fell open, a smile on his face. "Burning me to the ground with my own past now."

Talia nodded at him. "Yes, a big mistake," she said.

"What mistake?" Zanth asked.

"They should have kept voting him the sexiest man alive," said Talia, wrapping him in her arms. "Big mistake."

He laughed and slid his arms around her. "I'd marry you all over again, Talia Smith, hater of humans."

Zanth pulled in a heavy breath and stared around the sepulcher at the stoic angels of death standing guard at Azrael's back. And then her gaze moved to Talia and finally Jack again.

"So, will you help me, Jack Casey?" she asked, holding out her hands. "Help me convince him to come with me. There are many places we can go—except for Hell now."

"That's a selling point, Zanth," said Jack. He turned around and stared at Azrael a moment. "So, archangel, what happens to a human soul that escapes their assigned home room after they die?"

Azrael frowned. "What, Jack?"

"An escaped soul?" he repeated. "What happens if they slip out the back door? Do you guys send angels of death with tire irons after them? Bloodhounds? A hit squad?"

Muriel stepped beside the confused archangel.

"Sir, Jack needs to know what will happen to Tre Sheridan once he steps out of this door."

Jack sighed. "Isn't that what I said?"

Talia rubbed his shoulders. "Yes," she said. "In Jackspeak. But Muriel translated."

Azrael laid a hand against his chin and glanced up through the tower.

"For the short term, nothing will happen to him. Because until you open that door back out again, Jack, that event has never happened in Purgatory before. But at some point, he will have to face the decisions he made and the actions he took. Like all humans. Until that time, there are more pressing issues for Heaven than wandering souls. It is a common occurrence to see the unrisen souls find their way back to Earth, returning to familiar places and people they miss."

Jack's face scrunched into a confused look. "Like ghosts?"

Talia nodded. "Yes, Jack. But not like your Hollywood versions that haunt places or people. No humans can see these souls. They also know they're dead because an angel of death crossed them over and brought them through the Corridor of Pervasive Light to Puriel. If they find their way back to Earth before they have risen, it's a purposeful transition. If not a lonely one because no one else can see or hear them."

"So, no ghosts wandering the Earth because they don't know their dead or anything like that?" he asked. "And no scaring the hell out of new home buyers when they buy Lucifer's latest Gothic Demon Revival reno?"

Talia and Muriel laughed, but Azrael and the rest of the guard gave him another series of confused looks.

Tough crowd.

"No," said Talia with a grin. "They could rattle chains all day long, but no human would ever hear them. And the first thing an angel of death tells them is that they have died."

He glanced around the tomb. All the angels of death were nodding. Except Kesien.

"Unless those angels of death were part of Archangel Samael's guard," said Kesien in a dark tone.

"I remember when your guard went on strike," said Anahera in a pained voice. "I confess, a lot of us in this guard joined them initially, thinking Archangel Azrael had treated Talia so badly." The tall, red-haired angel moaned and bowed her head, wings splayed across the stones and still weeping light. "Talia showed us that the archangel had been trying to protect her all along."

Deemah shook her head. "Maybe so, Anahera, but Archangel Samael had only been trying to protect himself—and his loyal core of death angels. For months, we watched the death angels in our guard refuse to cross over their human charges. Left them to wander, confused and alone." She sighed. "Grieving and struggling, they were left to find their own way."

"It was horrific. And even now, I feel sick about it," said Kesien, a pained expression on his face. "What happened to those souls? Could be thousands. Did they ever find their way? Are they still wandering the Earth?"

Azrael held out his arms, wings flexing wide. "Fear not, angels," he said as a bright white light lit the sepulcher, a misty image of a beacon of light cutting across the world. "We compensated. I worked with Sariel and the other archangels of death to shine a beacon of light across the Gates of Hell, leading all those souls into the Corridor of Pervasive Light."

"Is that true?" Kesien cried, a look of reverence burning on his face for the archangel.

The archangel nodded.

"You rock, Azrael," said Jack with a smile.

Muriel nodded. "Jack's right. You rock, sir."

A smile touched the archangel's face, silver-black hair falling away from his face as he let the light fade.

"Thank you, Jack. And Muriel." He fixed Kesien with his gaze. "We made sure that our human charges didn't suffer for Samael's transgressions." Those charcoal grey eyes turned steely again as he stared at Jack. "And Jack, to answer your question, Tre will someday find his way back in front of Puriel. As do all the lost souls that enter the Mortise of Souls and disappear from the system. We eventually find them."

Zanth's eyes narrowed, anger burning in her gaze. "To be judged and imprisoned again!"

Already, Azrael shook his head. "No, Zanth," he replied. "To help him find his way again."

Her anger slid immediately to sorrow, those red eyes turning glassy again.

"But if his soul rises," she said in such a painfully quiet voice that it hurt Jack's chest to hear her speak. "Then he will be forever separated from me." She bowed her head and turned away. "At best, we will have only stolen moments until that happens."

"There *is* a path to redemption, Zanth," said Azrael. "Even for a demon. Even Lucifer had a path to redemption and he spit on it. It isn't a quick or easy path, but it's there."

"A path ruled by judges and rules!" she shouted, staring at the closed Purgatory door. "I will not have my every action and thought controlled."

"You mean like they are now?" Jack replied.

She whirled around. "Now? What are you talking about?"

"Hell—including Lucifer—controls everything you do and feel, Zanth," said Jack. "From what I've learned, Heaven only has one rule."

"One rule?" She scoffed at him. "Complete and total control?"

He shook his head. "Love frees all. That's the rule, Zanth. And it's kind of unwritten."

Her eyes widened. He nodded at her.

"Yep, that's it," said Jack, holding out his hands. "Sorry to ruin Luci's big, scary stories about Heaven's iron fist and all that." He turned to the archangel. "So, if I leave the back door open for Tre Sheridan, he'll have lots of time to get his shit together with Zanth before he has to go back to the support groups?"

"Yes, Jack," said the archangel with a wry smile. "And maybe by then, the two of them will have discovered a path that they both can walk. Side-by-side—like you and Talia did."

The archangel patted Jack on the back and moved past him to Anahera who sat against the wall. He picked her up in his arms and turned around.

"All right, guard. Remain at your posts and await the seraphim's orders while I get Anahera back to Eolowen. To Berith. These wings need immediate healing. Daidrean, I am leaving you in charge in my absence."

The tall, thin angel of death stepped forward, medium brown hair shaggy, his grey eyes a little paler than Jack remembered.

"All right, guard," said Daidrean in deepening tenor voice as he summoned his shield of gold light and turned toward the door. "I want all the squads in phalanx lines as Talia and her squad enter Purgatory. Shields out. Remain on sentinel status until told otherwise."

The archangel turned his gaze to Talia. "Talia, I've got to get Anahera back to Berith now. Quickly. As I said earlier, Jack will have to go in with you, supplying those all-important seraphim powers. And apparently, the archdemoness will be fighting alongside you." His eyes narrowed and he pointed a finger at her. "Double-cross my angels or harm Jack Casey and I will hunt you to the ends of time, Zanth. Are we clear?"

Her eyes brightened, almost a smile playing on those full ruby red lips.

"Oui, archangel. I will fight beside them. And once we all emerge from this door again, I will no longer be Lucifer's first lieutenant. Tre and I will disappear into the Mortise or somewhere on Earth. Perhaps even the Middling?"

"Good," said the archangel. "Godspeed, angels. Be careful, Jack. All of you, come back safe."

He blinked up through the tower, carrying Anahera aloft.

"All right, squad," said Talia, motioning them toward the door. "It's time we round up Archangel Samael and those traitors."

"Gladly," Kesien snapped and moved beside her, his features sharpening.

Muriel blinked across the stones to stand at Talia's right shoulder. Deemah flitted through the air and landed beside Kesien as Jack wrapped Talia tighter in his arms.

"Right beside you, babe," he said. "All the way. Now until forever."

She leaned up and kissed him as Zanth let her demon cone of silence fade away.

"Let's find that idiot, Samael," said Zanth. "Before he loses the Book of Secrets."

Jack hoped that Zanth didn't renege on taking him to his dad. That was an ache that had been with him for almost a decade, all those words left unsaid. All those things he never got to tell his ol' man.

Now, he finally had a chance to lay that pain to rest.

"Let's do this," said Jack as he reached toward the stone door's iron ring.

He yanked the door pull hard and the heavy door opened, rasping across the stones. He stood beside the door, holding it open as Kesien and Deemah blinked through the dusky threshold and into the twilight world of Purgatory. Zanth stepped through behind Muriel.

Talia paused beside him and held out her left hand.

"Ready, Mr. Casey?" she asked.

He nodded, taking hold of her hand. "Ready, Mrs. Casey. Let's take this douchebag down."

With her right hand, she brushed his blond bangs out of his eyes. "You sure you want to see your father like this, Jack?" she asked in a soft voice. "In here? He will be struggling with a lot of issues he left behind and trying to cope with things left unresolved in his life. Are you sure you want to see that?"

An ache thrummed through his chest. "I'd walk barefoot over lava for a chance to talk to him for an hour, Talia." His voice was shaky and he tried to control it. "I never got to say goodbye to him. Or tell him I loved him. Or benefit from his wisdom after I became a man. I was just a scared kid. For years, I didn't even know what I needed to say. Or ask him. Until now."

"Then we'll make sure we find him," she said with a smile.

"Thank you," he said in a quiet, unsteady voice. "This means so much to me."

"I know," she said, squeezing his hand. "You mean so much to me, Jack, so I have to make sure you get this chance. I'm just sad that it took a demon to give you this closure and not me. I wanted to ask Pravuil about reuniting the two of you for a short time, but there's never been a chance to ask."

"Hey," he said in a soft voice and reached up with his left hand to stroke her face. "Just the fact that you thought to do it means everything to me, babe. Thank you."

He kissed her in a soft, slow kiss that left her breathless for a moment.

She pulled in a few breaths and then nodded toward her squad that stood in the hollow, eerie half-light that surrounded a wide, winding footpath in front of them.

With a backward glance at the sepulcher, Jack turned and walked through the doorway's threshold beside Talia and let the door swing shut behind him. Closing them inside Purgatory. Until they found Archangel Samael.

And his dad.

15

IN ALL HER EXISTENCE, TALIA HAD NEVER STEPPED INSIDE PURGATORY. She'd never even seen this door before. When souls called out to angels (or demons) for help, she'd always been told that they blinked into Purgatory to be at that soul's side. Never passing through this door.

She'd only journeyed to this part of the Heavens a few times in all her time as an angel. And that was to visit the ethereal ocean. It was the only time she'd flown into the Mortise of Souls, where the human pain and loneliness was so profound that it had dimmed her halo and made her ache all over.

When she'd asked Azrael about why the Maker allowed them to spend so much time in pain, the archangel said that deliverance was always a breath away. They just had to ask. Of course, she'd asked why they never asked and stayed in such desolate places.

Humans were stubborn, Azrael had said. And proud. Purgatory wasn't meant to break their spirits. Unlike the Middling where banished, rebelling angels lived alongside humanoid people that chose to live there. Purgatory, according to Azrael, was a place where human souls mourned losses and confronted fears. They weren't places where humans could wallow and hide from their former lives.

But Talia worried that without a defined path lit for them, that fate was exactly what happened to so many souls.

This area seemed so desolate and dreary and the shadowy expanses filled her with trepidation. So many spirits congregated in the places beyond the Mortise of Souls. Unrisen souls. She sighed. Lost souls. So many had given up.

Why had the Maker let them give up? Why hadn't He sent his angels into these places? To comfort and guide them? But Azrael said that a soul had to find its own way. And learn to ask for help. Rely on others.

Angels and humans both had to learn that lesson in humility—many the hard way.

Yet, so many souls had refused to do that one simple action and had been left to wander these places for a very long time. In despair until eventually, they found their way. It seemed cruel to her, but on some level she understood.

Independence was important, but not when it created angels (and humans) like Lucifer. So independent and full of hubris that they thought themselves above it all. Better than the rest. A hard lesson to learn—one that Lucifer refused time and time again.

She stared at the stormy, dark sky, a pallid greyness clinging to this world. No sun burned bright across Parrish blue skies. No fleecy Constable clouds softened the skies or flitted along the air currents. Purgatory was a place of half-life. Of dusk. That time before the darkest night of a new moon descended on Earth.

Within the Delta, Spirit Lake, and even Purgatory, confused and grieving souls hid from their misconceptions and misunderstood Earthly doctrines. They clung to certain ideas and perceived truths in various ways. Struggling to find a way past the obsessions of their former human lives. Some souls chose not to confront their losses even after death, instead hiding from them. Avoiding the pain that their deaths had caused.

"I can't imagine staying in this place for long," said Jack as Muriel nodded slowly.

"You'd be surprised, Jack," said Talia. "I've been in here once or twice and the souls inhabiting this place find comfort here."

Ghost-like trees rustled, the air misty and gritty as wind scoured the rocky landscape, the dark and silent forest sloping upward. Rising toward a craggy, basalt mountain peak ahead. Everything—sky, rocks, brush—had a greyish blue cast to it.

The air had that electric ozone scent that hung on the breeze like woodsmoke. Like the air smelled after a lightning strike or when an archangel cast a bolt of Holy fire. Across the ridge that rose toward the base of a mountain in the wilderness, tiny gold lights gleamed in the twilight as dozens of small cabins dotted the ridge.

No, she knew that these souls in Purgatory were here intentionally. They had purposely sought out the Mortise of Souls trenches, following the deep ruts into various twilight regions that embodied their difficulties—like letting go of their former lives. They lived imagined lives in these hovels, surrounded by the busted remnants of conjured realities and pieces of their broken dreams.

Jack squinted at the surrounding landscape. "It looks like part run-down state park and a junkyard." He pointed toward the tall, towering heaps that dotted the countryside like haystacks. "What the hell is all this stuff piled up everywhere?"

"Broken dreams, Jack," said Talia, gesturing at the tall, forbidding hills. "All these piles are parts of the baggage that each soul carried with them into Purgatory. All of it sits ignored and scattered now."

Kesien shook his head, wings rustling, his halo deep gold against the shadows. "How could one soul hope to sift through all of that without help?"

"It's overwhelming," said Jack in a quiet voice that was a mixture of fear and shock. "And horrifying."

"Exactly, Kesien," said Muriel, an edge to her voice. "And yes, Jack. Without help, they stay here forever. It's too much."

Jack nodded. "It's not like they can just Google Purgatory to give them a clue about how to even start fixing things. This…is—awful." He pulled in a sharp breath, eyes wide. "And my dad's in here… somewhere?"

His voice ached at that last statement and Talia felt his pain. She couldn't imagine how he must feel right now after seeing this place.

"All will be transformed at the end of time, Jack," said Deemah. "I know it feels hopeless and these souls seem lost forever. But their time will come, too. Says the Maker."

"And Azrael," said Muriel, her gaze flicking from the distant cabins to the shadowy piles of junk piled so tall and high across the hard ground.

Talia wondered if the Shade River Delta looked like this, too. That swampy, dusky region was populated with many souls, too, ignoring the realities they left behind and existing here in denial. She hadn't seen these piles of broken things along the shores of the Ethereal Ocean—where souls with overwhelming worries and troubles gathered on the sandy beach. It reminded her of books and movies about people stranded on deserted islands. A place of perpetual sunset for lost souls. Where only angels could fly to the opposite shore where the sun still rose.

She knew that Spirit Lake was almost as peaceful, where weary souls found rest from their exhaustion. Like a rest stop on a long journey, where they'd stopped for a night and never left. But the souls that gravitated toward Purgatory came to this wild, desolate landscape to hide from the truth.

"Why doesn't someone come in here after them?" Jack replied, his voice sharp with anger. "Now? This is…brutal."

"Angels can only enter when called, Jack," said Muriel.

Already, Jack was shaking his head, hands on his hips. "Even on Earth, during natural disasters and wars, we send in help…comfort. Doing any less here is—cruel."

He was right.

"Azrael says that help for each and every soul is only a breath away," said Deemah. "They just have to ask for it."

"Then put up a sign already!"

Shaking his head, Jack walked toward the nearest forbidding pile of broken dreams that loomed dark and shadowy in the twilight and craned his neck to see the top.

"So, all this junk is a piece of something that these souls can't let go of?" he asked, walking around the nearest ten-foot-high pile that cast a thick, sharp shadow in the growing dusk.

"Broken dreams, lost loves, unfinished goals," Muriel said with a nod, following behind him. "Stuff adds up after a while when that's all you're using to keep score."

Talia had never been to the River of Stars, but she knew that the souls traveling the star rivers were obsessed with the wonder and beauty of the physical world they left behind. Their obsessions and the mysteries that they hadn't solved in their lifetimes were the stars along that path. Like the piles of broken things scattered throughout Purgatory. Most of these souls were content to follow the star rivers, pursuing those answers long after death.

She hadn't wanted to tell Jack about what his dad faced in Purgatory yet. If Jack's dad was here, then he was hiding from reality and refusing to face the truths in his life. When he got terminal cancer, Jack's dad never faced those things, pushing them further into the background, according to his Book of Life and Death. He never talked to Jack about his drug problems, never even acknowledged them. But he'd worried about Jack's future, fearing what would happen to his son after he was gone.

Tom Casey was afraid that Jack would drift and become homeless, following in his footsteps into a world of drugs and other addictions. But the man refused to acknowledge his role in the deterioration of his marriage. Or how Jack's mother had done her best to distance herself from him and her young son—and any future pain. She'd already sentenced Jack to a short life of addiction and overdose and kept away from him to protect herself.

Leaving his seventeen-year-old son alone had eaten away at Tom Casey as he got sicker. He'd even tried to convince his ex-wife to fly Jack out to California, but she never returned his calls or emails.

Even Tom Casey's two oldest daughters had avoided the question of Jack's future, dealing with problems of their own. One had a husband that lost every job he got and they moved from apartment to apartment. The oldest, Meredith, already had three boys and little extra money. And Jack's mother had already instilled the fear in them that Jack would turn out like his father. But Meredith Casey Vaughan had assured Tom Casey that Jack would always have a place in her house. It was barely more than a dresser and a bed, but it wasn't the streets.

Inside Purgatory, Tom Casey had no way to know how Jack's life had turned out. Or whether his oldest daughter had kept her word. Insulating him in case his worst fears for Jack had come through.

Maybe seeing his only son again would turn Tom Casey around? Help him face whatever truths he'd been hiding from?

Talia knew that Jack needed to see his father again, find some peace. Even now, that pain was still evident in Jack's eyes and written all over his Book of Life and Death. If she hadn't saved Jack from overdosing, that pain would have consumed him. She shuddered. Might have even brought him through this door. For a very, very long time.

Zanth sighed, a wistful look on her face as she stared out at the empty desolation surrounding her, the wilderness, and the distant mountain range rising in the mist.

"Broken dreams, dark realizations, lost love…like my Tre," she said softly. "I feel his presence in here, but it is faint." Her expression darkened, those full red lips pressing into an angry line. "And I feel that idiot near him, too. Cowering with the Book. What does Lucifer see in him?"

"Total obedience and a fear of crossing him—like all of his Hellpoodles," Jack replied with a shake of his head. "Like that dickhead Raziel. Thought he was hot—a chick magnet. Until I burned him to ash."

Zanth turned her gaze toward him, surprise in those glowing red eyes. "You turned an archangel into ash?"

He nodded. "Turned his own column of Holy fire back on him. Burned him to a crisp."

A look of admiration blossomed on Zanth's face as she took a step toward Jack and laid her hand on his arm.

"I am most impressed, Jack Casey," she said in a sultry tone.

"Eliminating an archangel is not an easy task—even for an archdemoness. For a human, it is extraordinary."

One corner of Jack's mouth lifted, not quite into that sexy smirk, but seeing him direct that hot, crooked smile toward Zanth made her feel a stab of jealousy.

"Wish I could take credit," he said, his gaze falling to his feet. "But it's the seraphim powers I carry. That Heaven can't seem to take back again."

Zanth squeezed his arm and Talia felt white fire flicker across her eyes.

"Your powers are much more potent than mine," said Zanth, gazing into his eyes as she moved closer to him. "The only thing that holds you back is your human frailty."

Zanth's fingers brushed up and down his arm and Talia felt a plume of fury shoot through her, white fire coiling around her fingers, and roiling across her wing feathers.

"I enjoy watching you use those powers, Jack Casey," the archdemoness continued. "You command them like a seraph. Almost like Lucifer."

Talia was a breath away from spitting Holy fire at this archdemoness bitch. She started to blink between them, but all her jealousy fled when Jack took a marked step back from her, anger burning in those sizzling light green eyes, a dark expression on his face.

"Let's get one thing straight, Zanth," he snapped, glaring at her now. "I am nothing like Lucifer. Nothing! I command nothing. I have no skills with these powers beyond my acting talent and mirroring my incredible wife's abilities. I just figured out how to keep my dumb, lucky ass alive by mimicking what I saw. That's not skill. It's miming. I'm just another idiot human with more than my share of luck. That's all."

She couldn't stand it any longer. She blinked toward him, arms wrapping around his waist. By High House, she loved this man. And every time she got jealous, he unknowingly quelled it in a way that made her fall in love with him all over again.

He smiled as she leaned up and kissed his mouth. And he kissed her back. An anxious kiss.

"Jack has incredible amounts of experience and talent using his seraphim powers," said Talia to the archdemoness, "but I understand why he thinks it's all dumb luck."

Muriel chuckled. "Sorry, Jack, but most of that is skill and every angel of death—including your wife—will tell you that." Muriel slid into formation on Talia's right, her gaze in constant motion as she searched for Samael—and demons. "He can't see the skill involved, Zanth. He just thinks it's imitation. Even the archangel will tell you that he's incredibly impressed with Jack's use of these powers. For a human…it's mind-blowing."

Zanth smiled at Jack, unaffected by his anger. "The angels tell a different story," she said. "Your anger gives away your humility, Jack Casey. Acknowledge your power and use it. It suits you. But do not tell Lucifer I said that."

"All right, squad," said Talia in a quiet voice as she gathered the angels of death closer around her in the twilight and between the thick, velvety shadows stretching between the piles of things scattered around them. "Stay close to each other. Shields out. Form around Jack."

Zanth stood an arm's length away as Jack slipped out of Talia's arms and hovered at the edge of the group. She sighed. Like he was aching to sneak off at his first opportunity.

That terrified her.

Talia sang out a series of angel notes, asking that the squad keep careful watch on Jack. In case he tried to sneak off and look for his dad. As a human alone in here, it wouldn't take long for Purgatory to affect him with the truths that he needed to face, too. He didn't have to be dead to feel a burning need to hide from the stark, fiery face of truth in this landscape. It changed with the souls that inhabited it. Affecting them with the illusions of lies that they told themselves.

Zanth heard the notes that Talia chanted. She had a quizzical look on her face as she glanced over at Jack and then around the formation at her and the other angels of death.

"He does not hear you?" she spoke in the thrumming, velvety dark Hell notes that Jack also couldn't hear.

Talia shook her head.

"Beware too many secrets," Zanth continued in the shadowy demonic notes. "That was the final blow that drove a fatal wedge between Tre and me."

Zanth's sudden candor made her uneasy. And it frightened her. She couldn't stand the thought of anything driving a wedge between her and Jack. To look into those sultry green eyes and see only distance would destroy her. How terrible that moment in the Middling must have been for him when he saw that distance in her eyes? It made her chest tighten.

"What is that distant mountain range ahead, Tal?" Jack asked. "Where this path leads? Through this crazy growing fog? Like a damned Hollywood set."

The mist had grown thicker and rolled across the ground in waves. A mournful call echoed in the distance, the smell of burning rubber and hot asphalt hanging in the air. And woodsmoke.

Fires guttered through the fog on all sides of the path in little writhing smears of light. Like fireflies on the horizon. She knew that humans had an attraction to bonfires, fireplaces, and other forms of fire. Even lightning. Perhaps lighting a fire within this dusky place was a comfort?

"It's a point of communion with Heaven, Jack," said Talia as she lifted her hand toward the sky and moved beside him, not wanting him out of her sight.

"Or Hell," Zanth added.

Talia ignored her, pointing toward the peak. "At this tallest point— or anywhere in Purgatory—every soul can rise above this place and ask for help. Once they've stopped hiding from their truths and decide to confront their illusions."

Glaring at the tall bluff, Jack shook his head. "They have to know to go to that one spot? It's not like anyone hands these dudes manuals when they arrive. Would it kill someone to put up sign in this place? Hey, dudes! Stand here, take a number to shout for help."

Laughing, Talia turned away from the mountain range, her gaze fixed on Jack.

"No, it's a symbolic place to look toward the Heavens, but souls can ask for help anytime and anywhere. And someone will hear them."

"A lot of someones, Jack," said Kesien, shifting to Talia's left now, his gaze focused and steely as he stood sentry. "Every angel—and the Maker—will hear them. If they ask."

"And all demons will hear them, too," said Zanth. "If they wish."

"Only if they prefer a place hotter than Death Valley, Zanth," Jack replied. "But hearing them and helping them are two different things."

He was right, but every angel in Heaven stood ready to answer that call. And lead those souls back to the Corridor of Pervasive Light.

"We stand ready to answer those calls for help, Jack," said Kesien. "As angels of death. Always."

Muriel's wings rustled as she closed ranks, standing close to Talia's right shoulder, her gaze uneasy as the fog thickened.

"Where do you suppose Archangel Samael's hiding?" Muriel asked, glancing at the tree line on both sides.

Dark knolls loomed thirty feet into the air, burgeoning with shadowy piles of objects and things. The towering mounds were everywhere, behind them, on the horizon, looming on both sides of the path.

Talia had never explored Purgatory before, but already, she felt its oppressive despair and heaviness. Especially the emotions that had stacked those heaps of trinkets, treasures—and junk. Was being inside here more difficult for Jack as a human or did his partial angel nature shield him from it?

"He could be anywhere," said Talia with a shrug, her gaze falling onto the archdemoness whose piercing stare traversed the twilight and cut through the shadows.

Zanth was searching for her lover's soul. And Talia worried about what would happen when she found it.

But only Jack could open the door out of this place for Zanth's lover, so she didn't expect trouble from this archdemoness.

Yet.

No, she expected problems when they started forcing Samael toward that door. And she feared that somehow, all of this was an elaborate setup by Lucifer. With Zanth playing the part of a dejected lover to lure Jack inside—and put Samael and his traitorous guard between Jack and that door.

And a legion of demons.

But she'd seen Tre Sheridan's Book of Life and Death. It existed and Zanth was listed among those pages, too. His life had ended when he jumped off a tall tower, committing suicide. Before that, he'd made a deal with a demon for a year of fame that had ended his career as a magician and illusionist. Until he stopped a mass shooting at a Las Vegas Strip hotel, making him famous again. She'd assumed that he was distraught about selling his soul and his year of fame ending. After everything in his life had turned around—without demonic help.

Until she read Pravuil's notes about him falling in love with archdemoness Zanth. The lovesick, failed magician had willingly given up everything to be with her when he agreed to help Lucifer in exchange for a place beside Zanth in Hell. And then jumped to his death in order to enter Purgatory.

But everything that had happened after his soul crossed over was absent from Tre Sheridan's Book. Like this convenient fight that Zanth had mentioned. And how he was trapped in Purgatory, separated from his demon lover forever. Unless Jack opened the door for him.

It sounded too convenient. Like a quick way for Lucifer to get hold of Jack again.

She hated being forced to trust a demon. Especially an angel executioner like Zanth. Even worse, she hated gambling with her husband's life—and soul—to flush out these traitors. Why couldn't they just wait for Samael to be forced out of Purgatory instead of sending Jack inside?

She knew that Azrael didn't want to send Jack in here. Jack's presence in the squad had been Azrael's last option. He hadn't wanted Jack anywhere past Purgatory's door. But conveniently, Azrael had been pulled away from the mission, forced to carry Anahera back to Eolowen and Berith.

Forcing Jack into the squad. And forcing him to enter Purgatory. Had this been part of Lucifer's plan all along?

Was Zanth leading them into an ambush? Was she plotting to drag Jack back to Hell and collect Lucifer's bounty?

Even if Zanth was telling the truth, Talia worried about Jack's reaction to seeing his dad in Purgatory. What if he didn't want to leave after he found his father? What if this reunion emotionally wrecked him? Put him back on that path of self-destruction that he'd been on when she met first him.

"Tal, you okay?"

Jack was staring her now, a twinkle in those hypnotic, pale green eyes as he studied her with concern.

"Worried about finding Samael," she said with a nod.

He shook his head. "It's way more than that."

"All right," she said and fixed him with her gaze. "I'm worried about what this place might do to you, Jack. You've never seen your father like this before. I don't want the memory of it and the image of him you encounter here to scar you."

He rubbed her arm, smiling. "No worries, Mrs. Casey. I'll be okay. I just want to help him if I can—get him out of here." His eyes narrowed as he looked around, shivering. "This place feels so dark. So empty and lonely. Almost cold. Has he really been in here for almost a decade?"

"Time is so different in Purgatory, Jack," she said, laying her hand against his devastatingly handsome face. "It won't feel like a decade to him."

He looked so young and vibrant, silver-grey wings flat against his back, halo burning gold and bright. And even in this twilight world of loss and broken dreams, he still took her breath away. She hoped that never changed.

He bowed his head, staring at his feet, those faded blue Vans slip-ons looking so bright against this anemic landscape.

"I just want to help him move on if I can," he said in a tight, quiet voice. "Tell him I love him."

"I'm sure he knows that," she said, gripping his hand and squeezing.

"But I never got to say it, Talia," he said with a sigh. "Saying those words has always been hard for me. At seventeen, I…" He pulled in a breath, his gaze falling away. "I couldn't say it. I didn't quite get the weight of it all. How not saying those words when it mattered most would eat at me as I got older? And I never realized the regret I'd feel, the ache in my chest whenever I wondered whether my ol' man knew I loved him or not."

She put her arms around him and held him. "He knows, Jack. And you have the chance to tell him now."

He nodded against her hair. She hoped this reunion fixed a lot of hurts for Jack. He let her go as Zanth approached, Kesien behind her.

"Talia," said the archdemoness, pointing beyond the dozens of junk piles littering the landscape, at the distant lights. "I have located my Tre's soul, but…he does not want to speak to me."

Talia frowned. "I'm sorry, Zanth."

The archdemoness shook her head. "Non, you misunderstand me. If he wanted to speak to me, I would feel a pull toward his location and there would be a trail to follow. Without that, I must feel my way to him now."

"So, you're saying it will be more difficult to locate him?"

She nodded. "Oui. But not impossible. I must warn you though. He is surrounded by Archangel Samael and his death angels. They cling to him. Otherwise, this place would expel them immediately into your angel forces."

Talia felt the heat of anger rise at her temples, Holy fire roiling through her body.

"How many of them are there?" she asked.

Zanth shrugged. "I sense many. At least thirty or so. Perhaps more?" She let a smile curve across her ashen face. "But I am not worried about the numbers. They will face an archdemoness, an angel of death with rare powers, and Jack Casey's seraphim powers. As well as three of the best angels of death I have ever encountered."

She seemed very cooperative now…now that Jack held the future of her lover's soul in his hands.

"Let's go jam with the archangel," said Jack, patting his front jeans pocket, Eternean armor rattling. "I'll put on my traitor-bashing playlist."

Grinning, Muriel moved toward him. "And what song would lead off this playlist, Jack?" She glanced at Talia. "Sorry, I've gotta ask."

Jack's expression brightened, the corners of his mouth curving into that sexy smirk. "There's a little Seek and Destroy by Metallica. Followed by Mötley Crüe's Shout at the Devil. A little Angel of Death by Slayer and Black Sabbath's Heaven and Hell—without Ozzie, but still the bomb." He smiled. "Playlist ends with AC/DC's You Shook Me All Night Long. On repeat, of course."

"You weren't even born when those songs were hits, Jack," said Muriel.

"Gianni said the same thing to me," said Jack, shaking his head.

"They mean that you probably haven't heard half of those songs, Jack," said Deemah who cast a playful smile at Kesien who seemed tense and distracted.

"I've heard them all many, many times," Jack said with a frown. "Blame my dad. He was an 80s metal head. Loved rock in all its forms —from the 70s onward. Thank God he named me after his favorite 70s bands and not his favorite metal bands. I might have been named Judas Ozzie Casey instead of Jackson Seeger Casey."

Talia laughed. "I can't imagine calling you Jude," she said. "Much less, Judas."

"Hey Jude…great Beatles' song," said Jack, fixing her with his gaze.

Muriel gave her a confused stare. "Jackson Seeger Casey. Afraid you'll have to explain that one."

"Dad changed the spelling on my middle name," said Jack, shoving his hands into his jean's pockets beneath his armor. "So, it wasn't quite so obvious, but he named me after Jackson Browne and Bob Seger.

Hey, maybe that's why he's in Purgatory? For putting a name like that together."

Talia and the other angels laughed at his joke, but Kesien was barely listening, his gaze tracking off toward the lights dotting the landscape. She knew he was aching to go after his former archangel of death. Get justice for the angels that were lost at Samael's hand. Even Zanth had disengaged, staring toward the horizon. She sensed her lover's soul out there and was no doubt anxious to find him.

If that were Jack out there, she'd have already left the slowpokes behind to find him.

The squad turned to stare at her now. Waiting for marching orders, she realized.

"All right, squad," she said, her loud tone shaking Kesien out of his thoughts and bringing Zanth back into the conversation. "We need to find Tre Sheridan in this expanse because that's where we'll find Archangel Samael. I want halos dimmed and no shields. Tight roundel formation around Jack."

"Talia, that isn't necessary," said Jack, his expression shifting into a wounded look. "I've got seraphim powers."

She took his hands in hers and stared into his eyes. "You are as formidable as the rest of the squad, Jack," she said. "But you're the most important person in my life and I intend to protect you with everything I've got. Because I love you more than my own existence." She frowned at him. "Now, no arguments and let me do my job."

"I love you, too, Mrs. Casey," he said with a smirk and kissed her hard on the lips. "And I hate it when you put it that way. Makes it impossible for me to be mad."

She grinned and let go of his hands. Zanth was watching them, envy burning in her glowing red eyes. She saw that expression a lot on the archdemoness' face, making her almost feel guilty. She wasn't trying to rub hers and Jack's relationship in Zanth's face.

"Kesien," she said, turning to the attractive, six-foot-sixish angel of death. "I want you on point, following Tre Sheridan's trail using his Book of Life and Death."

Kesien nodded, tangle of black curls falling into his eyes. "I've been consulting it for direction, but I'll use it to map his trail through Purgatory."

He reached into the air and pulled the glowing Book of Life and Death out of the mist as Talia turned to Muriel.

"Muriel, I want you sticking close to Jack and watching for demons. And ambushes."

"On it," said Muriel.

She swiveled around toward Deemah. "Deemah, I want you on flank, making sure nothing follows us. Demonic, angelic, human—or other."

Deemah nodded and flicked her long dark hair off her left shoulder as she positioned herself behind Jack. Muriel slipped in front of Jack, Kesien positioning himself on Jack's left as she slid into place to his right.

"Zanth, I want you with Muriel, using your unique connection to Tre to locate your lover's soul."

Nodding, the archdemoness took her place on Muriel's left, a red glow engulfing her form.

"All right, Kesien, as soon as you've found a path, we'll move out. And Jack—"

Jack cast an angry look at her. "Let me guess," he said. "I'm comic relief."

"You always are, Jack," said Muriel.

She shook her head. "I was about to ask you to use omnificence to try and locate Samael. I will use it as well, but you're so much better at focusing it than I am."

She had control of omnificence that didn't require a focus, but unlike his human limitations, Jack had found a way to focus it down quickly. It overwhelmed him much of the time, but usually when he was forced to use it in combat situations. She wanted to see if he could use it, without pressure, to locate Samael.

"Thanks, babe," he said, his anger dissipating. "Sorry I snapped at you. Thought you were going to give me the archangel equivalent of shut up and stay out of the way."

She reached out and rubbed his shoulder. "Never. You have

seraphim powers. And my rare angel powers. I have a bad feeling that we'll need all of that before we leave here."

"I've got something, Talia," said Kesien, his voice intense. "A coil of afterimage in the mist."

"Great work, Kesien," said Talia. "Let's follow it and see where it takes us. We move as a group, so no one goes off on their own. And anyone who blinks ahead, will face my wrath when I catch up with you."

"She's meaner than Azrael," Muriel replied.

Talia nodded. "All right, dim your halos and put away your shields. It's time to flush out Samael and his traitor angels of death."

Jack smiled and reached out, taking hold of her hand as they followed Kesien into the misty twilight. Toward the concentration of flickering lights in the distance.

16

Surrounded on all sides by angels of death—and Zanth—Jack held Talia's hand as the squad followed Kesien into the hilly landscape's misty half-light. That began to flatten out toward what looked like...civilization.

A small town? A Hollywood set? An illusion in the mist?

The urban-looking chain-link fence cast a stark, honeycombed shadow as man-made shapes slipped out of the dusk.

What the hell was this place? Was this how Purgatory really looked or was it how the souls inside had shaped it? Or was it his own imagination conjuring up what he thought Purgatory should look like?

And maybe, somehow, all three of those things were true?

Regardless, he didn't want to attract any unwanted attention to himself. Being the only living human in this place might piss off whatever wandered these shadowy landscapes. And they might want to try and end him.

Would a living, breathing human in here also attract demons like a fresh rack of ribs on the buffet?

His seraphim powers could handle both, but would it scare off

Samael and his death angels? He didn't want to blow their surprise advantage against the archangel.

Or upset Kesien more—if that was possible. Dude was already brooding and angry enough for the whole squad. But Jack understood.

Kesien felt responsible.

Jack glanced at Talia and pointed at his halo after trying to picture its light with a dimmer switch—that he turned down to almost dark.

All the other angels had nearly extinguished their halos. And the fog had helped obscure any divine light, too. He had no clue how to turn his down. He was still waiting for that *Intro to Angel Tech* class. His wings and halo hadn't come with a manual.

"Is my halo light dim enough, Mrs. Casey?" he asked in a quiet voice and squeezed her hand.

She shook her head, laying her hand against his cheek. "Your halo will always burn bright for me, Mr. Casey," she said, leaning up and pressing a steamy kiss against his mouth.

"Another kiss like that and it's gonna burn like a roman candle," he said, running his fingers through the raven black waves of her hair as he gazed into her luminous grey eyes.

She laughed and brushed her lips across his mouth, teasing him with a soft, brief kiss.

"I'll keep that in mind," she said and pointed at his halo. "I can barely see your halo's glow now, Jack, so whatever you did is working."

"Good," he said, his gaze darting to the sky, searching for a flutter of wings or movement around the squad. "Now, let's see if I can locate that douchebag Samael with my omnificence. But with no reference points in this place, it'll be a lot harder to locate this cowardly archangel. Much less that Book of Secrets."

"Omnificence will create those reference points for you, Jack," she said. "If you relax your hold on the power a bit."

Relax his hold? If he even twitched his index finger after focusing it down, the whole flow of power threatened to drown him in images and data.

"I'll give it a shot," he said. "Who knows? Maybe it won't try and drown me this time?"

"Be careful, Jack," said Talia, brushing her fingers against his cheek. "I'm sure it's a lot trickier to manage in human form and I'll admit, that still worries me. As angels, the light flows through us like the air currents. With flesh and blood, that power can overwhelm quickly."

He knew that better than anyone. Especially since he was the one that had awakened this rare power in the Middling. Thanks to that little maneuver by God's Scribe. At the time, Jack didn't realize that he'd awakened the omnificence angel power instead of Talia. If he hadn't had seraphim power flowing through him back then—even though he didn't know it at the time—omnificence would have overwhelmed him.

He held out his right hand, palm turned down, and let the crush of images, data, and places surge over him until he felt like he was drowning in currents and force and images. It was tough to move and control this wild force inside him.

Finally, he stopped walking and lifted his index finger. Beneath it, he focused all of that raging information flow downward. In front of him.

Like a funnel.

Only when he had control of that small sliver of persistent data and images that rushed over him like high tide did he try and sift through the entire stream for a sign of Archangel Samael. He barely remembered seeing this dude in Heaven because of Raziel. His memory was sketchy. Flashes of flowing white hair and angry soot grey eyes. Bad temper. Kept hitting Eolowen hard with a flood of death angels hell-bent on exterminating rivals like some sort gangland-style hit-and-run tactics. Even tried to roast Talia in mid-air right in front of the seraphim, according to Muriel.

While he'd been trapped in Hell, Talia fought this douchebag archangel right outside the High House spires. And knocked his winged ass out of the sky. This was the same whiny archangel that was Kesien and Deemah's former commander.

Why were so many of Heaven's archangels douchebags?

Azrael, Zephana, and Pravuil were slapping, but Raziel and Samael? Jack wanted to punch both of them in their smug-ass archangel faces.

Jack remembered Azrael fighting this dude's forces ever since he'd first met the archangel. Fighting Samael and his death angels for longer than he'd known Talia. Lots of throwing shade at Azrael and his guard, trying to get him in trouble with the seraphim. But like a little bitch, Samael didn't have the balls to challenge Azrael—or Talia's guard—directly. No one in Heaven did a thing about Raziel and they hadn't done anything about Samael either. Not even raining down a little Holy fire. Or dropping some old-fashioned, Biblical seraphim justice on this clown and his entourage.

Of course, no one knew the seraphim had been chained up in the spire basement. They couldn't even bitch slap Raziel or Samael.

Still, Jack couldn't help wondering what had happened to this archangel after the seraphim imprisoned him in their spire. Despite what the archangel had done, Samael hadn't been reeducated or even had his wings and halo taken—like they'd done to poor Talia after he'd caused her to lose Lucifer's wager.

Whatever High House had done about Samael, it hadn't been enough to cancel the dude's arrangement with Lucifer either. Or stop the attacks by Samael's rebel death angel guard on Eolowen. Nothing had been done to those salty bastards.

Ahead, the Purgatory pathway wound through thick forest and brush, veering back toward what looked like a modern-looking city block. Abandoned and decaying. Like the images of the rust belt and Detroit he'd seen after the auto industry had closed up shop and its supporting industries went bankrupt. Whole city blocks and neighborhoods left abandoned and empty. Was nothing like the car boom town assembly line that his grandfather had worked in his prime. Way before Jack was born.

This place looked like the apocalypse had flown in for a weekend layover and never left. Unnerving at best. Chilling at its worst. He hoped his dad wasn't in this creepy city that could double for a slasher film set.

It gave him the creeps.

The winding trail forked, its right half—a dirt path—turning abruptly away from the mountaintop where souls asked for help. Or whatever. He knew that his dad wasn't an ask-for-help kind of dude. Apparently, his dad had ignored his drug and alcohol problems. It had even been a struggle to get him to accept the hospice support.

He remembered having to beg Dad to take that support and care during that final month or two. He'd been so weak and in so much pain. Jack had struggled to take care of him after school or before he left for his lifeguard job at the Y. Leaving Dad alone got harder and harder, but the rent had to get paid somehow. Jack had been looking for a second job when his dad passed away.

The other pathway's fork angled left and narrowed into a dirt footpath that looped back and forth along the mountain's gentle slope toward the top of that plateau-like summit. He wondered what was up there besides a place to commune with Heaven. Did they get immediate responses? Did angels of death appear to them? Or demons, offering deals or contracts in Lucifer's name? That was a chilling thought.

That mountain top was probably the last place they'd find Samael or the soul of Zanth's lover. His omnificence didn't even flutter toward that location. For Samael or this Tre Sheridan.

His thoughts shifted back to his old man again. Where was his dad in this crazy dim-lit, sprawling expanse? His chest ached at the thought of seeing him again after struggling with a decade of grief. To talk to him again, even for a few minutes, was a dream he'd had for a long, long time.

Could he help his dad? Like Tre? Keep that Purgatory door open a little longer—long enough for his dad to slip out, too?

Would he burn for that? With the exception of trying to rescue Talia from Lucifer, Jack had never felt so torn or tempted to break the rules. Not since he'd let his flake habit rule his life—and ruin his acting career.

But where would his dad go? Was there a better place for him if his soul didn't join these Risen that Talia had mentioned? Would leaving Purgatory make things worse for his dad?

He forced his dad out of his thoughts and concentrated on Samael again.

The flood of images and data intensified, rolling past him in waves, and he pushed the name, *Archangel Samael,* to the front of his brain. Tried to focus omnificence on it and this douchebag's location. But he kept getting distracted as the squad moved forward.

Especially whenever his thoughts drifted to his dad.

Abruptly, the dirt path disappeared into a grid of broken concrete sidewalks and curbs that edged blackened streets. Framed by more chain-link fences.

He half-expected the hot smell of asphalt, exhaust fumes, and smog to settle around him. The *whup, whup* of a helicopter punctuated by the *pop, pop, pop* of gunshots. Like a night on his apartment patio outside L.A.

But the silence of this cityscape made his skin crawl. Like it should have been bustling with people and cars and activity.

The air had a scrubbed antiseptic scent, almost like the smell of bleach and rubbing alcohol. Traces of woodsmoke hung in the air even though he didn't see any sort of fires burning among the firefly-like gold lights that flickered in the distance. And thankfully, he hadn't smelled even a hint of brimstone in the air. Although, he bet that Archangel Samael and his brigade of traitorous death angels reeked of sulfur and ash.

This place had a strange way of distracting his omnificence power, making it wander. Like trying to scan for a radio station on a road trip in his SUV. For only an instant or two, he felt Samael's presence out here. Close, too. Then the connection got staticky and he lost all focus —and had to start over searching again.

"The coils are thickening," said Kesien in almost a whisper. "Lengthening. That means we're getting close."

Zanth's red eyes narrowed as she glanced from side to side at the towering piles of broken and twisted things rising out of the dusk. Surrounding them. Car parts, old computers, pipes, hinges, old cell phones, sheet metal, and stereo equipment piled high into the shadowy half-light. In other piles, busted picture frames layered over top of broken vases, worn-out chairs, old grey-faced stuffed animals, faded rugs, and shattered glass.

The stuff of broken dreams, according to Talia and her squad.

He studied the mechanical outlines and metallic sheen as traces of light touched the towering piles of scrap as tall brick buildings and concrete took shape around them. Obscured by the odd shapes and twisted lines of other mounds of things, the stacks created strange forms that loomed like shadowy spirits across the path ahead.

Was this what every human life got reduced to?

Piles of useless stuff that no one remembered why they still had it, how to use it, or what it was even for...but they still held onto it with an almost obsessive grip. Old newspapers and magazines. Legal pads and manilla folders. Piles of papers with messy handwriting scrawled across torn, faded pages that were creased and turning yellow. The context of all the words and sentences had been lost long ago.

So, all of it ended up here. Forgotten in Purgatory's shadows, the truth hidden.

Like the souls that hid inside Purgatory from things they couldn't forget and things they didn't want to remember. The pain of a life they couldn't expunge. So, they clung to the last bits of it with all their might. Because it was all they knew. All they remembered. And they were afraid to go on and find something new.

He understood that too well.

He'd held onto the last pieces of furniture that Dad had made—before he got sick. The old man's Firebird convertible and an album collection he couldn't even play. Even the last notes that Dad had written when Jack was in high school, the handwriting slanting and growing shakier.

It made him shiver with dread. And it scared the hell out of him. Was his dad still hiding from the truths of his life? Holding onto whatever he believed was true and ignoring the rest.

Until someone forced him to face all of it. Like Jack?

In his head, Jack pushed Samael's name harder against the

overpowering flood of information. Trying to sense the archangel's presence out there.

As the squad moved away from the silent forest, not an insect buzz or the warble of a bird call filled the silence. That made him even more uncomfortable.

Not even the wind blew in this place. It was all just dusk and fog and junkyards. Dirty, broken memories of cities and towns and places that had once been familiar and soothing.

But even that began to change as they walked onward toward a taller chain-link fence with a large metal gate. Hanging open. As they moved closer, he saw the decayed, rusting remains of what looked like an old-school playground. One that looked part horror film and part apocalypse.

To the right, a bank of tall swings creaked in the stillness, chains rattling as the seat swayed in a slow, jerky tilt. Like a sickly breeze blew it into a rusty wobble. Except there wasn't even a breath of wind blowing across this landscape.

Across from the swings stood a slick, shiny metal slide that glistened in the faint light as it curved downward toward a sea of smooth gravel surrounding it.

Gravel? Apparently this was a park from the 60s. Where if the metal slide, rusting merry-go-round/buzzsaw, and plywood seesaws didn't kill you, faceplanting in gravel would take you out. The playground designers must have had too many three-martini lunches when they decided that gravel would soften a kid's fall against concrete.

Abruptly, the area changed from playground to low-budget, small town amusement park. Or the county fairgrounds.

In the distance, a small, rickety white Ferris wheel cast forbidding shadows across a rusty, black-and-green kiddie train on an oval track that hadn't run in decades. The carnival merry-go-round creaked on its hinges, gaping-mouthed horses shrieking, rusted poles impaling them as they trembled on their axes. All of the rides were dark and frozen in place, not a single carnival lightbulb flickering.

Creepy as hell. This place must have been directed by John Carpenter or Wes Craven.

"This place reminds me of when I had a small part on The Walking Dead," he said, turning toward Talia. "There aren't zombies in Purgatory, are there?"

But she wasn't beside him. She was off to his right and he could barely see her halo in the fading light. Everything had that shadowy feel to it, like the sun had just gone down. All the angels of death had drifted away from him, focusing on the signs and artifacts around them.

Even Zanth, who seemed like all her attention was concentrated on finding her lover.

The entire squad seemed weirded out by this place.

"What did you say, Jack?" Talia asked, her voice so soft that he could barely hear her.

"Zombies, babe," he said, louder this time. "There any zombies in Purgatory?"

"Zombies aren't real, Jack," said Muriel. "Remember that, if any souls decide to conjure any."

Shit! There was no telling what might walk out of this creepy-ass place. He gritted his teeth and kept searching for Samael.

On either side of the park, white wooden cabanas with green rooftops housed empty game booths and what might have been carnival booths. Ring tosses. Dart throwing. Dark and shadowy Skee-ball machines.

That's when he felt the first stirring of his omnificence, a tremor of connection roiling through it like a boat that had hit bottom. He felt a thump and scrape, his attention snapping toward a silvery ripple in the darkness.

The hair on the back of his neck stood up. They weren't alone in this park.

The mark on his arm burned as he kept it stretched out in front of him. He halted in mid-stride as Talia and the other angels drifted farther away. The squad was spread out across the entrance to the amusement part of this hellscape. And he was at the rear.

But there was nothing amusing about it.

He blocked out everything else, concentrating only on Archangel Samael. Everything was still hazy and out of focus as the images overwhelmed him.

That's when he realized he was searching for the wrong dude.

Maybe it would be easier to locate a soul assigned here than an archangel that could probably make it harder to locate him?

Jack had been so focused on that douchebag Samael that he hadn't even tried to find the soul of Zanth's dead boyfriend yet, like Kesien focusing on Sheridan's Book of Life and Death.

He let go of his focus on the archangel and searched for Tre Sheridan instead.

Almost instantly, the dude's full name rushed at him in a wave of television images, billboards, online videos, and internet searches. Tremaine Garrett Sheridan. Magician and Illusionist. Winner of last year's *Top Entertainer* and Vegas Strip Headliner. Hero that thwarted the Renato Resort massacre.

A burst of green light shot away from Jack's hand and arced across the rusty old amusement park like fireworks that erupted through the twilight and gathering fog.

Hadn't expected a spotlight to shine on the dude, but he'd take it.

The neon green beam snaked between two empty cabanas, lighting up a large white circus tent that stood behind the old carnival games.

For an instant, the inside of the tent lit up, casting dozens of heavy, winged shadows against the white tarp. And outlines of demon horns.

His skin began to crawl, a cold chill enveloping him.

It was an ambush. And they'd walked right into it.

"Talia!" he said in a half-whisper, his tone sharp and urgent. "The tent..."

Talia and Kesien turned toward the huge white tent, crouching as a flood of demons and angels of death poured out of it.

Demons screeched. Blurring across the silent, dead amusement park. Toward Muriel and Deemah.

Talia shouted commands.

Jack watched as the squad turned as one unit, shields of gold light materializing in the fog. But they were a good thirty feet ahead of him. And those few feet might have been an ocean as the sea of demons and traitorous death angels filled it.

Flooding them from all sides, including the air as the fog writhed around him. Engulfing the old amusement park in a surge of demons, angels, and mist that made his omnificence power look like a squirt gun.

In an instant, he was cut off from the squad.

A silver sword cut through the mist, aiming for his chest.

He dodged the death angel's sword and held up his hand.

Summoning a rush of Holy fire, he tossed a wave of the roiling white flames at three death angels blinking toward him.

Holy fire crackled, knocking back the sword and writhing tangle of death angels that had blinked at him.

With a sweep of his right hand, he called up a white beam of seraphim powers, lighting up a seraphim ward that blazed around him like a bubble. It ignited the fog around him like arcs of lightning.

"Jack? Where are you! Jack!"

Talia's urgent call cut through the shrill demonic shrieks and beating of dozens and dozens of wings.

He gathered three or four murder marbles in each hand and threw them through the seraphim ward. Into a massing crowd of demons and death angels trying to end him.

The murder marbles went off in succession, *whump, whump, whump*! Taking down a horde of demons and several members of Samael's guard. Red goo sprayed across the ward in a fine mist as feathers fell like snow around him.

Somewhere in the middle of the maelstrom of angels and demons, a red blast of demonic energy rolled through the crowd, sending shockwaves across the amusement park.

They collided with his seraphim ward like thunderclaps, but the ward held, dispelling the bursts as they rolled over him. Knocking down angels and demons.

Holding a seraphim ward was difficult, but keeping it up against these frequent surges of demonic energy was beginning to drain his power. He already felt the overexertion trembling through his muscles and nerves. He'd never summoned a seraphim ward before, not one powered with pure white Holy fire.

Talia told him during their honeymoon that he couldn't have sustained seraphim wards on their cabin there. He thought he could at least hold onto one small ward. But it was already sapping his strength. He didn't know how much longer he could hold it before he lapsed into a power drunk and it winked out.

Guess he'd have to find out.

Zanth's archdemoness energies were at full power against Samael and his guard. And the blowback against his seraphim ward took down any demons in his path—except Zanth with her archdemoness shield.

"Jack!" Talia's voice rang out again.

Could he tell Talia that he was all right through this strengthened bond between them?

Even through the fog and the chaos and the bodies, he felt his connection to her like heat lightning.

He closed his eyes, focusing on that rush of electricity and the steady warmth of her presence, and blasted a shout in his head at her.

Seraphim ward! Behind you.

In a breath, Talia blinked through the fog and demons. She hovered in front of him a moment and then slid through the ward.

Kesien followed, blinking right behind her.

Then Muriel and Deemah.

Tal had called out the ward's presence to her squad in those angel notes he couldn't hear.

Drifting through the maelstrom like smoke, Zanth materialized in front of the ward. Being a demon, she couldn't step into its protection, but she stood in front of it and lifted her hands until a red gleam illuminated her. A demonic ward.

Her eyes began to spark, glowing brighter in the twilight as she threw bolts of shadow at the angels and demons rushing at her.

As an angel executioner—and an archdemoness—she was in her element.

Handfuls of grey feathers cascaded around her, smoking, and burning as red demon goo splattered the seraphim ward, the concrete, and the nearby white wooden cabanas.

"Jack!" Talia cried.

She threw her arms around his neck, holding him close for a moment. He felt her hurried breaths across his neck as her heart pounded against his chest. She was trembling.

He rubbed her back, fingers brushing across her wingtips. "You okay, Mrs. Casey?"

She nodded, exhaling sharply. "I thought they'd gotten you, Jack," she said, her voice breaking, those luminous grey eyes glassy with tears. "Everything happened so fast. I was frantic until I felt your voice vibrate against my breastbone."

The first tear fell and turned to crystal, shattering against the concrete.

"Those clowns?" He chuckled, shaking his head. "Not likely." He kissed her lips and let her go. "I was casting out my omnificence power, searching for Samael. Then I switched my target to Tre Sheridan and omnificence shot forward like a spotlight and lit up the tent where those bastards were ready to ambush us."

At last, she smiled. "That green light that the squad and I saw?"

He nodded.

"Your omnificence power gave away their hiding place, Jack. I was still focused on Samael, too. That's what they were counting on, wasn't it?"

"They probably didn't realize we knew about Tre Sheridan until they saw Zanth tossing Hellfire at them. At least this leveled the playing field a little," he said and nodded toward Zanth who was still blasting shadow bolts at the death angels. "And now, Zanth's demolishing them. I already took out a lot of the demons with murder marbles."

She put her arms around his neck again and pressed a brief but flaming kiss against his mouth that left him wanting more.

"I love you, Jack Casey," she whispered against his ear and turned toward the ward. "Now until forever."

He watched Talia's fluid movements as she lifted her arms into the air and rained down Holy fire on the remaining force of death angels and demons. But where was Samael in all that chaos?

"Tal, did you find Samael?" Jack asked.

She closed her eyes a moment. She was using omnificence.

He felt the energy thrum past the ward and fan out through the force of demons and death angels. With a lot more control and command than he could summon that power. The ribbons of energy flowed through her form like the air currents she floated across with ease. In an endless flight. Whereas, he had to land periodically and rest because of the friction and force against his human body.

Finally, she opened her eyes, shaking her head as she turned back to him.

"I don't sense him in this attack force," she replied. "I feel him out there though. Close. Like he's watching this fight unfold. From a hidden distance."

"Like a cowardly little bitch," Jack replied. "Maybe this is the decoy fight while he escapes with that book?" said Jack.

"We have to be prepared to blink after him if it is," Talia replied and turned toward her squad. "But I don't feel him moving yet. Just waiting. And watching."

As the silence gathered and lengthened, Talia and her squad remained silent. He knew that she was singing out more of those angel notes. The ones he couldn't hear. Had Samael and his guard heard her? Or was he the only one in this vicinity that couldn't understand those notes.

"It's rude to leave the human out of the conversation," he announced. "Just sayin'."

"Sorry, lover," said Talia, turning back to him. "I told the squad to be ready to blink after Samael if he tries to run with the Book."

He was sweating, feeling weak, the seraphim ward weighing on him. In a moment, it flickered. Gritting his teeth, he held onto it and forced more Holy fire into the ward to keep it lit as Zanth burned down the last remaining demons and stray death angels.

Most of the others were beginning to flee now.

Talia gave him a concerned look and glanced at the seraphim ward.

"Jack, you need to let the ward go. Before you overextend your seraphim powers and it falls. Then you'll be weak and very power drunk."

Grudgingly, he nodded, sweat dripping down the sides of his face. She was right. The strain had to be visible by now.

"Oui, let it go, Jack Casey," said Zanth, tossing down a massive burst of shadow and Hellfire that cut down several death angels and demons. "This assault is finished now."

The few remaining death angels and demons scattered before her as the sparks danced from her eyes like lightning bugs.

His muscles were corded and began to quiver, his limbs heavy, his breath quickening. He couldn't hold the ward any longer. He had to let it go.

With a deep breath, he closed his eyes and let the ward fall.

The bright white light dimmed and went out like a blown bulb. Immediately, dusk rushed in, overpowering the ward's remnant crystalline gleam as the Holy fire dissolved.

Already, he felt drained. He rubbed his forehead, his breathing heavier than he'd expected. Maintaining that ward had taken far more energy than he'd realized. He leaned against a cabana wall, sweat dripping down the sides of his face, and tried to catch his breath.

Zanth approached him.

Talia looked wary as the archdemoness paused in front of him, studying him a moment. That short black dress hugged Zanth's curves like a magnet, her ashen skin almost glowing in the twilight. Granted, Zanth was an archdemoness, but right now, she was damned hot in a New Orleans summer meets Hellfire kind of way. Talia would smite him if she could hear his thoughts. But he knew that Zanth was presenting herself in a sexy, Vegas showgirl persona for her lover. She had no interest in him and even if she did, he was happily married, and eternally in love with his wife.

Zanth reached out and laid her hand against his face and Talia's eyebrows shot up, anger smoldering in those grey eyes like a wild fire about to chew through everything in its path. Her eyes had turned a deep, ashen charcoal and they grew more molten as Zanth continued to touch him.

Didn't Talia realize that Zanth only flirted with him when she wanted something?

"You located Tre, didn't you?" she asked in a soft voice. "With omnificence."

He nodded, his gaze flicking from the fury building in Talia's face back to Zanth's calm, friendly demeanor. He half-expected Talia to rain down Holy fire on the archdemoness.

Talia moved closer, but didn't act. Yet.

"He's in that white tent," said Jack, nodding toward the billowing tent in the distance beyond the game cabanas. "I still feel his soul at the edge of my angel powers. You gonna be okay approaching him? Or do you need a negotiator?"

She tilted her head to the side, those red eyes glowing brighter, dark lashes batting at him with one purpose in mind as she let her hand fall away from his face.

Charming Tre Sheridan.

"Would you mind, Jack Casey? Having another human male perspective would help me face him." She bowed her head, her expression darkening. "After our fight."

Talia hung close, hovering off to Zanth's right side. Talia still looked like she was moments away from dropping buckets of Holy fire down on the archdemoness…and maybe him, too. With that look she was giving him, he wouldn't rule it out. But at least her eyes weren't burning white with Holy fire and directed at him. He still got a shiver at the memory of her flaming white eyes at Gianni's wedding, after he'd taunted Lucifer—and Talia—into a blind fury.

"I'd be happy to help the two of you patch things up," he said and motioned toward the white circus tent. "Lead the way, Zanth and I'll get Tre to understand what he's now dealing with as a soul—and a lover to a divine being. That's something I know a lot about."

Zanth nodded and turned away from him, moving with a sultry

swing of her hips. He let her get a few paces ahead before he followed. Talia stepped in front of him, shaking her head.

"No way, Jack Casey," she said in a quiet but determined voice and crossed her arms, wings twitching at her shoulders. "Not leaving you alone with that archdemoness. Not for a moment."

He smirked at her. "Don't trust me, aye?"

She shook her head and took a step toward him. She smashed her mouth against his in the fieriest kiss she'd ever planted on him. Leaving him breathless and distracted. He shook his head a moment, feeling dizzy.

"It's her I don't trust," she said and brushed her fingers through his bangs. She nodded toward the tent. "After you, Mr. Casey."

"Not after that kiss," he said with a smile. "I'd rather revisit that death angel mile-high club we discussed on our wedding night. Mrs. Casey."

She ran her hand down his back, sending an electric jolt of need through him.

"Later," she teased against his ear and brushed her lips across his right earlobe. "After we take care of Samael and the Book."

"Is that a yes?" he asked.

"That's a later," she replied in a sultry voice.

"I love being married to you," he said, his smirk widening.

That made Talia grin.

"I still need your help, Jack Casey," Zanth called out in that raspy, alto voice, sexy French accent like dark chocolate and threadbare velvet.

But he wouldn't mention that to Talia.

With Talia beside him (and not planning to let him out of her sight around the archdemoness), he hurried after Zanth, side-stepping the fallen death angels and demons crumpled in his path. He reached out into the foggy dusk and held Talia's hand. He wanted Tre Sheridan to see them as a couple—and know that if he really loved Zanth, then everything could still work out.

"Let's show Tre Sheridan that if a human and an angel of death can find their happily ever after together, then so can he and Zanth. Even with Hell involved."

Talia nodded and held out her left hand, her wedding ring sparkling.

"Good idea, Tal," he said. "I'll make sure he sees my ring, too."

Talia lowered her voice to a whisper. "I want to make sure they get back together," she said. "So, she'll stop hitting on my husband."

He squeezed her hand. "I think I like jealous Mrs. Casey. Her kisses are as smokin' hot as she is, but don't tell her that. I don't want her to think about fire too much and smite me."

"Not a chance, Mr. Casey," she said and nodded toward Zanth. "But I will smite anyone that makes a play for my husband."

"Jealous, possessive Mrs. Casey," he said and tugged at his collar. "Is it hot in here or just you, Tal?"

She smiled and tugged on his hand again, blinking both of them across the creepy, abandoned carnival lot, past the cabana games, and toward the white circus tent where Zanth paced back and forth, the tent flaps still closed.

The archdemoness was suddenly a bundle of nerves.

That must have been some fight between her and her lover. Because Tre Sheridan died and his soul was inside that tent, yet, she haunted the entrance like the gathering mists instead of going inside and throwing her arms around the dead dude.

"Zanth, what are you still doing out here?" he asked as Talia stood stoically beside him. "Figured you'd be all over this Tre Sheridan's soul. Sharing a demonic kiss—or gettin' horizontal...whatever demons and human souls do together."

She slapped her arms against her side and continued to pace. "He may send me away and not even speak to me," she said, her tone almost frantic. "I don't know where to even start with him."

She was really rattled. He'd never seen her like this before. So scattered and not in command of...well, anything. Most demons he'd encountered were control freaks (Luci was an off-the-scale control freak). Had to control every part of an interaction. Even Anqa, the succubus that Lucifer sent to babysit/control him in Hell.

Lucifer wanted total control and that had rubbed off on his demons, too.

"Start with the truth," Jack replied and motioned toward the tent flap. "And an apology for anything hurtful you said to him. Then offer him your heart."

Zanth paced a few more laps and then turned to stare at him.

"I told him the truth, Jack Casey," she snapped, angry as she whirled around, glaring at him, those eyes gleaming a brighter red. "But he chose to ignore it." Her eyes narrowed to slits and she cast a condescending glance at him. "Demons—and Tre—are much more sophisticated than your sappy, sentimental human offers."

He laughed. "Jealous much, Zanth?"

Her eyebrows shot up. "Jealous?"

"My sappy, sentimental offer was the sincerest moment of my life," he said, his voice louder than he'd intended. "I meant every word when I offered Talia my heart that night. It was the only true thing I had left to give her. The only thing that mattered to me."

He felt arms slid around his waist from behind as Talia laid her head against his shoulder.

"And it was the best moment of my existence, Zanth," said Talia in a soft voice. "Because he meant those words. And his every action has proven it, over and over." She motioned toward the tent. "And right now, that's the only thing you have to offer a human soul that has lost everything and is stuck alone in Purgatory."

Jack saw the indecision in Zanth's eyes as she kept glancing at the tent entrance. He felt her need. She wouldn't admit it, but she wanted to run in there and throw her arms around Tre Sheridan. Still, she fought against the light and the pureness of love, something all demons probably struggled against. He knew that she was only repeating back Lucifer's words with little understanding or evidence to disprove them. Demons were still fallen angels—or at least partly— so fragments of that light had to be inside them somewhere. Even if it was the thinnest of rays. He just had to convince her to reach for it. Because that's where her love lived.

He had to get her to see that.

"What exactly was this fight about anyway?" Jack asked.

Her hands were in motion again as she returned to her pacing.

"I told him not to sacrifice his life so that Samael could escape with that Book," said Zanth, her turns sharp and frenetic. "But he ignored my advice and did it anyway."

Jack was surprised. She'd actually told this dude not to give up his life for a nebulous arrangement that made little sense even to Lucifer's first lieutenant. Even before she assaulted him and Talia on their honeymoon, Zanth had decided to go against Lucifer's orders, Lucifer's plans. He couldn't help but wonder why.

Could he get any of this information out of her? Or would she hold to the demonic code and keep it to herself?

"Why would he do that?" Talia asked Zanth.

The archdemoness shook her head, shrugging, arms waving. "I do not know. I don't understand why he told me to stay out of it. To give him space." She sighed, those red eyes looking a little glassy now. "I asked him if eternity was enough space and I walked away."

Jack stared at the tent flaps. This dude hadn't made any moves to come out here and face her either. What was up with these two anyway?

Why would Tre Sheridan say that to her if he loved her?

Then it came to him. Tre reminded him a lot of Rachel Daniels and Lare Dumont because this dude had also made a deal with Lucifer. A contract for his soul—just like Lare and Rachel. So, there weren't any other choices for poor Tre, no matter how much he loved Zanth. Lucifer would call in his contract and force him to end his life with a suicide. Or the dude would burn on the racks forever—far away from Zanth. Tre Sheridan had no choice but to do Lucifer's bidding.

Didn't Zanth realize that?

Dude knew he had already lost her. It wasn't really a fight. He was trying to spare her feelings by pissing her off and getting her to forget about him. While he pined for her in here. That thought made Jack squirm. It was an all-too-familiar scenario that he'd faced once.

"Zanth...listen..." he began, his gaze moving between her and Talia. "There's something you don't understand here."

"What?" Zanth cried, rounding on him, glaring, misery burning in her glowing red eyes. "I understand it all perfectly. He—"

"Loved you so much that he made you furious enough to walk away from him. Because he knew that he'd be forced into the suicide with Lucifer calling in his contract."

"By Hell's gates! The contract…" Zanth's voice got quiet, trailing off.

Jack nodded and held Talia close. "Kind of like that afternoon at the beach house, babe," he said to Talia in a soft voice. "When I threw myself between you and Lucifer to keep you out of his hands. Knowing I'd be dragged off to Hell…and away from you for eternity." His voice caught in his throat and it took him a moment to get his voice back. "But—I did it to protect you." He sighed. "To save you."

"And losing you almost destroyed me, Jack," said Talia.

Her eyes welled with tears as Zanth turned to stare at her. A look of horror darkened Zanth's ashen face as she began to put the pieces together in her head as she realized Tre Sheridan's sacrifice.

"Yes, Zanth, losing Jack almost destroyed me," said Talia in a trembling voice as she brushed crystal tears off her cheeks. "I was planning to storm Hell to free him when he found a way to escape. So, you see, Tre was trying to protect you because he knew that he couldn't get out of Lucifer's contract."

Jack nodded. "He caused that fight to protect you, Zanth—and your feelings for him."

Zanth's full red lips began to tremble, her red eyes glassy again.

"How can you be sure?" she asked.

"Because that's how I'd have handled it in his shoes," said Jack as Talia's arms tightened around him." And I'm the best—eh, only human reference you've got on that subject, Zanth."

Something rustled.

Jack glanced past Zanth as the tent flaps swished open. The hollow figure of a thirty-something dude with bright sapphire blue eyes and a mop of curly, stone-brown hair emerged from the tent.

17

TALIA HUNG BACK AS THE SOUL OF TRE SHERIDAN STEPPED OUT OF THE billowing white tent, his sapphire gaze sullen and sad.

Zanth turned, surprise radiating across her ashen face, but despite the angel executioner's reactions, Talia saw both pain and love churning in those glowing red eyes. It was the first time since she had encountered the archdemoness that she could empathize with her. It felt like the moment when Jack appeared in the tower window in the Middling, trying to rescue her.

She had been furious at Jack for putting himself within Lucifer's strike range, knowing that the King of Hell had been waiting for him to do just that. Try and rescue her. But all she wanted to do was run to Jack and hold him in her arms for an eternity. Love had won that time and all she could do was put her arms around him and hold on with every last bit of control she had.

"Tre!" Zanth cried.

The archdemoness didn't move, but Talia felt the pull on Zanth's heart. It might have been shriveled and dark in her demonic chest, but Talia knew she had one in there somewhere. And it beat faster as Tre stood there, staring at her, his lanky frame dressed in old, worn jeans, black sneakers, and a faded black T-shirt underneath a navy blue tuxedo tailcoat.

"I told you I needed space, Zanth!" he shouted, those bright blue eyes narrowed, bottom lip quivering as he crossed his arms against his chest.

He was older than Jack and a few inches shorter than Jack's six-foot height. In life, Tre had carried about thirty more pounds than Jack. In Tre Sheridan's eyes, she saw an expression reminiscent to Jack's in those final moments inside the beach house escape room. When she and Jack had gazed at each other for what felt like the last time, knowing that he'd be dragged off to Hell and never see her again.

Pain stabbed her heart at the memory.

She wrapped her arms tighter around her new husband and the love of her life, snuggling against his warm body as she tried to blot out the echoes of that pain.

But Jack slid out of her grasp and moved toward Tre.

"Just stop, okay?" Jack held up his hands. "There's a way out of this now, so you can stop trying to push her away."

Tre glared at him. "Who the hell are you and what do you know about any of this? The last thing I want to see right now is a bunch of worthless angels."

Kesien and Muriel gathered around Tre, Deemah standing off to their right as Talia and Jack filled the gap between them. Encircling Zanth and Tre now.

"Dude, chill," Jack snapped and motioned at Talia and Kesien. "These angels of death are part of the reason there's another chance for you and your demonic bae."

Tre pressed his mouth into an angry line, fingers swiping through a tangle of stone-brown curls as he turned away from them. He stared at the Ferris wheel in the distance, eyes narrowed and misty.

"It's all too late, bro," said Tre in a tight voice as he shoved his hands into the pockets of his jeans. "Even if they could fly me out of here, Lucifer owns my ass. And he wants me right here with the archangel. That was the deal."

Jack smirked at Tre, shaking his head. "An eternity of being Samael's bitch in exchange for one year of human fame? That's a shit deal, dude. Even without hiding Samael's cowardly ass here in Purgatory, why would you sell your soul for one year of fame? What a waste of your soul. And Top Entertainer—seriously? Who the hell sells their soul for that show?"

"I did, okay?" Tre said with a snarl. "I wanted to make it. I was a damned good illusionist! I had the creds, but not the luck. I needed that break, y'know? I figured if I signed that contract, I'd get my break and be on top for a long time. So, all I needed was a year at the top."

Talia felt bad for the confused young man. Didn't he realize that Lucifer cheated and would have taken away all that success after the year was up? And Tre had no idea how close to that break he'd been before he sold his soul. It had been eighteen months away. Waiting for him in that Vegas Strip hotel lobby where he would foil a gun man's plot to shoot dozens of people at that venue.

Tre didn't realize that he and Zanth would have met in that hotel lobby anyway. And as thanks for foiling that attack, the hotel would have headlined him with his own show. He'd have made it. And found Zanth.

All of that was gone now, along with Tre Sheridan's life. But she had a bit of news that might brighten his outlook.

"Tre," said Talia, slipping forward. "One thing that you need to know is that this suicide pact you made with Lucifer completed your contract."

"Of course, I know that!" Tre shouted. "But the aftermath of that move has just begun."

She shook her head and blinked in front of him, grabbing him by the shoulders and shaking him.

"Listen to me," she said in a forceful voice that made even Zanth pause in surprise. "If you hadn't killed yourself, you'd have ended up in Hell, your soul tethered to Lucifer after you signed away your soul. But your suicide brought you here. Untethered."

Zanth gasped and turned toward Tre.

"Oui! Tre, don't you see? Lucifer has no tether on your soul, so he cannot drag you back to Hell."

Tre shrugged. "So what. I'm in here for the duration instead of Hell. Doesn't change anything."

Jack's sexy smirk turned into a knowing smile that set his face alight.

"Dude," said Jack, laying a hand against his chest. "That's why I'm here. See, I can open that door and let you and your demon hookup slip out before the check arrives."

Tre's anger didn't diminish. "Angels can't open that door, bro. Otherwise, that archangel wouldn't have needed my help." He sighed. "My suicide."

"I'm no angel, dude," said Jack.

"You got that right," Muriel said with a snicker that even made Kesien smile.

"And what are those wings and halo? Special effects? Illusions?"

Jack shrugged. "These are real," he said. "And it's a hella-long complicated story, but I'm human, dude. And my...well, hybrid form here is exactly why I can open the door as the only living human in Purgatory."

At last, the reality sank in and Tre's eyes widened, the corners of his grimace turning upward.

"You're serious."

"Serious as a dead mime, dude," said Jack.

"Then it's not too late for me and Zanth?" he cried.

Jack shook his head.

Tre turned toward Zanth, his bottom lip trembling as Zanth slid toward him, her hands against his face.

"I offer you my heart, Tre Sheridan," said Zanth in her rough alto voice. She glanced over at Jack a moment and then the archdemoness' gaze caught Talia's and held it. "Like Jack Casey offered his to Talia Smith once."

Tre's eyes bugged out and his gaze snapped back to Jack. "Wait a minute...you're...Jack Casey? The actor? From that cop show and that reality show everybody was watching? And you've got wings?"

Jack nodded. "And this beautiful angel of death is Talia Smith. My new wife."

"The chick from that show is an angel of death? No shit?"

Talia laughed. "That's me."

"So, believe me, dude," said Jack as he slid his arms around her. "I really do understand what you're going through."

Tre Sheridan looked like he'd slammed face-first into a brick wall. "I guess you do." He turned toward Zanth who was staring at him with reverent, glowing red eyes. "I love you, Zanth," he said. "With all my heart. It was killing me to push you away, but I had to—so you'd have to let me go. Because there was no way out of this place for me."

"Until now," Zanth said and swept her arms around Tre who frantically pulled her against his chest.

He kissed her hard on the lips, their kiss long and anxious.

"Okay, now, I've seen everything," said Muriel with a sigh. "My first demonic happily ever after. Maybe a demon match up will be on the next season of yours and Jack's show, Talia?"

"I think that arrangement would make Devin Van Fossen's head explode," said Jack.

Finally, Tre let Zanth go, but he frowned at Talia and her squad of death angels.

"So, how and why did you join forces with a bunch of angels, Zanth?" Tre asked. "Wouldn't that make Lucifer furious?"

Zanth cast a long, probing stare at Jack and it made Talia uncomfortable.

"Oui."

Finally, Tre pointed at Jack. "Especially Casey? Hell, even I know that Lucifer's head would explode if he knew you'd gotten help from Jack Casey."

Now, Zanth looked uncomfortable, even nervous.

"Jack Casey was the only one that could get you out, my love," said Zanth, motioning at Jack. "I had no choice."

Tre chuckled. "Since when has that mattered to Lucifer. He hates Casey."

Jack stepped forward. "Dude, Lucifer started this whole feud between us by wagering my soul without my knowledge. And then he tried to drag my woman off to Hell, taking me instead."

Jack's use of *my woman* made Talia smile.

"Bro, you were in Hell?" Tre shouted, staring at him in shock, mouth hanging open.

"For months as Lucifer's consolation prize," Jack said with a nod. "He's just pissed because I escaped Hell and locked him in the same garden that he ruined."

"The Garden of Eden?" Tre said with a gasp.

"I did not realize it was you that locked him the Garden, Jack Casey," said Zanth, a strange expression on her face.

Talia studied the archdemoness' expression closer and felt a chill. She was impressed. And now, the archdemoness stared at him with newfound interest that made Talia's hackles rise again.

Jack nodded. "It was me. But don't be too impressed because he killed me in there after I had to fuse the lock from the inside, trapping both of us there."

With wide eyes, Zanth reached out to Jack and Talia bristled. She rubbed his shoulder.

"You sacrificed yourself twice," she said in a soft, reverent voice and nodded at Talia. "For this angel of death that you love so much?"

"Talia means everything to me," he said, his voice getting tight. "And I'd do it all over again, too."

Talia stepped between Jack and Zanth. "I brought Jack back through our rare bond."

"Bro, how did Lucifer escape?" Tre asked, looking anxious again.

"Oui," said Zanth, fixing Jack with that glowing red demonic stare again. "How did Lucifer escape? He never told us. He returned to Hell with his wings and halo. And a renewed vengeance to hunt down your soul, Jack Casey."

"He broke the wards when he got his wings and angel powers back through a Phoenix shift," said Jack with a shrug as he moved toward Talia. "So, for him, it was only a waiting game. And he's been trying to kill me ever since."

And take Jack's soul.

The thought of Lucifer dragging Jack back to Hell terrified her. Like this strange situation with Archangel Samael and his death angels that had suddenly turned on her death angel guard, destroying dozens of angels of death before breaking Samael out of High House and assaulting the archive. All of that to break the halo tether chaining Lucifer to Hell? Behind a locked gate. If he got the Book and escaped Hell somehow, would his first action be to come after Jack?

Right now, that was her greatest fear.

Jack still had seraphim powers, but Lucifer could outlast him. And drain Jack's seraphim powers because as a human, Jack didn't have an endless source of power like a seraph. Or an archangel...or any angel, for that matter. She could bolster his power with her halo and their stronger bond, but regardless, Jack's humanity would cause him to hit that protective failsafe—and descend into a power drunk. Leaving him vulnerable to an attack from Lucifer and his demons.

They had to stop Samael. Here. And now.

Before he delivered the Book of Secrets to Lucifer—and endangered the human world—and Jack's life. With Procel, another fallen angel with rare angel powers beside him, Lucifer had a real chance to escape Hell. If Procel could awaken resurrect from the Book of Secrets.

And if Procel gained that power, he could resurrect Lucifer's fallen demons. With both sides possessing resurrect, Heaven and Hell could battle endlessly for eternity.

But it also meant that Lucifer could break his halo tether and come after Jack.

If that happened, Jack couldn't return to his life on Earth. He wouldn't admit it, but he could never walk away from his human life forever. Any more than she could permanently walk away from being an angel of death. And she refused to force him to lose everything. Despite what he'd said about walking away from all of it for her, she knew that Jack loved being an actor as much as she loved being an angel.

Somehow, they'd find a way to spend time in Eolowen and in Los Angeles, in both the angelic and human cities of angels.

Tre Sheridan smiled. "Lucifer will lose his mind when he finds out you helped his first lieutenant and her lover escape him. Bro, if I were you, I'd be very worried right now."

Kesien blinked beside Jack, his face taut with worry, but the flames of retribution still burned in his grey eyes.

"This soul is right, Jack," said Kesien, gripping Jack's shoulder. "If Lucifer finds out you were behind this, he will set your world on fire searching for you."

Jack's expression sharpened and she saw the momentary fear glint in those light green eyes before his game face burned bright in Purgatory's dusk and fog.

Talia couldn't stop herself from enfolding Jack in her arms and wrapping him in her wings.

"Then we need to assign two squads of death angels to protect Jack," said Talia.

"Your squad is already permanently assigned, Talia," said Kesien, lifting his head higher, golden halo burning bright. "Whether Heaven knows it or not."

Muriel's wings fluttered through the fog as she landed at Jack's back and kept a close watch.

"Talia, you know we will guard Jack with everything we have," said Muriel as she glanced past Jack and caught her gaze. "Regardless of what the official orders say. And that includes Anahera, too."

"And me," said Deemah, unfurling her wings as she stood beside Kesien, long walnut hair coiling around her shoulders. "Lucifer and his demons won't get through us to Jack. That's a promise, Talia and Jack."

Jack chewed his lip, those hypnotic green eyes turning glassy. "Best squad ever. Thank you."

Kesien nodded. "It is my honor, Jack," said the tall, curly-haired angel of death. "You have earned our protection—over and over. And this squad would follow Talia anywhere."

"This angel of death is correct," said Zanth, motioning at Kesien as she slowly circled Jack, arms crossed, those red eyes gleaming. "When Lucifer discovers you helped Tre and me disappear, he will stop at nothing to take your soul—ignoring all the rules for humanity. And he will set your world—the Earth—aflame in the process."

She turned away and paced in front of him.

"What does that even mean?" Jack asked, fixing Talia with his gaze. "Are we talking about Lucifer going after my friends and family again here? Or something crazier—like an apocalyptic assault on everything?"

He looked worried and a little shaken. Not for himself, she knew, but for innocents getting hurt because of him.

"Oui," Zanth snapped as she paced slowly back and forth in front of him. "He will try to hurt you in any and every way that he can, Jack Casey."

Jack frowned, his sexy mouth flattening into an angry line. "You're his first lieutenant! You know what he's planning. Spill it, Zanth! You owe me that much for reuniting you and your human hookup."

A curious smile lit Zanth's ashen face as she glanced over at Tre Sheridan whose eyebrows pressed into a frown as he glared at her.

"You presume much, Jack Casey," said Zanth, that annoying smile persisting as she made a turn and paced away from him. "Lucifer never tells his first lieutenants or his princes of Hell such important details. It is always on a need-to-know basis. It will be a nightmare pursuit, I can assure you of that, but unless Lucifer breaks all seven seals, there will be no apocalyptic assault on your world." She turned around, staring at him. "Only you, Jack Casey. He will mount an apocalyptic assault on you."

Jack swallowed a breath and exchanged a fearful look with Talia.

"So, it's business as usual then," said Jack, crossing his arms and watching Zanth pace. "Except that Luci can throw a surprise party at my place any time instead of only calling me on my phone."

Still smiling, Zanth shook her head as she uncrossed her arms and paused in front of Jack.

"Not business as usual, Jack Casey. He will get at you through your friends, through acquaintances—even strangers. He will harm them in ways that you cannot even imagine. And he will pursue you relentlessly. Day and night. Until he takes your soul. And destroys your world in the process."

Talia felt her chest tighten, knowing that Zanth was right. If Lucifer broke his tether and somehow opened Hell's gates, the only place he couldn't directly hit back at Jack was Heaven. But even in Heaven, the King of Hell could still attack Jack through an intercessory.

"Then there's no place I can get clear from him," said Jack, sounding defeated.

Zanth shook her head. "Oui," she said and gestured toward the shadows beyond the fluttering white tent. "That is why Tre and I must disappear. So, Lucifer does not learn of my abandoning his command for Tre—at your hand. If that information does not surface, then he will never know it was you, Jack. Right now, that is the best way that we can protect you from Lucifer's wrath."

Tre moved toward her and slid his arms around her waist, pulling Zanth into a lingering embrace.

"You have my word, bro," said Tre, giving Jack a sharp nod. "You open that door for me and we'll immediately disappear, so Lucifer can't come after us."

Zanth nodded. "Oui," she said and laid her head against Tre's shoulder. "As an archdemoness, I have ways to melt into the ethereal planes. And now that I have Tre at my side, I will fade from existence. Lucifer will assume that I perished in this fight and he will choose another first lieutenant. And in this way, he cannot learn how Tre and I disappeared."

Tre gave him a sharp, emphatic nod. "It'll be the best illusion of my life, Casey. I give you my word. We both aim to repay you and these angels of death. For now, this is the best way we can do that."

Jack exhaled sharply. "Thank you for that. Now, I have to worry about him attacking my friends and family." He pulled Talia into a tight embrace. "And the woman I love."

She kissed him hard on the lips. "Now until forever, Jack Casey."

He smiled and returned her kiss, turning back to them. "Now, my mother on the other hand…"

"Jack!" Talia cried as he busted out laughing.

"What? You think Luci's any match for Nina Westwood Casey? She'll take him apart, Tal. Trust me. Heaven doesn't know they have a secret weapon."

Zanth sauntered back toward Jack, those sultry demon hips swaying in that short black dress as she stopped in front of him and laid her hands on his shoulders. Staring into those smoldering light green eyes. Shoving Talia's need to smite right past her resolve.

"And now, there is one final thing we can do to repay you, Jack Casey," she said, her gaze unblinking as she stared into the luminous green depths of his eyes.

Jack's game face slipped, a look of surprise on his face. Her scintillating approach had caught him off guard and he looked confused. Not attracted. And that made Talia's smite reflex relax. A little.

Jack frowned. "Uh…what?"

Smiling, Zanth reached up, brushed Jack's pale blond bangs out of his eyes, and cupped his chin.

"Your father. I will take you to him if you still wish to see him," said Zanth, a smile in her voice, those intense red eyes softening.

Jack nodded, his eyes brightening, lips curving into a smile. "Dad…" he said in a tight, quiet voice, a mixture of pain and grief surfacing in those light green eyes.

His gaze shot to Talia, his sexy mouth pressing into a line as he held out his hand to her.

"Come with me?" he asked, his voice almost child-like.

In that moment, if he'd been planning to jump off a bridge or step out in front of a bus, she'd have followed him.

Nodding, she reached out and gripped his hand. His hold was like iron, his hand trembling as he let it fall against his right side.

Only then did he look back at Zanth. "Take me to him," he said in a thin voice. "Please?"

Zanth turned toward Tre and kissed him. "I will be right back, my love." She turned to Muriel and Kesien. "Will you protect him until we return?"

It was a question not a demand, surprising Talia again.

"You bet," said Muriel as she nodded toward Jack. "And...thank you."

"Yes, Zanth," said Talia as Zanth fixed her with that unblinking, glowing red demonic stare. "Thank you and Tre for this moment that none of us was able to give Jack."

With a deep bow of her head, Zanth gestured at Jack. "Your husband has earned this moment. And even now, it surprises me that he would help me reunite with Tre after everything I—and Hell—have thrown at him. It humbles me."

"All right, squad," Muriel announced as she blinked beside Tre Sheridan. "Roundel formation around Tre. Shields out. Swords at the ready."

Tre glanced at Muriel. "Roundel? Isn't that some kind of old people music or something?"

Jack grinned and glanced at Muriel. "See? And you thought it was just me."

Muriel shook her head. "Now, I know it's a human thing." She glanced at Deemah. "Deemah, remind me to ask Azrael to rename this formation."

"Will do," she said.

"I win," said Jack with a fist pump. He glanced at Muriel. "You dudes wanna borrow my demon-splattering playlist? In case any more demons and death angel traitors show up."

Muriel shook her head. "Nah. We're good, Jack."

Tre was smiling. "My illusion act on the Strip played some kick-ass tunes."

"Like what?" Jack asked as his gaze moved to Tre Sheridan.

The squad had taken up a circle formation around the former magician, warily watching the fog and the shadows for signs of another attack.

"A little hip hop, a little metal," Tre said with a shrug.

"How metal?" Jack looked intrigued.

"You know how that cop show you were on always played

something current? Like angry rock or hip hop during the action scenes?"

Jack was nodding again.

"Well, that's what I did," Tre said, smiling, a hand against his chest. "Played some intense stuff during the setups and then something lit during the trick's climax. Audiences loved it. Said it gave my act a real current feel. Wish I had my playlist."

Talia smiled. Two performers talking shop. Jack was in his element. Especially when the word *metal* came up and it didn't refer to armor or swords.

"I'll Google your act when I get back to Earth," said Jack. "You may not have a physical body anymore, dude, but maybe you and Zanth can still visit the things you loved about the world below?"

"Thanks, bro, I hope we can, too."

"Let's go, Jack Casey," said Zanth, her voice loud and sharp.

Jack's gaze snapped back to Talia. She squeezed his hand as he leaned deeper into the embrace of her wings folding around him.

"I'm ready, Zanth," he said. "And again. Thank you for this."

Zanth turned sideways, hands glowing red and then a deep gold as she slid her palms into the mist and shadows.

"Hurry back, Talia," said Muriel, eyes narrowing as she scanned the horizon beside Kesien who was back to his brooding expression.

A glowing door appeared beside the archdemoness. She took hold of a crystal doorknob and turned it, the door opening inward into a luminous white mist.

"He is this way, Jack Casey," said Zanth and stepped through the doorway, disappearing into the dusky fog.

With a tug on Talia's hand, Jack hurried toward the glowing doorway. He took a deep breath, closed his eyes, and stepped through. Talia blinked through the illumination and the haze beside Jack.

18

Jack's eyes burned as a surge of light exploded around him, Talia, and Zanth in a fiery orange burst. Momentarily blinding him.

Purgatory peeled back like an overripe banana as he stepped out of the illuminated mist into an overexposed, over-contrasted cinematic landscape of dramatic clouds that rushed past in shades of storm-grey and midnight blue, the setting sun painting them orange and pink. White-capped, sunset-washed mountain peaks towered across the western horizon, the luminous waters of Haro Strait mirror-calm, reflecting back brilliant oranges, pinks, and purples as the sun sank behind the mountains.

His heart ached when he saw the little white cabin taking shape in the fog. Identical to the one in his memory of those childhood family vacations. It perched on a bluff overlooking the Salish Sea, the air crisp and smelling of brine, winds sharp as they buffeted the point, and fanned across the tall sea grass. This slice of Purgatory was a place of perpetual sunset, where it never got completely dark and the sun never fully lit the landscape. But despite all of the dusk and shadows and dramatic skies, like a Ridley Scott or David Lynch film, he'd recognize this place anywhere.

The cabin at Lost Souls Point on the island's western side.

He swallowed the lump in his throat. It was the San Juan Island cabin that Dad had rented every summer for the Casey family vacation in Washington State. Or at least a depiction of it.

A memory of the place at any rate. Was it his memory? Or his dad's?

Jack had been only six or seven when Dad took him on his first plane flight from Indianapolis to Seattle with his four sisters and his mother. To the San Juan Islands and this cabin for the very first time. He remembered them all piling into a huge rented SUV at the airport and driving north to a small coastal town called Anacortes. And how amazing it felt to watch Dad drive that big SUV straight onto the ferry. Driving it right onto a big boat! As a kid, it had been like magic back then.

For an hour, that ferry floated through the archipelago's misty, cool waters until finally, it reached this island tucked away in the fog and teal green waters of the Puget Sound. Into Friday Harbor where dad drove off the ferry into the quaint small town that had always reminded him of a movie set. Back then, he'd never seen anything like this place. It felt like his dad had found this little corner of magic that no one else seemed to know about—at least in Indiana.

For four magical years, Dad had packed up the family and took that daylong trip from Indiana to San Juan Island. When Dad died, Jack couldn't bear the thought of stepping foot onto the island again. But a decade later, after finally marrying Talia, he'd made peace with part of his grief, wanting to share the island's wonder and beauty with her when he found out the show wanted to send them there for a honeymoon.

He'd never dreamed that his dad was in Purgatory, surrounding himself with the elements of those trips. That, of all things in his short life (he was only forty-eight when he died), Dad had chosen to immerse himself in the illusions of those trips. Those short four years when they were all still a family. And together. In this tiny white, three-bedroom cabin overlooking Haro Strait.

This choice of setting, where Dad had absorbed himself in the past, spoke volumes to Jack.

A thin gold light burned in the cabin's front picture window.

Jack broke into a run through the windswept grass toward the door and Talia didn't follow. Was she giving him space? He sighed. Space to confront the worst loss of his lifetime?

He felt her lift into the air behind him, hovering close overhead while Zanth hung back. Both of them let him have his privacy while maintaining a distant but careful watch. He felt Zanth's apprehension beneath the burn of Talia's protectiveness sweep around him with the beat of her wings.

Both archdemoness and angel of death felt uneasy.

Talia's fear and nervousness pulsed like a racing heartbeat through the strengthened bond they shared. Like she and Zanth both were expecting another ambush. Until they got married, he'd never felt the intensity of Talia's emotions like this before. But as he ran toward the cabin, he felt the waves of her worry wash over him and he felt guilt mix with grief.

But she knew how much he needed to see his dad.

"Dad?" Jack shouted, his legs pumping as he ran down the uneven footpath. "Dad!"

He flung open the door, his wings flat against his back, halo casting a gold gleam alongside the cabin's warm orange glow.

The cabin looked just like he remembered it. All cedar inside, including the hardwood floor, a fire burning in the hearth, a brown leather sofa flanking it. Behind the sofa was a beat-up cherry wood dining table with seven mismatched wooden chairs surrounding the oval table. Beyond it, an L-shaped kitchen with a 90s black granite countertop, white cabinets, and black and white tile on the floor.

But Jack halted when he saw the tall, pallid man seated on the brown leather sofa, dressed in a washed-out black T-shirt. Dad always wore that Bob Seger and the Silver Bullet Band T-shirt, the one with the horses, and an old, faded pair of torn khakis. So thin. Face stubbled, light green eyes hollowed. His pale blond hair was windblown and feathered across his forehead like Jack remembered it, his eyes tired and watery. He looked just like those last pictures that Jack had carried around in his head since high school. But his form looked faded somehow. Almost like he was a reflection of his former self.

Like a photograph left out in the sun.

Dad's lined, oval face looked so weary and weathered, except for that mischievous smirk he wore to cover up the cancer pain and his failing health. Jack hadn't realized it until much later that Dad had been acting his way through the final months of his life—so Jack wouldn't realize how sick he was and how close to the end he'd gotten. To protect Jack from the pain that was coming as the end of his life edged closer, the cancer accelerating through his already ravaged body.

"Dad!" Jack cried, his eyes brimming with emotion.

The ol' man looked exactly like he remembered from that long ago Indiana summer in 2012. When Dad's stage four cancer had exhausted all possible treatments, something that Dad had also kept to himself. Trying to protect Jack from the pain and loss.

His dad's gaze snapped up as Jack, overcome with emotion, approached him, his hands outstretched. He squinted, almost not believing this was real as he stood barely three feet from his ol' man. After a decade without him.

"Jack?" His dad's eyes widened as he shook his head, a gasp slipping between his lips. "My God…Jack!"

Dad jumped up from the couch and rushed toward him, wrapping Jack in his arms. His hug was tight and encompassing, almost frantic as he held Jack so close against his faded form.

Shaking, Jack threw his arms around his dad and held onto him. A moment he'd been denied a decade ago.

God, it hurt.

He didn't feel the rise and fall of breath in Dad's chest or the beat of his heart. There was no human warmth against Jack's skin either, but Jack remembered the feel of Dad's comforting presence. The familiar weight of his dad's arms remained as the man held him in a bear hug that Jack knew so well. That hug finally broke open the unhealed wound Jack had hidden for a decade.

Unable to stem the tide, the pain from the sudden loss of his idol and biggest fan poured out. All the exhaustion and grief he'd tamped down deep to go on with his life, without his dad's influence, bubbled up. The long, lonely years that had scarred his young life and compartmentalized it into two periods: before Dad died and after Dad died.

All of it flooded back and hit him like a bullet train.

As his warring emotions collided, everything came apart at the seams, exploding into a torrent of grief that he couldn't control. Couldn't contain. Couldn't hold back the deluge as it burst out like a flash flood.

Hard, wracking sobs tumbled out and he couldn't stop them. They shook his entire body as the waves of tamped down grief rose like a tsunami and pounded through his chest.

"Jack..." his dad said in a soothing voice, a hand against his hair, stroking as he held him against his chest. "My son, it's really you. I've missed you so much, boy. So sorry I had to leave you so soon and so quickly."

"Dad," Jack choked out, but the rest of the words wouldn't come. "Dad, I..."

The rest of the words hung in his throat, the raw grief still gushing out. His dad just held him like he hadn't seen him in years.

And he hadn't.

Nearly a decade had passed since that horrible afternoon when Dad had lapsed into a coma while Jack was at the YMCA, working his life guard job. The man died hours later, leaving Jack angry, confused, alone, and deeply grieving.

For years afterward, he'd tried to make sense of the devastating loss and ended up medicating it with alcohol and flake, hoping to pave over it every time the cracks appeared.

Those cracks had become deep, gaping sinkholes by the time he'd gotten fired from *SanFran Confidential*.

He pressed his face against his dad's chest and held onto him as his body shook with grief.

"It's okay, son," Dad whispered and held him closer. "I understand."

Suddenly, his dad thrust him out at arm's length, a terrified expression haunting his face.

"Oh, my God…no. Jack—you're so young. You didn't…die, did you?" Dad's eyes were glassy and he swiped at the tears clinging to his eyelashes. "Please tell me that you didn't inherit my issues! Tell me you didn't overdose or drink yourself into oblivion."

Jack felt so overwhelmed he could barely speak. But how could he tell his ol' man that he'd had a raging flake habit alongside a drinking problem. And how it had gotten him fired from his hit series. Left him with nothing. But he knew he had to tell him the bad parts first. To get to the better parts of his life. The moments that involved Talia.

He bowed his head, sucking in a sharp breath, trying to say everything at once, but his mouth bobbed open without a word escaping.

"Jack," he said, his grip tightening, as Dad, at last, noticed the halo and the wings flat against his back. "What happened? How did you die? My God, you weren't even eighteen yet. Please tell me I didn't curse you with my addictions?"

Jack shook his head, fighting to find his voice.

"What addictions?" Jack finally asked in a tight, thin voice. "I know you…drank a little."

The pain in his dad's face radiated as the ol' man winced and stared at the floor. But Jack couldn't let on that he knew. He needed to hear him say the words. Tell him to his face that he'd been a drug addict and an alcoholic. Prove or deny his mother's words.

"Jack, there's so much you don't know about me," said his dad in a pained voice. "So much I was too ashamed to tell you. And the rest, I was terrified that you'd hate me when you figured out I was an alcoholic. A binge drinker who disappeared for weeks at a time. Addicted to any high I could buy. But your mother, bless her heart, always told you I was away on a business trip or something harmless. Knowing I was off in some crack house, smoking heroin and doing coke."

Jack flinched.

So, what his mother said had been true after all. That Dad had a drug problem every bit as bad as his drinking problem. And Jack's coke problem had been the thing his mother had most feared. Enough to wash her hands of him at ten—so she wouldn't have to witness another slow suicide. Especially her only son's slow freefall toward an overdose.

He was beginning to understand his mother's reactions and responses over the years, not sure how he'd have reacted if their roles had been reversed. Would he have reacted differently if Dad had overdosed instead of landing in hospice?

Would he have reacted differently to Dad's drug habit and alcoholism? Like avoiding all drugs and alcohol? Instead of letting Rachel Daniels and Lare Dumont wear him down?

Would he and his soul both need saving? By Talia?

If he'd sidestepped all the drugs and the fast lane—and never tried to break through Hollywood's wall of fame—then maybe he'd have never met Talia?

That thought made him shudder. It was a heavy, high price to pay, but he'd do it all again—all the bad parts. For Talia.

"Dad, I..." He fought down a wave of grief, took a deep breath, and gripped his dad's arms. "I want to hear it all," he said finally. "But first, you need to know that I became an actor, just like I said."

Dad's eyes widened. "Where, son? Theatre? Broadway?"

He let a grin brighten his face. "Hollywood, Dad," he said. "I got cast on one of the hottest cop shows in the country."

"What? Hollywood? You—you made it? In Hollywood?"

Jack gave his dad an emphatic nod. "Even made a movie."

But he couldn't finish the flex. It had all fallen apart because of his flake addiction.

His gaze fell away from his dad's face and he couldn't look him in the eye and tell him about the coke. He couldn't.

Jack turned away, his voice catching. "But I messed it all up, Dad," he said in a shaky voice.

"How, Jack?" His father's voice ached through him.

He winced. "Because of the cocaine, Dad," he said, glaring at the cabin's hardwood floors. "I had a raging flake habit and a bad drinking problem. Got myself fired from the biggest break in my career."

"Oh, Jack—no."

His dad's voice ached with defeat as he dropped down on the cabin's brown leather sofa.

"But, Mr. Casey, your son worked his heart out to overcome it all."

Jack glanced up as Talia floated through the cabin rooftop and landed in her full angel of death Holy light, wings unfurled, halo burning bright.

"An angel…" Jack's dad gasped, his gaze fixated on Talia as she landed between them. "Here? In Purgatory?"

"Your son brought me and my squad here, Mr. Casey," said Talia, pale gold light radiating from her.

"Did he die of an overdose?" Jack's dad asked, his voice tight and mournful. "This is all my fault."

Talia shook her head as she reached out and gripped Jack's hands, pulling him toward her.

"Talia saved me from that fate, Dad," he said as he held her hands tighter.

His dad shook his head, looking shocked. "How?"

Jack smiled as he reached out and ran his fingers across her cheek. "By falling in love with me."

His dad's eyes got huge as he stared at Talia and then at Jack. "An angel fell in love with you?"

Jack nodded. "And I fell in love with her. On a reality television show called The Cinderella Hour. Where she landed on Earth to save me."

"It's the number one show in the country, Mr. Casey," said Talia in a soft voice. "And Jack's the reason for it. You'd be so proud of him. They even want him back on his old show."

At last, Jack felt his dad's hands grip his shoulders and turn him around.

"I've always been proud of my son," said his dad, his gaze not leaving Jack's face. "No matter what. And I knew he would make it big. He had the most breathtaking looks I'd ever seen. Combined with his unshakable work ethic and talent and he was a natural."

Jack stared at his dad a moment. Dad had never said a word about the plays and musicals he'd done in high school, in summer theatre, and around the region. Never once encouraging him to follow that path. Instead, he'd pushed him toward college to get his bachelor's degree. But Jack never resented that—or Dad ignoring his love for acting.

He'd always known that the odds were high that he'd never succeed in Hollywood, despite his looks that had gotten him lots of high school and summer theatre leads. When he had nothing left but Dad's old Firebird convertible and a life that could fit in a U-Haul trailer, he knew he had nothing left to lose by pursuing his acting dream in Hollywood.

Talia smiled at Jack and then gazed at his dad. "He looks just like you, Mr. Casey."

Dad shook his head. "He's always looked like the best version of me and Nina."

Jack pulled Talia close. "And Talia's my better half, Dad," he said and held out his left hand. "We just got married."

His dad's apprehension faded as a bright grin lit his face. "You're married, son?"

He nodded. "Millions of people watched us get married on live television, Dad." His voice got quiet. "Mother—coordinated the ceremony and the wedding venue."

"Nina was there? At your wedding?" Dad's eyes got glassy. "That makes me so happy, son," he said in a tight voice.

Then Jack saw it. That love for his mother still burned in Dad's eyes. Even after death. That had to be the reason why Dad had remained here in Purgatory. Waiting for his family to pass this way before he left his old life—and Purgatory—behind at last.

Jack felt a wave of relief wash over him. Dad wasn't stuck here. He was waiting.

Dad laid his hands on Jack's shoulders again, smiling. "Son, you need to understand that your mother left because of me. Not you."

Jack sighed. "She made it pretty clear that she wanted nothing to do with me, Dad when I got fired from my show."

Already, his dad was shaking his head.

"She wanted nothing to do with the drugs, Jack. She loves you. And she couldn't stand to watch you self-destruct like I did. She couldn't go through that a second time—not with her only son. Dealing with my addiction nearly destroyed her."

Jack bristled. On some level, he understood that, but if she'd cared about him at all, why hadn't she come and gotten him when Dad died? To make sure he didn't turn to drugs and alcohol? Instead of turning her back on her still-seventeen-year-old son. That fact still hurt despite their conversations at the vineyard. Back in Santa Rosa, she'd wanted a second chance when she'd given him none. She'd indicted him along with the rest of the world after he got fired from *SanFran Confidential* and forgot she had a son again. Like she had in the divorce.

The fact that she'd abandoned him at the two lowest moments in his life made him still want to keep his distance from her.

"Dad…" he began, struggling with the words.

"What is it, Jack?"

Dad needed to understand what had happened after he passed away. His brow wrinkled, his green eyes darkening, mouth pressing into a tense line as he studied Jack.

"Dad—" Jack repeated as he tried to force it all to the surface. "After you passed away that summer…Mother didn't even call me. She left me to fend for myself."

His eyes narrowed. "What? Alone?" His face scrunched into that angry, pinched look he got whenever Jack had broken his curfew or not told him the whole story about something. "But you were only seventeen!"

Jack nodded. "I was alone in the apartment for nearly two weeks until Meredith came and got me. If it hadn't been for Meredith—"

He pulled in a breath and stepped back from his dad.

He'd called Meredith that night, desperate, frantic, but she and his sister, Whitney had been in Santa Rosa visiting his other two sisters:

Tara and Jenna. At that point, Jack hadn't spoken to Tara and Jenna in nearly eight years, not since Mother took them to Santa Rosa. He occasionally saw Whitney, but Meredith was the one that had stepped in and gave him a place to live. His mother never even called him.

The only help he'd gotten that night had come from the hospice nurse who got him through the hardest parts. He'd spent a horrible two weeks alone in that cavernous apartment until his sister, Meredith got his voice mail and rushed back to Indiana to get him.

Dad's eyes turned glassy as he clasped Jack to his chest again. "I'm so sorry you went through that, Jack. Why didn't Nina come get you? Or send you a plane ticket?"

Anger sharpened his voice, but all Jack could do was shrug.

He'd never understood why she hadn't come and gotten him. Or at least gotten him to Santa Rosa.

"It's a question I've asked myself hundreds of times, Dad."

"You were still a minor!"

Jack nodded. The hurt from that summer had lingered for a long time. And that feeling of wanting to go home again persisted all year until he realized that he had no home anymore. The familiar and the routine were gone, replaced by an uncomfortable transition to a dresser that Dad had made him and a narrow bunk bed in one of Meredith's son's rooms. Jack's nephew hadn't been too keen on sharing his room with Jack either, even though Jack would leave for college in two months. He was grateful to Meredith for taking him in, but it had never felt like anything but temporary. And he felt like a visitor that had stayed too long.

After struggling to get through fall and spring classes—and his profound grief—Jack decided to leave all of it behind to pursue acting. After getting some work doing commercials early that summer, he gave up on the degree, and moved to Los Angeles where he waited tables, worked as a lifeguard, and auditioned for anything and everything. Until he got a couple of small television roles. And then the callback for *SanFran Confidential.*

"Meredith took me in, Dad," he said. "Gave me a place to live until I left for Los Angeles. I'm twenty-six now," said Jack. "About to turn twenty-seven soon."

His dad's expression turned to shock. "Have I been dead for almost a decade now?"

Jack nodded as Dad laid his hand against Jack's face. "Are you and your sisters happy, son?"

A sigh slipped through Jack's teeth. "My sisters stopped talking to me when my flake habit hit the news."

Dad winced, shaking his head. "Oh, Jack—no..."

"But Dad," Jack added quickly. "Talia is the love of my life. I wanted you to meet her. She's the most amazing thing in my life."

Dad's voice got quiet. "But she's an angel, Jack. If you're not dead, how is it that you have wings and a halo, son? Without being an angel, too? Are you telling me the truth?"

He had a lot of explanation ahead of him, trying to explain all of this to his dad.

"Yes, of course, I am! But it's a long story, Dad," he said and launched into the explanation about *The Cinderella Hour* and the wagers and Talia falling from Heaven into his arms.

Dad frowned. "So, you started seeing angels around you? Just like that? Like special effects in a movie?"

Jack nodded. "Because of the bond between me and Talia," he said with a sigh. "And because her rare angel powers became mirrored in me, Lucifer was hunting both of us."

"Lucifer?" said his dad, shaking his head. "As in Satan? Prince of Darkness."

"That's the dude," said Jack. "Has terrible taste in music though."

"What? How so?" Dad asked, squinting at him.

"Prefers the original Sympathy for the Devil to the live version."

"No way. The original?" Dad's eyes were wide.

"Yeah, I know, right?" Jack said with a shrug. "Tried to tell him. I think he's warming up to the live version though."

"Wait a moment," said his dad, eyebrows pressing into a frown. "The Devil was hunting you, Jack? Why?"

Jack told him about Lucifer trying to claim his soul after the lost wager and then about his sacrifice to save Talia. And finally, how he'd tricked Lucifer and escaped Hell. And how Heaven gave him wings and a halo to hide him from Lucifer.

"You've been to Hell, Jack?" The look on Dad's face was dire, fear shining in his light green eyes.

Reluctantly, Jack nodded. "I hope you don't think I earned a trip there. Because I didn't."

"And you've been to Heaven?" Dad's eyes were wide as he stared at Jack in disbelief.

"Several times," said Jack as Talia gripped his hand. "Fought beside Talia and her death angel guard when Lucifer marched on Heaven. Helped the angels defeat him and send him back to Hell—where he's currently trapped right now. But he's turned one of Heaven's archangels of death and the dude's hiding in Purgatory with a rare book that can't fall into Lucifer's hands. That's why we're here." He sighed. "And I came to uh…to uh, see—you."

Once more, his dad clasped him against his chest in a long, warm bear hug that left Jack fighting back tears and shaking again.

Finally, his dad let him go, his gaze falling onto Talia. Smiling, Dad stepped toward her and gripped both of her hands in his large, squared hands.

"Talia, is it?" said Dad with a warmth in his voice, a smile still lighting his face.

Talia nodded.

"It was no easy feat to turn Jack's head, Talia," said his dad as Talia's smile became a grin. "Much less turn it away from acting and toward marriage. Don't get me wrong. He loved the girls, but never enough to give up his love for acting. You must have had an incredible effect on him."

"She saved my soul and she saved my life," said Jack, moving beside Talia whose gaze turned toward him. "And I never want to be apart from her. So, if that means giving up acting, I'll do it. She's my life, Dad."

Talia's eyes glistened and turned glassy as she bit her lip.

When Dad let go of her hands, Jack reached out and took her right hand in his, gripping it.

"That speaks volumes, son," said Dad as he bowed his head. "But I'd always hoped that you'd carry on the Casey name. Have a son, a namesake."

Talia's smile faded and he saw the look on her face. Like his dad had rejected her because she couldn't have kids, but Jack had never even thought about having kids. With Dad's addiction issues showing up in him, he hadn't wanted to bring kids into the world with the possibility of his passing down those tendencies, too.

"I didn't want to pass down my addiction issues to kids, Dad," said Jack as his gaze met Talia's and he gave her a reassuring nod. "So, instead of kids, I'm hoping for a star on the Hollywood Walk of Fame, Dad," said Jack. "And letting my body of work be my legacy and namesake."

Through a teary gaze, Talia smiled at him.

"I understand, Jack," said his dad. "My greatest fear was passing my proclivity toward addiction to you." Dad sighed. "And the look on your face tells me that weakness almost destroyed you. Guess my three older brothers will carry our name forward."

Jack studied his dad who leaned against the wall of the cabin, looking tired and a little lost now. Like he didn't belong in that cabin —or that time and place—anymore. No, he definitely didn't look like a man trapped in Purgatory.

And now that he knew about Jack's life, he hadn't made a move to leave this place. Because he was still waiting for something.

Waiting for Mother, he realized. That was his last bit of unfinished business.

"Dad, why are you still here?" Jack demanded, stepping toward his dad again. "You're waiting for Mother, aren't you? After all this time."

His dad turned away toward the cabin's picture window and with his back turned, he watched the clouds roll across the stormy horizon and past Haro Strait's mirror-calm as Bob Seger's *Against the Wind* began to play in the background.

That was his and Mother's song. They met at a party and were instantly attracted to each other, danced together all night, and made out in the backseat of Dad's 1969 Firebird convertible. A year later, they were married after Mother found out she was pregnant with Meredith.

Against the Wind turned out to be their theme song because their entire relationship had been like running against the wind. All attraction and friction. No shelter from the constant opposing forces. Well, that, and Mellencamp's *Hurts So Good*.

"Admit it," Jack snapped. "You still love her. Even now."

Dad nodded, a heavy sigh rising above the chorus of *Against the Wind*. But there was more.

"And you're waiting here for one last glimpse of her. Before you face the angels, aren't you?"

Again, he nodded. "I've been avoiding these truths since I died, Jack. Until you arrived and reminded me. Now, there's one last thing I need to do before I can rise. This is my last chance to tell Nina how sorry I am about everything. And how grateful to her I am."

Jack squinted. "Grateful?"

At last, Dad turned around. "Grateful to her for sticking by me longer than anyone should have. It's time that she finally hears that from me." Dad laid his hands on Jack's shoulders. "And for giving me four daughters and my only son." He brushed his fingers through Jack's hair. "You went through so much, Jack. At ten years old, you were more the man of the house than I ever was. Always protecting me. Taking care of me. Especially when my cancer became terminal."

Jack pulled in a breath, nodding, the pain of those days rushing back to him. Nights sitting beside Dad's hospital bed, holding his hand, and telling him stories about the day's events. He'd embellish his sisters' brief phone calls from California with lots of stories and he told Dad how much they loved him in much longer tales.

When Dad couldn't remember Meredith and Whitney visiting, Jack told him stories about how his sisters in Indiana had sat with him. He made sure the ol' man knew *all* his kids had been calling and visiting. Tara and Jenna came out once. When they tried to get to

Indiana before he passed away, Dad had slipped quietly away while they were arranging flights.

"You always made sure I was comfortable, Jack," he said, laying his hand against Jack's face until Jack's eyes burned. "And you made sure to remind me when the girls called or visited, so I never forgot that all my kids loved me. You were the best son a man could have and I'll always be grateful to Nina for bringing you into my life. Never forget how much I love you, Jack."

Jack threw his arms around his dad, nodding against his shoulder. He couldn't speak. Couldn't find his voice to tell his dad how much he meant to him. He said the words, finally, but they were broken and so quiet he doubted his ol' man even heard them. Until Dad nodded at him.

"You say it with every action, son," he said and let Jack go. "Now, go live that life you dreamed of. The one you told me about so many times when I was in hospice. With the love of your life beside you, Jack. Never put anything above that love. That's the secret to staying together. I will see you much later. Somewhere far from this faded image of happier times. Long life, son until this road brings us together again."

One last time, Jack hugged his dad. Talia floated beside him a moment and then she reached out and hugged his dad.

Jack gripped Talia's hand and opened the cottage door.

"See you soon, Dad," said Jack, pausing in the threshold a moment.

But he didn't look back as *Against the Wind* continued to play. Talia tugged him outside and into the cinematic rush of steel grey clouds across the stormy skies and mirror-calm of Haro Strait.

Toward the glowing orange glow of a doorway that led back to the old amusement park and Talia's squad of death angels.

Talia slid her arms around his neck and gently kissed him as they paused in front of the glowing doorway.

"Are you all right, Jack?" she asked, staring into his eyes.

He twisted his mouth to hold back the pain of saying goodbye to his dad again and kept his pain in check as he nodded.

"It's just…hard to say goodbye to him all over again," he said in a tight voice that came out much softer than he'd anticipated.

Talia nodded. "I can't imagine how much that must hurt, but I'm so glad you got to spend a little time with him. And tell him how you feel."

He slid his arms around her waist, drawing her closer. "And I got to introduce him to the love of my life. My wife—something, I never thought I'd get to do."

He kissed her hard on the lips.

"I'm so glad I got to meet your dad," said Talia, stroking his hair. "Your mother was right though. You look just like him."

Talia's eyes widened and she glanced around the atmospheric landscape, apprehension shining in her eyes.

"What is it, babe?" he asked, frowning.

"Samael's on the move," she said in a dark voice. "With the Book of Secrets. We need to get back."

"Come on," he said, nodding toward the orange light. "Let's get back to your squad and make sure Kesien hasn't bludgeoned that rat bastard into oblivion with that book."

"Or Zanth hasn't wrapped them around a tree somewhere," Talia replied.

Jack cast one last look back at the cabin, knowing he wouldn't see his dad again for a very long time. Taking a deep breath, he sprinted toward the glowing orange doorway and Talia followed him into the rush of flame-like light that burned across the overlook.

Everything tilted for a moment and then the sky darkened as the old, creepy amusement park materialized around them again.

As he and Talia stepped into the middle of a hellacious argument between Kesien and Zanth.

19

AS SOON AS TALIA EMERGED FROM THE STRANGE CORNER OF PURGATORY where Jack's dad had hidden himself away, she and Jack stepped into the middle of a fierce argument. The dreary dusky landscape of the old carnival blurred against the abandoned city block around it as one of the cabanas burned with Holy fire.

Kesien, eyes grey flames, shouted at Zanth in a fierce voice. His charcoal grey wings were spread wide, halo spinning wildly as Muriel and Deemah tried to hold him back.

Tre looked terrified as he stood behind Zanth, a hand on her shoulder, but the archdemoness looked unaffected by Kesien's fury. She stood with arms crossed, eyes still glowing a soft red as she leaned a little toward him despite his volatile behavior and angry eyes.

"Whoa!" Jack shouted, wide-eyed as he glanced from Kesien to Zanth. "Dude—chill!"

Kesien lunged for the archdemoness.

Jack launched himself between Kesien and Zanth, arms out to keep them apart, but Kesien pushed with such force that he slammed Jack forward, right into Zanth, nearly knocking her and Jack both to the ground.

But Zanth pushed back with the totality of her archdemoness

powers, throwing Jack into Kesien, stunning him, and shoving both of them to the ground as silence settled over the decaying amusement park.

Kesien scrambled to his feet, teeth gritted, hands balled into fists, but Talia threw a Holy fire barrier in front of him as Muriel and Deemah tackled him to the ground again.

"Kesien!" Talia shouted. "Enough."

She repeated it in the Enochian tongue, the notes rolling off her tongue in rapid succession until the melody penetrated Kesien's fury and calmed him. What had set him off like that? She'd never seen the even-tempered death angel fly into a rage like that before.

Slowly, the fire began to cool in the tall angel of death's eyes, his irises returning to a calmer shade of grey, the white Holy fire dissipating.

Until Zanth laughed that bitter, condescending demonic laugh, eyes smoldering with superiority. Setting Kesien afire with wrath again.

His eyes burned white as he rose into the air, wings beating the dusky shadows, halo whining as it wobbled around his head, almost out of control. He gritted his teeth, white fire rolling across those usually kind grey eyes again as he moved toward Zanth.

Finally, Jack got to his feet and leaped onto Kesien's back, wrestling him to the ground. At six feet tall, Jack looked like a kid against Kesien's over six-foot-six frame.

This time, Jack's eyes were pale green flames as he turned his heated glare onto Zanth.

"Dammit, Zanth!" he shouted through gritted teeth, huffing for air. "What the hell did you say to him?"

Zanth propped her hands on her hips, smiling with that knowing, pompous expression that Talia despised. The archdemoness glanced at Kesien, looking almost bored, and then fixed Jack with her sultry, flirtatious stare.

Like she wanted to devour him. Setting Talia's annoyance factor off the charts.

She pondered whether or not to unleash Kesien on that smug

demon bitch when all of this was over. The only thing that kept her from it was the fact that she'd given Jack the chance of a lifetime to see his father again.

"I merely told your tall angel of death what his boss has been up to," she said with a casual shrug.

"*Former* boss," Kesien said with a snarl, Jack barely able to hold onto him as Muriel and Deemah struggled to hold Kesien back.

"Spill it, Zanth," Jack shouted and glared at Tre. "Or your soul hookup's temporary address in Purgatory becomes permanent."

Zanth's eyebrows pressed into a hard line. "What does that mean?"

"It means I drop him like yesterday's Hollywood scandal. And that door stays closed. You got me, Zanth?"

Zanth cast a bored look at Jack and rolled her eyes. She took hold of Tre's hand and nodded over her shoulder at Kesien.

"His boss has been working with Lucifer since Lucifer made his first wager with Azrael. And that includes the angels of death that were in his guard."

"No!" Kesien shouted. "We were working for Heaven. Crossing over our human charges. Protecting them from that darkness. Not working for Hell."

Zanth threw her head back and laughed, long black hair shimmering blue in the twilight. "He was using his guard to do Lucifer's bidding, angel of death. Why can you not accept that?"

"Because I am a soldier of the Light!" Kesien's voice ached this time as Jack held onto him with everything he had. "The Maker's angel to command. I have never done Lucifer's bidding. Ever!"

"Did you participate in Samael's early rituals?" Zanth asked.

Pain radiated across Kesien's face. In his eyes. Pinched his handsome face. He winced. "Not—after the first one."

Zanth clicked her tongue, shaking her head. "Those rituals set Lucifer's Phoenix shift into motion, my tall angel of death." Zanth gestured around her. "Everything Samael did was in support of Lucifer's plans to march on Heaven. To destroy every angel of death left standing and any archangel still loyal to the Light. And to make vulnerable every part of the Creation and destroy the angelic way of life."

"What does that mean?" Kesien cried, his voice imploring.

Like he'd finally seen the truth, but was pleading with Zanth to tell him it wasn't true.

Zanth sighed. "He used you. Every angel of death he could sway was a resource molded for Lucifer's use. Your squad was always under Lucifer's control. Now, Samael's final act is to present this Book of Secrets to his lord and master. To reap the rare powers that it holds through his fallen angels."

"No," Kesien said with a groan as he began to wilt, sinking to the ground in a heap of feathers and pulsing orange halo light. "No! Even my squad?"

Zanth gave him a deep, sweeping nod. "Oui. Reptev, Pharzus, and Lix—they were already Lucifer's agents."

Kesien shook his head. "No...even Lix?"

"Oui, my tall angel of death. Lix was their leader."

Kesien hung his head, cringing at every word that Zanth spoke. "But everything we did was to oppose Lucifer. To protect Baladon— the Heavens. And the Maker. Not to help Lucifer. I couldn't have helped Lucifer—I–I couldn't have." He shook his head, his voice barely above a whisper now. "I couldn't have helped him."

Deemah wrapped her arms around Kesien as Muriel laid her hand against his wings. Jack gripped his shoulders.

"Dude, you didn't know how twisted Samael had become," said Jack, rubbing Kesien's shoulder. "No one did. But you fought him, remember? Opposed him. Told him to shove it because you weren't playing by his script. Remember? If it hadn't been for you and Deemah, that flying dickhead, Raziel would have killed me with Holy fire. After Samael sacrificed me to Lucifer."

Kesien bowed his head, staring at the ground. "Deemah and I were mentored by Lix and Reptev. Pharzus was a legend among my guard, having gone up against one of Lucifer's Devourer of Angels and defeating it. He'd been teaching us the techniques to fight them. To fight the demons and the darkness." He smashed his hands into fists. "And Lix and Pharzus both tried to get us to join Samael's rituals."

"And you refused, Kesien," Deemah said in a comforting, soothing voice. "Remember? You told them it didn't feel right? Oh, they tried so hard and for so long to talk you into it, after that first ritual, but you said no, Kesien. You stood for the Light. You stood for the Maker—like you always have."

Jack nodded. "Yeah, dude. You tried to release me from capture, remember? And you walked away from Samael the moment you saw the darker side to his bullshit."

Talia blinked across the amusement park's chalky soil and stood in front of Kesien. She dropped down on her haunches, hands on his forearms.

"You were never part of the angels of death that went on strike either," Talia said in a soft voice. "Remember how they all stood around watching humans die and leaving them to stumble around and find their own way across the expanse? And the moment you walked away from Samael, you came to Eolowen to join Azrael's guard. And care for our human charges, not fuel some new game that Samael was playing."

At last, Kesien nodded. "You're right, Talia," he said, staring down at his feet. "I brought all the angels of death I thought I could save with me." He groaned, laying a hand against his face. "And they turned on me. On Azrael." He smashed his eyes closed. "On the finest death angel guard I've ever worked with. Destroying dozens and dozens of angels of death—sending their light to oblivion."

Jack slid his arm around Kesien's shoulders. "You couldn't have known, dude. They were shielding all that darkness from you on purpose. Hiding it like some pipe bomb they'd planted."

"But they were my squad," Kesien said with a moan, shaking his head. "It was my guard. I should have known. I should have felt their coming betrayal."

Already, Jack was fervently shaking his head again.

"Even if they hadn't joined Azrael's guard," Jack continued, staring at Kesien now. "They'd have still poured into Heaven alongside those demons to jailbreak Samael and steal that book from the archives—taking down lots of angels of death in the process. That part wouldn't have changed."

Kesien propped his hands on his hips and stared down at the ground. "Maybe not."

"No maybe about it, Kesien," said Jack, his tone sharp as he studied Zanth's expression and then turned back to Kesien. "Luci had probably been planning that little heist for years. When you were still a loyal member of Samael's guard. Probably when I still thought Rachel Daniels loved me and I was on top of the world playing Detective Davy Pierson." He sighed. "Back when I couldn't see angels and demons. Or past my raging addiction to flake."

"Jack's right, Kesien," said Deemah. "Lucifer probably had that whole exercise plotted out decades ago. And the stages he had to initiate to get his hands on the Book of Secrets."

Jack stepped away from Kesien, a mixture of anger and apprehension burning on his beautiful face.

"She's probably right," said Jack, pacing around Zanth. "Decades ago. Maybe even before I was born?" A curious smirk lit his face as he circled Zanth. "Regardless, all of his recent actions have been put in motion for a reason. Why is that? Zanth? Is all of this just Luci's clumsy attempt to break his halo tether? Or is it something more malevolent?"

Zanth was unusually quiet now. She fixed Jack with her gaze, but didn't respond.

"Because that's what everyone expects him to do," said Jack, his voice growing quiet. He held out his arms wide. "Everyone expects him to try and break his tether—even though he's behind a locked gate. And we all know that Luci is a master manipulator. But clumsy isn't a word I'd used to describe him. Calculating. Driven. Vindictive. But not clumsy."

Zanth's eyes narrowed and began to glow a deeper red. "What are you getting at?" she asked, as if he was rambling and making no sense.

But Jack was honing in on something that made the archdemoness uncomfortable because she kept shifting her weight and casting furtive glances at Jack as the discomfort on her face grew.

"And ever since we kicked him to the curb and saved Heaven," Jack continued as he paced around Zanth. "He's been herding me and Talia toward something. And trying to kill me." Jack whirled around and stared at Zanth, his nose almost touching the archdemoness' sculpted nose. "Because that's what everyone expects him to do."

Talia felt the air rush out of her chest.

She gripped Kesien's shoulder and weathered the shift until she could right her wings and let the air currents rush through her again.

Jack was right. All this time, Lucifer had appeared to do exactly what everyone expected of him after they'd tethered his halo to Hell.

While hiding his true goal.

Zanth had a peculiar expression now. Almost like she was proud of Jack for landing on this observation.

"He is after his freedom," said Zanth, but Jack was already shaking his head.

"No," Jack snapped. "He's after something more. Something bigger. With much higher stakes."

Zanth lifted an eyebrow. "With the Book of Secrets?"

Jack's expression was grim now as he nodded. "You tell me, Zanth," he said. "What else is in that book?"

The archdemoness shrugged. Either she had Jack's level of acting prowess, or she truly didn't know.

But Jack was right. What was Lucifer really after? And how much danger did his ambitions place on Heaven…and the Earth.

A rush of shadows shot across the dark skies above the amusement park and moved overhead through the soot grey clouds.

Wings!

Talia gritted her teeth. Angels of death.

Archangel Samael and the traitors from his former guard. Surging across the sky toward the sepulcher. Had Zanth led Talia and her squad into an ambush?

Jack's eyes narrowed, his green eyes like polished marble as he stood about two inches from Zanth's face.

"Were you the stopwatch, Zanth? Keeping us out of the way—just long enough for Samael to do whatever he came in here to do? 'Cause it wasn't to hide in Purgatory. What was he here to do, Zanth?"

The archdemoness stared at Jack, her smile condescending again. Had this all been a setup? Had Zanth counted on all of them buying into this made-up love story? To lure her and Jack inside here. Deep into Purgatory. Buying time for Lucifer?

Had Jack really been reunited with his dad? Or had it all been a cruel setup? To hurt him and then deliver all of Talia's squad—and finally Jack—into Lucifer's clutches?

The first red coil of demon light, almost imperceptible, swirled around them, hidden in the thick, shadowy mist that rolled across the ground. The mist lifted on a soft breeze, casting out tendrils that softly wrapped around Talia, Jack, and the squad in a diffuse red—and sparkly—haze until the mist enveloped the entire squad.

Concealing them.

"So, it's demon cone of silence time again?" Jack remarked as Zanth reached out to Jack, fingers brushing across his cheek.

In an obvious flirt that even Tre noticed. Tre's eyes narrowed and he scowled at Jack.

It unsettled Talia.

Zanth didn't even try to hide her attraction to Jack this time. And Talia had to fight down the rising tide of Holy fire that burned at her wing tips, wanting to obliterate the archdemoness for constantly hitting on her husband.

"I did not lure you into a trap, Jack Casey," she said in a rough but velvety alto voice, but her gaze was unblinking as it fixed Talia with an almost heartfelt stare. As if she'd heard Talia's thoughts.

"And that was really your father. No tricks."

Zanth's gaze shifted to Jack again as Talia watched his corded muscles and taut jaw line relax. He'd been thinking the same horrible thing. That his dad had been some demonic illusion.

"But I do not know what Lucifer plans. He has kept all of it to himself. But you are right. It is bigger than breaking his tether and it involves that book. And a fallen angel—here. In Purgatory. I do not know which one. Hiding here was merely pretext—as you have discerned." The archdemoness sighed.

Jack got very quiet as he stared around him at the landscape and then back at Zanth, a forlorn look on his face.

"He's going after that gate lock, too? Isn't he?"

"If I knew more, I would tell you." She took Tre's hand in hers again and a smile brightened her ashen face. "For reuniting me and my love."

"Jack," Talia replied, stepping forward. "Lucifer has no way to open those gates."

"Why not?" Jack asked. He looked perplexed by her statement and she needed him to understand why Abaddon had locked it.

"Because, Jack, Abaddon is still the keeper of Hell's gates as well as punisher of humanity's wicked in the end times," she explained and that response did little to quell the confusion shadowing his face.

"Isn't that three-headed Hellpoodle the keeper of the gates," Jack asked, frowning. "Whatsitsname…Cerberus. And his bro, Orthrus."

"No, they guard the gates, Jack, but they don't control them," said Talia, flexing her wings until they settled against her shoulders. "Abaddon is the keeper of those gates. After you convinced him to return to Heaven, he finally locked the gates to keep Lucifer inside—as the Maker had commanded him millennia ago. So, even if Lucifer breaks his tether, he can't leave Hell. And now, there are only two ways to open those gates."

Jack's brow furrowed. "Can't Aby just turn the key in the lock again and reopen it?"

Talia shook her head. "That key was a Heavenly seal. Now, only the Maker or the apocalypse can open those gates again, Jack," she said, gesturing toward the mountaintop.

"Oui, Jack Casey," said Zanth with a nod. "And God must destroy the Book of Creation to open the first seal, setting the apocalypse into motion."

Jack's face scrunched into a mixture of fear and confusion. "Destroy it?"

Talia nodded. "Don't worry, Jack, the Book of Creation is well-guarded by the seraphim in High House. Lucifer could never get to that Book and destroy it to set off the apocalypse."

"Then what's Luci up to, babe?" he asked in a pained voice, looking almost sick to his stomach.

"I wish I knew, Jack," said Talia in a soft voice. "But I do know that he could never get past the seraphim—or High House. Besides that, he'd have to destroy the other six seals. Not even the seal outside of Hell is within his reach."

Jack shook his head. "Wish I could say that was comforting," he said with a sigh. "Samael got past a lot of angels in High House to get out of angel prison. What's to stop Luci from forcing his way into High House—right to that creation book or whatever."

Zanth's gaze hardened and she looked past Talia. "Samael knows a great deal about what Lucifer is planning. That is why we must grab him now, before he finds a way around the seraphim and archangels at the sepulcher door. He is planning to slip past them somehow. We must be there to grab him. Before he and the book reach Lucifer."

And without another word, Zanth's condescending demon glare returned as the red mist fell away.

"I am afraid you will never have that answer," she sneered at Jack and taunted him with her statement, her tone a challenge. "Not from me. Human." Zanth practically spat the word human through her full red lips. "You have the human soul. Now, release me from this demon trap!"

Acting, Talia realized. She was acting! It was the first time Talia had seen Zanth react in this way. Telling them how to respond and avoid raising alarms.

That meant they were now being watched in Purgatory. By what or who, Talia didn't know. But she'd felt Samael pass overhead moments ago.

Was this fallen angel that Zanth mentioned watching and listening? Listening in Lucifer's name. Alongside Lucifer's demons.

"Roundel formation, squad! Around Jack—now!" Talia ordered. "Positions in the air. Now! We're going after Samael." She stared at Zanth a moment and motioned toward her. "And bring the demon and this confused soul we've captured. We'll sort him out later—after we've dealt with Lucifer's archdemoness."

Jack stared at Talia a moment, a twinkle lighting those sexy, light green eyes.

"I haven't bashed any demons for a good hour or so," he said with a smirk. "Can't wait to piñata them and Zanth all over Purgatory."

Zanth's gaze caught hers and held it a moment. Her smile became a brief grin and she offered Talia a small, decisive nod.

"I look forward to your trying, Jack Casey," she said with a laugh.

Jack smiled, spreading his wings, and helped Deemah drag Kesien to his feet. With Muriel on one side, Jack on the other, and Deemah behind him, the squad shot into the air. Jack floated in the center as Talia leaped into the air, wings extended. Talia cast a glow of Holy fire near Zanth, surrounding her with a ring of white fire as the archdemoness' black wings thumped the air, Tre Sheridan in her arms.

As a unit, they surged away from the old, frightening amusement park, giving the illusion that they had Zanth and Tre trapped with Holy fire. They darted across the shadowy landscape, beneath the rolling dark clouds.

Toward the sepulcher door. Hot on Samael's trail—and the Book of Secrets.

20

Squinting, Jack glanced around the creepy amusement park with its ashen soil, shadowy movements, and cinematic storm clouds rushing past overhead. He felt something dark and heavy hanging over this place now.

And evil. In that massive horde-of-demons kind of way, like he'd felt the first time he woke up in Hell.

Something dark and menacing had rolled up on them and revealed itself after that flying dickhead traitor, Samael passed overhead with his contingent of winged douchebags.

And even more unsettling was the strange interchange that he'd watched between Zanth and Talia, with Zanth suddenly trash-talking angels and acting like she had back on San Juan Island. When she was trying to kill him and Talia on their honeymoon.

Zanth had turned on an abrupt but expert dark performance to satisfy something out in this wasteland. But what? Was Lucifer suddenly riding around in her head again? Or were herds of Luci's demons watching her every move? Or maybe that fallen angel that Zanth had mentioned?

And he'd watched something unsaid pass between Zanth and Talia. He'd felt it rush through the bond he shared with Talia, but through ethereal channels that he couldn't subscribe to as a human. Those damned angel notes again. Joined by a dark but delicate harmony in a minor key from Zanth. But he had no idea what they'd said to one another.

Regardless, he didn't have time to consider much beyond that because a big force of death angels, Kesien's former guard, swooped out of the dusky shadows on top of the squad.

Holy fire flashed like lightning and ripped through the charged air like tracer bullets as the bad guy angels of death surrounded them in a show of angelic force. The force of Holy fire they'd gathered struck like a hailstorm and burned through the twilight like laser blasts and pyrotechnics that would have even impressed George Lucas.

Deemah shrieked, wing feathers catching fire as she dropped out of the sky, careening toward the ground. She hit with a dull thump against the ashen soil.

Acrid smoke hung in the air, engulfing the squad from the sharp, charred smell of angel wing feathers, crackle of flames like tin foil. The sound grew louder until it pounded the dusky landscape like hailstones pounding metal, the heat thrumming against Jack's face.

He glanced back at the flicker of light behind him, the burning scent intensifying.

His wings were on fire!

He catapulted out of formation and hit the misty ground hard, rolling until the flames disappeared. Already, the intense burning pain radiated across his back and shoulders, throbbing into his wing tips as he moved beside Deemah.

Like a bad neighborhood in L.A., the force of angels of death surrounded him and Deemah, who looked unnerved.

"Jack!" Talia shouted, fear in her voice.

Jack smirked at Deemah and lifted his arms into the air. "They're messing with the wrong angels. About time we showed them that."

Deemah nodded and raised her shield of Holy fire as Jack spread his arms wide and summoned a burst of seraphim powers in both hands.

The white light pulsated around him, churning into a halo of light that spun around him like a spotlight. He snapped his arms toward the ground, releasing the burst of seraphim power.

The energy waves radiated outward in an expanding circle of light that popped like a bass drum as it surged across the ashen soil in a glowing blue wave. Dropping the force of death angels to their knees, hands against their ears as they writhed against the sound.

He blinked out of the circle, appearing behind Kesien's former guard, and summoned another wave of Holy fire. It cascaded over the surprised angels of death in a shockwave of light and seraphim retribution. Knocking them face-first into the ashen soul, wings splayed, halos crooked.

The beating of wings churned overhead.

Jack looked up.

Samael, dark wings extended, flew over him.

Something dark and heavy was in his arms as the archangel leaped into the air and took flight. Trying to make a break for it.

"Don't let that dickhead escape!" Jack shouted, jumping into the air.

He vaulted over the other angels and somersaulted toward the fleeing archangel that sailed past him, wings flexed wide to catch as much air as he could. He let the force of the wind propel him toward Samael, gaining on him as Talia and Kesien blinked into the air beside Jack.

Jack flung seraphim energy across the sky and behind him, into a shield that protected Talia and her squad as they rushed after Samael. Leaving all the dude's poorly trained minions behind.

They had to herd Samael into Azrael's—and the seraphim's—arms. And spring the trap.

Samael's halo flickered a rusty gold and Jack kept it in his sights as the archangel dove through clouds and spiraled into shadows, trying to shake off the squad. But Kesien followed Samael and his former guard with a bloodhound's senses and a hunter's tenacity, a determined glow in those grey angel of death eyes, wings stretched wide.

Kesien wouldn't let Samael escape this time. Not after the dude had obliterated all those angels. Not after all the havoc that bastard had caused. Jack knew that Kesien wouldn't rest until Samael had been brought to justice.

The mountain plateau rushed past on the right and the old, decaying city slipped into the shadows on their left as shadows gathered like flood waters across the ground.

Kesien's speed increased.

Talia fought to keep pace with the tall angel of death as Jack kept a steady stream of seraphim powers at his fingertips to light her way toward the looming darkness of the sepulcher door ahead.

He felt Zanth behind him, carrying Tre as she struggled to keep pace with the angels. The archdemoness had wings like the assassin demons, but none of them was built for speed like Talia and her angel of death guard. But Jack still felt Zanth behind him and knew that she would follow, making it look like she had been captured and wrapped in Holy fire.

Only in the chaos of a brawl with Samael could he open that door long enough for Zanth and Tre to escape. While keeping Samael and his traitorous guard in Azrael's snare.

The sepulcher door gleamed with a pale burst of light in the twilight as shadows encroached, growing tighter and thicker around them.

Samael's speed increased and he suddenly darted ahead of his guard. Toward the sepulcher doorway.

Where Azrael and the seraphim waited on the other side for this rat bastard.

Jack smiled and beat his wings faster, trying to keep pace with Samael, hoping to push him headlong into Heaven's ambush. Where the archangel could take him down hard.

Jack dipped the trailing edge of his wings as he felt Talia's presence warm the air beside him like a quilt fresh from the dryer. Muriel was at her left shoulder, Kesien a steel-edged, determined presence to Jack's right, Deemah at Kesien's right elbow.

Just a little closer…

But the screeching sound startled him.

He looked up.

As brimstone and Hellfire rained down from the shadowy storm clouds. But they weren't clouds.

It was a storm of Hell creatures! They'd been ambushed!

Assassin demons and shadowy energies filled the sky, bat wings thumping the air, shrill chittering making his skin crawl.

And dusk became night, engulfing them in darkness, red eyes, and demon claws as sharp as scythes.

Startled, Zanth stared up at the sky, a look of surprise on her face. And this time, she wasn't acting. Tre looked terrified as he huddled closer to Zanth

Jack swiveled around, both hands raised and filling with murder marbles.

"Welcome to the party!" he shouted. "Here's some beads for this Mardi Gras, bitches!"

He flung the murder marbles like strings of beads that set the sky aflame, dropping assassin demons out of the sky.

Demons hit the ground and rolled, turning to smoke.

Talia brandished a flaming sword of Holy fire as her squad turned, lifting glowing shields of light into the growing darkness as the sepulcher door began to tremble and shake behind them.

21

TALIA WHIRLED AROUND IN MID-AIR, WINGS SPREAD WIDE AS DEMONS exploded around her and the squad, materializing above and below them. Assassin demons by the hundreds, leathery bat wings beating the dusky air screeched past in a blur of smoky black shadows.

She and the squad landed between Samael and the sepulcher door. Blocking his path. Samael couldn't open that door. Why had he even approached it?

He held up the Book to the door, the gem sockets glowing brightly and thrumming together in a pulsing pattern that ran across the cover. Except for the empty center socket. She squinted at the Book with its dark center and gasped.

There were two empty sockets on the front of the Book, not just one.

"Lucifer!" Samael shouted and kicked the door. "Get me out of here! I couldn't get the gem—but I made a deal!"

What gem fit that lower empty socket? A new, rare angel power? One that even Pravuil was unaware of?

And with Lucifer's powers restored, could he now awaken rare angel powers? That thought terrified Talia. Could he awaken

Vassago's power from the fallen angel's story gem and use that forced possession power on her again?

Or Jack?

The archangel looked terrified as he pounded the door with his fist, wild soot grey eyes wide, white hair flowing like a lion's mane at his shoulders as he backed away from her and her squad, clutching the Book to his chest.

What did he mean about not getting the gem? But making a deal?

She remembered when Raziel removed Vassago's story gem from the Book, to keep her from learning about the rare power that the blinded fallen angel would soon use on her. But Pravuil had switched it. And the actual stone had never been returned to the Book's cover. She had no idea there was another empty socket below the first one.

Was that why Samael and his guard attacked Pravuil and the archive? Not only to steal the Book, but to get hold of Vassago's real story gem to find and awaken his rare angel power? Or socket another gem that she hadn't seen before. One that had been housed in High House or the archive?

Regardless, he was a traitorous, murdering monster and she wanted him to pay for extinguishing the lights of so many angels of death. And for selling out to Lucifer.

Her eyes filled with Holy fire as she blinked toward him.

The sepulcher door bumped against Samael's wings and back, startling the archangel.

He'd run out of space.

He cradled the Book of Secrets against his chest, halo spinning in a wild, rusty gold dance above his head. His worried gaze shot past her at Zanth. Like he expected her to either open the door or incinerate Talia and her squad at his command.

Why would Samael betray Heaven's angels of death like this? Much less the Maker? Had he bought into Lucifer's skewed stories? Did he see Lucifer and the other fallen angels as the victims instead of the aggressors?

What could Lucifer have possibly promised an archangel of death to sway him away from the light like this?

"Finish them!" Samael ordered, his grey eyes brightening like hearth embers as he glowered at Zanth and motioned toward Talia and her squad. "But the bounty on the human is mine!"

Jack shook his head, scoffing at Samael. "Dude, seriously? You're calling dibs? Hate to break it to you, but you're gonna need *another* army to drag my ass back to Hell."

Samael's eyes burned with outrage as he glanced at Jack and then Zanth.

"You dare order me around, you pathetic backstabbing angel of death?" Zanth's velvety alto voice was a feral growl. "I will burn you into a pile of ash. And the only way you will collect Jack Casey's bounty is by capturing him and delivering him yourself."

Samael slowly shook his head. "Now, now," he said in a condescending tone that set Zanth's eyes burning white hot. "What would Lucifer say? You're supposed to treat me like royalty, remember?"

Zanth turned and slammed him with a burst of demonic injury that singed his hair and grey robes.

"Royalty?" She glowered at him. "I will. Like they were treated during the French Revolution. And what would Lucifer say?" She propped one hand on her hip. "He would thank me as I hand him that book. With your hands still attached to it."

The archangel shifted away from Zanth as Talia moved toward him.

"You're about to be the sorriest archangel in Heaven, Samael," said Talia as she blinked toward him.

Zanth cast bursts of demonic energy over her head and tossed them at Jack and the squad, the dark force barely missing them. Talia knew how much precision it had taken for Zanth to miss like that.

That's when Talia realized that Zanth had been telling the truth. That she and Tre Sheridan really did want to disappear together and leave Lucifer's army behind.

Jack blinked with seraphim precision past Zanth and slammed Samael against the vibrating sepulcher door, Kesien blinking right behind him.

"And the flattest," Jack snapped. "When I smash you against this wall like a mosquito, you murdering bastard."

"Try it," Samael snarled. "Human. As soon as Lucifer gets hold of you, you're done."

"Done?" Jack said with a chuckle. "Dude, I'm just getting this party started. And with seraphim powers, I can match Luci blow for blow."

Jack's fingers lit with seraphim light, but Kesien interrupted.

The tall, curly-haired angel of death grabbed Samael by the throat, lifting him into the air as Jack reached for the Book of Secrets tucked under Samael's arm.

Stars and galaxies floated across the Book's cover, the five gemstones glowing like spotlights in Purgatory's dusky mist. The empty sockets in the center gleamed with a pale white glimmer.

"But I get first shot at you, Samael," Kesien said, fixing the frightened archangel with his granite grey glare as he gripped Samael's robes in his fists. "And I plan to extinguish the last breath of the Maker's light from your eyes, traitor!" Kesien shouted and gritted his teeth, his eyes burning white with Holy fire. "You've earned oblivion."

Kesien shook Samael hard enough that the archangel nearly dropped the Book of Secrets, but he fought against Jack trying to wrest it away from his grasp.

Again, Jack reached for it, but Kesien swung Samael around and slammed him against the sepulcher door.

"After you atone for all the angelic beings that you extinguished from Heaven during your little rebellion. Monster!"

A massive force of demons materialized out of the dark Purgatory skies and dropped on top of them. They grabbed hold of Jack and Kesien, dragging them off the archangel as Samael skittered backward, still clutching the Book.

In an instant, Talia and the squad were overwhelmed and surrounded on all sides by demons.

Talia blinked toward Jack as he tossed murder marbles in a circle around him and Kesien, mowing down rows of red, leathery-skinned demons and shadow panthers.

Behind her and Zanth, Deemah, and Muriel bashed dozens more demons as they made their way toward Samael and the sepulcher door.

Talia cut down dozens more with her guttering sword of Holy fire and cleared a path for them.

But more and more demons appeared around them.

Deemah cried out, her arm bleeding gold light as assassin demons materialized around her in panther form. They slashed at her arms and wrists with sharp claws.

She struggled to maintain her hold on her shield until Muriel pushed through the pack of panthers and bashed them away. They turned to smoke and disappeared into Purgatory's foggy landscape.

Muriel backed toward the sepulcher door, pulling Deemah alongside her as Talia blinked in front of them, thrusting out her sword and cutting through the line of demons.

She held back the massing forces, but more moved over the horizon toward them. She backed toward the sepulcher door. It wouldn't be long before they overwhelmed her and the squad.

"There's too many!" Muriel shouted.

Jack rolled into the center of the next wave of demonic swarms and slammed a basketball-sized orb of Holy fire against the ashen soil. It exploded around him, halos of light writhing over the squad from the shockwaves.

Obliterating the huge force.

Until the sky turned black again.

"Kesien, the Book!" Talia shouted over her shoulder.

Nodding, the tall, curly-haired angel of death grabbed hold of the Book, still in Samael's hands, as he tightened his grip around the archangel's throat.

"You're done, Samael," said Kesien.

But something massive and monstrous dropped out of the sky on top of him. Towering, heavy, corpulent, and red. Screeching with a hideous gaping maw.

A Devourer of Angels!

Kesien skittered backward as it clawed at his wings, grabbing hold of his leg. It latched onto Samael's wing and he howled, barely holding onto the Book as it dragged him toward it.

"Not me, you idiot! The other angels!" Samael shouted, struggling. "Let go!"

Like smoke, Zanth stepped behind Samael, blocking his path.

"Going somewhere? Archangel?" she asked with a smile, those full red lips looking hungry as she crossed her arms. "I can't wait to watch it eat you and spit out your wing feathers."

"You'd dare double-cross your lord and master?" Samael sputtered, trying to free himself from the Devourer. "Lucifer will flay the skin off your back! Make it let me go!"

"I answer to no one but me, Samael," she said with a growl. "You should have figured that out sooner. A pity."

She shoved him forward as the Devourer wrapped a tentacle tighter around the archangel's wings. The archangel screamed as the greater demon dragged him toward its massive, mouth and all those sharp, pointy teeth.

Zanth laughed and turned toward Talia. "Don't worry," she said in a bright voice. "It won't eat your Book. Just the archangel."

Deemah and Muriel rushed the Devourer, slamming it with their shields of light as they tried to free Kesien, but it shot out tentacled arms, wrapping them both in its grasp.

Dragging them toward its massive, gaping maw.

"No!" Talia blinked toward it. "Stop it! Release them!"

Zanth turned, glaring, and lifted both hands into the air. Summoning smoky darkness. She threw the writhing energies at the tentacles gripping Kesien, Deemah, and Muriel. Leaving Samael to fight his own way out.

Talia leaped into the air, sword raised, and launched herself at the Devourer of Angels. Stabbing it in the chest with her sword of Holy fire.

But it grabbed hold of her, pulling her into range of its huge mouth. Ahead of Samael.

Kesien was only inches from its fanged mouth, Talia right beside him. With Samael next to be devoured.

"Talia!" Jack screamed.

Jack blinked past the demons. And grabbed hold of the sepulcher door as it shook and trembled.

He slammed his shoulder against the door and rocked it open. Thunder made the ground tremble as angels of death and seraphim light poured through the doorway, Archangel Azrael leading the charge.

The sudden burst of seraphim light blinded the Devourer of Angels.

It shrieked, eyes smashing closed as tentacles and stringy arms flailed in front of its gaping mouth.

Jack blinked into the air, wings spread wide as he put himself between the Devourer's maw and her and Kesien.

"Jack, no!" Talia shouted.

The Devourer of Angels bit down hard on Jack's right wing.

Jack cried out. Struggling to stay in the air, he managed to stuff a dozen murder marbles into the Devourer's mouth before his right wing folded and he fell out of its grasp. Slamming against the ashen soil.

A heartbeat later, the Devourer of Angels exploded in a shower of red blubbery demon bits and a spray of scarlet goo as a barrage of death angels and cherubim flooded into Purgatory.

Engaging the demons.

Zanth glanced at the open door a moment and then glanced at Jack, Tre's hand locked in hers.

Jack waved her forward. "Go!" he shouted, wincing. "Hurry."

Zanth turned toward the doorway and ran toward it with Tre beside her. He ran through the threshold and she followed.

But stopped.

She turned, her glowing red eyes catching Talia's in a look of understanding. And thanks. But her gaze softened with concern as Talia dropped down beside Jack, still huddled on the ground, struggling against pain, the massive gash across his wing leaking blood and light.

"Zanth—go!" Jack yelled.

She glanced out the door at Tre and back again.

And then she turned to smoke.

When the archdemoness materialized beside her and Jack, Talia was startled.

"Zanth!" Jack cried, wincing as the sound of swords cracking against Eternean armor rang out above the guttering of Holy fire and demon screeches. "What are you doing? You and Tre get out of here!"

She bent down to him, shaking her head as she reached toward his bloody right wing.

"Not until you and your love are safe, Jack Casey," she said, a determined glint burning in those red eyes. "I concealed Tre in smoke outside Purgatory. He will be fine until this is over."

Jack smiled, clearly as impressed by the archdemoness' decision as Talia.

"I misjudged you, Zanth," said Talia, reaching out and touching the archdemoness' shoulder. "Thank you."

Zanth smiled and laid a hand against Talia's for a moment.

With Zanth's help, Talia got Jack on his feet and together, the three of them pounded down the force of demons as Azrael, with the distant burn of seraphim light, tore down the rest of the demon invasion until thousands and thousands of demon corpses littered the misty ground of Purgatory.

And everything was still again.

"By the Maker!" Kesien's anguished cry startled Talia and silenced Jack. "No! NO!"

Talia turned, her heart dropping as Samael and three angels of death, Kesien's former squad members, spiraled up into the tower. Away from the sepulcher.

Escaping. She winced. With the Book of Secrets.

And she and Kesien were too far away to stop him.

Azrael blinked past, Kesien beside him with three more archangels in pursuit. Others rushed into the tower ahead of them.

From the top of the tower, a flood of assassin demons descended through the tower's expanse. Filling it and the sepulcher with demons.

Buying Samael and his guard those last few precious moments to escape. With the Book of Secrets.

22

Surrounded by the dank sepulcher's heavy shadows, Jack leaned against Talia as they stood on the inside of Purgatory, staring up at the vertical rise of the temple tower overhead. He felt weak as blood and light ran down his right wing, soaking the shoulder of his navy blue hoodie and dripping onto his faded Levi's.

Talia and her squad looked shell-shocked, but he hurt too much to channel any fury at that flying dickhead getting away with the Book of Secrets. Judging by the despondent looks on Muriel's and Deemah's faces, he knew this was bad, even though he couldn't quite understand the gravity of the situation. Or how dangerous that book was in the wrong hands because he couldn't read it.

Talia always said that only angels with rare powers could read the book and he had no clue whether that included Lucifer or not. He'd never gotten a chance to ask.

Besides Talia, Berith was the only other angel in Heaven with rare powers—except Vassago, the blind fallen angel under close supervision in High House—that could read it. But both Talia and Berith had mentioned another fallen angel, still in Hell, that had rare angel powers.

Was that why Samael had taken the book to Lucifer? To let this other fallen angel awaken some new power that Heaven didn't know about?

Jack could only imagine what kind of terrible power it could be, but he also knew that Lucifer wouldn't have set any of this in motion if it didn't directly benefit him in some way. And inflict maximum suffering on humanity and the angels that stood with Heaven.

The thought made him shudder.

Kesien still raged over Samael's escape, ranting and pacing, wings unfurled, and Holy fire dripping from his eyes as his halo spun like a methed up drone huffing neon.

Deemah and Talia tried to calm him down, but he wanted to burn down the road to Hell and land some Old Testament whoop ass on Samael and the three death angels from his former guard. By himself. Before they reached the Gates of Hell.

Only moments ago, Jack had heard Azrael mention something to Talia about recalling Abaddon from his earthly walkabout to deal with Samael. It was just before the archangel had launched into those damned angel notes that Jack couldn't hear much less understand. He had no clue what Azrael hadn't wanted him to hear and he doubted Talia would tell him either.

He sighed and shoved his hands into his jeans' pockets, feeling his phone warm against his thigh. Whatever ended up in the angel tongue had always been off the table for discussion between them. At first, it felt like she was keeping secrets from him and it hurt. Took him awhile to get it through his thick skull that angel of death business was none of his business. So, he did his best to let it go.

Most of the time.

"Talia, get Jack and Kesien back to Eolowen," said Azrael, white flames of Holy fire burning around his shoulders, reflecting off his Eternean armor as he motioned her out the sepulcher door. "Make sure someone stays with Kesien at all times." The archangel's voice was low, but loud enough for Jack to hear him. "I don't want him going after Samael alone."

"I'll take care of it," said Talia as the seraphim light touched Purgatory, burning away the demon corpses.

Azrael squinted at Jack. "One loose cannon's enough to deal with."

"Why you looking at me?" Jack asked with a shrug of his left shoulder, his right one barely responding.

"Keep an eye on your husband, too, Talia—no theatrics or heroics."

"What about drama?" Jack asked.

Azrael glared at him.

Jack held up his hands. "Dude, it was a joke, okay?"

"Don't let this one or Kesien out of your sight," Azrael repeated in a sobering tone. "As my right hand, I'm counting on you while I help the seraphim and cherubim sort out this Purgatory mess."

Talia nodded and moved closer to Jack. "You have my word, archangel."

The archangel bent toward Jack, his voice soft as he cast an apprehensive glance toward Zanth's smoky outline near the door's threshold.

"And get that demon out of here before the seraphim see her and smite her into oblivion. And that soul attached to her."

Wide-eyed, Jack nodded.

Abruptly, the archangel turned back toward the guard that had swarmed across Purgatory's landscape. But he quickly turned back around.

"And thank her for me," he whispered, the hint of a smile in his grey eyes. "*After* you've closed that door."

"You got it," said Jack as Talia helped him toward the open sepulcher door.

He stopped in the threshold and didn't look back, not wanting to draw any attention to Zanth or Tre.

"Stay in your smoke form," said Jack in a quiet voice, not looking in her direction. "Follow us out of the sepulcher. We need to fly up and out of this tower with a boatload of cherubim and seraphim floating overhead. So, stay close and stay out of sight until we get through the Mortise of Souls. To the road. Got it?"

A velvety alto voice thrummed in his ear. "Got it, Jack Casey. When you and Talia are ready."

Muriel and Deemah held onto Kesien who kept arguing with them, trying to leap into the air and pursue Samael and his guard.

"Kesien," Talia snapped. "We follow him as a squad. Or not at all."

"But we're not going after him, remember?" Kesien replied in an acidic tone, grey eyes narrowing. "Azrael told us to return to Eolowen."

"Dude," said Jack, glancing back at the furious angel of death. "He didn't say when, did he? So, chill until we get out of here."

For a moment, Kesien stared at him in surprise. When the realization sank through his anger, he settled down and nodded.

Jack turned to Talia and held out his left arm. "Mrs. Casey? You ready to return to our honeymoon?"

She smiled and took hold of his arm, leaning over to kiss him. It was a long, steamy kiss.

"I'm going to need a little attention," he said with a smirk.

Her cheeks blushed. "Jack…"

He lifted up his right wing. "The wing, babe—the wing. Think you could get me to Berith after we locate Samael's trail?"

"Of course, lover," said Talia, laying her hand against his face.

"Then we can head back to Earth. Rehearsals for The Divine Newlyweds Show will be starting soon. We can stay in the set trailer until Gianni's realtor finds us a new place."

She caressed his cheek. "By the ocean, okay? I know how much that would mean to you, Jack. I want to watch the rest of my sunrises and sunsets with you on the beach."

He gave her an anxious kiss. "Honeymoon first. Happily ever after on the beach second. Roll credits. Sign me up."

She gripped his arm tighter as he glanced to his right, seeing Zanth and Tre's smoky outlines beside him now.

"Sign me and Tre up, too," said Zanth.

Talia rose into the air, supporting Jack as he stretched out his left wing, the right wing too painful to unfurl. Immediately, he listed left, his right wing hanging at his side. Then he felt Muriel at his right, sliding an arm around his waist, leveling him out.

"Easy there, Jack," she said. "We've got you."

"Thanks, Muriel," he said and smiled at her, making her blush.

"All right, squad," said Talia as she caught Jack's gaze, a twinkle in her arctic grey eyes. "Supremes formation. Around Jack."

Jack laughed. "I totally married the right woman."

"Indulging him is dangerous, Talia," said Muriel with a shake of her head. "Can't wait to hear you call that formation out in training."

"Neither can I," said Deemah. "That will make my day and it will confuse the daylights out of Azrael. Especially when the guard breaks into a chorus of Stop in the Name of Love."

"Just tell him it's Jack and he'll get it," said Muriel.

"Good point," said Deemah. "Do you think Azrael's eyes will get stuck in that eye roll?"

Muriel laughed when Jack shot a glare at them.

Kesien shot ahead of the squad as they rose out of the sepulcher and into the warm seraphim light engulfing the tower.

"Kesien, stay in formation," Talia called. "That's an order."

"I'm worried, Talia," said Muriel, nodding toward Kesien. "I've never seen Kesien so angry and reckless before."

Jack shook his head. "Or so laser-focused. He's not going to stop until he captures Samael and those three dudes from his former guard."

"Agreed," said Talia with a deep nod. "We need to keep a close eye on him. Can't let him walk into a demon trap trying to get Samael or the Book back."

"They will shred his wings from his body and obliterate him," said Zanth, her sultry voice rasping against the musical sounds of angel voices. "I am sorry, but Samael is already out of your reach."

That rat bastard couldn't have cleared the Mortise of Souls and gotten away clean so fast. Or to Hell yet. They still had time.

"He's not in Hell with that Book yet," said Jack as the squad rose out of the old, grey stone temple into misty, charcoal grey skies. "So, it ain't over yet."

The air smelled sweet, but smoky and still charged with brimstone. They flew through the steamy rainforest toward the road that led away from Purgatory, Kesien still out ahead of the squad. They flew toward the pocked stone walls of the Garden and Eolowen's glistening white facade.

Jack sighed. Toward Hell.

They soared above the treetops, the tall temple with its moss-covered grey stones fading into the mist as they flew over the deep scar in the ground that was the Mortise of Souls trench. In tight formation, they flew along the winding road ahead, hoping to pick up Samael's trail as the first wash of blue touched the sky.

Zanth carried Tre through the mist and above the forest below as the Mortise of Souls slipped away and disappeared in the cool greyness that brightened with a hint of turquoise. The road shot uphill and turned right toward a thick forest with massive trees bearing delicate red leaves, a sweet rain-scented smell clinging to the air.

Abruptly, the walls of the Garden loomed in the mist.

Jack shuddered at the sight of the stone walls still marred with scorch marks and holes, painful reminders of when he'd fought Lucifer while trapped inside its warded walls. And died.

"Take us to the haunted woods," said Zanth.

He felt Talia turn slightly left toward a wall of spindly, skeletal trees and misty indigo twilight that clung to the haunted woods. He set down beside Talia as they landed on the edge of the meandering ashen footpath that wound into the heart of those woods.

"We're here, Zanth," said Talia.

In a moment or two, the demon smoke dissipated, revealing Tre Sheridan's dark hair and lanky form as he gripped Zanth's hand tightly, his tailcoat fluttering. Smiling, Zanth turned to Jack and Talia, the squad standing behind them, on guard for demon attacks. Deemah kept her arm wrapped around Kesien's, keeping him from taking off.

Zanth stepped toward Jack and took both of his hands in hers, gripping them in her long, ashen fingers.

"Thank you, Jack Casey," she said. "You did not have to help me, but you did. And I thank you."

He nodded. "Happily ever afters are rare, Zanth," he said and held Talia close. "Hope you and Tre find yours. Like Talia and me."

Zanth leaned up and kissed Jack gently on the cheek. "I do not know what Lucifer is planning or I would tell you. But if you ever need my help again, go to the crossroads ahead and burn three things: an angel feather, a fallen angel feather, and the scale of a demon's wing. Only the intertwining of red, white, and black smoke will summon me, Jack Casey. But I will come and help you. I give you my word."

"Thanks, Zanth," said Jack as he leaned forward and kissed Zanth on the cheek. "Appreciate that."

"I wish you and Tre well, Zanth," said Talia. "Thank you for helping us. Oh, and Azrael told me to thank you. From him."

Zanth's red eyes sparked, a smile touching her full red lips. "Thank your archangel for me." She nodded down the path. "Now, go. Stop Samael if you can. Before he gives Lucifer the Book. I don't know what Lucifer intends to do with the Book, but you must stop him."

With a subdued expression, Tre glanced at Jack and then Talia. "Thank you both for saving me from the biggest mistake of my existence. I can't undo what I did, but thank you for reuniting me with Zanth. As long as we're together, I'll deal with the mess I created. So, thanks."

Jack nodded. "You're welcome, dude. Don't waste this chance. You may not get another one. Right, Mrs. Casey?"

"I was going to say that," said Talia with a playful smile. "But Jack's correct. Souls in Purgatory can still ascend—like Jack's father will ascend once he's faced his former wife again. And demons that turn toward the light can find a path back to redemption."

Dad would really ascend? Jack felt his eyes sting, a warmth filling his chest. Then it wasn't too late for his dad.

"He'll rise?" Jack asked in a tight voice. "Really?"

Talia nodded, her arm tightening around his. "He's atoning for past wrongs. It's part of the Maker's promise to humans, Jack."

He squinted, blinking back moisture as he focused on the horizon. Talia had confirmed what he'd been hoping. Dad would ascend. He would definitely see him again someday. Maybe then they could sit down together and he could tell his dad everything that had happened in his life—good and bad—with Talia beside him? More than just the quick highlights.

Tre leaned over and kissed Zanth in a long, lingering kiss and then, hand in hand, they turned to smoke and drifted into the haunted woods together. Disappearing into the indigo mist.

Someone gasped and tugged on his hoodie sleeve beneath his armor. He looked up at Talia's taut expression as she pointed at the sky.

In huge, black smoky letters filling the sky, the message read, "Too late, angels. See you in Hell. Samael."

Dammit! They were too late.

That flying dickhead and his douchebag entourage had escaped with the Book of Secrets. Jack felt a cold wind brush across him, dread heavy in the pit of his stomach. How hard was this going to bite them in the ass?

Kesien glared at the sky and screamed Samael's name down the empty road.

Jack already knew the answer though. The question now was what was Lucifer planning to do with this Book of Secrets? Or most importantly—what could he do with it?

And Jack dreaded the answer to those questions.

———

BACK AT EOLOWEN, the chaos had calmed, all the wounded had been treated. Including Anahera who was back on her feet and Pravuil who was up and moving around a lot better now. But deep-seated anger burned in the Scribe's gold eyes, a look that Jack hadn't seen there before. Alongside a worried expression. And that made Jack nervous.

Like the Scribe knew something he wasn't telling the rest of Heaven. Jack worried that it was about the Book of Secrets. Or the archive.

Jack leaned on his left elbow as he sat on the bed in the room off the terrace while Berith hovered over his wings, applying gold healing light to huge tears that Devourer had made. He'd already set his armor beside the bed, down to Levi's, Henley, hoodie—and his Vans.

"Another Devourer? Jack, when are you going to learn that you're not invincible?" Berith scolded him as she treated his wing.

"When I'm dead," he replied.

Talia shook her head violently and moved toward him through the powdery ribbons of sunlight filling the white room. The room smelled like cotton sheets fresh from the dryer.

"Oh, no you don't," she said. "Your dying privileges have been revoked, mister."

Azrael slipped through a portal in the roof and landed in the room, curtains on the doorway billowing. Jack glanced through the momentary opening, seeing Kesien leaning against the terrace wall, his face dark and brooding as he stared into the distance. Opposite him, Pravuil stared toward the spires, looking a little lost.

"What's up with the Scribe?" Jack asked.

Frowning, Azrael glanced through the fluttering curtains a moment and sighed.

"He's still troubled about the attack on the archive," said Azrael as he slid toward Berith and kissed her gently on the lips. "He lost several angels in that assault."

Jack shook his head. "I think it's more than that."

Azrael studied his face a moment. "Why do you say that, Jack?"

He winced when Berith started healing the deepest gouge in his wing. "Because, he's not mourning," said Jack. "Dude's really worried about something."

Once more, Azrael stared out through the white curtains and returned his gaze to Jack. "That's a very astute observation, Jack," said Azrael, looking surprised. "How did you—"

Jack tapped his temple with his left index finger. "Actor, remember? Facial expressions are my business. And that dude's face is full of dread. Like he—"

"Hasn't told us something," said Azrael in a worried tone as he finished Jack's sentence. "I think you're right, Jack."

Azrael craned his neck and sang out a series of angel notes that shook Pravuil out of his thoughts. God's Scribe glanced toward the curtains and then rose into the air, parting the curtains with both hands. Pravuil landed at the foot of the bed, staring at Azrael.

"Well, I'm here," said Pravuil, glancing from Jack to Berith to Azrael and finally Talia. "What's wrong?"

"I was about to ask you the same question," said Azrael.

God's Scribe shoved his hands into the pockets of his long white robes and floated in front of the bed.

"Worried about this situation with Samael," said Pravuil.

Jack shook his head. "Come on, Scribe, fess up," said Jack. "You're salty over something you're not telling us. What happened in the archive that you're not talking about?"

Pravuil's head snapped up and he glared at Jack. "Listen to me, you young upstart angel!" He pointed a finger. "My head's been ringing ever since that schmuck, Samael clobbered me, killed several of my angels, and ransacked the archive! I'm bloody angry and as upset as Kesien about Samael escaping with the Book of Secrets!"

He'd expected an angry backlash from God's Scribe. Because Pravuil knew something he wasn't ready to tell them yet. Calling him out would force him to spill whatever he was trying to hide.

"And the academy award for overacting to hide the truth goes to… Pravuil, God's Scribe," Jack replied, watching the archangel's face redden and those gold eyes narrow.

He rushed around the bed and got in Jack's face.

"Listen up, Jack Casey!" he shouted, wagging his finger at Jack. "I've already told this story a hundred times! Everyone knows what happened in the archive when Samael broke out of High House!"

Jack stared at him unblinking a moment. Dude was expecting him to buy that?

"And the academy award for using anger to mask some really bad news also goes to God's Scribe."

Pravuil's hands balled into fists. "Keep pushing, kid, and I'll add you to God's shit list."

"There's no such thing," said Talia, hands on her hips.

Pravuil frowned. "Then I'll start one. Every slot filled with Jack Casey's name."

Jack laughed, but Pravuil was making him nervous. Dude was trying so hard to hide something. Why? It might help them figure out what Samael and Lucifer were up to with that book.

"Come on, Scribe," Jack said with an exasperated sigh. "We already know that Samael got the Book. What else did he take? From the archive?"

Azrael's expression turned fearful, his face pale. "Pravuil? Is Jack right? What haven't you told us about the attack on the archive?"

Visibly flustered, Pravuil's face beamed bright red as he flung his arms out and darted toward the curtains. But Berith blinked in front of him, blocking the way out.

"Pravuil..." she said in a quiet voice. "Please. We need to know."

Pravuil whirled around and pointed at Jack. "You've got an annoying habit of being right, Jack. You know that?"

Jack couldn't hold in his smile. For a moment, it annoyed Pravuil, but he came back into the room as Berith flitted ahead of him. She returned to healing Jack's wing as the Scribe stood at the foot of the bed.

"What are you saying, Pravuil?" Azrael asked, sliding around the bed to meet the Scribe.

Sighing, God's Scribe hung his head. "Samael and his guard didn't just take the Book of Secrets. They wanted the gem I removed from the Book to trick that putz, Raziel. Ransacked the place trying to find it."

"Which gem?" Talia asked, looking alarmed.

"Vassago's," said Pravuil with a shake of his head.

"What?" Azrael looked alarmed.

Pravuil ran long, thin fingers through his short white hair and stared at the floor a moment. "Yes, Vassago's gem." He cringed. "I captured his story and rare power in a gem for the archive. But... there's one other gem, too. And another empty socket."

Talia moved toward him. "What other gem and socket?" she demanded. "I saw the Book up close many times. I held it in my hands, reading it, studying it. There was only one empty socket. Not two, Scribe."

Already, Pravuil was shaking his head, looking sheepish. "I hid the other socket, too, Talia. I had to! I didn't want anyone—especially Lucifer—to know about this newly discovered gem. And the rare power associated with it."

"Pravuil!" Azrael snapped, anger warming his eyes to embers. "What rare power?"

"The power of transference," said God's Scribe at last.

Talia shook her head. "Transference? What does that power do?" she asked.

"Botisa the Fallen discovered it millennia ago," said Pravuil. "Her rare power is transforming things—not people—and moving them somewhere else. I have no idea why Samael would have been after that gem any more than I'd know why Lucifer would bother with transference over resurrect or omnificence."

"Dude, because he's tethered to Hell," said Jack. "It'd be like an angel delivery service for him. He could transfer whatever he wanted directly to Hell."

"Hell is a barrier that would stop most of those transfers, Jack," said Azrael. "It would be very limited in Hell. Like the powers in that Book. They're all Heavenly powers, requiring Heavenly essences to awaken them."

Then what did Lucifer plan to transfer to Hell? He had no clue. And how could he awaken any of those powers in the Book when he needed items only found in the Heavens?

He bit back a groan as Berith shifted her healing light farther down the long, jagged gash that had nearly bisected his wing.

"Then we need to figure out what he's planning to transfer and where," said Jack, glancing around the room. "And fast. Before Luci manages it somehow."

Pravuil shook his head. "Good thing Samael and his filth didn't get hold of the stone, thank the Maker. I made sure of it." He turned toward Talia and motioned. "But maybe Talia can awaken that power? Or Berith?"

"How, Scribe?" Talia asked, holding out her hands. "The Book is gone."

At last, the expression on God's Scribe's face lightened. "But I have the gem and we have a blank book as a reader. Enough for you, Talia to awaken this power."

But the expression on Talia's face darkened, a worried look shining in her big grey eyes.

"Scribe, I remember Samael saying he didn't get the gem," said Talia. "Inside Purgatory."

God's Scribe nodded. "Not on my watch, he didn't."

"But I distinctly heard Samael say that he made a deal."

"A deal?" Azrael cried, rushing toward Talia. He took Talia by the shoulders. "Talia, what deal? Tell me everything you heard."

She shook her head. "That's it, sir," she said. "All I heard him say was that he made a deal."

Jack got to his feet, but Berith held him back, still healing the last part of the long, deep gashes on his wing.

"Who could Samael have made a deal with in Purgatory?" he asked.

"Asmodeus," said Berith as she tugged Jack back toward the bed.

A deadly silence hung in the room and Jack saw the concern on their quiet, brooding faces turn to fear.

"Like the composer or something?" Jack asked, but Berith was already shaking her head.

"No, Jack," said Berith. "An archdemon so evil that Lucifer kicked him out of Hell. Locked him away in Purgatory. Banished him there."

"Wow," Jack said with a whistle. "So evil that Luci kicked him out of the clubhouse?"

Talia moved closer to him, fear shining in her eyes. "Zanth's replacement?"

A chill brushed across his heart. Talia was right.

"Holy shit, Tal—you're right. So, Luci's gathering up the meanest demon in existence and a new rare power of transference. Please tell me it's not for the biggest bash Hell's ever thrown."

"Archdemon, Jack," said Berith and Pravuil nodded.

"And it will be Hell's biggest bash, Jack," said Pravuil. "If Lucifer manages to break his tether and get past Hell's gates."

Azrael floated into the air. "And he'll set his sights on destroying the Maker's Creation if he gets free. Mark my words. Excuse me, I need to assemble every soldier in the Heavens into a fighting force ready to act on the seraphim's orders. In case Lucifer succeeds. Talia, ready your squad. In case the call goes out."

Talia nodded. "Yes sir."

With a flutter of soot grey wings, Azrael ascended through a portal in the ceiling as tenor angel notes rolled off his tongue in a somber melody that sounded more like a requiem than a call to action. Jack felt his stomach drop, remembering when Lucifer decided to march on the Heavens.

War with Hell was on the horizon again. But as long as Lucifer was still tethered, there was hope of stopping it.

"What does all that mean?" Jack asked, turning to Talia. "Setting his sights on the Maker's Creation?"

Talia ran her fingers through his bangs. "It means that Lucifer will target your world and every one of the Maker's Chosen, Jack. Especially you."

"All we can hope is that he stays tethered in Hell then," said Jack. "And that the gates to Hell stay locked."

She nodded, but he saw the fear shining in her arctic grey eyes.

Berith patted his right forearm. "There, Jack," she said, smiling at him. "Your wing should be completely healed within the week, but it's sturdy enough to fly again. Should get you back to Earth."

"Thanks, Berith," he said and hugged her.

Pravuil turned toward the curtains again. "I'm going back to the archive. To dust off a reader and retrieve the transference stone from where I hid it. As soon as it's ready, I'll call you back to Heaven, Talia. With the Book of Secrets in Samael's hands, I'd feel safer if you and Berith awakened this rare power for the light."

"As soon as you're ready," said Talia. "I'll come to the archive and study the story of this new power."

Berith moved beside Talia. "And so will I, Scribe," Berith added. "Anything to circumvent Lucifer's plans."

The Scribe nodded and started through the curtains, but paused, his back still turned.

"My one comfort is that all of the pieces needed to awaken the powers in that Book are mostly found in Heaven," said Pravuil. "Where Lucifer can't reach them." His yellow eyes narrowed. "Or get through the Gates of Hell."

"Couldn't agree more, Scribe," said Talia, glancing at Berith who was nodding. "Berith and I will stay alert to your call."

God's Scribe took to the air and blinked across the Heavens toward the spires.

Jack stared out through the curtains at Kesien who looked angry and dejected. He motioned Berith toward the tall, six-foot-sixish angel of death, his black curly hair disheveled, grey eyes filled with pain.

"Berith, think you could use your healing light on Kesien? He's feeling responsible for Samael's bullshit because he didn't stop him in the beginning. He's not listening to any of us, but maybe your healing light will help him."

"I can try, Jack," she said, patting him on the back. "But he looks devastated. I'll talk to him."

She flew out the doorway, rose-gold halo bright against the white stones.

"I hope she can help him," said Talia, watching Kesien slump against the wall and bury his face in his hands.

"Me, too," said Jack as he sat down on the bed, a pensive look on his face.

For a long time, he stared at the shifting rays of sunlight on the floor as Talia and her squad talked about how to help Kesien. The rays of light seemed to move across the floor, shining through one portal and then another. Radiating from one opening, fading, and then suddenly appearing in another portal across the room. Like they'd been summoned into each opening.

He winced. Or transferred there.

"Holy shit!" Jack shouted, lurching forward.

Talia rushed over to him and gripped his forearms. "Jack? What is it?"

He stared into her luminous grey eyes, his mouth hanging open as nothing came out. He understood what Lucifer was after now.

"Talia…" He groaned, staring at her with fear-filled eyes, his gaze flicking to the sunlight and back to her face again.

"Jack?" she cried. "What is it?"

He shook his head as her grip on his forearms tightened. "That rare power…it's—" He paused, struggling to put the words together.

"What rare power, Jack?" Talia asked him, watching him fumble through his words.

Could Luci somehow use transference to get through Hell's gate? Or transfer something into Hell? Something powerful enough to break the lock on the gate?

"Transference!" He forced the word out, shaking his head as he said it. "What if Lucifer can awaken it and somehow use it to open Hell's gates?"

His words hit Talia hard and for several moments, she couldn't speak.

"Then we send Abaddon back to Hell to close those gates again," she said finally in an anxious voice. "We send him before Lucifer breaks that lock. And we keep him in Hell to monitor Lucifer."

Her response was comforting. Finally, he nodded at her. "Hope Azrael recalls that dude fast and sends him to shore up Hell again. Close the place down for the season."

She nodded, stroking his cheek with her fingers until his tense muscles relaxed. "That's Abaddon's function, Jack."

Jack rose from the bed and stood in front of her, hands on her waist. "We let Aby handle it then," he said with a sigh. "Ready to head back to the City of Angels' south side, Mrs. Casey? Looks like Azrael and the Scribe have this one handled for now."

He hoped that was true.

Talia wrapped him in her arms and kissed him. "Lead the way, Mr. Casey. Let's go home."

He smiled. First time she'd ever said that about Earth before. Or his shithole studio apartment.

"Home it is, babe," he said and took hold of her hand.

They flew through the wafting white curtains and soared over Eolowen's crystal rooftops into the crisp turquoise sky as the scent of jasmine and gardenias filled the air. They dropped through the clouds. Headed back to Earth.

Rehearsals for the new show were starting soon. He looked forward to setting his sights on things a little less dire—and a little domestic. Like his new wife and keeping up the ratings on this new show format that had no princess—or couples—competitions. He sighed, remembering that Rachel Daniels would be part of the cast this time. There'd be lots of drama involved with Rachel back. He'd have to get through it without Talia smiting her. But he looked forward to hanging with Gianni and Banks again.

And he worried that he hadn't seen the last of Lare Dumont and Tyler Hughes either, after leaving them knocked out on his apartment floor.

Talia caught an updraft and he followed, rising alongside her. She spread her wings wide, riding the warm currents and then dropped into a thick swirl of clouds, spiraling gently downward. Toward Earth. And Los Angeles.

23

IT WAS LONG PAST SUNSET WHEN JACK PUSHED OPEN THE FRONT DOOR of his shithole studio apartment. Turning around, he scooped Talia into his arms and carried her over the threshold. The dull, scuffed pine floors squeaked against his blue Vans as he pushed the door closed with his foot and set her down beside the old green couch. A hint of stale beer and greasy pepperoni hung in the air, laced with cedary traces of his Tom Ford cologne.

His place was still a mess from when he and Gianni had battled a shitload of demons and Zanth, pizza box still on the table, a line of empty beer bottles sitting beside it. Murphy bed was down, pale blue sheets tangled, green blanket twisted into a ball at the foot of the bed.

"Sorry, babe," he said and rushed toward the table to clear the pizza box and beer bottles. "Didn't get a chance to clean up after the last demon brawl."

Pine hardwoods creaked as Talia blinked across the floor, her Eternean armor clanking as she wrapped him in her arms.

He leaned down to kiss her when the whole room shifted and he felt the thump of the mattress against the back of his calves. He smiled. She'd blinked them both across the room. To the Murphy bed.

"I don't want to clean up beer bottles or sweep floors, Jack Casey," she said, draping her arms around his neck.

"No?" he asked, shaking his head as his arms slid around her waist.

Smiling, she shook her head slowly. "I want to tangle sheets and kick blankets onto the floor."

"We making a fort?" he asked with a smirk.

"Later," she said.

And pushed him backward. Onto the bed.

He propped himself up on his elbows as she unfastened her armor, piece by piece, dropping it onto the hardwood floor with a clank. He kicked off his Vans as she reached for him, wearing a short, dappled grey angel robe.

Straddling him, she unzipped his hoodie and shoved it off his shoulders. Peeled his grey Henley over his head. Tossing both onto the floor.

"I like where this conversation is headed, Mrs. Casey."

"And it's just getting warmed up, Mr. Casey," she said, unzipping his Levi's and snaking them down his hips.

His pulse raced, blood pumping as his wings folded against his shoulder blades. Her hands slid across his bare chest, down his stomach. His body was on fire as she took hold of his grey boxer briefs and pushed them off his hips, down his legs, until they hit the floor.

Breath quickened as he rolled her angel robe up and over her head, tossing it onto the floor. She was naked under her robes.

He rolled her onto the bed underneath him, pushing his body against hers as her legs parted. He slid his hands across her breasts, down her stomach, caressing her soft, winter-pale skin. His hand slid between her legs, stroking, pleasuring her. He was already hard.

She moaned, pressing her body against his hand, moving rhythmically against his fingers as he softly kissed her breasts.

"Make love to me, husband," she whispered against his ear, nibbling his earlobe.

He lifted his hips, shifting his erection until he gently entered her, pressing deep with anxious strokes, wings flexing between his shoulders until her body moved with his, those long legs wrapping around him. His thrusts quickened, deepened as she arched her back and her hot breath huffed against his neck.

Her hands slid up and down his back and over his hips, gripping his body tighter against hers. Sweat was a crystalline sheen across her breasts as his hips rocked against hers, heat and need spiking through his body like a California heatwave.

His body pulsed, breath huffing, his thrusts faster, urgent, building like a wild dance beat. His hair was damp with sweat, her body slick against his as he pumped faster until she gasped, her body beginning to shudder against him.

She arched her back, moaning, his thrusts fluid and frantic until he felt the first tremble of climax. He whispered her name against her ear as he felt that first moment of release, rushing, building until his thrusts slowed and he collapsed, panting, pressing against her sweat-slicked body. His wings draped over the edges of the bed as he still lay on top of her, his fingers entwining hers, her raven black hair clinging to his cheek as he pressed his face against her breasts.

"I love you, Mrs. Casey," he said, winded.

She wrapped her arms around him, her body so warm against his as he closed his eyes, wanting to fall asleep with her, naked, wings and legs tangled together.

"Now until forever, Mr. Casey," she whispered.

"You're my Heaven, Tal," he said, his voice growing soft and sleepy. "Always." His eyes began to close until everything faded into a soft, velvety charcoal grey.

* * *

HE AWOKE to the sound of an alarm clock bleating at him as his own voice filled the room.

"This is Jack Casey. Yeah, that Jack Casey. You know what to do."

The old answering machine beeped.

"Jack, Phil Getz here. Reminding you that Evan Bellows will be conference-calling us today at 11:10 A.M. To talk about SanFran

Confidential. I know it's your first day of rehearsals and all, but I made sure to schedule the call during your first break at the studio. Bellows is ready to throw obscene amounts of money at you…and me. Who knew? So, don't be late. Talk to you soon."

Dammit! He'd forgotten about Evan Bellows and his ridiculous offer. He didn't want to go back to *SanFran Confidential.* This new show had to do well.

He lifted his head from the pillow. Realizing he was alone. And they had a nine A.M. set call today. He glanced at the clock. Seven A.M.

"Tal?" he called out.

No response.

"Tal!" he shouted, rolling onto his back underneath the tangled sheets.

The faint patter of water whispered through the quiet apartment. She was in the shower, something that was still a novelty to her. Angels didn't need to take showers, but she loved the feel of the warm water against her body—and her wings.

Grinning, he wrapped the sheet around his waist and slid out of bed, tiptoeing around the Murphy bed. Toward the closed bathroom door.

Quietly, he opened the door and crept toward the green shower curtain.

Talia's slim, alluring curves, wings, and long legs were silhouetted through the curtain as he leaned against the wall, smirking at the sexy image fogging his bathroom mirror.

"Good morning, Mrs. Casey," he called out and dropped the sheet on the white tile floor.

"It is now," said Talia as she reached out through the shower curtain and grabbed his arm.

And tugged him into the shower.

They made love in the shower's steamy warmth, wings beading and shiny with spray, halos bright. Talia climbed out first, leaving him to wash his hair and shave. He dried off with a soft green towel and pulled on a blue pair of boxer briefs. He dressed quickly in Levi's, a light blue T-shirt, and his favorite navy blue hoodie. After pulling on some socks and his Vans, he stepped out of the bathroom. Talia floated beside the Murphy bed, wings unfurled. She wore a faded jean miniskirt, black flats, and a sheer purple blouse.

He whistled at her. "I have the hottest wife ever," he said and pulled her into his arms.

She kissed him hard on the lips and brushed his damp blond bangs out of his eyes.

"My husband is way hotter," she said, smiling at him.

"He taller than me?" he asked.

She laughed as he returned her kiss.

"Ready for a brand-new reality television show, Mrs. Casey?"

Her brow was shadowed with that sexy little shadow she got when she was surprised or confused by something. He ran his fingers through her raven black hair.

"Please tell me I don't have to learn a new silverware layout or someone's getting a fork through their heart."

Jack laughed, shaking his head. "No princess lessons this time, babe. This show's supposed to follow us around as newlyweds, remember?" he said, matching her smile. "It's supposed to be all romantic and sexy and honeymooning and stuff."

Finally, she nodded. "If only those cameras could see us fighting demons and locating rare angel powers, Jack."

"Don't think America's ready for that story yet," he said and nodded toward the door. "Ready to hit the road? Gonna take a good forty minutes at this hour to get to Burbank."

"Let's go," said Talia, holding his hand. "I can't wait to see Izzy and Morgan."

"Looking forward to seeing my dudes, Gianni and Banks, too."

He knew Gianni was probably worried about them after he'd helped Jack fight demons at his place last week. Jack couldn't wait for the dinner invite to Gianni and Izzy's place either. He wanted some old-fashioned, mundane married life for a change. Movie night on the couch. Dinner at his favorite Chinese restaurant. A walk on the beach with his wife, watching the sunset.

And he yearned for a little ordinary barbecuing, some wine, and lots of laughs with friends, something he hadn't had in a long time. Not since he got fired from *SanFran Confidential*. Way before he'd met Talia or stumbled onto the set of *The Cinderella Hour*.

But he couldn't get that dickhead Archangel Samael out of his head. Taking that Book of Secrets to Hell. For Lucifer. And Azrael's words still burned in Jack's head.

Ready your squad, Talia. In case the call goes out.

He hoped that things didn't escalate again. But if Lucifer awakened transference, he could wage another war from Hell. That was a terrifying thought.

"I'm sure Armand will be relieved to see you in one piece, Jack," she said.

"Relieved enough to invite us over for dinner?"

Talia cocked her head and gave him a confused look. "Dinner?"

He nodded. "I'm ready for some typical, Hollywood married life clichés, Tal. With you beside me. As my wife."

That made her smile.

He gave her a quick kiss as they hurried to the front door. He grabbed his keys off the hook beside the door and they clambered outside, holding hands. He locked the door and walked arm in arm with Talia to his black Explorer. They climbed in and he started the engine, pulling out of the apartment parking lot, headed for the 110 and the 5. To Four Acre Studios in Burbank. And the first rehearsal for *The Divine Newlyweds Show*.

———

AFTER TEDDY ROSWARSKI let him through studio security, Jack drove past the rows of squat grey buildings, sunlight sparkling, and parked in his new parking space on the lot at Studio 22, home of *The Cinderella Hour: The Divine Newlyweds Show*. Or so the huge billboard outside the studio read. Beyond his parking space stood his new set trailer, a 43-foot luxury Star Waggon, the one Herb told him he'd have as the top-billed star on the show. Much larger than the one he'd inhabited for *SanFran Confidential*. Gave him a funny feeling seeing it parked nearby. He didn't want to go back to that life—or the person he'd been.

Heat roiled across the asphalt as he climbed out of the Explorer, Ray-Ban Aviators shining in the June heat, summer only a breath away. The cloudless sky was a crisp cerulean blue, buzz of a lawnmower nearby as he gripped Talia's hand and they walked toward the door to Studio 22.

It was too hot outside for a hoodie, but his old studio building had always been over-cooled in the summer. Studio 22 would be the same and while they were rehearsing, there wouldn't be any set lights to warm him.

This was the first rehearsal for the new show, so the next couple of weeks would be little more than sitting around a big table slurping coffee and reading the script as they scribbled down blocking, read out loud, juggled script changes, and made notes.

He knew that this part of the process would bore Talia into a coma, too, but she'd be fine once they were on set or on location. He sighed. Unless Azrael called her back to Heaven to fight this new war between Heaven and Hell—without him.

He couldn't keep that thought out of his head.

Or that there was still a bounty on his head, so Lucifer's demons were still hunting him. With a vengeance, trying to claim that bounty. But without Zanth this round. Unfortunately, Lucifer had summoned this new archdemon, Asmodeus out of Purgatory where he'd been banished. So evil that even Lucifer had banned his ass.

Was that one of the reasons Samael had gone into Purgatory? To release Asmodeus? Make a deal with him? Had Luci made peace with this archdemon, so it would hunt him for Lucifer? Or was this archdemon bound for some bigger, more malevolent purpose?

And all he knew it was its name.

A cold chill rolled across him at the sudden realization. He'd opened the door out of Purgatory, letting that bastard out. Had he been played again by Lucifer? Was Zanth's defection planned? Something Lucifer was counting on?

He shuddered at the thought of this archdemon loose on the world.

What if he came face-to-face with this evil bastard one night alone, walking back to his SUV? With Talia in Heaven. Would he have enough seraphim power to take down this new archdemon?

Or would Talia return to find him gone forever?

He had no idea what to expect from Lucifer now. Luci had been strangely silent throughout this hunt for Samael.

Everything felt out of balance, like when the washer got out of round and thumped like drums from Hell. Even this new show format was an unknown to him.

But he couldn't tell Talia that this sketchy new archdemon frightened him. A lot. He had to keep his game face intact and play off Asmodeus as just another demon to splatter.

But right now, he had to shift his focus to mundane things like *The Divine Newlyweds Show.*

Taking a deep breath, he opened the door into Studio 22's cool darkness. The sound of hammering and sawing vibrated through the darkened building as he and Talia made their way past the warm set lights on their left, scent of warm sawdust mixing with carpenter's glue.

Light illuminated the offices at the back of the big, cavernous space and the stage where he'd first laid gaze on Talia, remembering her pale wintry beauty, that coal black hair, and those luminous grey eyes setting him alight in a way that he'd never felt before. He gripped Talia's hand and made his way toward the largest glass office with its huge conference room table and walls covered in whiteboards.

As they got within fifty feet of the largest glass-enclosed room, he saw Gianni and Izzy seated around the big simulated walnut conference room table. Banks and Morgan sat across from them and Rachel Daniels and Eric Saunders sat to Izzy's left. The rest of the two dozen chairs were filled with crew. Only two seats were empty. On Gianni's right.

He let out the breath he'd been holding too long and glanced at Talia. "Ready, babe?"

She smiled at him, caressed his cheek, and then nodded. "Ready to be television's newest newlyweds," she said and flexed her wings, already hidden with angel magic. "With wings."

Pulling in a nervous breath, he opened the office door.

"Morning, everyone," he said and held the door open for Talia who entered the office ahead of him.

"Jack!" Gianni was on his feet, rushing over to him. "Good to see you!"

"Dude, it's great to see you, too," he cried and pulled Gianni into a hug.

"How did everything go?" Gianni asked in a quiet voice against his ear.

"Tell you later," Jack whispered and let go of the taller soap star.

Izzy was a few steps behind Gianni, but Talia hugged her and then Gianni as Jack gave Izzy a big hug. Banks pounded him on the back and hugged him. Then Morgan.

When he felt the weighty stare boring into him, he turned. Rachel Daniels sat beside Eric Saunders, displaying her most unaffected smile, but her too blue gaze was fixated on him.

"Hello, Jack," she said, twisting a lock of auburn hair around her index finger. "Good to see you again."

He couldn't help but see an ulterior motive hiding in her nonchalant but friendly demeanor toward him.

"Hey, Jack and Talia," Eric called to them, waving.

"Hi, Eric," he replied and fixed Rachel with his unblinking gaze. "Rach. You, too married yet?"

With a slow and pointed shake of her head, Rachel smiled at him. "Not yet, but soon."

Thankfully, Jennifer Collins interrupted the stand-off, rushing over to him, and hugging him and then Talia. Steve Kosinski was behind Jennifer, eager to shake Jack's hand and hug Talia. Finally, Herb greeted them like long-lost relatives. He shook Jack's hand hard and hugged Talia.

"Great to see you, two!" Herb announced, all smiles as he motioned for them to sit down beside Gianni and Izzy. "We're just getting started. Please…have a seat." Herb held up two keys and extended them to Jack and Talia. "Keys to your trailer while on set." He grinned. "It's one of the best trailers on the lot, Jack. You and Talia earned it."

"Thanks, Herb," said Jack, taking both keys. "Mrs. Casey and I thank you."

"Yes, thank you, Herb," said Talia as she slid one key out of his hand.

"Hope you got similar trailers for my costars," Jack replied.

A funny look crossed Herb's face. "What? That…wouldn't upset you?"

Jack almost snorted out a laugh. "Of course not. Why should it?"

That made Herb smile. "All right, then. Jennifer, contact—"

Jennifer, clipboard under her arm, was typing away on her phone. "Just texted the vendor," she said, glancing up through a pair of purple glasses. "They'll have the other trailers swapped out by one o'clock."

Jack followed Gianni around the table, still holding Talia's hand. He plopped down in the chair beside Gianni and Talia sat down to Jack's right. With Morgan Banks on the other side. She reached out and hugged Talia again. Banks gave Jack a wave of thanks as Jack settled into his chair and picked up the script lying there.

"Thanks, Jack," Gianni whispered.

"Don't thank me, dude," said Jack. "You and Izzy earned it."

Jack flipped through the script, reading through the location shoots, the lines, and the blocking.

"Now that everyone's here," said Herb, looking relieved and excited now that he and Talia were on set, "we can start talking about this season's new format."

"Is it true that there won't be any more competitions?" Talia asked.

"Yes, Talia," said Herb, moving toward the whiteboard on the wall behind the table. He picked up a blue marker. "But there will be plenty of conflict and unexpected challenges though."

Jack's gaze shot toward Rachel Daniels who smiled at him from across the table. And it made him uneasy. He gave Talia a sideways look and found that she was glaring at Rachel Daniels as the woman undressed him with her gaze. With Lare gone and controlled by

Lucifer, Jack couldn't be sure what motivated her hungry look that ate men alive and spit out their spines. He just knew he didn't want to be a blip on her GPS again.

He felt Talia's grip tighten on his hand.

"I thought she gave up hunting you," Talia whispered.

"Until the blood under her nails dried," he snapped.

"Looking forward to the challenges," said Rachel with a sultry nod. "And the drama." She smiled. "I mean the script."

Herb grinned and clapped his hands together. "All right, let's get started!"

FOR OVER AN HOUR, they talked about the new format and then Herb's vision—which was a long-winded, artistic way of saying that he wanted their best improvs, riffing off each other and going off script. And then they read through *the script* which was little more than a collection of scenes strung together with transitions and a huge Hollywood hope that lightning would strike and brilliance would occur.

Jack couldn't stop his attention from wandering as they started the first read. It felt so wooden. So planned and stifling in some ways. With couples' outings planned down to the *unplanned moments*. Rigid events. And carefully plotted out activities. With a planned expectation that they would go off script and say or do something heartfelt or brilliant.

But it all fell flat for him. Lacking the heart and chemistry that America fell in love with and kept the ratings off the charts.

Feeling frustrated, Jack struggled through the script's second pass, wanting to toss the whole thing into the trash. This wasn't the show he'd signed on to do. This wasn't *The Cinderella Hour*. It was a standard, tired reality television show that no one wanted to watch.

And that frightened him.

"Herb," he said finally, climbing out of his chair as the clock ticked past eleven. "You sure about this script?"

Herb frowned at him from across the table. "What do you mean, Jack?"

Jack picked it up and glanced at the next scene. A boring *day in the life* scene. With no tension. No uncertainty. Just four couples sitting around a picnic table, waiting for something to happen.

"Nothing happens in this scene," he replied, hoping Herb would come to his senses.

"That's where you come in, Jack," said Herb, sounding so optimistic—and deluded. "Taking it to the next level with those off-the-script moments you're so famous for."

"Herb...it's..." He stumbled, searching for a polite way to tell Herb the truth.

Herb frowned, standing up. "It's what, Jack?"

Then the whole room was on its feet.

Sighing, Jack tossed the script onto the table, shaking his head. "Dude, this isn't the newlyweds show that America signed on for. This is straight up boring."

"But Jack," Herb replied, rushing around the table toward him. "I wanted to give all the couples—you especially—a chance to go off script." He grinned. "It's what put this show on the map."

Jack backed away from the table, shaking his head harder. "Dude... you can't force off-script moments like this. Or you'll end up with none. This isn't working."

Clock on the wall said eleven oh five. He had to go. Maybe he had something to say to Evan Bellows after all? And that made him sad. He hated the idea of returning to *SanFran Confidential*, but after seeing this script, he worried that he'd have no choice if he wanted to keep acting.

"But Jack, just listen—" Herb cried, rushing into his vision for the new show again, but Jack stopped him.

"Let's take a break, Herb," he said. "I need to take a phone call."

"A phone call?" Herb's eyes were wide and fearful and the silence in the room was palpable now. "Jack...no..."

Dammit, did everyone on the lot know he was talking to Evan Bellows?

He glanced around the table at the silent, tense faces, seeing their thoughts racing across their faces. Yeah, the whole cast and crew knew who was calling him.

"I'll be back in thirty minutes," he said and hurried out of the office door.

His phone vibrated in his pocket as he moved past the set lights toward the studio door.

"Jack, wait!" Talia called.

He kept walking past the stage and out the studio door, veering right toward his and Talia's trailer. He got within ten feet of the Star Waggon when his phone began vibrating in his Levi's pocket. He slid his phone of his right front pocket and tapped the screen.

"This is Casey," he said.

"Hi, Jack," said Phil. "Glad you could make it."

"Jack! How are you?"

Evan Bellows' sunny, energetic voice joined Phil's, filling his ear.

"Good," he answered, glancing up as Talia stopped beside him. "And you?"

"I've been better, Jack," said his former director with a pause. "Not gonna lie. SanFran Confidential is in real trouble."

He sighed. "Yeah, heard about Lare's meltdown and disappearance."

The line went quiet for a moment.

"Even before Lare disappeared, the show was in trouble, Jack," said Evan, the drama in his voice manifesting now.

Dude knew how to spin things.

He squinted. "What does that mean?"

"It means, Jack," said Evan, his voice getting louder, "that America wants Davy Pierson back. Headlining SanFran Confidential."

But he wasn't that naïve kid anymore. That twenty-year-old clean and sober young actor hungry for his first break. Davy was a wide-eyed, street-smart young detective that did things his way, not the official department way. Which put him at odds with Drummond Turillo, the hardened *one-way-or-the-highway* detective.

Their fights had been legendary until the audience began siding with Jack instead of Laren Dumont. Forcing the writers to acknowledge that this young detective had heart—and a near-cult following. Until they fired him to appease Lare's ego and Rachel's demands—and solve the rampant drug problem on the set.

"Jack, did you hear me? I said headlining SanFran Confidential. Without Laren Dumont at the helm."

Jack frowned. "It's Lare's show, Evan," he said, beginning to pace the walkway outside Studio 22. "You threw that in my face at least four times when you fired me, remember?"

Evan's sigh was heavy. "I remember," he said, regret in his voice. "That was a very dark day for the show. One that I admit, it has never recovered from." Silence hung between them for a moment. "And when the second season of your new show aired, landing in the same time slot as SanFran Confidential, I laughed. I said that America was so over Jack Casey. They'd never watch a stupid fairytale reality show —even with Casey at the helm."

Jack pulled in a breath, those words hard to hear even now.

"And Jack...I can't begin to tell you how wrong I was and how every week, the ratings proved it." Evan's voice had no trace of malice or annoyance. It was matter-of-fact and almost contrite. "And the critics. And the fans. You destroyed us in the ratings. Every. Single. Week. And still, the fan letters poured in for you and Davy Pierson, begging us to bring you back."

"You did what you had to do, Evan," said Jack as he walked up and down the walkway in front of the new trailer. "I got myself fired from the show. I have no one to blame but me for that."

"No, Jack," said Evan, his voice was small and quiet. "I let big stars like Lare Dumont and Rachel Daniels talk me into firing one of the show's biggest draws. You weren't the only cast member with a raging flake habit, but I blamed all of it on you. Fired you as the example to keep Lare and Rachel happy." He pulled in a breath. "I was wrong, Jack. I shouldn't have fired you without firing Dumont and Daniels, too. And a whole list of others."

Jack smiled. He'd waited years to hear that from Evan Bellows, never expecting that the Emmy-winning director would ever say it.

"You have no idea how much I appreciate hearing that, Evan," he replied, glancing up at Talia whose face was filled with worry and apprehension as she stood beside him.

She nodded to his left. When he glanced in that direction, he saw Jennifer Collins standing on the walkway beside Gianni, Banks, and Herb. All of them looked horrified.

Abruptly, Jack turned away from them.

"So, what do you say, Jack? Come home to SanFran Confidential." Evan's voice had lapsed into his recruiter's edge. "Make it your show. At two point four million an episode, you'd be the highest paid actor on television."

Two point four million per episode? He struggled to catch his breath. He could almost hear Phil Getz panting in the background.

"An actor would have to be crazy to turn down that kind of money," said Jack as he paced the walkway again.

"Is that a yes, Jack?" Evan asked, his voice loud and electric. And hopeful.

"I'm going to need a little time to think through this, Evan."

"Give us a week, Mr. Bellows," Phil replied, finally cutting into the discussion.

"That's fair," said Evan. "I know it's a big decision, Jack. Think about it and I'll call you next week."

"Will do. Thanks, Evan. Thanks, Phil."

He ended the call as Herb, Gianni, and Jennifer wandered back inside Studio 22's dark, over-cooled confines, leaving him standing on the walkway. Feeling like a dick.

"Jack," said Talia in a quiet voice. "Are you planning to go back?" she asked in a fearful voice. "To all the pain and probably dozens of demons on set."

He shook his head a moment. "Don't know yet, Tal," he said in a quiet voice. "Feeling a little confused and conflicted right now."

She laid her hand against his cheek. "Promise me you won't make a snap decision," she said. "I know that's a lot of money."

More money than he'd ever seen as an actor.

She stroked his face a moment. "But Jack...I just don't want to see you return to that life."

He bristled. "What you really mean is you don't want me to be the person I used to be."

"No, lover," she said in a soft, soothing voice. "I don't want you to go back to the ways that could return you to the fate I saved you from." Her voice quivered. "I don't want to lose you, Jack."

She had a point, something that had already gone through his mind a few times. If he went back to the show, would he go back to his flake habit? His drinking habit? And overdose at twenty-seven?

He smiled, taking hold of her hands. "I'll never go back to that life, Mrs. Casey," he said. "Because it's a life without you."

She wrapped her arms around him and he held her. But the flash of gold light startled him.

He glanced up as the world froze. Talia let him go, turning around.

Azrael stood before them, clear gold Eternean armor bright in the California sunlight, grey robes fluttering beneath it. His face was haggard, charcoal grey eyes watery, soot grey wings drooping at his shoulders, mouth turned downward as his silvery black hair blew in the breeze.

"Archangel!" Talia cried.

Jack started to make a smart comment about Azrael just wanting to watch the rehearsals, but he stopped when he saw the pain flooding the archangel's eyes.

"What's wrong?" Jack asked, stepping toward Azrael. "What's the matter?"

Azrael laid his hand on Jack and Talia's shoulders and blinked them into the trailer. With maple hardwood floors, taupe walls, a leather couch, and Italian kitchen cabinets that had modern brushed nickel handles and a taupe finish. It smelled like lemons and leather.

But the devastated look on Azrael's face quickly drew Jack's attention away from the trailer's luxury layout. Talia reached out to the archangel.

"Sir...what is it? What's happened?"

His face pinched, charcoal grey eyes turning glassy as he started to speak, but the sound of *Sympathy for the Devil* screeched from Jack's pocket, sending a chill down his spine.

Azrael's eyes narrowed, eyebrows furrowed. "Lucifer."

Wincing, Jack fished out his phone and with reluctance, he answered the call.

"I told you I'm not interested in a Hell timeshare, Luci. It's time for us to see new people."

"Ah, Jack," said Lucifer, his voice bright and animated. "So terrible to hear from you."

"I'm kinda busy right now," said Jack, still staring at Azrael.

"Make time. Jack."

The pain in Azrael's face deepened.

"So, talk already," he snapped.

"I've acquired a new accessory for my tower," Lucifer replied, sounding so pleased with himself.

Jack shook his head. "Dude, you need to stop sniffing so much brimstone. Or get your own decorating show on that home décor channel. I hear demon red's in this year."

"Yes, Jack, a new accessory," Lucifer continued, ignoring him. "Your precious Berith. Back here. In Hell—alongside the Book of Secrets."

Slowly, the words, punctuated by Lucifer's wild laughter, sank into his head and he sucked in a painful breath, understanding Azrael's expression now. His chest tightened, his heart beginning to hurt. Berith was like the mother he'd never had, but always wanted. She got him through those horrible months in Hell. He owed her everything. Pain mixed with fury.

"Let that sink in for a beautiful, painful moment, Jack."

"You let her go," he said with a feral growl. "Now."

"Come and get her, Jack," said Lucifer, delight in his voice. "If you think you're man enough."

He couldn't speak. Couldn't get a single word out, the pain and fury twisting him into knots. He wanted to rage. To punch the wall and shout.

"Oh, we're going to have so much fun when you get here, Jack. Just you and me. You'll curse the day you were born." His voice turned dark and deadly. "And I'm looking forward to every single moment of it."

As the call cleared, Jack stared up at the archangel, feeling his heart pounding against his rib cage, fury burning through his veins.

"Get your guard busy training," said Jack through gritted teeth.

"Training?" Azrael replied, looking disheveled and shaken.

Jack nodded. "Lucifer's got Berith and we're going in after her."

The archangel's eyes brightened, the hint of a smile touching the corners of his mouth as they shared a moment of agreement and purpose.

"Already got the guard gearing up and in formation," said Azrael in a dark tone.

Talia reached out and gripped Jack's hand.

"If Lucifer wants to throw an exclusive bash at his place, we're going to crash it," said Jack, glancing at Talia who nodded and then Azrael.

"Beside you all the way, Jack," said Talia as Azrael gave him a sharp nod.

"Okay then!" Jack shouted. "Let's get this party started!"

The End of THE DIVINE NEWLYWEDS SHOW: A Game of Lost Souls, Book Nine

The story continues in…

A GAME OF LOST SOULS

THE CELESTIAL COUPLES SHOW

Read Chapter 1 Now!

AWARD-WINNING BESTSELLING AUTHOR
LISA SILVERTHORNE
THE CELESTIAL COUPLES SHOW
A GAME OF 10 LOST SOULS

Novels by Lisa Silverthorne

Standalones:

ISABEL'S TEARS

LANDFALL

PACIFIC BLUE TATTOO

A Game of Lost Souls series:

THE CINDERELLA HOUR

THE PRINCE CHARMING HOUR

THE EVER AFTER HOUR

THE FALLEN HEARTS SEASON

THE RISING SPIRITS SEASON

THE ETERNAL SOULS SEASON

THE ROYAL WEDDING HOUR

THE HEAVENLY HONEYMOON HOUR

THE DIVINE NEWLYWEDS SHOW

THE CELESTIAL COUPLES SHOW

THE ENOCHIAN APOCALYPSE SHOW

Curse and Crown series:

THORN & BLADE

The Spiral series:

BETWEEN

REPRISE

AVENGE

The Resurrectionist Papers

GRAVE RECKONING

Short Story Collections

THE SOUND OF ANGELS

THE MAGIC OF ORDINARY THINGS

TIMELESS

Science Fiction Writing as L.S. Silverthorne

Standalones:

REDISCOVERY

Experiencing True Purple series:

RECOMBINANT, Book 1

HELIX, Book 2

SPLICE, Book 3

FORTHCOMING!

A Game of Lost Souls series:

The Angelic Anniversary Hour, Book Twelve

The Perdition Picture Show, Book Thirteen

Curse and Crown series:

Storm & Steel, Book Two

Dagger & Flame, Book Three

The Spiral series:

Ruin, Book 4

Descent, Book 5

The Resurrectionist Papers:

Corpses Delicti

Stiffed Again

Cease and Deceased

Science Fiction Writing as L.S. Silverthorne

Experiencing True Purple series:

Cipher, Book 4

Renascence, Book 5

SNEAK PEEK: THE CELESTIAL COUPLES SHOW

1

JACK CASEY KNEW IT WAS A DREAM. BUT BEHIND THE HORRIFYING torrent of Hell images, Berith was warning him not to try and rescue her from Hell. And to stay far away.

Either way, it made him recoil.

Tossing and turning in the dark, unfamiliar set trailer bedroom, wearing only green boxer briefs, he tried to shove away the sweltering visceral heat, the stink of brimstone, and the constant roaring wail of damned souls that echoed above the ubiquitous snap of whips.

He was drowning in a sea of red-eyed demons leering back at him.

Flinching with every biting crack of the whip, he remembered the lash endlessly cutting into his flesh, shredding his clothes. Felt the deep, burning ache that never left his skin—or his heart—down there in Hell.

"Talia!" he shouted, unsure if his call was out loud or just in the nightmare.

Seas of those glowing red demon eyes surrounding him were seared into his memory, haunting him. Even now. They burned like embers through the shadows. In the dark, rocky crevices. Along the dim, ruddy gleam of steaming lava rivers that gave Hell's cavernous depths a lurid neon glow, deepening the shadows—and his despair.

Dense, suffocating heat pressed against his body, weighing him down, his clothes heavy and wet with sweat. Hanging in tatters. With every heated breath, his lungs ached, every inhale and exhale singeing his insides, and his heart broke at being so far away from Talia.

"Talia!" His voice echoed through the caverns, lost again in the wail of souls.

He shifted again in the bed, trying to escape the heat and the pain and the images. And that constant feeling of being watched, of being hunted and cornered, had persisted long after he'd escaped Lucifer's domain. In Hell, his every movement had been on display, like the cage fights he'd endured.

Sweat slicked his body as he struggled against the covers, breath huffing as he fought against the barrage of images that rushed at him like a bad acid trip. Like those flaked-out parties at Lare's beach house. Dredging up out-of-focus, hazy memories of distorted figures tangling around him until he couldn't breathe. Couldn't focus. Couldn't move.

Everything tilted. Like when a bad trip spiraled into an overdose. Everything hurt. Slowing. Fading. Blacking out.

He tried to shout again. Couldn't.

But in that nothingness, those crystal-clear memories flooded over him in waves of torture, pain, and anguish. The ones that he'd blocked out since escaping Hell. Stored and kept out of focus deep inside his head, right beside those distorted—and missing—beach house party memories. Those unnerving flashes of demons and horns after he'd woken up beside Rachel. Without his clothes.

Sparks of things that he didn't want to remember. Couldn't face even then. All this time, he'd hoped that all of the memories would somehow disappear and he wouldn't have to deal with them.

Ever.

Things he couldn't give voice to, things he'd never even told Talia. Things he couldn't tell her. Or himself. Much less face.

Jack!

The lyrical alto voice was sharp. Crystalline. Angelic. It was Berith! Desperate. Despairing. Determined.

Jack!

She shouted in his ear and her voice filled his entire being.

Do NOT try and rescue me. It's you that Lucifer wants—and I don't know why. Stay away or he'll consume you! Stay. Away. You can't save me this time...it's too late. Tell Azrael—that I love him. For eternity.

Abruptly, Berith's warm and kind mothering presence melted into a blistering wave of hatred and vengeance as he felt Lucifer wrest control from her.

And takeover his dream.

Sympathy for the Devil screeched through his head, electric guitars wild and distorted against the staccato beat of drums that pulsed through his bloodstream.

His heart raced, breaths coming in gasps. His skin burned, temples pounding. Chills roiled across his body that shook in time to the drums and guitar riffs. And he thought his heart might explode.

Hello, Jack! Welcome home. I've set up a brand-new rack in your honor. Can't wait to beat the life out of you. And drench the ground with your blood. Every last drop. Until I consume your soul.

You will be mine again, Jack. Soon. So very soon. Can't wait for your arrival.

Lucifer's dark laughter spiraled around him, stirring up all of Hell's memories that Jack had suppressed.

Gut-wrenching images flooded his brain, blazing through him all at once like a California wildfire. Lucifer's laughter intensified as everything went up in flames around Jack. Blistering. Searing. Suffocating.

Oh, and Jack...those memories at the beach house...the horns—the bedroom...that was me.

Lucifer's malevolent laughter was caustic.

Horrified, Jack recoiled. It was the realization he'd felt deep in his soul, but couldn't bring himself to say out loud. Or ask.

Those fleeting pictures of waking up naked in bed with Rachel and —he shuddered—those shadowy flashes of horns and demons... He felt the grim dread deep in his soul that it had been Lucifer.

God, he felt sick all over.

Smothering heat mixed with the cloying stink of sulfur and ozone. He was drowning in lava and demons. And screaming as he jerked up from the bed, queasy, drenched in sweat, and hurting all over.

He grabbed the small grey trashcan near the bed and threw up in it, his stomach heaving only air. When the dry heaves subsided, he set down the trashcan and stared around the dark room, shades still down. He stared into the abyssal darkness until the room began to look almost familiar again.

He was still at the studio. In his and Talia's set trailer beside Studio 22 at Four Acre Studios in Burbank.

In the pre-dawn greyness, the trailer's modern bedroom took shape around him. Taupe, grey, and white with lacquered cabinets. His sweat-slicked skin was chilled, his mouth dry, his gut hurting.

Disoriented, he searched through the darkness for something he recognized. For Talia's comfort that he needed more than ever at this moment. But he was alone in the queen-sized bed, wearing only boxer briefs, his blond hair drenched, and his face a mask of sweat.

The grey and white comforter lay crumpled on the floor. Crisp white sheets smelling of sunlight were tangled around him as the world buzzed with a cacophony of noises that had become one dull roar he couldn't separate into things. Until, at last, he realized that the buzzing rumble was his cell phone lying on the nightstand beside the bed.

Vibrating. Screeching out *Sympathy for the Devil.*

His blood turned to ice.

"Jack!"

Talia's musical soprano voice cut through his turmoil. He realized that he was finally awake. His phone was really ringing.

And it was Lucifer.

The soft gold light of Talia's halo warmed the room as she moved toward the bed.

"Jack, don't answer it," she whispered.

But he'd already grabbed the phone off the nightstand. With shaking hands, he answered the video call.

Lucifer's blond hair was a tangle of sunlit golden curls, blue eyes hypnotic against a white hoodie over a grey *SanFran Confidential* T-shirt, and faded jeans.

"You bastard," Jack growled, glaring at the screen, his voice scratchy and thin.

Talia was beside him now, sitting on the side of the bed, hands kneading his bare shoulders. His skin had turned to gooseflesh and he had to fight to keep his teeth from chattering.

"And it's good to hear from you, too, Jack," said Lucifer, smiling through his steepled fingers, sounding so smug. "Sleep well?"

Lucifer's laughter was thick. Dark. Mocking. Like his tone of voice, so precise and enthusiastic. Cheerful. British. But so damned arrogant with dark, dark undercurrents.

"What do you want?" Jack demanded, his gaze steely as he tried to control his shaking and the panic rising inside him.

At the revelation that his nightmares—and Berith's warnings—had been real. Every. Single. Moment.

"You really are grumpy in the mornings, Jack," said Lucifer, his smile broadening into a grin as he leaned back in a white leather chair, hands behind his head. "Even grumpier than you were here—if that's possible." Lucifer clicked his tongue and abruptly leaned back toward the screen again, letting his arms fall into his lap. "What's the matter, Jack? Have a bad dream? Show not going well? Run out of those horrid toaster pastries again? You really should stock up on those if it makes you that irritable."

"I said!" Jack shouted, "what do you want?"

Jack felt Talia's arms slide around him protectively. She had no idea how her touch was holding him together right now. He fought down his rising panic, trying to take deep, measured breaths and not show Lucifer how unnerved he felt at this moment.

He stared down the King of Hell, challenge white-hot in his game face as he struggled to hold it in place.

"No jokes, Jack?"

The light-hearted glow in Lucifer's tranquil blue eyes began to fade into a stormy, piercing stare as the smile slid from his face.

"You know what I want. Jack." Lucifer didn't blink. "Tick tock.

Tick. Tock. Berith's time is fleeting. I didn't think you were man enough to actually return to Hell. Afraid of my restored powers?"

Jack glared at him. "I'll match my seraphim powers with yours any day, Lucifer. Try me."

"Jack, don't," Talia whispered.

That deadly twinkle lit Lucifer's dangerous gaze.

"Berith doesn't have time to waste, Jack. Hoping that a coward like you will muster enough false courage to come save her. Perhaps a line or two of cocaine—that is your poison, isn't it—will bolster your courage? Like it used to, Jack. Remember?" That vicious, charming smile returned. "At those beach house parties. I remember." He chuckled. "And so do you now. Don't you?"

Jack swallowed the panicked gasp that tried to escape through his gritted teeth. He did his best to hold onto his game face that was already slipping, the horror of those memories sizzling through his brain now.

"Don't you worry, Luci," he said, forcing a smile. "Party's just getting started. And I wouldn't miss it for all the flake in the world. Neither would Azrael and Talia. And hey—I'll bring the tunes. Got an awesome demon-splattering playlist I can't wait to play for you. Along with a shit-ton of murder marbles. Enough for everyone, I promise. So, dust off your dance floor, dude. I've got some new moves that are gonna rock your world, you colossal douchebag."

He reached down and cleared the connection. Hanging up on Lucifer for a change. Felt good.

"Jack!" Talia cried. "What did you just do?"

He collapsed onto the bed, shaking, the chills shuddering through him as his breaths came in gulping gasps.

"About time I hung up on him for once."

His stomach lurched. He scrambled up from the bed and grabbed the trashcan again. Heaving into it. But only air came up.

"Jack, what is it? What's wrong?" Talia blinked in front of him, dropping down on her knees and putting her arms around his waist.

His game face fled and he couldn't stop his face from scrunching into an anguished frown. What would she think of him when she found out what really happened at Winter's Revenge in Malibu? After he'd been blacked out on flake.

The awakened memories made him sick all over and he gagged.

Gently, she took the trashcan that he'd been white-knuckling and set it beside the nightstand. She held his hands, her luminous grey eyes lit with fear and worry.

"Talia, I...I..."

His mouth bobbed open, but he couldn't pull it all into a coherent sentence. Or even twelve.

Talia's wings curved around him as she held him in her arms.

"You're shaking," she said. "Tell me what's wrong. It's more than that phone call from Lucifer. You were having terrible dreams. What is it, Jack?"

Every word hurt. "The beach house, Tal—" He stuttered through more gulping breaths, the shakes coming in tremors now.

She held him closer, wings cradling him.

"What about the beach house?" she asked in a soft voice.

God, he didn't want to say it out loud. Didn't want to make it real instead of a shadowy figment of a flake-fueled hallucination. A what if. Just a distant but unlikely possibility. But if he was remembering those moments now, wouldn't they already be appearing in his damned Book of Life and Death? Penned there by Pravuil. Affirming that they were real.

He shuddered. And they were about Lucifer.

"The memories," he hissed, sucking in another quick breath. "They're all coming back."

"The blacked-out things you couldn't remember?" she asked in a patient voice.

He nodded and her arms tightened around him.

"Oh, God, Talia," he moaned.

She stroked his hair, the gold light of her halo merging with his. "Jack...what happened to you in that room?"

"In the bed, Talia," he said through gritted teeth, his voice so small and raw. "It was him."

For several long, aching moments, she didn't say anything.

"Lucifer!" he spat.

She forced him to look at her, holding him steady. "Lucifer put that memory in your head just now."

He shook his head. "No, he was at the beach house. In that bedroom—"

"Jack, it was the dream," she said, her voice rising. "He planted those images in your head through the dream. Using your hazy memories against you. It's what he does."

Jack winced. "But how can I ever be sure?"

The silence was deafening.

"Rachel," Talia said finally as she enfolded him in her arms again until he felt the beat of her angel heart against his chest, felt the warmth of her human soul enveloping him. Calming him. "Jack, Rachel knows what happened to you at those parties. She'll tell you the truth."

He didn't fully trust Rachel, even now, but maybe because he'd saved her, she'd tell him the truth.

"What about my book?" he asked in a hoarse voice. "Is it in Pravuil's book about me now? For every angel of death to read?"

"Your Book of Life and Death?" she asked.

He nodded against her midnight curls that smelled like roses and rainwater.

"I'll find out," she said. "After you've had some more sleep."

He pulled away, shaking his head. "After those nightmares and Face-timing Lucifer, I'm not gonna sleep for a long time."

Talia picked up the comforter off the floor and draped it across the bed again. After untangling the sheets, she sat him down on the bed and crawled in beside him.

"Let's go back to bed, Mr. Casey," she said, fingers tracing across his shoulders and down his chest.

He let her pull him under the covers. Still shaking, he snuggled against her, his wings and body feeling weary. Heavy. Broken. And not knowing whether Lucifer had planted that memory in his head gnawed at him.

Along with Berith's warning.

"Talia, Berith told me not to try and rescue her."

"When?" Talia asked.

"She spoke to me in my dream, but Lucifer hijacked it."

Again, Talia was quiet for several moments.

"You're sure it was Berith?" Talia asked finally.

He nodded against the silky black waves of her hair. "She told me that Lucifer was after me not her. And…" He sighed. "To tell Azrael she loved him. For eternity."

Talia pulled in a heavy breath. "Then it was a warning from her. To keep you away. To say goodbye to Azrael."

"Like it's a big secret that Lucifer's after me?" he replied. "Doesn't matter. I'm going after her, Talia."

"We're going after her, Mr. Casey," Talia corrected him.

He couldn't hold back his grin. "Marrying you was the best decision I ever made, Mrs. Casey."

He kissed her, stroking her face as he laid his head against her shoulder.

"Loving you was the best decision of my existence, Jack Casey," she said, snuggling against him. "Now, sleep. We have to be on set early today."

Nodding, he tried to let go of the horrors that had sprung out of his nightmares and the dread and worry knotting his gut. He had to get to Berith fast. Before Lucifer extinguished her life force and returned his attention to hunting Jack again. But first, Jack needed to ask Rachel what really happened in the Breckinridge Suite.

He had to know if Lucifer was lying. He had to.

Not long after the alarm rang and Jack climbed into the shower, the entire trailer filled with light. Not someone had turned on every light in the place kind of light. More like someone had poured light into every corner and crevice and painted the trailer, floor to ceiling, in warm, radiant light.

That only an archangel gave off.

Jack wrapped a grey towel around his waist and with damp hair, he padded barefoot into the bedroom in the wake of Archangel Azrael's angelic light. He had his back to Jack, Talia standing in front of him. His wings were unfolded to their full wingspan, halo spinning with red-gold light. But Jack couldn't hear what they were saying. Damned angel notes.

Talia's gaze abruptly shifted to him, causing Azrael to turn around.

"Jack!" Azrael cried and grabbed him by the shoulders. "I came as soon as I heard!"

"Heard what, archangel?" he asked, shaking his head.

Azrael cast a forlorn look at Talia and then fixed Jack with his tough, unaffected archangel stare. But his massive, soot-colored wings drooped against his shoulders, silvery black hair unusually disheveled.

The archangel couldn't hide that he was hurting. Or how much he loved Berith.

After enduring millennia without her, expecting it to be forever, she came back to him. Only to have that douche-canoe, Lucifer snatch her away from him again.

Despite his marble exterior, pain radiated from every feature of the archangel's face. Even the dude's red-gold halo looked pale and washed out.

"Berith contacted you," said the archangel, her name aching on his lips.

Jack smashed his eyes closed. Of course. The archangel hadn't dropped in for a visit. Azrael wanted to know what he saw.

"The dream—sorry."

"Jack, what did she say to you?" Azrael's grip on his shoulders tightened. "Tell me...please."

"She was adamant, archangel," he said, trying to make her message clear. "She said not to try and rescue her."

Even as he ramped up to tell his account, he felt his words stabbing the archangel in the heart. Azrael's face pinched, mouth pressing into a tight line.

"Why?" he asked.

Jack bowed his head, hands on the towel around his waist.

"She said it was me that Lucifer was really after." Each word was an apology. "She said he'd consume me." His heart twisted into a knot. "Azrael, she said I couldn't save her this time. That it's too late now."

Azrael's shoulders slumped, his charcoal grey eyes losing their radiance.

"She said to tell you that she loved you, Azrael. For eternity."

That was the final blow that made the archangel's knees buckle. He grabbed hold of the lacquered taupe dresser and eased himself onto a wooden chair beside it. He stared past Talia now, the pain etched into his face.

"Then it's over," Azrael lamented and laid his hand against his forehead. "I've lost her again—this time for eternity. I'm too late to save her."

Jack understood that pain. He'd felt it when Erica Thomlin fired that gun and Talia stepped in front of him. He'd felt it again at the beach house when Lucifer dragged him off to Hell. And he'd felt it a third time when he had to wipe Talia's memories to save her from Vassago, knowing she wouldn't remember him—or that she loved him. Worst pain he'd ever felt and he hoped he never felt it again.

He moved over to the wilted archangel and gripped Azrael's forearm.

"And that's why we're gonna ignore that warning and storm Hell's Gates anyway."

Talia was beside him now, an arm around his waist, holding him close.

Confused, Azrael frowned, shaking his head as he glanced from Talia to Jack. "What? But Berith said Lucifer planned to capture you, Jack."

Jack scoffed. "Like that's a big revelation? It's old news and I'm still going after Berith."

Azrael looked alarmed now. "Jack, no! I won't risk your life and immortal soul by delivering you to Lucifer in Hell."

"It's my risk, dude," he said, a hand against his bare chest. "And I'm taking it no matter what you say. Berith deserved that chance at redemption. At love. I'm not gonna let Luci stomp all over it because he's jelly that dad let Berith move back home and not him."

Azrael was smiling now.

"Besides," said Jack, moving out of the way as Azrael stood up, those huge soot-grey wings expanding again. "Berith's the mom I never had. I'd do anything for her." His voice got all tight and quiet. "And you, archangel."

Those charcoal eyes went from steely to watery. Azrael looked moved by his statement, but it was true. Azrael had done a lot for him. It was time he returned the favor.

Talia pulled Jack into an embrace and he wrapped her in his arms.

"So, we're agreed?" Jack asked, glancing from Talia to Azrael. "We're still gonna crash Luci's party? With every uninvited guest we can muster."

Azrael nodded. "When you put it like that, Jack," he said, holding out his arms. "How can I disagree?"

"But Lucifer's up to something, archangel," he said, his tone darkening. "I don't know what he's after, but it's more than petty vengeance against me."

Azrael's brow furrowed and he cast an unsettled look at Talia.

"Explain, Jack," said the archangel.

Jack shrugged. "We all know the dude relishes his petty vengeance, but this is much, much more than that. And I can't figure out what he's after. Or why he's so focused on dragging my ass back to Hell. He says it's because he wants to murder me personally, but I'm not buying it. Why have me, Berith, and the Book of Secrets? Doesn't make sense. Besides, those three things don't exactly go together."

"Jack's right," said Talia, slipping her arms across his bare chest, turning his skin to gooseflesh. "What's the connection between Berith, Jack, and the Book of Secrets? We still need to figure that out."

Azrael shook his head, hands on his hips. "It doesn't make much sense, does it? Especially when you toss in the rare transference power. Why all of those things? Why now? He's locked in Hell even if his tether breaks because Abaddon still holds the key. The Book of

Creation is out of his reach and he can't awaken any of those powers in the Book of Secrets."

"I thought only the Maker could break the first seal on the Book of Creation," said Talia.

Azrael nodded. "That's correct, Talia. If Lucifer had stayed the Light Bringer, God's left hand, he may have had the power to destroy the Book of Creation and break the first seal. According to Pravuil anyway. But Lucifer lost that standing when he fell from Heaven."

A knock thrummed through the studio trailer.

Startled, Jack glanced at the clock. It was after seven. First reminder that they had a set call in thirty minutes. He glanced down at the towel he was wearing. He hadn't even dried his hair yet.

"Dude, we've gotta go," said Jack. "Herb's expecting us on set at seven-thirty. First day of filming today."

"Go ahead and get dressed, Jack," said Azrael, motioning him toward the bathroom. "And thank you."

Jack gave him a sharp nod and headed back into the bathroom.

"Talia," said Azrael, his attention returning to his right hand angel of death. "Pravuil needs you to return to Heaven right away. He said it was about the transference power. And if you see Kesien, tell him to return to Eolowen immediately. On my order."

"Kesien?" Talia replied in surprise. "He's not training with the guard?"

"He disappeared while on patrol. Muriel's fuming and Deemah's furious. I can't protect him from Muriel's wrath for long."

With a rush of air, Azrael blinked through the ceiling, wings whispering as the trailer went dark again.

ABOUT THE AUTHOR

LISA SILVERTHORNE, an award-winning bestselling author, has published 25 novels and 150 short stories and novelettes in many genres. She is the author of *A Game of Lost Souls* series, *Experiencing True Purple* series, *The Spiral*, *The Resurrectionist Papers*, and a new series, *Curse and Crown*. She lives in Las Vegas, Nevada.

Before you go, you are invited to please leave a **review of this book**!

Reviews are a wonderful way to help an author. They are also an exciting opportunity to share your honest thoughts with other readers, so **please post yours,** in as many places as possible!
